He took a slig...
needed spac...

"Brock, I never r...
know if my parer...
They're good pe...
in for you for years—I thought you'd just walked away."

He shook his head. Shrugged. "Well, which room are you in?"

"I'm the last down the hallway. Number five," Maura said.

"I'll watch you through your door," he said with a half smile. "I mean, I'm here—might as well make sure you're perfectly safe."

"I assume I'll see you," she murmured.

"You will," he assured her.

She turned and headed down the small hallway to the end. There, she dug out her key, opened her door, waved and went in.

And finally, alone and in the sanctity of her room, she leaned against the door, shaking.

How could time erase their past so easily? How could the truth hurt so badly...and mean so very much at the same time? What would have happened if she had received his messages? Would they have been together all these years, perhaps with a little one now, or two little ones?

Just now, she could have turned to him, slipped her arms around him. She knew what it would feel like, knew how he held her, cupped her nape when he kissed her, knew the feel of his lips...

New York Times and *USA TODAY* bestselling author **Heather Graham** has written more than a hundred novels. She's a winner of the Romance Writers of America's Lifetime Achievement Award, a Thriller Writers' Silver Bullet and, in 2016, the Thriller Master Award from International Thriller Writers. She is an active member of International Thriller Writers and Mystery Writers of America, and is the founder of The Slush Pile Players, an author band and theatrical group. An avid scuba diver, ballroom dancer and mother of five, she still enjoys her South Florida home, but also loves to travel.

For more information, check out her website, theoriginalheathergraham.com, or find Heather on Facebook.

NEW YORK TIMES AND USA TODAY BESTSELLING AUTHOR

HEATHER GRAHAM

TANGLED THREAT
&
SUSPICIOUS

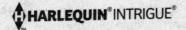
HARLEQUIN® INTRIGUE®

ISBN-13: 978-1-335-77493-4

Tangled Threat & Suspicious

Copyright © 2019 by Harlequin Books S.A.

The publisher acknowledges the copyright holder of the individual works as follows:

Recycling programs for this product may not exist in your area.

Tangled Threat
Copyright © 2019 by Heather Graham Pozzessere

Suspicious
Copyright © 2005 by Heather Graham Pozzessere

Printed in U.S.A.

www.Harlequin.com

CONTENTS

For Roberta Young Peacock, a true Florida girl,
with lots of love and best wishes.

TANGLED THREAT

Prologue

The History Tree

"They see her...the beautiful Gyselle, when the moon is high in the sky. She walks these oak-lined trails and sometimes pauses to touch the soft moss that drips from the great branches, as if she reaches out for them to touch what is real. In life she was kind and generous. She was beloved by so many. And yet, when brought so cruelly to her brutal and unjust death at the infamous History Tree, she cast a curse on those around her. Those involved would die bitter deaths as well, choking on their own blood, breath stolen from them as it had been from her," Maura Antrim said dramatically.

The campfire in the pit burned bright yellow and gold, snapping and crackling softly. All around them, great oaks and pines rose, moss swaying in the light breeze. The moon overhead was full and bright that night, but cloud cover drifted past now and then, creating eerie shadows everywhere.

It was a perfect summer night, and perfect for storytelling. She was glad to be there, glad to be the storyteller and glad of the response from her audience.

Maura's group from the resort—teenagers and adults alike—looked at her, wide-eyed.

She refused to smile—she wanted to remain grave—though she was delighted by the fascination of the guests assembled around her. She had been grateful and pleased to be upgraded to her position of storyteller for the Frampton Ranch and Resort, an enterprise in North Central Florida that was becoming more renowned daily as a destination. The property had been bought about five years back by billionaire hotelier Donald Glass, and he had wisely left the firepit and the old riding trails as they were, the History Tree right where it grew, the ruins of the old plantation just as they lay—and amped up the history first, and then the legends that went along with the area.

Maura wasn't supposed to be on tonight—she shared the position with Francine Renault, a longtime employee of Donald Glass's hotel corporation, probably second in command only to the main resort manager, Fred Bentley. The two of them were known to argue—but Francine stayed right where she was, doing what she wanted. Despite any arguments, Donald Glass refused to fire either Francine or Fred, who, despite his stocky bulk, moved around the resort like a bat out of hell, always getting things done.

Fred Bentley had watched Maura at the start of the evening; she thought that he was smiling benignly—that he approved of her abilities as a social hostess and storyteller.

It was hard to blame him for fighting with Francine. She was...a difficult personality type at best.

And sharing any job with Francine wasn't easy; the woman had an air of superiority about her and a way of treating those she considered to be "lesser" employees very badly. Francine was in her midthirties—and was a beauty, really, a platinum blonde, dark-eyed piece of perfection—and while Maura had turned eighteen, Francine considered all of Donald Glass's summer help annoying, ignorant children.

The young adults—or "camper" summer help—were fond of gossiping. It was rumored that Francine once had an affair with Donald Glass, and that was how she held on to her position—and her superiority.

Glass was married. Maybe Francine was blackmailing him, telling him that if she wasn't given a certain power, she'd tell his wife, Marie, and Marie—or so rumor had it—could be jealous and very threatening when she chose to be. Hard to believe—in public Marie was always the model of decorum, slim and regal, slightly younger than Donald but certainly older than Francine.

Teens and young adults loved to speculate. At Maura's age, the thought of any of the older staff together—all seeming so much older than she was at the time—was simply gross.

Tonight, by not being there, Francine had put herself in a bad position.

She hadn't shown up for work. A no-show without a call was grounds for dismissal, though Maura seriously doubted that Francine would be fired.

Maura looked around, gravely and silently surveying her group before beginning again.

She didn't get a chance—someone spoke up. A young teenager.

"They should call it the Torture Tree or the Hangman's Tree…or something besides the History Tree," he said.

The boy's name was Mark Hartford, Maura thought. She'd supervised a game at the pool one day when he had been playing. He was a nice kid, curious and, maybe because he was an adolescent boy, boisterous. He also had an older brother, Nils—in college already. Mark's brother wasn't quite as nice; he knew that many of the workers were his own age or younger, and he liked to lord his status as a guest over them. He was bearable, however.

"The Torture Tree! Oh, lord, you little…heathen!"

Nils had a girlfriend. Rachel Lawrence. She was nicer than Nils, unless Nils was around. Then she behaved with a great deal of superiority, as well. But, Maura realized, Nils and Rachel *were* at the campfire that night—they had just joined quietly.

Quietly—which was amazing in itself. Nils liked to make an entrance most of the time, making sure that everyone saw him.

Rachel had her hands set upon Mark's shoulders—even as she called him a heathen. She looked scared, or nervous maybe, Maura thought. Maybe it was for effect; Nils set his arm around her shoulders, as a good, protective boyfriend should. They made a cute family picture, a young adult male with his chosen mate and a young one under their wings.

Maura was surprised they were on the tour. Nils had said something the other day about the fact that they were too mature for campfire ghost stories.

"Torture Tree—yes, that would be better!" Mark said. He wasn't arguing with Rachel, he was determined that he was right. "Poor Gyselle—she was really tortured there, right?"

Mark and the other young teens were wide-eyed. Teenagers that age liked the sensational—and they liked it grisly.

"She was dragged there and hanged, so yes, I'm sure it was torture," Maura said. "But it was the History Tree long before a plantation was built here, years and years ago," Maura said. "That was the Native American name for it—the Timucua were here years before the Spanish came. They called it the History Tree, because even back then, the old oak had grown together with a palm, and it's been that way since. Anyway, we'll be seeing the History Tree soon enough," she said softly. "The tree that first welcomed terror when the beautiful Gyselle was tormented and hanged from the tree until dead. And where, so they say, the hauntings and horrors of the History Tree began."

Maura saw more than one of her audience members glance back over the area of sweeping, manicured lawn and toward the ranch, as if assuring themselves that more than the night and the spooky, draped trees existed, that there was light and safety not far away.

The new buildings Donald Glass had erected were elegant and beautiful. With St. Augustine just an hour and a half in one direction and Disney and Universal and other theme parks just an hour and half to the south— not to mention a nice proximity to the beaches and racetrack at Daytona and the wonder of Cape Kennedy being an hour or so away, as well—Frampton Ranch and Resort was becoming a must-see location.

Still, the ranch had become renowned for offering

Campfire Ghost Histories. Not stories, but histories—
everything said was history and fact...to a point.

The listeners could hear what people claimed to have
happened, and they could believe—or not. And then
they'd walk the trails where history had occurred.

"You see, Gyselle had been a lovely lost waif, raised
by the Seminole tribe after they found her wandering
near the battlefield at the end of the Second Seminole
War. She was 'rescued' by Spanish missionaries at the
beginning of the Third Seminole War, though, at that
point, she probably didn't want or need rescuing, having been with a Seminole family for years. But 'saved'
and then set adrift, she found work at the old Frampton
plantation, and there she caught the eye of the heir, and
despite his arranged marriage to socialite Julie LeB-
lanc, the young Richard Frampton fell head over heels
in love with Gyselle. They were known to escape into
the woods where they both professed their love, despite
all the odds against them—and Richard's wife, Julie.
Knowing of her husband's infidelity, Julie LeBlanc arranged to poison her father-in-law—and let the blame
fall on Gyselle. Gyselle was hunted down as a murder-
ous witch, supposedly practicing a shaman's magic or
a form of voodoo—it was easy to blame it on traditions
the plantation workers didn't really understand—and
she was hanged there, from what was once a lover's
tree where she had met with Richard, her love, who
had promised to protect her..."

She let her voice trail. Then she finished.

"Here, in these woods, Gyselle loved, not wisely,
but deeply. And here she died. And so they say, when
the moon has risen high and full in the night sky—as
it is now—those who walk the trails by night can hear

her singing softly 'The Last Rose of Summer' with a lovely Irish lilt to her voice."

"What about the curse?" a boy cried out.

"Yeah, the curse! That she spoke before she died—swearing that her tormenters would choke on their own blood! You just said that she cursed everyone, and there are more stories, right?" Mark—never one to be silent long—asked eagerly.

Maura felt—rather than saw—Brock McGovern at her side. He was amused. Barely eighteen, he'd nevertheless been given the position of stage manager for events such as the campfire history tour. He'd been standing to one side just behind her as she told her tale with just the right dramatic emphasis—or so she believed.

He stepped forward, just a shade closer, nearly touching her.

"Choking on their own blood? Kind of a standard curse, huh?" he teased softly and for her ears alone.

Maura ignored him, trying not to smile, and still, even here, now, felt the rush she always did when Brock was around.

Brock was always ready to tease—but also to encourage and support whatever she was doing. He had that ability and the amazing tendency to exude an easy confidence that stretched far beyond his years. But he was that sure of himself. He was about to leave for the service, and when he returned, he planned to go to college to study criminology. Barely an adult, he knew what he wanted in life. She was sure he was going to work hard during basic training; he'd work hard through the college or university of his choice. And then he'd make up his mind just where he wanted to serve—FBI,

US Marshals, perhaps even Homeland Security or the Secret Service.

He shook his head, smiling at her with his unusual eyes—a shade so dark that they didn't appear brown at times, but rather black. His shaggy hair—soon to become a buzz cut—was as dark as his eyes, and it framed a face that was, in Maura's mind, pure enchantment. He had already had a fine, steady chin—the kind most often seen on more mature men. His cheekbones were broad, and his skin was continually bronzed. He was, in her mind, beautiful.

He'd often told the tales himself, and he did so very well. He had a deep, rich voice that could rise and fall at just the right moments—a voice that, on its own, could awaken every sense in Maura's body. They had known each other for three years now, laughed and joked together, ridden old trails, worked together...always flirting, nearly touching at first, but always aware that, when summer ended, he would head back down to Key West and she would return to West Palm Beach—about 233 miles apart, just a little too far for a high school romance.

But this summer...

Things had changed.

She had liked him from the time she had met him; she had compared any other young man she met to him, and in her mind, all others fell short. He'd been given a management job that summer, probably because he was always willing to pitch in himself, whether it came to working in the restaurant when tables needed bussing or hauling in boxes when deliveries arrived. He'd gained a lean and muscular physique from hard work as much as from time in the gym, and he had a quick mind and a quicker wit, cared for people, was generous with his time, and was just…

Perfect. She'd never find anyone so perfect in life again, Maura was certain, even though she knew that her mother and father smiled indulgently when she talked about him in glowing terms—she was, after all, just eighteen, with college days and so much more ahead of her.

This summer they'd become a true couple. In every way.

A very passionate couple.

They'd had sex, in her mind, the most amazing sex ever, more meaningful than any sex had ever been before.

Just the thought brought a rush of blood to her face.

But…she believed that they would go on even through their separation, no matter the distance, no matter what. People would think, of course, that she was just a teenager, that she couldn't be as madly in love as she believed she was. So she was determined that no one would really realize just how insanely fully she did love him.

She turned to Brock. He was smiling at her. Something of a secret smile, charming, sexy…a smile that seemed to hint that they always shared something unique, something special.

She grinned in return.

Yep. He had become her world.

"Take it away," she told him.

"The curse!" he said, stepping in with a tremor in his voice. "It's true that while being dragged to the tree—which you'll see soon on our walk—the poor woman cried out that she was innocent of any cruel deed, innocent of murder. And she said that those who so viciously killed her would die in agony and despair. The very woods here would be haunted for eternity, and the evil they perpetrated on her would live forever. They had brought the devil into the woods, and there he would abide."

He smiled, innately charming when he spoke to a group, and continued, "I think that storytellers have added in the choking-on-blood part. Very dramatic and compelling, but…there are records of the occasion of the poor woman's demise available at the resort library." He set his flashlight beneath his chin, creating an eerie look.

"And," Maura said, "what is also documented is that bad things continued to happen on the ranch—under the same tree, the condemned killer, Marston Riggs, tortured and killed his victims in the early 1900s, and as late as 1970, the man known as the Red Tie Killer made use of the tree as well, killing five men and women at the History Tree and leaving their bones to fall to the ground. But, of course, we don't believe in curses. The History Tree and the ranch are perfectly safe nowadays…" She looked at Brock. "Shall we?" she asked.

"Indeed, we shall," he said, and the sound of his voice and the look that he gave her made her long for it to be later, when they had completed the nighttime forest tour—and were alone together.

They walked by the grove, where there was a charming little pond rumored to invigorate life—a handsomely written plaque commemorating the Spaniard Reynaldo Montenegro and his exploration of Florida.

Brock said to the tour group, "Here we are at the famous grove where Reynaldo Montenegro claimed to have found the Pond of Eternal Youth."

It was as great tour; even the adolescents continued to ask questions as they walked.

"I'm happy to have been the tour guide tonight," Maura murmured to Brock. "But I can't believe that Francine just didn't show up."

"If I know Francine, she'll make a grand entrance somewhere along the line, with a perfect reason for not being on time. She'll have some mammoth surprise for everyone—something way more important than speaking to the guests. Hey, what do you want to bet that we see her somewhere before this tour is over? Here, folks," Brock announced, "you'll see the plaque—an inquisition did come to the New World!"

The copse, illuminated only by the sparkling lights that lit the trail, offered a sadder message—that of tortures carried out by an invading society on the native population it encountered.

They passed the ruins of an old Spanish farm and then they neared the tree.

The infamous History Tree.

The tree—or trees—older than anyone could remember, stood dead center in the small clearing, as if nothing else would dare to grow near. Gnarled and twisted together, palm and oak suggested a mess of human limbs, coiled together in agony.

Maura stopped dead, hearing a long, terrified scream, then realizing that she'd made the sound herself.

From one large oaken branch, a body was hanging, swaying just slightly in the night breeze.

She didn't need to wonder why Francine Renault had been derelict in her duty.

She was there…part of the tour, just not as she should have been.

Head askew, neck broken. She was hanging there, in the place where others had been hanged through the years, again and again, where they had decayed, where their bones had dotted the earth beneath them.

Brock had been right.

Francine Renault had indeed shown up before the tour was over.

THE POLICE FLOODED the ranch with personnel, the medical examiner and crime scene technicians.

The rich forest of pines and oaks and ferns and earth became alive with artificial light, and still, where the moss sagged low, the bright beams just made the night and the macabre situation eerier.

Detective Michael Flannery had been put in charge of the case. Employees and guests had been separated and then separated again, and eventually, Maura sat at the edge of the parking lot, shivering although it wasn't cold, waiting for the officer who would speak with her.

When he got there, he wanted to know the last time she had seen Francine. She told him it had been the night before.

Where she had been all day? In the office, in the yard with the older teen boys and at the campfire.

Had she heard anyone threaten Francine?

At least half of the resort's employees. In aggravation or jest.

The night seemed to wear on forever.

When she was released at last, she was sent back to her own room and ordered to stay there until morning.

When morning came, her parents were there, ready to take her home.

She desperately wanted to see Brock.

Her parents were quiet and then they looked at each other. Her father shook his head slightly, and her mother said softly, "Maura, you can't see Brock."

"What?" she demanded. "Why not? Mom, Dad— I'm about to leave home. Go to college, really be on my own. I love you. I'm going to come home. But… I'm almost eighteen. I won't go without seeing Brock."

Her father, a gentle giant with broad shoulders and a mane of white hair, spoke to her softly. "Sweetheart, we didn't say that we wouldn't let you see Brock. We're saying that you *can't* see Brock." He hesitated, looking over at her mother, and then he continued with, "I'm so sorry. Brock was arrested last night. He was charged with the murder of Francine Renault."

And with those words, it seemed that her world fell apart, that what she had known, that what she had believed in, all just exploded into a sea of red and then disappeared into smoke and fog.

Chapter One

"I'm assigned to go back to Florida. To stay at the Frampton Ranch and Resort—and investigate what we believe to be three kidnappings and a murder. And the kidnappings may have nothing to do with the resort, nor may the murder?" Brock McGovern asked, a small note of incredulity slipping into his voice, which was surprising to him—he was always careful to keep an even tone.

FBI Assistant Director Richard Egan had brought him into his office, and Brock had known he was going on assignment—he just hadn't expected this.

"Yes, not what you'd want, but, hey, maybe it'll be good for you—and perhaps necessary now, when time is of the essence and there is no one out there who could know the place or the circumstances with the same scope and experience you have," Egan told him. "Three young women have disappeared from the area. Two of them were guests of the Frampton Ranch and Resort shortly before their disappearances—the third had left St. Augustine and was on her way there. The Florida Department of Law Enforcement has naturally been there already. They asked for federal help on this. Shades of the past haunt them—they don't want any more unsolved murders—and everyone is hoping against hope that Lily Sylvester, Amy Bonham and Lydia Merkel might be found."

"These are Florida missing persons cases," Brock said. "And it's sad but true that young people go to Florida and get caught up in the beach life and the club scene. And regrettable but true once again—there's a drug and alcohol culture that does exist and people get caught up in it. Not just in Florida, of course, but…everywhere." He smiled grimly. "I go where I'm told, but I'm curious—how is this an FBI affair? And forgive me, but FBI out of New York?"

"Not out of New York. FDLE asked for you. Specifically."

"I see."

Egan didn't often dwell on the emotional or psychological, but the assistant director hesitated and then said, "You could put your past to rest."

Brock shrugged. "You know, one of the cooks committed suicide not long after the murder. Peter Moore. He stabbed himself with a butcher knife. He'd had a lot of fights with Francine Renault—the victim found at the tree. They suspected he might have killed himself out of remorse."

Egan offered him a dry grimace. "I know about the cook, of course. You know me—I knew everything about you on paper before I took you into this unit. I'm not sure anyone would have made a case against him in court. That's all beside the point—the past may well be the past. But there's the now, as well. They're afraid of a serial killer, Brock," Egan said. And he continued with, "The badly decomposed remains—mostly bones—of another young woman who went missing

several months ago were recently found in a bizarre
way—they were dumped in with sheets from several
hotels and resorts at an industrial laundry that accepted
linens from dozens of places—Frampton Ranch and
Resort being one of them."

"I see," Brock said.

He didn't really see.

That didn't matter; Egan would be thorough.

"Yes, this may be a bit hard on you, but you're the
one in the know. To come close to a knowledge of the
area and people that you already have might take someone else hours or days that may cost a life… You're the
best man for this. Especially because you were once
falsely accused. And, I believe, you may just solve
something of the mystery of the past. And quit hating
your own home."

"I don't hate my own home. Ah, come on, sir, I don't
want to play any cure-me psychological games with
this," Brock said.

Egan shook his head and leaned forward, his eyes
narrowed—indicating a rise in his temper, something
always kept in check. "If I thought you needed to be
cured, you wouldn't be in my unit. Women are missing. They might be dead already," he said curtly. "And
then again, they might have a chance. You're the agent
with a real sense for the place, the people and the surrounding landscape. And you're a good agent, period.
I trust in your ability to get this sorted."

Brock greatly admired Egan. He had a nose for sending the right agent or agents in for a job. Usually.

But Brock was sitting across from Egan in Egan's office—in New York City. He, Brock, was an NYC agent.

And while Brock really didn't dislike where he came

from—he still loved Florida, especially his family home in the Keys—he had opted to apply to the New York office of the Bureau specifically because it was far, far away from the state of his birth.

The New York City office didn't usually handle events in Florida, unless a criminal had traveled from New York down to the southern state. Florida had several field offices—including a multimillion-dollar state-of-the-art facility in Broward County. That was south—but Orlando had an exceptional office, close enough to the Frampton place. And there were more offices, as well.

Even if the Frampton Ranch and Resort was in a relatively isolated part of the state, a problem there would generally be handled by a more local office.

"Frampton Ranch and Resort," he heard himself say. And this time, years of training and experience kicked in—his voice was perfectly level and emotionless.

It was true: he sure as hell knew it and the area. The resort was just a bit off from—or maybe part of—what people considered to be the northern Ocala region, where prime acreage was still available at reasonable prices, where horse ranches were common upon the ever-so-slightly rolling hills and life tended to be slow and easy.

There were vast tracts of grazing ground and great live-oak forests and trails laden with pines where the sun seemed to drip down through great strands of weeping moss that hung from many a branch. It could be considered horse country, farm country and ranch county. There were marshes and forests, sinkholes and all manner of places where a body might just disappear.

The Frampton ranch was north of Ocala, east of

Gainesville and about forty-five minutes south of Olustee, Florida, where every year, a battle reenactment took
place, drawing tourists and historians from near and far.
The Battle of Olustee, won by forces in the state; the
war had been heading toward its final inevitable conclusion, and then time proved that victory had been necessary for human rights and the strength and growth of
the fledgling nation, however purposeless the sad loss
of lives always seemed.

Reenactors and historians arrived in good numbers, and those who loved bringing history to life also
loved bringing in crowds and many came for the camp-
grounds. The reenactment took place in February, when
temperatures in the state tended to be beautiful and
mosquito repellent wasn't as much a requirement as
usual. During the winter season—often spring break
for other regions—the area was exceptionally popular.

The area was beautiful.

And the large areas of isolation, which included the
Frampton property, could conceal any number of dark
deeds.

He'd just never thought he'd go back to it.

Certainly, time—and the path he had chosen to take
in life—had helped erase the horror of the night they
had come upon the body of Francine Renault hanging
from the History Tree and his own subsequent arrest.
He'd been so young then, so assured that truth spoke for
itself. In the end, his parents—bless them—had leaped
to the fore, flying into action, and their attorney had
made quick work of getting him out of jail after only
one night and seeing that his record was returned to
spotless. It was ludicrous that they had arrested him;
he'd been able to prove that it would have been impos-

sible for him to have carried out the deed. Dozens of witnesses had attested to the fact that he couldn't have been the killer, he'd been seen by so many people during the hours in which the murder must have taken place. He could remember, though, sitting in the cell—cold, stark, barren—and wondering why in God's name they had arrested *him*.

He discovered that there had been an anonymous call to the station—someone stating that they had seen him dragging Francine Renault into the woods. The tipster had sworn that he would appear at a trial as a witness for the prosecution, but the witness had not come to the station. Others had signed formal protests, and the McGoverns' attorney had taken over.

So many people had come forward, indignant, furious over his arrest.

But not Maura. She had been gone. Just gone. He couldn't think of the Frampton Ranch and Resort without a twinge of pain. He had never been sure which had broken him more at the time—the arrest or the fact that Maura had disappeared as cleanly from his life as any hint of daylight once night had fallen.

They had been so young. It had been natural that her parents whisked her away, and maybe even natural that neither had since tried to reach the other.

But there were times when he could still close his eyes and see her smile and be certain that he breathed in the subtle scent of her. Twelve years had gone by; he wasn't even the same person.

Egan was unaware of his reflections.

"Detective Michael Flannery is lead investigator now. He was on the case when you were arrested for the crime, but he wasn't lead."

"I know Flannery. We've communicated through the years, believe it or not. I almost feel bad—he suffered a lot of guilt about jumping the gun with me."

"He's with the Florida Department of Law Enforcement now, with some seniority and juice, so it seems," Egan informed him. "Years ago, when the murder took place, the federal government wasn't involved. Flannery doesn't want this crime going unsolved. He knows you're in this office now. His commander told me that he keeps in touch with you." Egan paused. "It doesn't sound as if you have a problem with him—you don't, right?"

"No, sir, I do not."

Even as a stunned kid—what he had been back then—Brock had never hated Detective Flannery for being one of the men who had come and arrested him.

Flannery had been just as quick to listen to the arguments that eventually cleared Brock completely of any wrongdoing. While Brock knew that Flannery was furious that he had been taken and certain that there had been an underlying and devious conspiracy to lead him and his superiors so thoroughly in the wrong direction, he had to agree that, at the time, Brock had appeared to be a ready suspect.

He'd had a fight with Francine that day, and it had been witnessed by many people. He hadn't gotten physical in any way, but his poor opinion of her, and his anger with her, had probably been more than evident—enough for him to be brought in for questioning and to be held for twenty-four hours at any rate.

"I'm curious how something that happened so long ago can relate to the cases happening now," Brock said.

"It may not. The remains of the dead girl found in the

laundry might have been the work of one crazed individual or an acquaintance seeking vengeance, acting out of jealousy—a solitary motive. It might be coincidence the way she was found—or maybe a killer was trying to throw suspicion upon a particular place or person. But…a lot of the same individuals are still there now who were there when Francine Renault was killed."

"Donald Glass—he's around a lot, though he does spend time at his other properties. Fred Bentley—I imagine he's still running the works. Who else is still there?" Brock asked.

Egan handed him a pile of folders. "All this is coming to your email, as well. There you have those who are in residence—and dossiers on the victims. Yes, Glass and Bentley are still on the property. There are other staff members who never left—Millie Cranston, head of Housekeeping. Vinnie Marshall, upgraded to chef—after Peter Moore's death, I might add. And then…" He paused, tapping the folders. "You have some old guests who are now employees."

"Who?"

"Mark and Nils Hartford," Egan told him. "Both of them report directly to Fred Bentley. Mark has taken over as the social director. Nils is managing the restaurants—the sit-down Ranch Roost and the Java Bar."

Brock hadn't known that the Hartford brothers—who'd seemed so above the working class when they'd been guests—were now employed at the very place where they had once loved to make hell for others.

"Flannery said this is something he hadn't mentioned to you. One of your old friends—or acquaintances—Rachel Lawrence is now with FDLE. She's been working the murder and the disappearances with him."

"Rachel? Became...a cop?" Brock shook his head, not sure if he was angry or amused. Rachel had never wanted to break a nail. She'd been pretty and delicate and... She'd also been a constant accessory of Nils Hartford.

"I guess your old friend Flannery was afraid to tell you."

"I don't know why he would be. I'm just a little surprised—she seemed more likely to be on one of those shows about rich housewives in a big city, but I never had a problem with her. That the Hartford brothers both became employees—that's also a surprise. They made me think of *Dirty Dancing.* They were the rich kids—we were the menial labor. But the world changes. People change."

"Flannery's point, so it appears, is that a number of the same players are in the area—may mean something and may not. There have been, give or take, approximately a thousand murders in the state per year in the last years. But that's only about four percent per the population. Still, anything could have happened. Violent crime may have to do with many factors—often family related, gang related, drug related, well...you know all the drills. But if we do have a serial situation down there—relating to or not relating to the past—everyone needs to move quickly. Not only do you know the area and the terrain, you know people and you know the ropes of getting around many of the people and places who might be integral to the situation."

"Yes. And any agent would want to put a halt to this—put an end to a serial killer. Or find the girls—alive, one can pray—or stop future abductions and killings."

Egan nodded grimly and tossed a small pile of photos down before him. Brock could see three young, hopeful faces looking back at him. All three were attractive, and more grippingly, all three seemed to smile with life and all that lay before someone at that tender age.

"The missing," Egan said. He had big hands and long fingers. He used them to slide the first three photographs over.

The last was a divided sheet. On one side was the likeness of a beautiful young woman, probably in her early twenties. Her hair had been thick and dark and curly; her eyes had been sky blue. Her smile had been engaging.

"Maureen Rodriguez," Egan said. He added softly, "Then and now."

On the other side of the divided sheet was a crime scene photo—an image of bones, scattered in dirt in a pile of sheets. In the center of the broken and fragmented bones was a skull.

The skull retained bits of flesh.

"According to the investigation, she was on her way to Frampton Ranch and Resort," Egan said.

Brock nodded slowly and rose. "As am I," he said. "When do I leave?"

"Your plane is in two hours—down to Jacksonville. You've a rental car in your name when you arrive. I'm sure you know the way to the property. Detective Flannery will be waiting to hear from you. He'll go over all the particulars."

Brock was surprised to see that Egan was still studying him. "You are good, right?" he asked Brock.

"Hey, everyone wants to head to Florida for the winter, don't they?" he asked. "I'm good," he said seriously. "Maybe you're right. Maybe we can put the past to rest after all."

"I LOVE IT—just love it, love it, love it! Love it all!" Angie Parsons said enthusiastically. She offered Maura one of her biggest, happiest smiles.

She was staring at the History Tree, her smile brilliant and her enthusiasm for her project showing in the brightness of her eyes and her every movement. "I mean, people say Florida has no history—just because it's not New England and there were no pilgrims. But, hey, St. Augustine is—what?—the oldest settlement continually…settled…by Europeans in the country, right? I mean, way back, the Spaniards were here. No, no, the state wasn't one of the original thirteen colonies. No, no Puritans here. But! There's so much! And this tree… No one knows how old the frigging oak is or when the palm tree grew in it or through it or with it or whatever."

Angie Parsons was cute, friendly, bright and sometimes, but just sometimes, too much. At five feet two inches, she exuded enough energy for a giant. She had just turned thirty—and done brilliantly for her years. She had written one of the one most successful nonfiction book series on the market. And all because she got as excited as she did about objects and places and things—such as the History Tree.

The main tree was a black oak; no one knew quite how old it was, but several hundred years at least. That type of oak was known to live over five hundred years.

A palm tree had—at some time—managed to grow at the same place, through the outstretched roots of the oak and twirling up around the trunk and through the branches. It was bizarre, beautiful, and so unusual that it naturally inspired all manner of legends, some of those legends based on truth.

And, of course, the History Tree held just the kind of legend that made Angie as successful as she was.

Angie's being incredibly successful didn't hurt Maura any.

But being here… Yes, it hurt. At least…it was incredibly uncomfortable. On the one hand it was wonderful seeing people she had worked with once upon a time in another life.

On the other hand it was bizarre. Like visiting a mirror dimension made up of things she remembered. The Hartford brothers were working there now. Nils was managing the restaurants—he'd arrived at the table she and Angie had shared last night to welcome them and pick up their dinner check. Of course, Nils had become management. No lowly posts for him. He seemed to have an excellent working relationship with Fred Bentley, who was still the manager of the resort. Bentley had come down when they'd checked in—he'd greeted Maura with a serious hug. She was tall, granted, and in heels, and he was on the short side for a man—about five-ten—but it still seemed that his hug allowed for him to rest his head against her breasts a moment too long.

But still, he'd apparently been delighted to see her.

And Mark Hartford had come to see her, too, grown-up, cute and charming now—and just as happy as his brother to see her. It was thanks to her, he had told her, and her ability to tell the campfire histories, that had made him long to someday do the same.

The past didn't seem like any kind of a boulder around his neck. Certainly he remembered the night that Francine had been murdered.

The night that had turned *her* life upside down had been over twelve years ago.

Like all else in the past, it was now history.

Time had marched on, apparently, for them—and her.

She'd just turned eighteen the last time she had been here. When that autumn had come around, she'd done what she'd been meant to do, headed to the University of Central Florida, an amazing place to study performance of any kind and directing and film—with so many aspects thrown into the complete education.

She'd spent every waking minute in classes—taking elective upon elective to stay busy. She was now CEO of her own company, providing short videos to promote writers, artists, musicians and anyone wanting video content, including attorneys and accountants.

Not quite thirty, she could be proud of her professional accomplishments—she had garnered a great reputation.

She enjoyed working with Angie. The writer was fun, and there was good reason for her success. She loved the bizarre and spooky that drew human curiosity. Even those who claimed they didn't believe in anything even remotely paranormal seemed to love Angie's books.

Most of the time, yes, Maura *did* truly enjoy working with Angie, and since Angie had tried doing her own videos without much success, she was equally happy to be working with Maura. They'd done great bits down in Key West at the cemetery there—where Maura's favorite tomb was engraved with the words *I told you I was sick!*—and at the East Martello Museum with Robert the Doll. They had filmed on the west coast at the old summer estates that had belonged to Henry Ford and Thomas Edison. And they'd worked together in St. Augustine, where they'd created twenty little video bits for social media that had pleased Angie to no end—and garnered hundreds of thousands of hits.

Last night, even Marie Glass—Donald's reserved and elegant wife—had come by their dinner table to welcome them and tell them just how much she enjoyed all the videos that Maura had done for and with Angie, telling great legends and wild tales that were bizarrely wonderful—and true.

Maybe naturally, since they were working in Florida, Angie had determined that they had to stay at Frampton Ranch and Resort and film at the History Tree.

Maura had suggested other places that would make great content for a book on the bizarre: sinkholes, a road where cars slid uphill instead of downhill—hell, she would have done her best to make a giant ball of twine sound fascinating. There were lots of other places in the state with strange stories—lord! They could go back to Key West and film a piece on Carl Tanzler, who had slept with the corpse of his beloved, Elena de Hoyos, for seven years.

But Angie was dead set on seeing the History Tree, and when they'd gotten to the clearing she had started spinning around like a delighted child.

She stopped suddenly, staring at Maura.

"You really are uncomfortable here, aren't you? Scared? You know, I've told you—you can hire an assistant. Maybe a strapping fellow, tall, dark and handsome—or blond and handsome—and muscle-bound. Someone to protect us if the bogeyman is around at any of our strange sites." Angie paused, grinning. She liked men and didn't apologize for it. In her own words, if you didn't kiss a bunch of frogs, you were never going to find a prince.

"Angie, I like doing my own work—and editing it and assuring that I like what I've done. I promise you, if we turn something into any kind of a feature film, we'll hire dozens of people."

Angie sighed. "Well, so much for tall, dark—or blond—and handsome. Your loss, my dear friend. Anyway. You do amazing work for me. You're a one-woman godsend."

"Thanks," Maura told her. She inhaled a deep breath.

"Could you try not to look quite so miserable?"

"Oh, Angie. I'm sorry. It's just…"

"The legend. The legend about the tree—oh, yes. And the murder victims found here. I'm sorry, Maura, but… I mean, I film these places because they have legends attached to them." Angie seemed to be perplexed. She sighed. "Of course, the one murder was just twelve years ago. Does that bother you?" Staring at Maura, she gasped suddenly. "You're close to this somehow, right? Oh, my God! Were you one of the kids working here *that* summer? I mean, I'd have had no idea… You're from West Palm Beach. There's so much stuff down there. Ah!" It seemed that Angie didn't really need answers. "You wound up going to the University of Central Florida. You were near here…"

"Yes, I was here working that summer," Maura said flatly.

"Your name was never in the paper?"

"That's right. The police were careful to keep the employees away from the media. And since we are so isolated on the ranch, news reporters didn't get wind of anything until the next day. My parents had me out of here by then, and Donald Glass was emphatic about the press leaving his young staff alone."

"But a kid was *arrested*—"

"And released. And honestly, Angie, I am a little worried. Even if it has nothing to do with the past, there's something not good going on now. Haven't you watched the news? They found the remains of a young woman not far from here."

"Not far from here, but not *here*," Angie said. "Hey," she said again, frowning with concern. "That can't have anything to do with anything—the Frampton ranch killer committed suicide, I thought."

"One of the cooks killed himself," Maura said. "Yes, but… I mean, he never had his day in court. Most people believed he killed Francine—he hated her. But a lot of people disliked her."

"But he killed himself."

"Yes. I wasn't here then. I did hear about it, of course."

Angie was pensive for a moment, and then she asked, "Maura, you don't think that the tree is…evil, do you?"

"*Trees*—a palm laced in with an oak. And no. I'm quite accustomed to the spooky and creepy, and we both know that places don't become evil, nor do things. But people can be wicked as hell—and they can feed off legends. I don't like being out here—not alone. There will be a campfire tonight with the history and ghost stories and the walk—we'll join that. I have waivers for whoever attends tonight."

"What if someone doesn't want to be filmed?" Angie asked anxiously. "You tell the story just as well as anyone else, right? And the camera loves you—a perfect, slinky blonde beauty with those enormous gray eyes of yours. Come on, you've told a few of the stories before. You can—"

"I cannot do a good video for you as a selfie," Maura said patiently.

"Right. I can film you telling the story," Angie said. "Just that part. And I can do it now—I think you said that the stories were told by the campfire, and then the historic walk began. I'll get you—right here and now—doing the story part of it. Oh, and you can include... Oh, God!" Angie said, her eyes widening. "You weren't just here—you saw the dead woman! The murdered woman... I mean, from this century. Francine Renault. And they arrested a kid, Brock McGovern, but he was innocent, and it was proved almost immediately, but then... Well, then, if the cook didn't do it, they never caught the killer!"

Maura kept her face impassive. Angie always wrote about old crimes that were unsolved—and why a place was naturally haunted after ghastly deeds had occurred there.

She did her homework, however. Angie probably knew more than Maura remembered.

She had loved the sad legend of the beautiful Gyselle, who had died so tragically for love. But, of course, she would have delved as deeply as possible into every event that had occurred at the ranch.

"Do they—do they tell that story at the campfire?" Angie asked.

Maura sighed. "Angie, I haven't been here since the night it happened. I was still young. My parents dragged me home immediately."

She was here now—and she could remember that

night all too clearly. Coming to the tree, then realizing while denying it that a real body was hanging from it. That it was Francine Renault. That she had been hanged from a heavy branch, hanged by the neck, and that she dangled far above the ground, tongue bulging, face grotesque.

She remembered screaming...

And she remembered the police and how they had taken Brock away, frowning and massively confused, still tall and straight and almost regally dignified.

And she could remember that there were still those who speculated on his guilt or innocence—until dozens of people had spoken out, having seen him through the time when Francine might have been taken and killed. His arrest had really been ludicrous—a detective's desperate bid to silence the horror and outrage that was beginning to spread.

Brock's life had changed, and thus her life had changed.

Everything had changed.

Except for this spot.

She could even imagine that she was a kid again, that she could see Francine Renault, so macabre in death, barely believable, yet so real and tragic and terrifying as she dangled from the thick limb.

"Oh," Angie groaned, the one word drawn out long enough to be a sentence. "Now I know why you were against doing a video here!"

Angie had wanted the History Tree. And when she had started to grow curious regarding Maura's reluctance to head to the Frampton Ranch and Resort—especially since the resort was supposedly great and the expense of rooms went on Angie's bill—Maura had decided it was time to cave.

She hadn't wanted to give any explanations.

"Angie, it's in your book, and you sell great and your video channel is doing great, as well. It's fine. Really. But because they did recently find what seems to be the remains of a murder victim near here, I do think we need to be careful. As in, stay out of these woods after dark."

"There is a big bad wolf. Was a big bad wolf... But seriously, I'm not a criminologist of any kind, but I'd say the killer back then was making a point. Maybe the bones they found belonged to someone who died of natural causes."

Angie wasn't stupid, but Maura was sure that the look she gave her tiny friend at that moment implied that she thought she was.

"Maybe," Angie said defensively.

"Angie, you don't rot in the dirt on purpose and then wind up with your bones in a cache of hotel laundry," Maura said.

"No, but, hey—there could be another explanation. Like a car accident. And whoever hit her was terrified and ran—and then, sadly, she just rotted."

"And wound up in hotel sheets?"

Maura asked incredulously. Angie couldn't be serious.

"Okay, so that's a bit far-fetched."

"Angie, it's been reported that the remains were found of a murder victim. Last I saw, they were still seeking her identity, but they said that she was killed."

"Well, they found bones, from what I understand. Anyway," Angie said, dusting her hands on her skirt and speaking softly and with dignity and compassion, "I wish you would have just said that you were here when it happened. Let's get out of here. I'm sorry I made you do this."

"You didn't make me do it. If I had been determined not to come back here, I wouldn't have done so. But it's going to get dark soon. Let me shoot a bit of you doing your speech by the tree while I still have good light."

Maura lifted her camera, looked at the tree and then up at the sky.

They wouldn't have the light much longer.

"Angie, come on—let's film you."

"Please—you know the stories so well. Let me film you this time."

"They're your books."

"But you'll give me a great authenticity. I'll interview you—and you were here when the last crime occurred. I'm surprised they haven't hacked this sucker to the ground, really," Angie said, looking at the tree. "Or at the very least, they should have video surveillance out here."

"Now, that would be the right idea. They have video surveillance in the lobby, the elevators—and other areas. But for now, please?"

They were never going to be able to leave.

"All right, all right!" Maura said. She adjusted the camera on its lightweight tripod and looked at the image on the camera's viewing screen. "I've got it lined up already. I'll go right there. You need to get it rolling. The mic is on already, and you can see what you're filming."

"Hey, I've used it before—not a lot, but I kind of know what I'm doing," Angie reminded her.

Maura stepped away from the camera and headed

over to the tree. Angie had paid attention to her. She
lifted her fingers and said, "In three…" and then went
silent, counting down the rest by hand.

Maura was amazed at how quickly it all came back
to her. She told the tale of the beautiful Gyselle and then
went into the later crimes.

Ending, of course, with the murder of Francine Renault.

"A false lead caused the arrest of an innocent young
man. But this is America, and we all know that any man
is innocent until proved guilty, and this young man was
quickly proved innocent. He was only under arrest for
a night, because eyewitness reports confirmed he was
with several other people—busy at work—when the
crime took place. Still, it was a travesty, shattering a
great deal of the promise of the young man's life. He
was, however, as I said, quickly released—and until
this day, the crime goes unsolved."

She finished speaking and saw that Angie was still
running the camera, looking past her, appearing perplexed—and pleased—by something that she saw.

"Hello there! Are you with Frampton Ranch and Resort? You aren't, by any chance, the host for the campfire stories tonight, are you?"

Angie was smiling sweetly—having shifted into her
flirtatious mode.

Curious, Maura turned around and started toward
the path.

If a jaw could actually drop, hers did.

She quickly closed her mouth, but perhaps her eyes
were bulging, as well. It seemed almost as if someone
had physically knocked the breath from her.

Brock McGovern was standing there.

Different.

The same.

A bit taller than he'd been at eighteen; his shoulders had filled out and he appeared to have acquired a great deal more solid muscle. He filled out a dark blue suit and tailored shirt exceptionally well.

His face was the same...

Different.

There was something hard about him now that hadn't been there before. His features were leaner, his eyes...

Still deep brown. But they were harder now, too, or appeared to be harder, as if there was a shield of glass on them. He'd always walked and moved with purpose, confident in what he wanted and where he was going.

Now, just standing still, he was an imposing presence.

And though Angie had spoken, he was looking at Maura.

"Wow," Angie said softly. "Did I dream up the perfect assistant for you—tall, dark and to die for? Who the hell... The storyteller guy is wickedly cute, but this guy..."

He couldn't have heard her words; he wasn't close enough.

And he wasn't looking at her. He was staring at Maura.

"That was great," he said smoothly. "However, I don't consider my life to have been *shattered*. I mean— I hope I have fulfilled a few of the promises I made to myself."

Maura wanted to speak. Her mouth wouldn't work.

Angie, however, had no problem.

"Oh, my God!" Angie cried.

Every once in a while, her Valley girl came out.

"You—you're Brock McGovern?" she asked.

"I am," he said, but he still wasn't looking at Angie. He was locked on Maura. Then he smiled. A rueful smile, dry and maybe even a little bitter.

"Here—in Florida," Angie said. "I mean—at the History Tree."

He turned at last to face Angie. "I'm here for an investigation now. I'm going to suggest that you two head back to the resort and don't wander off alone. A woman's remains were found at a laundry facility not far from here, and there are three young women who have gone missing recently. Best to stay in the main areas—with plenty of people around."

"Oh!" Angie went into damsel-in-distress mode then. "Is it really dangerous, do you think? I'm so glad that you're here, if there is danger. I mean, we've seen the news…heard things, but seriously, bad things aren't necessarily happening here, right? It's just a tree. Florida is far from crime-free, but… Anyway, thank God that you're here. We didn't really think we needed to be afraid, but now you're here…and thank God! Right, Maura?"

Maura didn't reply. She'd heard Angie speaking as if she'd been far, far away. Then she found her voice. Or, at least, a whisper of it.

"Brock," she murmured.

"Maura," he returned casually. "Good to see you. Well, surprised to see you—but good to see you."

"Investigation," she said, grasping for something to say. She seemed to be able to manage one word at a time.

"I just told you—they found a woman's remains, and three young women who have been reported missing had a connection to the Frampton Ranch and Resort. The FDLE has asked for Bureau help," he explained politely.

"Yes, we were just talking about the young woman's remains—and the missing girls. I, uh, I think I'd heard that you did go into the FBI," she said. "And they sent you…here." There. She had spoken in complete sentences. More or less. She'd been almost comprehensible.

"Yes, pretty much followed my original plans. Navy, college, the academy—FBI. And yes, I'm back here. Nothing like sending in an agent who knows the terrain," he said. "Shall we head back? I am serious. You shouldn't be in the woods alone when…well, when no one has any idea of what is really going on. We're not trying to incite fear. We're just trying to get a grip on what is happening, but I do suggest caution. Shall we head back?"

He was the same.

He was different.

And she was afraid to come too close to him. Afraid that the emotions of a teenager would erupt within her again, as if the years meant nothing…

If she got too close, she would either want to beat upon him, slamming her fists against his chest, demanding to know why he had never called, never tried to reach her and how it had been so easy to forget her.

Either that, or she would throw herself into his arms and sob and do anything just to touch him again.

Chapter Two

"The soil—clay based, some sand—like that covers most of the north of the state," Rachel Lawrence said.

She was seated across from Brock with Michael Flannery in the Java Bar on the Frampton property.

Rachel had changed. Her nails were cut short, clean of any color. Her hair was shorter, too. She still wore bangs, but her dark tresses were attractively trimmed to slide in angles along her face.

Everything about her appearance was serviceable. The girl who had once cried over a broken nail or scuffed sneakers had made an about-face.

She had greeted Brock politely and gravely, and seemed—like Flannery—to be anxious to have him working on the case with them.

"There's the beginning of a task force rumbling around," she'd told him when they'd first met in the coffee bar. "I'm lucky to be working with Michael Flannery—very lucky. But at this moment, while our superiors are listening, and they were willing to accept FBI involvement, they don't necessarily all believe that we are looking at a serial killer and this situation is about to blow up and get out of hand. It's great to have another officer who knows the lay of the land, so to speak."

"Yes, I do know it. And I've got to say, Rachel, I'm happy to see that you are working for the FDLE—and that you're so pleased to be where you are."

She made a face. "Oh, well, there was a time when I thought I wanted to be rich and elite, own a teacup Yorkie in a designer handbag and be supported in fine fashion. But I do love what I do. Oh—I actually do have a teacup Yorkie. Love the little guy!"

It had been far easier to meet back up with Rachel— and even Nils and Mark Hartford—than Brock had expected.

Time.

It healed all wounds, right?

Wrong. Why not? He believed he was, as far as any normal psychology went, long over what had happened regarding his arrest for murder at such a young age— he'd barely been in jail before his parents arrived with their attorney, his dad so indignant that the icy chill in his eyes might have gotten Brock released before the attorney even opened his mouth.

Truly, he had seen and heard far worse in the navy. And, God knew, some of the cases he'd handled as an agent in a criminal investigation unit had certainly been enough to chill the blood.

Still…the haunting memories regarding the forest and the History Tree clung to him like the moss that dripped from the old oaks.

"A Yorkie, huh?" he asked Rachel, remembering that she was there.

They both grinned, and he assured her that he liked dogs, all dogs, and didn't have one himself only because it wouldn't be fair to the animal—he was always working.

Rachel went on with the information—or lack of it—that she had worked to obtain.

"Some of our elegant hotels have special bedding, but…lots don't. The sheets around the remains might have come from five different chain hotels that cover North Florida, Central Florida and the Panhandle, all of which have twenty to forty local franchises. That means that Maureen Rodriguez might have been murdered anywhere in all that area—buried first nearby or somewhere different within the boundaries—and then dug up and wrapped in sheets."

"You checked with the truck drivers making deliveries that day, naturally?" Brock asked her.

She gave him a look that was both amused and withering. "I did go to college—and I majored in criminology. I'm not just a piece of fluff, you know."

Detective Michael Flannery grunted. "She's tailing me—I'm teaching her everything I know. And," he added, "how not to make the same mistakes."

Brock nodded his appreciation for the comment and asked, "Were you able to narrow it down by the drivers and their deliveries?"

"The way it works is that they pick up when they drop off," Rachel said. "So it's not as if they're kept separately. It's almost like recycling receptacles—the hotels have these massive canvas bags. The sheets are all the same, so they drop off dirty and pick up clean replacements. The laundry is also responsible for getting rid of sheets that are too worn, too stained, too whatever. But the driver drop-offs do narrow it down to hotels from St. Augustine to Gainesville and down to northern Ocala. I have a list of them, which I've emailed and…" She paused, reaching into her bag for a small folder that she presented to Brock. "Here—hard copy."

He looked at the list. There were at least thirty hotels with their addresses listed.

"All right, thank you," he told her. "I'd like to start by talking to Katie Simmons—the woman who reported Lydia Merkel missing. And then the last person to see each of the missing young women."

"Cops have interviewed all of them. I saw Katie Simmons myself," Flannery told him. "I'm not sure what else you can get from her."

"Humor me. And this list—I'd like you to get state officers out with images of all the women. Let's see what they get—they'll tell us if they find anyone who has seen any of them or thinks they might have seen someone like them. We need the images plastered everywhere—a Good Samaritan could call in and let us know if they saw one of the women walking on the street, buying gas…at a bar or a restaurant."

"The images have been broadcast," Flannery said. "I asked for you, but come on. We're not a bunch of dumb hicks down here, you know."

Brock grinned. "I'm a Fed, remember?"

Flannery shrugged. "You're a conch," he reminded Brock, referring to the moniker given to Key West natives.

"I get you, but I'm not referring to local news. I mean, we need likenesses of the young women—all four of them—out everywhere. We need to draw on media across the state and beyond. And we need to get them up in all the colleges—there are several of them in the area. All four of the women were college age—they might have friends just about anywhere. They might have met up with someone at a party."

"I'll get officers on the hotels and take the colleges with Rachel. She and I can head in opposite directions and cover more ground." Flannery hesitated. "I've arranged for us to see the ME first thing, so we'll start all else after that—I assumed you wanted to see the remains of Maureen Rodriguez."

"Yes, and thank you," Brock told him. "Do I meet you at the morgue?"

"No, we'll head out together—if that's all right with you. I have a room here and so does Rachel. I'm setting mine up as a headquarters," Flannery said. "I'll start a whiteboard—that way, we can keep up with any information any of us acquires and have it in plain sight, as we'd be doing if we were running the investigation out of one of our offices."

"A good plan," Brock said. "But tomorrow I would like to get started over in St. Augustine as quickly as possible."

"All right, then. We will take two cars tomorrow morning. Compare notes back here, say, late afternoon. Get in touch sooner if we have something that seems of real significance. It's good that you decided to be based here. Easier than trying to come and go."

Flannery hesitated, looking at Brock. Then he shrugged. "Mr. Glass actually came to me." He lowered his voice, even though there was no one near them. "On the hush-hush. Said his wife didn't even know. Seems he's afraid himself that someone is using this place or the legends that go with it."

Brock drained his cup of coffee. "Can you set me

up with Katie Simmons for some time tomorrow?" he asked Rachel.

"Yes, sir, I can and will," she assured him. "She's in St. Augustine."

Brock stood.

They looked up at him.

"And now?" Flannery asked.

"You wanted me here because I know the place," Brock said. "I'm going to watch a couple of the people that I knew when I worked here. See what's changed—and who has changed and how. I'm not leaving the property tonight. If there's anything, call me. And I'll check in later."

"You're going to the campfire tales and ghost walk?" Flannery asked.

"Not exactly—but kind of," Brock said. He nodded to the two of them and headed out, glancing at his watch.

He did know the place, that was certain. Almost nothing on the grounds had changed.

His father had heard about the place—that it was a great venue for young people to work for the summer during high school. There was basic housing for them, a section of rooms for girls and one for boys. They weren't allowed off the grounds unless they had turned eighteen or they were supervised; any dereliction of the rules called for immediate dismissal. The positions were highly prized—if anyone broke the rules, they were damned careful not to be caught.

Of course, fraternizing—as in sex—had not been in the rules.

Kids were kids.

But with him and Maura…

It had felt like something more than kids being kids.

He still believed it. He wondered if, just somewhere in her mind, she believed it, too.

MARK HARTFORD PROVED to be excellent at telling the stories—despite the fact that he'd told Maura that he was afraid that night. Well, not afraid but nervous.

"You were so good!" he had said to Maura when he saw that she and Angie were going to be in his audience. "So good!"

He'd been just about fourteen when she knew him years before; he had to be about twenty-five or twenty-six now. He'd grown up, of course, and he still charmed with a boyish energy and enthusiasm that was contagious. His eyes were bright blue and his hair—just slightly shaggy— was a tawny blond. He'd grown several inches since Maura had seen him, and he evidently made use of the resort's gym.

Angie was entranced by Mark. But she'd always been unabashed about her appreciation of men in general—especially when they were attractive. Maura didn't consider herself to be particularly suspicious of the world in general, but she did find that she often felt much older and wiser when she was with Angie—warning her that it wasn't always good to be quite so friendly with every good-looking man that she met.

"I'm sure you're just as good a storyteller," Angie had told Mark.

"I try—I have a lot to live up to," he'd said in return, answering Angie, smiling from one of them to the other.

Maura was somewhat pleased by the distraction. Angie had been talking incessantly about Brock and she'd finally stopped—long enough to do a new assessment of Mark Hartford.

She had decided that she liked young Mark Hartford very much, as well.

They'd already seen Nils in the restaurant. Mark and Nils were easily identifiable as brothers, but Mark's evident curiosity and sincere interest in everyone and everything around him made him the more naturally charming of the two.

"Ooh, I do like both brothers. But the other guy…the FBI guy… Hey, he was the one they arrested—and he turned out to be FBI! Cool. I appreciate them all, but that Brock guy…sexier…way sexier," Angie had said.

Actually, Maura found Angie's honesty one of the nicest things about her. She said what she was thinking or feeling pretty much all the time.

Now the tales were underway. Mark was telling them well. Maura allowed herself to survey his audience.

There were—as there had always been, so it seemed—a group of young teens, some together, some with their parents. There were couples, wives or girlfriends hanging on to their men, and sometimes a great guy admittedly frightened by the dark and tales and hanging on to his girlfriend or wife or boyfriend or husband, as well. There were young men and women, older men and women—a group of about twenty-five or thirty in all.

She couldn't help but remember how her group had been about the same size that night twelve years ago—and how they had all reacted when they reached the History Tree.

She had screamed—so had several people.

Some had laughed—certain that the swinging body was a prop and perhaps part of a gag set up by the establishment to throw a bit of real scare into the evening.

And then had come the frantic 911 calls, the horror as everyone realized that the dead woman was real and Brock trying to herd people away and, even then, trying to see that the scene wasn't trampled, that as a crime scene it wasn't disturbed...

Only to be arrested himself.

Tonight, Maura had her camera; she also had waivers signed by everyone in the group. She'd been lucky that night—everyone had been happy to meet her and Angie—and they all wanted their fifteen minutes of fame. They were fine with being on camera with Angie Parsons.

They were still by the campfire.

She was thinking about Brock.

Determining how much she was going to video after Mark's speech, she looked across the campfire to the place where the trees edged around the fire and the storyteller and his audience.

Brock was leaning against a tree, arms crossed over his chest, listening.

He was no longer wearing a suit; he was in jeans and a plaid flannel shirt—he could pass himself off as a logger or such. Her heart seemed to do a little leap and she was angry at herself, angry that she could still find him so compellingly attractive.

Twelve years between them. Not a word. They weren't even friends on social media.

He must have sensed her looking at him. She realized that his gaze had changed direction; he was looking at her across the distance.

He nodded slightly and then frowned, shaking his head.

He didn't want to be on camera; she nodded.

She turned away, dismissing him.

She tried to focus on the words that Mark Hartford was saying.

The stories were the same. Until they came to the History Tree.

There, a new story had been added in. Mark talked about the tour that had come upon Francine Renault.

He wasn't overly dramatic; he told the facts, and admitted that, yes, he had been among those who had found her.

The story ended with the death of the cook, Peter Moore, who had stabbed himself and been found in the freezer, his favorite knife protruding from his chest.

A fight had gone too far, or so the authorities believed, and Moore had killed Francine. And then later, in remorse or fear that prison would be worse than death, he had committed suicide.

On that tragic note, the story of the History Tree ended. As did the nightly tour.

Mark then told his group that they needed to head back—there had been some trouble in the area lately and the management would appreciate it if guests refrained from being in the forest at night and suggested that no one wander the woods alone.

As they began to filter back, Maura saw that Brock didn't go with the others.

She might have been the only one to note his presence; he had apparently followed silently at a bit of a distance, always staying back within the trees.

She turned when the group left. As they headed back along the trail, Brock stepped from his silent watching spot in the darkness of the surrounding foliage. He walked to the History Tree.

He stood silently, staring up at it, as if seeking some answer there.

Mark was asking if the tourists wanted coffee or tea or a drink before they called it a night.

Angie had already said yes.

Maura turned away from Brock purposefully and followed Angie and Mark. Once they reached the lodge, she would beg off.

All she wanted to do that night was crawl into a hole somewhere and black out.

Her room and her bed would have to do—even if she didn't black out and lay awake for hours, ever more furious with herself that she was allowing herself to feel…

Anything about him. Anything at all.

"I'VE SEEN SOME strange things in my day," Rita Morgan, the medical examiner, said. She was a tall, lean woman, looked to be about forty-five and certainly the no-nonsense type.

"Many a strange thing, and some not so strange. Too many bodies out of the ocean and the rivers, a few in barrels, some sunk with cement." She pursed her lips, shaking her head. "This one? Strange and sad. As long as I've done this, been an ME, it still never ceases to amaze me—man's inhumanity to fellow man." She looked up at Brock and Flannery and shook her head again. "Thing that saves me is when I see a young person get up and help the disabled or the elderly—then I get to know that there's as much good out there as bad— more, hopefully. Yeah, yeah, that doesn't help you any. I just… Well, I can show you the remains. I can't tell you too much about them. No stomach content—no stomach. I had disarticulated bones with small amounts of flesh still attached—and a skull."

She stepped back to display the gurney that held the remains of a young woman's life, tragically—and brutally—cut short.

"It looks as if she was killed a long time ago—but from my brief, she was only missing about three months," Brock said, looking from Flannery to the medical examiner.

And then to the table.

Bits of hair and scalp still adhered to the skull.

"Decomposition is one of those things that can vary incredibly. I believe she was killed approximately two months ago. Particular to situations like this, the internal organs began to deteriorate twenty-four to seventy-two hours after death. The number of bacteria and insects in the area have an effect on the outer body and soft tissue. Three to five days—you have bloating. Within ten days, insects, the elements and bacteria have been busy and you have massive accumulations of gas. Within a few weeks, nails and teeth begin to go. After a month, the body becomes fluid."

"The skull retains a mouthful of teeth," Brock noted.

"Yes, which is why I believe decomp had the best possible circumstances. Lots of earth—and water. Rain, maybe. Even flooding in the area where the body was first left. As I said, there's no way to pinpoint an exact time of death. It's approximately two months' time. I also believe, per decomp, that she was left out in the elements—maybe a bit of dirt and some leaves were shoveled over her. It's been a warm winter, and the soil here can be rich—and as we all know, this is Florida. We have plenty of insects.

"The question is, after all that decomp in the wild, how in the world did she come to be in sheets at an industrial laundry? But that's your problem. Mine is cause of death. Not much to go on, as you can see, but enough." She pointed with a gloved hand. "That rib bone. You can see. The scraping there wasn't any insect—that was caused by a sharp blade. There's a second such mark on that rib—would have been the other side of the rear rib cage. In my educated estimation, she was stabbed to death. Without more tissue or organs I can't tell you how many wounds she sustained—exactly how many times she was stabbed—but I do imagine the attack would have been brutal, and that she probably suffered mortal damage to many of her organs. There's no damage to the skull."

"Were there any defensive wounds you were able to find on the arm bones?" Brock asked.

Flannery was standing back, letting Brock ask his own questions, since the detective had already seen the remains and spoken with the ME earlier.

"No, there were no defensive wounds, Special Agent McGovern," Dr. Morgan said. "She was stabbed from behind. She might never have seen her killer. Or she might have trusted him—or her. It was violent assault, I can tell you that. But—I am assuming that she didn't want to be stabbed to death—she had to have been taken by surprise. She never had a chance to fight back at all. Some of what I've been saying I'm assuming, but I am making assumptions based on education and experience. I'm the ME—you guys are the detectives. Can't help having an opinion."

"Of course, that's fine, and thank you," Brock said. "The sheets are at the lab? Still being tested?"

"Yes. They can't pinpoint the sheets to a certain hotel because too many of them buy from the same supplier."

She covered the remains.

She looked at Brock curiously, studying him. Then she smiled broadly. "You came out all right, it seems." She glanced over at Flannery. "Despite what you did to him."

"Hey, I acted on the best info I had at the time," Flannery said.

"Rash—hey, he was a newbie at the time. Didn't know his—oh, never mind. But good to see you—as a law enforcement officer, Agent McGovern."

"Well, thank you. I'm sorry, did we meet before?" he asked her.

She shook her head. "I was new in this office. But I assisted at the autopsies for both Francine Renault and the cook, Peter Moore..." She left off, shrugging. "I knew that they'd brought you in—one of the summer kids. Because you were seen in some kind of major verbal altercation with her. And arrested, from what I understand, on a *tip*."

She didn't exactly sniff, but she did look at Detective Flannery with a bit of disdain.

"I say again, I acted on the best info I had at the time. And yeah—I guess he came out all right," Flannery said with something that sounded a bit like a growl in his voice. He eyed Brock, as if not entirely sure about him yet.

"I spent only one night in jail. Trust me, I spent many a worse night in the service," he assured Dr. Morgan and Flannery.

Flannery looked away, uncomfortable. Dr. Morgan smiled.

"Thank you," he told her. "If there's anything else that comes to mind that might be of any assistance whatsoever..."

"I'll be quicker than a rabbit in heat," she vowed solemnly.

He arched his brows slightly but managed a smile and another thank-you.

Brock and Flannery left the county morgue together. They'd come in Flannery's official vehicle; it would allow them to bypass heavy traffic if needed, Flannery had said.

Brock preferred to drive himself, but that day, while Flannery drove, it gave him a chance to look through his notes on the victim.

"She stayed at the Frampton Ranch and Resort three months ago," he murmured out loud. "Her home was St. Pete. She wasn't reported missing right away because she was over eighteen and had been living alone in St. Augustine, working as a cocktail waitress—but hadn't shown up for work in over a week. Says here none of her coworkers really knew her—she had just started."

"The perfect victim," Flannery said. He glanced sideways at Brock. "The other missing girls... You have the information on them, too, right?"

"Yeah, I have it online and on paper. I have to hand it to Egan. He believes in hard copy and there are times it proves to be especially beneficial."

"And saves on eyestrain," Flannery muttered. He glanced Brock's way again. "You know, I asked for you specifically. Hope you don't mind too much. Can't help it. Still think there's something with that damned resort, even if I can't pin it. Well, I mean, back then, of course, it had to do with the ranch. Francine Renault worked there—and died there. But…that tree has seen a lot of death."

He said it oddly, almost as if he was in awe of the tree. Brock frowned, looking over at him. Flannery didn't glance his way, but apparently knew he was being studied.

"Well, bad stuff happens there," Flannery said.

"Right—because bad people like the aspect that bad things happened there."

"You think it should be chopped down."

"It might dissuade future killers."

"Or just cause them to leave their victims somewhere else," Flannery said. "Or create a new History Tree or haunted bog or…just a damnable stretch of roadway."

"True," Brock agreed.

"What drives me crazy is the why—I mean, we all study this stuff. Some killers are simply goal driven—they want or need someone out of the way. Some killings have to do with passion and anger and jealousy. Some have to do with money. Some people are psychotic and kill for the thrill or the sexual release it gives them. Years ago, it was just Francine. Now, that Francine—I didn't find a single soul who actually said they liked her, but it never seemed she'd done anything bad enough to make someone want to kill her. She seemed to be more of an annoyance—like a fly buzzing around your ear."

"Maybe she was a really, really annoying fly—buzzing at the wrong person," Brock said. Then he reminded the detective, "Peter Moore committed suicide. There was no note—but maybe he did do it, because he was afraid of being apprehended, or felt overwhelming remorse or was dealing with an untreated mental illness that led him down a very dark path. Seems to me that

everyone accepted the fact that he must have done it—
though he sure as hell didn't get his day in court."

Flannery glanced his way at last. "But you don't
think that Peter Moore killed Francine any more than
I do."

Brock hesitated and then said flatly, "No. And I knew
Peter Moore. He hated Francine, but he held his own
with her—he didn't really have to answer to her. He was
directly under Fred Bentley. I don't think he killed Francine. I don't even think that Peter Moore killed himself."

Flannery nodded. "There you go—see? There was
a reason I needed you down here. Damn, though, if it
doesn't seem like homecoming somehow."

"What do you mean?"

"I mean, I can't just buy the theory that Peter Moore
did it, either. In my mind, the killer might have helped
him into that so-called suicide. No prints but Peter's
on the knife in his gut, but hell, the kitchen is filled
with gloves."

"So it is."

"That beauty is back, as well," Flannery said, glancing his way once again.

Brock didn't ask who Flannery meant. That was dead
obvious. Maura.

"Did you ask her up here?" Brock asked him.

"Me?" Flannery was truly surprised. "I barely met
her back in the day, and she was fairly rattled when I
did… Well, you were there. You didn't ask for her to
be here? I'd have thought, at least, that the two of you
would still be friends. You were hot and heavy back
then, so I heard—the beautiful young ones!"

"I hadn't seen her since that night until I saw her
again late yesterday afternoon—out by the tree."

"Ah, yes, she's with that web queen or writer—or whatever that little woman calls herself," Flannery said. He looked over at Brock. "Is that what they call serendipity?"

Brock didn't reply. He was looking at his portfolios on the missing women. He'd already read through them on the plane, but talking things out could reveal new angles.

"All right," Brock said. "Maureen Rodriguez was out of the house and just starting a new life. So she wasn't noted as missing right away. But Lily Sylvester was supposed to check in with her boyfriend. She'd come to the Frampton ranch because she wanted to see it. She stayed at a little hotel on the outskirts of St. Augustine one night after her visit, and then she was supposed to meet with a girlfriend at a posh bed-and-breakfast in the old section of the city. She never showed that day and her friend called the cops right away."

He flipped through his folders.

"Friends and family were insistent about Lily," Flannery told him. "She was as dependable as they come. Is," he added. "We shouldn't assume the worst."

But it was natural that they did.

"All right, moving on to Amy Bonham. She stayed at the Frampton ranch. She told one of the waitresses that she was excited about a surprise job opportunity the next day. She was supposed to be heading in the other direction—toward Orlando and the theme parks. She also stayed at a chain motel the night right after she was at the Frampton ranch and disappeared the next day. I know you certainly looked into her 'job opportunity.'"

Flannery nodded. "We've had officers interviewing people across more than half the state."

"But no one knew anything about it."

"No. But the waitress at the Frampton ranch—Dorothy Masterson—swears that Amy was super excited. Dorothy believed that she was looking for work at one of the theme parks."

"And you checked with all the parks."

"Of course. Big and small."

Brock went on to his third folder. "Lydia Merkel."

Flannery nodded; he'd already committed to memory most of what Brock was still studying.

"Lydia. Cute as a button."

"You met her? You knew her?" Brock asked, frowning.

"I met her briefly—I was in St. Augustine. The wife had her nephews down and I was taking them on one of the ghost tours. Lydia was on our tour. All wide eyes and happiness. Can't tell you how stunned I was when the powers that be called me in and told me that we had another missing woman—and that I recognized her." He glanced quickly at Brock. "You know how it goes with missing persons reports. Half of the time someone is just off on a lark. There's been a fight—a person has taken off because they want to disappear. But I just don't think that's the case." He was silent. "Especially since we found the remains of Maureen Rodriguez."

"And you can't help but think that Frampton Ranch and Resort is somehow involved."

Flannery nodded grimly.

"Lydia had told a young woman she was working with—Katie Simmons—that she wanted to take her first days off to drive over and see the History Tree. We're not just working this alone. I have all kinds of help on this. We do have officers from the Florida Department of Law Enforcement out all over—not to mention the help we've gotten from our local police departments. I keep feeling like I'm looking at some kind of puzzle with pieces missing—except that the frame is there. Because there was only one thing the girls—or young women—had in common."

"They had left or were coming to the Frampton Ranch and Resort," Brock said.

He felt a sudden pang deep in his heart or maybe his soul—someplace that really hurt at any rate.

He glanced over at Flannery. "The four of them are between the ages of twenty-two and twenty-nine," he said.

"Lydia Merkel was—is—twenty-nine. She was at the ranch with friends for her birthday. On the tour, she talked about loving ghost stories—and how excited she was going to be to see the infamous History Tree."

Seriously—the tree should have been bulldozed.

Not fair—the tree wasn't guilty. Men and women could be guilty; the tree was just a tree—two trees.

"Funny, isn't it?" Flannery asked. "I mean, not ha ha funny, just…strange. Maybe ironic. The History Tree is two trees. Entwined. And you're here—because I asked for you particularly because I knew you were FBI, criminal section—and I'm here. And Miss Maura Antrim is here. We're all kinds of entwined. And I can't help but think that we still know the killer—even if twelve years have gone by."

"Yep. We're all tangled together somehow, like that damned tree. And so help me God, this time I really want to have the answers…and to stop the killing," Brock said quietly.

"You don't disagree with me?" Flannery asked him.

Brock shrugged grimly.

"But you don't disagree—you don't think I'm being far-fetched or anything?" Flannery pressed.

"No, I just wonder what this person—if it is the same killer—has been doing for twelve years," Brock said. And then added, "Although…maybe he hasn't been lying dormant. It's a big state filled with just about everything in one area or another. Forests, marshes, caverns, sinkholes, the Everglades—a river of grass—and, of course…"

"That great big old Atlantic Ocean," Flannery said. "So, there you go. My puzzle. Are there pieces missing? Did the three young ladies who disappeared just run off? Or…"

"Has someone been killing young women and disposing of corpses over the last twelve years?" Brock finished. He took a deep breath. "All right, I guess I'm going to do a lot of traveling. There will be dozens of people to question again. But I think I'll start at the library at Frampton ranch."

ANGIE WAS A late sleeper, something Maura deeply appreciated the next morning. She wanted some on-her-own time.

She had gotten a lot of great footage for Angie's internet channel on the tour the night before.

Martin had ended up loving being on camera—and it had loved him. They were going to do the campfire again that night, get more video and put together all the best parts.

She'd behaved perfectly normally, even though she was ready to crawl out of her own skin. While on the tour, she'd expected to see Brock materialize again.

It hadn't been until the very end that she'd realized he'd been there all along—watching from the shadows, from the background.

But he'd never approached her. She'd seen him later in the lounge, briefly, when she and Angie walked in after the trek through the woods. He'd been deep in conversation with a slightly older man in a suit—she'd seen him earlier and remembered him vaguely. He was a cop of some kind; he'd been there the night that Francine Renault was killed. She had seen him earlier in the day as well, walking around the ranch with a woman. Maura hadn't seen the woman's face, just the cut of her suit, and for some bizarre reason she had noticed the woman's shoes. Flat, serviceable.

And she'd thought that perhaps the woman was a cop or in some form of law enforcement, too.

Angie hadn't seemed interested in talking to any of them—Maura had been glad. She'd left Angie in the lounge, waiting for her appointed drink with Mark, and Maura had slipped quickly upstairs, wanting nothing more than to be in her room, alone.

Once there, she'd lain awake for hours, wondering why something that had happened ages ago still had such an effect on her life—on her.

Why... Brock McGovern could suddenly walk back into her life and become all that she thought about once again. So easily. Or why she could close her eyes and see the man he had become and know that he was still somehow flawed and perfect, the man to whom she had subconsciously—or even consciously—compared to everyone else she ever met.

He hadn't so much as touched her.

And he hadn't looked at her as if he particularly liked

her. He'd simply wanted her—and Angie—to be safe. Nothing more. Stay with people. He was a law enforcement officer, a Fed. He worked to find those who had turned living, breathing bodies into murdered, decaying bodies—and he tried to keep all men and women from being victims. His job. What he did.

A job he always knew he wanted.

She had to stop thinking about him, and that meant she needed to immerse herself in some other activity—research. Books, knowledge, seeking...

She had always loved the library and archives at the Frampton ranch. One thing Donald Glass did with every property he bought was build and maintain a library with any books and info he had on that property. It was fascinating—much of it had been put on computer through the years, but every little event that had to do with the property was available.

The hotel manager—solid, ruddy little Fred Bentley—had never shown any interest in the contents of the library.

Nor, when she'd been alive, had Francine Renault. But the libraries were sacred. No matter what else the very, very rich Donald Glass might be, he loved his history and his libraries, and anyone working for him learned not to mess with them.

For this, she greatly admired Glass. Not that she knew the man well—he'd left the hands-on management to Francine and Fred when Maura had been working there. And back then, she and Brock had both spent hours in the library—often together—each trying to one-up the other by finding some obscure and curious fact or happening. It was fun to work the weird trivia into their presentations.

That had been twelve years ago.

But Brock was suddenly back in her life.

No, he wasn't in her life. He just happened to be here at the same time.

Because a woman had been murdered—and others had disappeared.

Concentrate... There was a wealth of information before her. Bits and pieces that might offer up something especially unusual for Angie Parsons.

The library room was comfortable and inviting, filled with leather sofas and chairs, desks, computers—and shelves upon shelves of files and books.

Donald Glass had acquired an extensive collection; he had books on the indigenous population of the area, starting back somewhere between twelve and twenty thousand years ago. Settlers had arrived before the end of the Pleistocene megafauna era. The Wacissa River—not far away in Jefferson County near the little town of Wacissa—had offered up several animal fossils of the time, and other areas of the state—including Silver Springs, Vero, Melbourne and Devil's Den—had also offered up proof of man's earliest time in the area.

Way back that many thousands of years, there had been a greater landmass and less water, causing animals—and thus hunters—to congregate at pools. Artifacts proving the existence of these hunter-gatherers could be found in countless rivers—and even out into the Gulf of Mexico.

Mammoths had even roamed the state.

By 700 AD, farming had come to the north of Florida. There were many Native American tribes, and many of those were called Creek by the Europeans and spoke the Muskogee language. But by the time the first

Frampton put down roots to create this great ranching and farming estate, Florida Indians of many varieties—though mostly Creek—were being lumped together as Seminoles, largely divided into two groups: the Muskogee-speaking and the Hitchiti-speaking.

There were wonderful illustrated books describing fossils and tools found, creating images of the people and the way they lived.

According to the one she pulled from the shelf there had been a colony of Seminole living in the area when Frampton first chose his site.

They had held rites out at what was already a giant clearing in the forest. It was the Native Americans who had first called it the History Tree. The Timucua had first named it so; the Seminoles in the area had respected the holiness of the tree.

Maura—like the writer of the book—didn't believe that the Native American tribes had practiced human sacrifice at the tree. But as war loomed with the Seminole tribe, the European populace had liked to portray the native people as barbarians—it made it easier to justify killing them.

So the tree had gotten its reputation very early on.

Gyselle—who became known as Gyselle Frampton, since no one knew her real surname—had arrived at the plantation soon after it was built in the late 1830s. Spanish missionaries had "rescued" her from the Seminole, but she was fifteen at the time and had been kidnapped at the age of ten—or that was the best that could be figured. Oliver Frampton—creator of the first great mansion to rest on the property—had been a kind man. He'd taken her in, clothed her, educated her and had still, of course, given her chores to do.

She was a servant and not of the elite. She was not, in any way, wife material for his son.

That hadn't stopped Richard Frampton from falling in love with his father's beautiful servant/ward.

But Richard had underestimated his wife. Back then, a wife was supposed to be a lovely figurehead, wealthy to match her husband and eye candy on the arm of her man. Unless she was very, very, very rich—and then it wouldn't matter if she was eye candy or not.

But Julie LeBlanc Frampton had been no fool and not someone to be taken lightly.

She discovered the affair—and knew that her husband loved Gyselle deeply. Perhaps she was angry with her father-in-law for not only condoning the affair but perhaps finding it to be fine and natural. Wives weren't supposed to get in the way of these things after all.

Or maybe the situation was just convenient for her plan.

She hid the taste of the deadly fruit of the manchineel tree in a drink—one that Gyselle usually made up for the senior Mr. Frampton right before he went to bed made up of whiskey, tea and sugar.

The old man died in horrible pain. Julie immediately pointed the finger at Gyselle.

She created such an outcry and hysteria that the other servants immediately went for poor Gyselle. The master had been well loved. And without trial or even much questioning, they had dragged Gyselle out to the History Tree—thought to surely be haunted at that time and also a place where the devil might well be found.

Gyselle died swearing that she was innocent—and cursing Julie, those around her and even the tree.

After she was hanged, she was allowed to remain there until she rotted, until her bones fell to the ground.

Three years later, Julie Frampton died. At the time no one knew what her ailment was—tuberculosis, it sounded like to Maura.

But in the end, the true poisoner did die choking on her own blood—and confessing to the entire room that she had murdered her father-in-law.

"Maura!"

She had become so involved in what she was reading that the sound of her name made her jump.

She'd been very comfortable in one of the plush leather chairs, feet curled beneath her, the book—*Truth and Legends of Central Florida*—in her arms.

Luckily, she didn't drop it or throw it as she was startled. It was an original book, printed and bound in 1880.

"Mr. Glass!" she exclaimed, truly started to see the resort's owner. He usually kept to himself; Fred Bentley was his mouthpiece.

She quickly closed the book and stood, accepting the hand he offered to her.

Donald Glass, in his early sixties now, Maura thought, was still an attractive man. He kept himself lean and fit—and had maintained a full head of salt-and-pepper hair. His posture was straight; his manners tended to be impeccable. He'd never personally fired anyone that she knew of, in any of his enterprises. He left managers—like Fred Bentley—to do such deeds. He was customarily well liked and treated kindly by magazines when he was included in an article.

Donald Glass used his money to make more money, granted. That was the American way. But he did it all in one of the best possible manners—preserving history and donating to worthy causes all the while.

Whether he was into the causes or simply into tax breaks, no one really looked too closely.

But he tended to do good things and do them well.

"Miss Antrim, how lovely to have you here again," he said, smiling. "And I'm delighted that you've brought Angie Parsons with her incredible ability to show the world interesting places—and provide wonderful publicity for those places!"

"I'd love to take the credit, Mr. Glass," Maura told him. "Angie heard the story about the History Tree. She couldn't wait to come."

"Well, however you came to be here, I'm most delighted. Still sorry—and I will be sorry all my life—about Francine. She was…"

He paused. Maura wondered what he'd been about to say. That Francine Renault had been a good woman? But she really hadn't been kind or generous in any way.

"No one deserved to die that way," he said. "Anyway… I did consider having the tree torn out of the ground. But I thought on it a long time and decided that it was the *History Tree*. They didn't burn down the building when a famous woman died in a room at the Hard Rock in Hollywood, Florida, and…" Again, he paused. "I decided that the tree—or trees—should stay. Not to mention the fact that the environmentalists and preservationists would create a real uproar if we were to cut it down. It's hundreds of years old, you know. And yes—as you learned last night, we do tell the story at the campfire and continue the walk by the tree."

"Trees aren't evil," Maura said.

She wondered if she was trying to reassure him—or

if it was something she said but doubted somewhere in a primal section of her heart or mind.

"No, of course not. A tree is a tree. Or trees are trees," he said and smiled weakly. "Anyway, I'm delighted to see you. And thankful for the work you're doing here with Miss Parsons."

"I'm not sure you need us. You've always had a full house here."

He didn't argue.

"I'm sure Marie will be delighted to see you, too."

"A pleasure to see her," Maura murmured.

Marie was perhaps ten years younger than her husband; they had been together for thirty years or so. Like her husband she kept herself fit, and she was an attractive and cordial woman. Her public manner was pristine—every once in a while, Maura had wondered what she was *really* thinking.

Glass lifted a hand in farewell and said, "Enjoy your stay." He started to walk away and then turned back. "I don't mean to be an alarmist, but…be careful. I'm sure you heard. Remains were found nearby. And several young women have disappeared, as well. Whether they ran away or…met with bad things… I know you're smart, but…be wary."

"Yes, I've heard. And I'll be careful," Maura said.

She watched him for a moment as he headed out of the room and then she opened the book again. Words swam before her as she tried to remember where she'd left off.

She heard Glass speaking again and she looked toward the door, thinking that he had something else to say.

But he wasn't speaking to her.

Brock was at the doorway, his tone deep and quiet as he replied to whatever Glass had said.

The length of Maura's body gripped with tension, which angered her to no end.

She hadn't seen or heard from him in twelve years.

He and Glass parted politely.

Brock headed straight for her. He smiled, but it seemed that his smile was grave.

His face seemed harder than the image of him she'd held in her mind. Naturally. Years did that to anyone.

And he'd always wanted to be law enforcement. But that job had to take a toll.

"I thought I'd find you here," he said softly.

"Yes, well, I... I'm here," she said.

She didn't invite him to sit. He did anyway. She wondered if he was going to talk about the years between them, ask what she'd been doing, maybe even explain why he'd just disappeared after the charges against him had been dismissed.

Elbows on his knees, hands folded idly, he was close—too close, she thought. Or not really close at all. Just close because she could feel a strange rush inside, as if she knew everything about him, or everything that mattered. She knew his scent—his scent, not soap or aftershave or cologne, but that which lurked beneath it, particular to him, something that drew her to him, that called up a natural reaction within her. She knew that there was a small scar on the lower side of his abdomen—stitches from a deep cut received when he'd fallen on a haphazardly discarded tin can during a track event when he'd been in high school. She knew there was a spattering of freckles on his shoulders, knew...

"You really shouldn't be here—you need to pack

up and go," he said. His tone was harsh, as if she were committing a grave sin by being there.

She couldn't have been more surprised if he'd slapped her.

"I beg your pardon?" she demanded, a sudden fury taking over.

"You need to get the hell out—out of this part of the state and sure as hell off the Frampton Ranch and Resort."

Why did it hurt so badly, the way he spoke to her, the way he wanted to be rid of her?

"I'm sorry. I have every right to be here. It's a public facility and a free country, last I heard."

"No, you don't—"

She stood, aware she badly needed to leave the room.

"Excuse me, Special Agent—or whatever your title may be. You don't control me. I have a life—and things to do. Things that need to be done—here. Right here. Have a nice day."

She stood—with quiet dignity, she hoped—and headed quickly for the door.

How the hell could he still have such an effect upon her?

And why the hell did he have to be here now?

Another body. Another life cut tragically short. His job.

Brock was right; she was the one who shouldn't be here.

Chapter Three

To say that he'd handled his conversation with Maura badly would be a gross understatement.

But he couldn't start over. She was angry and not about to listen to him—certainly not now. Maybe later.

The library seemed oddly cold without her, empty of human life.

Brock needed to get going, but he found himself standing up, studying some of the posters and framed newspaper pages on the walls.

There was a rendering of the beautiful Gyselle, running through the woods, hair flowing, gown caught in a cascade.

Donald Glass didn't shirk off the truth or try to hide it; there were multiple newspaper articles and reports on the murders that had taken place in the 1970s.

And there was information on Francine Renault to be found, including a picture of her that was something of a memorial, commemorating her birth, acknowledging the tragedy of her death—and revealing that, while it was assumed she had been murdered by a disgruntled employee, the case remained unsolved.

Going through the library, Brock couldn't help but remember how shocked he had been to find himself under arrest. He'd been young—and nothing in his life had prepared him for the concept that he could be unjustly accused of a crime. He'd known where he wanted to go in life—but his very idealism had made it impossible for him to believe that such a thing as his being wrongly arrested could happen.

The world just wasn't as clean and cut-and-dried as he had once believed.

Of course, he had been quickly released—and that had been another lesson.

Truth was sometimes a fight.

And now, years later, he could understand Flannery's actions. There had been an urgency about the night; people had been tense. The police had been under terrible pressure.

Brock had usually controlled his temper—despite the fact that Francine had been very difficult to work with. But the day she had been killed, his anger had gotten the best of him. He hadn't gotten physical in the least—unless walking toward her and standing about five feet away with his fists clenched counted as physical. Perhaps that had appeared to be the suggestion of underlying malice. Many of his coworkers had known that he was always frustrated with Francine—she demanded so much and never accepted solid explanations as to why her way wouldn't work, or why something had to be as it was.

Like almost everyone else, he had considered Francine Renault to be a fire-breathing dragon. Quite simply, a total bitch.

She had been a thorn in all their sides. He had just happened to pick that day to explode.

After his blowup, he'd feared being fired—not arrested for murder.

He didn't tend to have problems with those he worked with or for—but he had disliked Francine. In retrospect, he felt bad about it. But she had enjoyed flaunting her authority and used it unfairly. Brock had complained about her to Fred Bentley many times, disgusted with the way she treated the summer help. Her own lack of punctuality—or when she simply didn't show up—was always forgiven, of course, because she was above them all. That night, Brock had been quick to put Maura Antrim on the schedule—as if he had known that Francine wouldn't be there.

Until she was—dangling from the tree.

As the police might see it, after they'd been pointed straight at Brock by the mysterious anonymous tipster, he'd been certain to be on the tour when Francine's body had been discovered, a ready way to explain any type of physical evidence that might have been found at the History Tree or around it.

At the time, Brock had wanted nothing to do with Detective Flannery. He'd been hurt and bitter. He was sure that only his size had kept him from being beaten to a pulp during his night in the county jail, and once he'd been freed, he found that his friends had gone.

Including, he now thought dryly, the woman he had assumed to be the love of his life.

Maura had vanished. Gone back home, into the arms of her loving parents, the same people who had once claimed to care about Brock, to be impressed with his maturity, admiring of his determination to do a stint in the service first and then spend his time in college.

Calls, emails, texts, snail mail—all had gone unanswered. It hurt too much that Maura never replied, never reached out, and so he stopped trying. He had joined the navy, done his stint and gone on to college in New York.

And yet, oddly, through the years, he'd kept up with Michael Flannery. Now and then, Flannery would write him with a new theory on the case and apologize again for arresting Brock so quickly. Flannery wasn't satisfied; he needed an explanation he believed in. He explored all kinds of possibilities—from the familiar to the absurd.

Francine had been killed by an interstate killer, a trucker—a man caught crossing the Georgia state line with a teenage victim in his cab.

She had been killed by Donald Glass himself.

By college students out of Gainesville or Tallahassee, a group that had taken hazing to a new level.

She had even been killed, a beyond-frustrated Flannery had once written, by the devils or the evil that lived in the forest by the History Tree.

Frustration. Something that continued to plague them. But then, Brock had been told that every cop, marshal and agent out there had a case that haunted them, that they couldn't solve—or had been considered closed, but the closure just didn't seem right, and it stuck in his or her gut.

Standing in the library wasn't helping any; Francine Renault had been a dead a long time, and regardless of her personality, she hadn't deserved her fate.

The truth still needed to be discovered.

More than ever now, as it was possible that her murderer had returned to kill again.

Brock left the library.

Before he left for his interviews in St. Augustine

that day, he had to try one more time with Maura. He had to find her. He hadn't explained himself very well.

In fact, he had made matters worse.

He had known Maura so well at one time. And if anything, his faltering way of trying to get her far, far from this place, where someone was killing people had probably made her stubbornly more determined to stay.

He'd admit he was afraid.

Beautiful young women were disappearing, and with or without his feelings, Maura was certainly an incredibly beautiful woman.

And there was more working against her.

She was familiar with the Frampton ranch and many of the players in this very strange game of life and death.

"MAYBE WE SHOULD move on," Maura said. She and Angie were sitting in the restaurant—Angie had actually wakened early enough for them to catch the tail end of the breakfast buffet, a spread that contained just about every imaginable morning delight.

The place was renowned for cheese grits; savoring a bite, Maura decided that they did remain among the best tasting she'd ever had. There were eggs cooked in many ways as well, plus pancakes, fruit, yogurt, nuts and grains and everything to cater to tastes from around the country.

Angie, too, it seemed, especially enjoyed the grits. Her eyes were closed as she took a forkful and then smiled.

"Delicious."

"Did you hear me?"

"What?"

"I was thinking we should move on."

Angie appeared to be completely shocked. "I... Yes, I mean, I know now about you—I mean, when you were a kid—but I thought we were fine. This is the perfect place to be home base for this trip. We can reach St. Augustine easily, areas on the coast—some of those amazing cemeteries up in Gainesville. I..."

She quit speaking. Nils Hartford, handsome in a pin-striped suit, was coming their way, smiling.

They were at a table for four and he glanced at them, brows arched and a hesitant smile on his face, silently asking if he could join them.

Angie leaped right to it.

"Nils! Hey, you're joining us?"

"Just for a minute. My people here are great—we have the best and nicest waitstaff, but I still like to oversee the change from breakfast to lunch," he said, sliding into the chair next to Maura. "You're enjoying yourself?" he asked Angie.

"I love it!" she said enthusiastically. "And last night—your brother was amazing. I mean, of course, I know that Maura had his job at one time, and I know Maura, and I know she was fantastic, but I just adored your brother. Keep him on!"

Nils laughed. "Oddly enough, that would have nothing to do with me. My brother reports directly to Fred Bentley, as do I. Couldn't get him hired or fired. But he's loved that kind of thing since we were kids. I was more into the cranking of the gears, the way things run and so forth." He turned toward Maura and asked anxiously, "And you—you okay being back here?"

"I'm fine," Maura said.

"Well, thank you both for what you're doing." He

lowered his voice, even though there was no one near. "Even Donald is shaken up by the way we keep hearing that young women have been heading here or leaving here—and disappearing. Seriously, I mean, a tree can't make people do things, but... I guess people do see things as symbols, but—we're keeping a good eye on it these days. We never had arranged for any video surveillance because it's so far out in the woods—and nothing recent has had anything to do with the tree, but... anyway, we're going to get some security out there.

"Donald has a company coming out to make suggestions tomorrow. We have cameras now in the lobby, elevators, public areas...that kind of thing. But dealing with security and privacy laws—it's complicated. I mean, the tree is on Donald's property and it's perfectly legal to have cameras at the tree. And with today's tech—improving all the time, but way above what we had twelve years ago—the tree can easily be watched. Anyway, it's great that you're helping to keep us famous."

"A true pleasure," Angie told him.

He smiled at Angie and then turned back to Maura, appearing a little anxious again. "I just—well, I know you thought I was a jerk—and I was, back then. I did feel superior to the kids who had to work." He laughed softly and only a little bitterly. "Then the stock market crashed and I received a really good comeuppance. Odd, though. It's like 'hail, hail, the gang's all here.' Me, Mark, Donald, of course, Fred Bentley, other staff...and now you and Brock and Rachel."

"Rachel?" Maura echoed, surprised.

"Oh, you didn't know? Rachel is with the Florida Department of Law Enforcement now—she's working with Detective Mike Flannery. They've stationed themselves here—good central spot—for investigating this rash of disappearances. I think it's a rash. Well, everyone is worried because of the remains of the poor girl that were found at the laundry."

"Oh! Are you and Rachel still…a twosome?" she asked.

"No, no, no—friends, though. I have a lot of love for Rach, though I was a jerk to her when we were teens. I'm grateful to have her as a friend. And can you imagine—she's like a down and dirty cop. Not that cops can't be feminine. But she made a bit of a change. Well, I mean, she has nice nails still—she just keeps them clipped and short. Short hair, too. Good cut. She's still cute. But I hear she's hell on wheels, having taken all kinds of martial arts—and a crack shot. Great kid, still. Well, adult. We're all adults—I forget that sometimes. And hey, what about you and Brock? I was jealous as hell of you guys back then, you know."

She certainly hadn't known.

"Of the two of us?" she asked. "And no—I hadn't seen him since that summer. I'm afraid that we aren't even social media friends."

"I'm sorry to hear that. But I guess that… Well, it was bad time, what happened back then." He brightened. "But you're here now. And that's great! I believe you recorded a tour? And more, so far? I'd like to think that you could spend days here—"

"We *are* spending days here," Angie assured him. "I guess we're like the cops—or agents or officers or whatever. We're in a central location. We'll head to St. Augustine and come back here, maybe over Gainesville's way. It's just such a great location."

"Well, I'm glad. That's wonderful. If I can do anything for either of you…"

His voice trailed oddly. He was looking toward the restaurant entrance. Maura saw that Marie Glass had arrived and seemed to be looking for someone.

"Excuse me," he said, making a slight grimace. "Our queen has arrived. Oh, I don't mean that in a bad way," he added quickly. "Marie never meddles with the staff and she's always charming. I mean *queen* in the best way possible, always so engaging and cordial with the guests and all of us." He made a face. "She's even nice when she knows an employee is in trouble, never falters. Just as sweet as she can be—while still aloof and elegant. Regal, you know?"

"Yes, very regal," Maura agreed.

Marie was looking for Nils, Maura thought, and as she noted their table and graced them with one of her smiles, Nils stood politely, awaiting whatever word she might have for him.

But she wasn't coming to speak with Nils. As she approached them, she headed for the one chair that wasn't occupied and asked politely, "May I join you? I'll just take a few seconds of your time, I promise."

"Of course, Mrs. Glass, please." Maura said.

Marie Glass sat delicately. "My dear Maura, you are hardly a child anymore, and though I do appreciate the respect, please, call me Marie."

Maura inclined her head. It was true. She was hardly a child. Marie simply had an interesting way of putting her thoughts.

"I know my husband and the staff here have tried to let you know how we appreciate the publicity your work here will bring us—and free publicity these days is certainly wonderful," Marie Glass began. "But we'd also be willing to compensate you if you want to show more of the resort—if you had time and if you didn't mind." She paused, flashing a smile Maura's way. "We love your reputations—and would love to make use of you in all possible ways. I am, of course, at your disposal, should you need help."

"Oh, that's a lovely idea," Angie said. "I'd have to switch up the format a little—as you know, I bring to light the unusual and frankly, the *creepy*, so—"

"Oh, bring on the creepy," Marie Glass said. She grinned again, broadly. "We do embrace the creepy, and honestly, so many people visit because of the History Tree. But we thought that allowing people to see how lovely the rest of the resort is… Well, it would make them think they should stay here and perhaps not just sign up for the campfire histories and the ghost walk into the forest. If it's a bit more comprehensive, we could use your videos on our website and in other promotional materials."

"I'm happy to get on it right away. Well, almost right away," Angie said cheerfully. "We did have plans to wander out a bit today, but we'll start on a script tonight. Maura's a genius at these things."

Maura glanced over at Angie, not about to show her surprise. So far, she hadn't known they were wandering out that day, and she wasn't sure that she was going to come up with anything "genius" after they got back.

From wherever it was that they were apparently going.

"Thank you ever so much," Marie said, standing. Her fingers rested lightly on the table as she turned to Maura. "We always knew our Maura was clever—

we'd hoped to have her on through college and beyond, but, well…very sad circumstances do happen in life. Ladies, I will leave you to your day." She inclined her head to Nils. "Mr. Hartford, would you come to the office with me?"

As soon as they were out of earshot, Maura leaned forward. "Where is it that we're wandering off to today?"

"Well, it was your idea—originally, I'm certain," Angie said.

"Where?"

"St. Augustine, of course. You said it wasn't much of a drive and that we could easily get there and back in a day. I want to head to the Castillo de San Marcos—did you know that it's the oldest masonry fort in the continental United States? And I'm not sure how to say this, but St. Augustine is the oldest city in the country *continually* inhabited by European settlers. Think that's right. I mean, the Spanish started with missions and then stayed and… I have it all in my notes. Though I know you—you may know more than my notes!"

Maura glanced at her watch. It wasn't late—just about ten. If they left soon, they could certainly spend the afternoon in the old city, have dinner at one of the many great restaurants to be found—perhaps even hear a bit of music somewhere—and be back for the night.

"Okay," she said. "I had thought you wanted to finish up around here today—maybe even leave here and stay in St. Augustine or perhaps head out to the old Rivero-Marin Cemetery just north of Orlando. I just had no idea—"

"I thought you loved St. Augustine."

"I do."

"So it's fine."

"Sure. But we don't have permits, and while people film with their phones all the time now, what you're doing is for commercial purposes and—"

"We'll film out in front of places where I might need a permit to film inside. And if you don't mind, when we get to the square, I'll have you tell that tale about the condemned Spaniard who kept having the garrote break on him so that they finally let him go. Now, that's a great real story."

"The square is called the Plaza de la Constitución."

"Right. Yeah, but it's still a square," Angie said, grinning. "It is a square, right?"

"The shape is actually oblong."

"Okay, technicalities are important. But the story is great. About the man."

"His name was Andrew Ranson and he wasn't a Spaniard. He was a Brit and he had been working on an English ship and was accused of piracy. He absolutely declared that he was innocent but met his executioner with a rosary clutched in his hands. While he was being garroted, the rope broke, and the Catholic Church declared that his survival was a miracle. He recuperated, but when the governor asked that he be returned to be executed, the Church refused to give him back. He was eventually pardoned."

"And it's real—proving my desire to show all these stories. We're back to truth being far stranger than any fiction. And there's so much more. It is okay to go today, right?"

"Yes, it is, sure—let's sign this tab and get going right away."

Maura asked for the bill, but as she did so, her old

boss came striding over to their table, a massive smile on his face.

Fred Bentley was powerfully built, stocky, not fat, but to Maura, it had always seemed that a barge was coming toward her when he strode in her direction.

He still had a head full of dark hair—dyed? She didn't know, but he had to be over fifty now, and it was certainly possible. He kept a good tan going on his skin, adding to his appearance of being fit, an outdoor man who loved the sun and activity.

He hadn't been a bad man to work for—he had certainly been better than Francine, who had changed her mind on a dime and blamed anyone else for any mistake.

Maura lowered her eyes for a moment, feeling guilty. Francine had not been nice. That didn't make what had happened to her any less horrible. Maura had to shake the image of Francine's lifeless body hanging from the tree. It haunted her almost daily.

"Maura, Angie," Fred said cheerfully. "Please, not a bill to be signed," he assured them. "What you're doing—in the midst of all this—is just wonderful. We're so grateful, honestly. Anything, anything at all that we can do, please just say so."

Maura smiled, uncomfortable. Angie answered him enthusiastically, telling him how she loved the grounds, the beauty of the pool and the elegance of the rooms, and, of course, most of all, the extra and unusual aspect of the campfire tales and the history walk. She was delighted to tout such a wonderful place.

To her surprise, Maura stood and listened and smiled, and yet, inside, she found that she was suddenly wondering about Fred.

Where was he when Francine Renault had been hanged from the great branches of the History Tree?

ST. AUGUSTINE WAS, in Brock's opinion, one of the state's true gems. Founded in 1565 by Pedro Menéndez de Avilés, the city offered wonders such as the fort, the old square, dozens of charming bed-and-breakfast inns, historic hotels, museums, the original Ripley's Believe It or Not! Museum, ghost tours, pub tours and all manner of musical entertainment.

The city also offered beautiful beaches.

But that day, he hadn't come to enjoy any of the many wonderful venues offered here.

As asked, Detective Rachel Lawrence had set up a meeting with Katie Simmons, the coworker who had reported the disappearance of one of the missing women, Lydia Merkel. She was possibly the last one to see Lydia alive.

They were meeting at La Pointe, a new restaurant near the Castillo—Katie hadn't wanted to talk where she worked, though Brock intended to go by after their meeting, just to see if anyone else remembered anything that they might have missed when speaking with officers before.

The restaurant was casual, as were many that faced the old fort and the water beyond, with wooden tables, a spiral of paper towels right on the table and a menu geared to good but reasonable food for tourists.

Katie Simmons was there when he arrived; if he hadn't seen a picture of her in his files, he would have recognized her anyway. She was so nervous. She saw him as he entered through the rustic doorway, and her straw slipped from her mouth. She quickly brought her fingers to her lips as iced tea dribbled from them. She was a pretty young woman with soft brown hair and an athletic build, evident when she leaped to her feet, sat and stood once again.

She must have realized who he was by the way he had scanned the restaurant when he had entered. Maybe it was his suit—not all that common in Florida, even for many a business meeting.

She waited for him to come to the table.

He smiled, offering her his hand, hoping to put her at ease quickly.

"Katie, right?" he said.

"Special Agent McGovern?"

"Call me Brock, please," he said as he joined her at the table. "And please sit, and I hope you can relax. I can't tell you how grateful I am that you've agreed to speak with me. I know you've already told the police about Lydia, but as you know, we're hoping that we can find her."

Katie sat and plucked at the straw in her tea, still nervous. It looked as if tears were starting to form in her eyes.

"Time keeps going by… It's been weeks now. I don't know how she could still be alive."

A waiter in a flowered shirt was quickly at their table. Brock ordered coffee and he and Katie both requested the daily special, a seafood dish.

"I don't want to lie to you, but I also don't think you should give up," Brock told her when the waiter had gone. "People do just disappear—"

Katie broke in immediately. "Not Lydia! Oh, you had to know her. She was so excited to have moved here. She loved the city, loved working here—and there was

more, of course. Lydia is a wonderful musician. She's
magic with her guitar. She has the coolest voice—not
like an angel, more like… I don't know, unique. She
can be soft, she can belt it out… I love listening to her!
She was going around getting gigs—and our boss is a
great guy. He does schedules every week and talks to
us before he sets them up. That allowed Lydia to set up
her first few gigs."

"She was performing before she left here?" he asked.

"Oh, she only had two performances. One was for a
private party out on a boat—but good money. They just
wanted a solo acoustic player. And then another was at
a place called Saint, which is a historic house that just
became a restaurant—or kind of a nightclub. Can you
be both? Or maybe you could say the same of a lot of
places here—restaurant by day, club, kind of, by night
with some kind of musical entertainment."

"Thanks. Do you know who hired her for the boat?"

"Sure. An association of local tourist businesses—
it's called SAMM," she said and paused to grin. "St.
Augustine Makes Money. That's really the name. Only
you don't have to be in the city to belong—people belong from all kinds of nearby locations. In fact, half
of the members, from what I understand, are really
up in Jacksonville. We're the cute historic place, you
know—Jacksonville is the big city. And where most
people come in, as far as an airport goes." She grew
somber again. "But she wasn't working the night before she disappeared. We were out together that night.
She was leaving in the morning. She was so excited.
Her career—her musical career—wasn't skyrocketing,
but it was taking off."

"And according to what I've learned, she did leave in her own car."

"Yes, and she loved her car. It was old, but she kept it up—she kept great care of it. Oh, and that's why she chose her apartment. She could park there for free. Right in this area—well, out a bit—but still in what we consider the old section. I mean, you could walk to her place if you had to."

"Her car was never found," Brock noted. He'd read everything he could about Lydia before coming here today. And, of course, one of the reasons it was easy for law enforcement to consider the fact that she might have disappeared on purpose had to do with the fact that her car had never been found.

Katie was instantly indignant. "I know that—and I'm so sorry, but it made me wonder if the cops are stupid. The state is surrounded by water—oh, yeah, not to mention swamps and bogs and sinkholes and the damned frigging Everglades! Someone got rid of her car. I'm telling you—there is no way in hell that Lydia left here willingly—that she just drove away. Okay, I mean, she did drive away that morning, but… I didn't worry until I didn't hear from her. I know she would have called and texted me pics of the History Tree. When she didn't… I swear, I didn't panic right away, but when I didn't hear from her by that night, I knew something was wrong. I called the ranch, and they told me that she'd never checked in. That's when I called the police. And they all told me she might have just taken a detour. I told them that her phone was going straight to voice mail, and they still tried to placate me. I had to wait the appropriate time to even report her as a missing person with people really working on the case. Then I found out that two other young women had disappeared, and then…"

She broke off.

Brock continued for her, "And then they found the remains of Maureen Rodriguez. Katie, as I said, I don't want to give you false hope. But don't give up completely. People are working very hard on this now, I promise you." He hesitated—an agent should never make a promise he couldn't guarantee he could keep, but…

"Katie, I promise you, I won't stop until we know what happened to her."

She smiled with tears welling in her eyes.

"I believe you," she said.

Their lunches arrived. As they ate, Brock allowed her to go on about her friend. They hadn't known each other that long; they had just hit it off. She loved old music and Lydia loved old music. They had loved going to plays together, too, and were willing to travel a few hours for a show, and they both loved improv and ghost tours and so on…

He thanked her sincerely when the meal was over; she had taken his business card, but also put his direct line into her phone. He promised to call her when he knew something—good or bad—and they parted ways.

He decided to stop by the offices of SAMM next, wanting a list of those involved in the boat event during which Lydia Merkel had played, and then he'd be on to the restaurant where she'd entertained at her one gig on the mainland.

Someone, somewhere, had to know something.

Her car hadn't been found.

She'd only had one credit card; it hadn't been used outside the city. No one disappeared without a trace. There was always a trace.

He just had to find it.

Chapter Four

"I am standing here on Avenida Menendez in historic St. Augustine in front of a home that was originally built in 1763. While it was in 1512 that Juan Ponce de Léon first came ashore just north of here, and 1564 when French vessels were well received by the Native population, it was in 1565 that Pedro Menéndez came and settlement began.

"It was while the Spanish ruled in 1760—nearly two centuries later—that Yolanda Ferrer's father first built the house that stands behind me. In 1762, Spain ceded Florida to the British in exchange for Cuba, and Yolanda and her young husband, Antonio, left for Havana. But in 1783, Florida was ceded back to the Spanish in exchange for the Bahama Islands. Yolanda came back to claim the home her father had built, and the governor granted the home and property to her. At that time, she was a young and beautiful bride, and she thought that she and her husband would live happily ever after— but it wasn't to be.

"Yolanda, deceived by her husband, argued and pleaded with him not to leave her—and then either fell to her death or was, perhaps, pushed to her death, in the courtyard behind the house, where, today, diners arrive from all over the world to enjoy the fusion cooking of one of St. Augustine's premier chefs, Armand Morena.

"Through the years, the house has changed. It stood for a while as an icehouse and as a mortuary. For the last fifty years, however, it has changed hands only once, being a restaurant for those fifty years. But it wasn't just as a restaurant that the building was haunted by images of the beautiful, young Yolanda, sometimes weeping as she hurries along the halls, sometimes appearing in the courtyard and sometimes in what was once her bedroom and is now the manager's office. Yolanda is known to neither hurt nor frighten those who see her. Rather, witnesses to her apparition claim that they long to reach out and touch her and let her know that her story is known and that, even today, we are touched by her tragedy."

Maura finished her speech and waited for Angie to cut the take on the camera. Angie did so but awkwardly, and Maura thought briefly about the editing she was going to have to do. She much preferred it when Angie did the talking, but Angie had already spoken in front of the Castillo and Ripley's, and at the Huguenot Cemetery, the Old Jail, the Spanish Military Hospital Museum and several other places. She had begged Maura to let her do the filming on this one and Maura had acquiesced.

The sun was just about gone. And Maura was tired. As much as she loved St. Augustine, she was wearying of seeing it as if she was reliving that old vacation movie with Chevy Chase.

"Ready for dinner?" she asked Angie.

"Oh, you bet. We're going to have to come back. I loved what I called the square—the Plaza de la Constitución. I mean, that's the whole thing, isn't it? Executions took place there once, and now it's all beautiful, and there is a farmer's market, and people come for musical events and more. I love the streets surrounding it, the beautiful churches and all. I'm so glad we came."

"I've always loved this city," Maura agreed. "But I'm tired and starving. Have you picked out a place you'd like to go?"

There were plenty of choices.

Angie hesitated. She winced. "If I picked a particular restaurant, would you think that I was being ghoulish?"

Maura arched a brow warily. "Ghoulish? I don't know of any new horrific restaurant murders in St. Augustine."

"The restaurant is quite safe—no blood and guts in the kitchen or elsewhere, as far as I know," Angie assured her. "But…" she said and hesitated again. "It is the last place one of the missing girls had a music gig—I think I saw some video—because Lydia Merkel was playing her guitar and singing there not long before she disappeared. It's called Saint."

"Oh," Maura murmured. "Really, I'm not—"

"You wouldn't have even known, I don't think, if I hadn't told you."

Maura had read news reports; she had seen videos of the young women, including Lydia Merkel, who had worked here in St. Augustine, before her mysterious disappearance.

She hadn't remembered the name of the restaurant where the girl had played, nor even the name of the restaurant where she had worked.

"Please? I can't help but want to see it," Angie said.

Of course, Angie wanted to see it. If the poor woman's body was found and her murder was never solved, she would become another Florida legend.

She didn't have the energy to fight Angie, and besides, she doubted that the restaurant itself had been any cause of what had happened.

"Okay. Is it close? I'm sure you know. Are we walking? I don't think it existed the last time I was up here. I'll google it," she told Angie.

"Two blocks to the east and then one to the south," Angie said.

"We'll leave the car and walk."

Saint was like many restaurants in the historic district—once upon a time, it had been someone's grand home. Maura thought that it might have been built in the 1800s during the Victorian era; a plaque on the front assured her she was right: 1855. Originally the home of Delores and Captain Evan Siegfried.

Abandoned after the Civil War, it had become an institution for the mentally ill in the 1880s, a girls' school in 1910, a flower shop in the 1920s, a home again briefly in the 1950s before it was eventually abandoned—then recently restored by the owners of Saint.

The restaurant's original incarnation as a home was evident as they entered; there was a stairway to the second floor on the right, and on the left was what had once been a parlor—it now held a long bar and a few tables.

They were led around to what had probably been a family room; there, to the far rear, was a small stage, cordoned off now, but offering a sign that told them that Timmy Margulies, Mr. One-Man Band, would be arriving at 8:00 p.m.

As the hostess led them to their table, Maura stopped dead—causing a server behind her to crash into her with his tray and send a plate of gourmet french fries and something brown and wet and covered with gravy to go flying to the floor.

Maura was instantly apologetic, beyond humiliated, and—what was worse—she had stopped in surprise.

Brock McGovern was seated at a table near the door, deep in conversation with a woman who was wearing a polo shirt with the restaurant's logo but not the tunic worn by the waitstaff.

Of course, now he—like the rest of those in the place—was staring at her.

She truly wanted to crawl beneath the floor.

Apparently he admitted to the woman that he knew Maura; he was standing, about to head her way.

She winced and ignored him, trying to help the waiter whose tray she had upturned, stooping down to help.

"It's fine, it's fine—really!" the young waiter told her, smiling as he met her eyes, collecting fallen plates.

"Oh, dear," Angie murmured.

Then Brock was at her side with the woman who had been at his table.

"Miss, seriously, please, it's all right—this is a restaurant. We do have spills," the woman said.

"I know, but this one was my fault," Maura said.

She was startled when Brock took her arm. She looked up into his eyes and saw that she was overdoing her apology.

She was still looking at him, but she couldn't help herself.

"I am so, so sorry!" she said again.

"Maura, it's all right," he said quietly. And, looking back at him, she realized she was as attracted to the man he had become as she had been to the boy he had once been. And maybe, just maybe, she had been apologizing to him, and he had been telling her that it was all right.

But…

"You never tried to reach me," she blurted as the waiter and busboys—and whoever the woman with Brock was—all scrambled around, cleaning up.

His frown instantly assured her that something was wrong with that statement.

"I did try," he said. "Repeatedly. I called, and I wrote and… I guess it doesn't matter now. There's no way to change the past."

Angie cleared her throat, "Um, excuse me. I think that they want us to sit. Maybe get out of the way? Brock! Wow, weird coincidence. Nice to see you—want to join us? Maura, we really need to sit."

"Yes, of course," Maura said, wincing again—wishing more than ever that she could sink into the floor and disappear. Her mind was racing; she was stunned and felt as if she had been blindsided.

She had great parents. Loving parents. But had they decided that there was no proof that Brock had really been cleared—and that he shouldn't contact their precious daughter? What else would explain that he said he'd reached out but had never actually reached her?

She was still standing. And everyone was still looking at her.

She smiled weakly and took her chair, continuing to be somewhat stunned by Brock's words, wishing that they might not have been said under these circumstances. She supposed that was her fault. But she hadn't been able to stop herself.

"This is charming, absolutely charming," Angie said

when they were seated, her eyes on Brock. "We had no idea that you'd be here—and even if we had, how convenient that we came to be in the same place! Have you had dinner? Will you join us for the meal?"

"I have not had dinner, though I did have a great lunch," he said.

"You were here investigating?" Angie asked.

"Yes."

"I know some of what's going on, of course," Angie said. "There's news everywhere these days—even on our phones. Hard to miss. I understand that the last girl who disappeared near the ranch had been living here in the city."

"Yes," Brock agreed. Angie frowned slightly; she'd obviously been expecting more info.

"Do you think there's any possibility of finding any of the missing women alive?" Maura asked him.

"There's always the possibility," Brock said.

"Ah," Angie said, studying him. "A politically correct answer."

"No," Brock said. "They haven't been found dead. That means there is a possibility that they will be found alive."

"Even after the woman's bones were found in sheets?" Angie asked.

"Even after that. It's still unknown if the cases are connected. That three young women have disappeared in a relatively short period of time does suggest serial kidnapping, but whether they were connected to the murder of Maureen Rodriguez is something that we still don't know. But," he added, "as I tried to say, I think it's a dangerous time right now for any woman from the ages of seventeen to thirty-five or perhaps on upward. Frankly, I'd be much happier if all those I knew were in Alaska right now—or Australia or New Zealand, perhaps."

He glanced over at Maura and she felt bizarrely as if her heart stopped beating for a minute.

She had been so angry for so long.

And now she realized that he hadn't been trying to get rid of her, per se—he was worried about everyone.

And maybe, because of the past, *especially* about her.

"But I do say it's a good thing that you stick together," he said, offering them a smile. "So, did you enjoy your day?" he asked politely.

Maura didn't have to worry about answering—Angie had no problem excitedly telling him about all that they had seen and done.

Their waiter—the same man who had collided with Maura—came and suggested that they have the snapper; the preparation of it, a combo of lemon and oil and garlic, was simple but exceptional. The three of them ordered. Maura and Brock were both driving, but Angie was at her leisure, so she indulged in the restaurant's signature drink—the Saint. It came out blue and bubbly, and she assured the waiter she didn't care much about what was in it. It was delicious.

"Have you all finished up here for the day?" Brock asked.

"Oh, yes, Maura is amazing. She knew where to go, what to get—we don't do full-length documentaries, you know. Just little bits. There have been all kinds of surveys about the modern attention span. You'll have tons of people look at something if it only takes them briefly out of their scanning. Unless it's something they really want to see, they pass right by when things be-

come long. Two to three minutes tend to work really
well for me. I was doing terribly, then I started working with Maura. She edits, although half the time we
get just about perfect in one take."

He glanced over at Maura. "Are you in business together?" he asked.

"No," Maura said.

"Are you kidding? She's in megapopular demand!"
Angie answered. "Artists, authors, performers—Maura
knows how to make everyone really show off in that
two to three minutes," Angie said.

"And I should definitely put in," Maura said quickly,
"that Angie is truly a shooting star—her books on truth
being stranger than fiction, weird places and so on do
amazingly well."

"I have some pretty generous sponsors for my video
channel. Whoever knew that being a nerdy and somewhat gruesome kid would pay so well, huh?" Angie
asked.

"We never do know where life will take us, I guess,"
Brock said, turning his attention to Maura once again.
"But sometimes you pop before the camera?"

"When Angie wears out," Maura said.

"No, she's great," Angie said. "The video-cam thing
loves her—and she's so smooth. A grand storyteller.
She'd have been perfect in the old Viking days or in
Ireland when history was kept orally and people listened around the fire. Of course, I keep telling her that
it can't be her life. We've worked together about three
years now and I'm always amazed that she never says
no. Work, work, work, I tell her. I put things off when
I'm in the middle of a relationship. Maura won't take
the time for a relationship."

Maura glared at Angie, amazed that her friend would say such a thing—especially when she'd been flirting with Brock in front of Maura and was unabashedly interested in men. If not forever, for a night—as she had often said.

Maura wanted to kick her. Hard. Beneath the table.

And she might have, except that Angie was a little bit too far away to accomplish the task.

But Brock looked at Maura, something strange in his eyes. "Some of us do make work into everything," he said.

Angie pounced on that. "So—you're not married. Or engaged. Or steadily sleeping with anyone?"

Once again, Maura wanted to kick Angie. She damned the size of the table.

Brock laughed. "No, not married, engaged or sleeping with someone steadily. I think you only want to wake up every morning looking at someone's face on the other pillow when that person is so special that they know the good and the bad of you and everything in between. When you know... Well, anyway...my work takes up a lot of time. And it takes a special person to endure life with someone who works—the way I do." He sat back. "I'd like to follow you back to the Frampton ranch. Being perpetually, ever so slightly paranoid is a job hazard. I know you're fine, but...humor me?"

He was looking at Maura.

She still loved his face. His eyes, the contours of his cheeks, the set of his mouth. He'd been so determined and steady when they'd been young, and she had been so swept into...loving him. For good reason, she thought. He'd grown into the man she'd imagined somewhere in the back of her mind.

The man whose face she had wanted to see on the pillow next to hers when she woke up every morning.

"Maura?" Angie asked.

"Um, yes, sure," Maura said.

Brock stood, heading to find the waiter and pay the check.

"He is so hot!" Angie said. "He's got a thing for you. But if you're going to waste it—"

"Angie, he's working down here."

"You must have been the cutest kids."

"Oh, yeah, we were just frigging adorable, Angie. It was twelve years ago. Come on, let's get the car and head back. I have a lot of editing to do."

"No, you don't. Almost every take was perfect. I should have gotten that check—I'm really making money. Unless, of course, he has a budget for dinners out. I'd hate to ruin his budget."

"Angie, it's all right—look, he's motioning to us. We're all set to go."

Brock wasn't parked far away; he walked them to their car and then asked that they wait for him to come around on Avenida Menendez so that he could follow them.

As Maura waited behind the wheel, she thought about the years that had gone by.

She'd been stunned at first that things had ended so completely with Brock, but slowly, she'd felt that she was more normal—that heartbreak was a part of life. There had been other men in her life. But anytime it had gotten to *we're either going somewhere with this, or...*

She had chosen the "or."

She hadn't planned on making that choice forever,

she'd just never met anyone else she wanted on the pillow next to hers every morning.

She wondered what it meant that he'd never found that person, either.

Brock drove up slightly behind her, allowing her to move into traffic. She headed out of the historic district of the city with him behind her, easily following.

"I wonder if I should have ridden with him," Angie said. She glanced over at Maura. "I mean, if you're going to waste a perfectly good man..."

Maura was surprised that she could laugh. "Angie, I rather got the impression that you liked Nils Hartford or Mark Hartford. Maybe even Fred Bentley..."

"Bentley? No, no, no!" Angie said. "I like them tall and dark—or a little shorter but with that ability to smile and charm, something in their eyes, love of life, of who they are...not sure what. But Bentley? Nah. He's like a little tram coming at you—no, no. Although..." She turned in the passenger's seat to extend her seat belt, allowing her to look straight at Maura. "Now, I'd love to find out more about Donald Glass. Power and money! We all know that those are aphrodisiacs. Even when a man is sexually just about downright creepy. Somehow, enough money and power can change the tide, you know?"

"Uh, you know he's married," Maura reminded her.

"Ah, well, I heard that didn't always matter to him so much." Angie said. She laughed. "He even has a younger wife—younger than him. But that's the problem—there will always be younger, and younger will always be replaced with younger still."

"See, a warning philosophy," Maura said.

"But I know plenty of couples where there's an age

difference—both ways!—who are happily going strong.
I mean, there are older men who stay in love, and even
older women who stay in love with younger men who
stay in love."

"Of course," Maura murmured. She wasn't really
paying attention to Angie anymore—she was only
aware of the car following her.

It seemed forever before they reached the Frampton
Ranch and Resort.

Angie talked the whole way.

It was all right. All Maura had to do was murmur an
agreement now and then.

At long last, she pulled into the great drive and out
to the guest parking. Brock was still right behind her,
turning into a parking space just a few down.

He headed over to them while Maura went into the
back seat of her car to grab her camera bag.

"An escort all the way," Angie said, greeting Brock
as he joined them.

"All the way to the lobby," he agreed.

As they walked, Maura realized that despite the fact
that he had joined them for dinner, she had never asked
him about the woman in the Saint shirt who had been
his companion at his table before she and Angie arrived.

But oddly, she didn't want to ask him in front of
Angie. She glanced his way as they neared the entrance
to the lobby, once the great entry to the antebellum
house. He glanced back at her and, for a moment, it was
strangely as if no time had passed at all. She'd always
been able to tell him with just a look if they needed to
talk alone.

He seemed to read her expression. Or, at least, she
thought that he gave her a slight nod.

They walked up the porch steps and then through the great double doors to the "ranch house."

That was rather a misnomer. When the house had been built, it had been based on the Southern plantation style.

The integrity of the plan had been maintained with the registration desk to the far side and the doors leading to the coffee shop and the restaurant on opposite sides—one having once been the formal parlor and one the family parlor. The floors were hardwood, polished to a breathtaking shine without being too slippery—a great accomplishment by maintenance and the cleaning crew. There were great suites in the main house on the second floor while the attic had been heightened and rooms added there. Two wings—once bunkhouses— had become smaller one-room rentals.

Angie had, naturally, taken one of the big suites on the second floor.

Maura just hadn't needed that much space; she'd been perfectly happy up in the attic, and though she enjoyed working with Angie, she liked her own room, her own downtime and her own quiet at times.

"Safely in," Brock murmured.

"Welcome back…did you all decide to hit the entertainments somewhere nearby together?" a voice asked.

Maura was surprised to see that Fred Bentley was behind the registration desk. There was someone on duty twenty-four hours, but it wasn't usually Bentley. He lived on the property, having something of an apartment at the far end of the left wing, and she'd never really figured out what he considered his hours to be, but he was usually moving about in different areas, overseeing tours, restaurants, housekeeping and everything else.

"Our night clerk didn't show," he said, apparently aware that they were all looking at him curiously. "Not appreciated," he added.

Maura didn't think that the night clerk would be on the payroll much longer.

"I ran into Maura and Angie in St. Augustine," Brock told him, answering Fred's earlier question. "It can be a surprisingly small world."

"That is a strange coincidence," Bentley said. "Well, as I said, welcome back. Oh, Angie, Mrs. Glass was hoping that you'd tour the place a bit with her tomorrow, get an idea of what you could do…more videos on the resort as a whole. The swimming pool and patio out back are really beautiful." He nodded toward Brock and Maura. "Those two used to love it—our summer employees have always been allowed use of the pool and gym during their off-hours."

"It was a great place to work," Brock said. "Well, it's been long day. I'm going to head up."

"I think we all are," Maura said. "Good night, Fred."

An elevator had been installed; Maura usually took the stairs, but Angie headed for them and she thought that maybe Brock was on the attic floor, as well. "Night, Angie," he said, heading for the elevator.

"Good night. But long day—I'll take the elevator, too!" she said, joining him and Maura, who pressed the call button.

"I'm in the Jackson Suite," Angie said. "Have you seen the suites?" she asked Brock cheerfully in the elevator. "You're welcome to come see my room."

"I've seen all the suites, and thank you, but tonight… I'm ready for bed," he told her.

Angie laughed softly and said, "Me, too."

Angie was always flirtatious—and she'd honestly stated what she wanted to Maura. Usually her easy way with come-ons didn't bother Maura in the least.

Tonight...

It wasn't the night. It was that she was coming on to Brock.

The elevator stopped on the second floor. Angie stepped out. "Well, lovely day, lovely dinner. Thank you both!"

"Thank you," Angie told her.

The elevator door closed.

"She's subtle, huh?" Brock murmured.

To her surprise, Maura smiled. "Very."

"So, what did you want to ask me?"

He could still read her glances. And in the small elevator, they were close. She wondered if it was possible for so much time to have gone by and there still be that something...

The elevator door opened. They stepped out into the hallway. Brock stood still, waiting for her to talk.

"None of my business really, but that was rather bizarre running into you. And you were with that woman at a table, and then just came on over with us so easily... I..."

"I went in search of Lydia Merkel," he said. "She had a coworker, Katie Simmons, who insists that Lydia didn't disappear on purpose. She'd gotten two gigs playing her guitar and singing, as well as working as a waitress. One of those gigs was at Saint."

"Oh! Well, yes, of course, you were working. And the woman you met... She hired Lydia Merkel?"

"Exactly. Lydia played there the Wednesday night of the week she disappeared. I was hoping to learn something more. But I pretty much gained the same information. The manager did have a few minutes to speak with Lydia. Katie said that she was the perfect entertainment for their night clientele—charming, speaking between songs, performing at just the right volume for diners. She asked her back for a few nights each week and Lydia was delighted. But she had a bit of a vacation planned. She was heading to the Frampton Ranch and Resort, and it was a long-held dream. The manager told her that was fine. Lydia could come in the next week and they'd discuss the future. Of course, as we all know, Lydia never went back."

He paused for a minute and said very softly, "I'm sorry. I never meant to come off the way that I did earlier. But a woman was murdered. Three young women are missing."

"I'm sorry, as well. I thought... Never mind. I don't know what I thought. But you seriously think that... there will be more kidnappings? And that the same person who murdered the poor woman whose remains were found at the laundry has taken these other women?"

He nodded grimly. "From what I've learned, there is no way Lydia Merkel just walked away from her life. I haven't had time for other interviews yet, but I imagine I will find that neither Lily Sylvester nor Amy Bonham just walked away, either. And—while other businesses had sheets and used the laundry and fall in place with other leads as well, the Frampton Ranch and Resort still comes out on top of every list. Maybe I am touchy as far as this place goes, but in truth, I was sent here because of my familiarity with not just my home state but with the Frampton Ranch and Resort. You...you need to be so careful, Maura."

"I will be—I always am. But I'll be very careful. And…thank you."

He nodded. He knew that she was thanking him for the warning—and for telling her just how hard he had tried to reach her years ago.

He still hadn't moved; neither had she.

There were five rooms in the attic. The space was small. The walls were old and solid, and they were speaking softly, but it had grown late.

There was nothing more to say.

And there were years and years of words that they might say.

And, still, neither of them moved.

"I, uh… I'm so sorry for the families and friends of those poor women. And it's truly horrible about that young woman who was murdered, but do you think that they're all related?"

"We don't know. But they did have this place in common. And there's the past."

Maura shook her head. "You mean Francine?"

"Yes."

"But…that was twelve years ago."

"Yes."

"Peter committed suicide," Maura said. "I remember reading about it, and I remember him fighting with Francine. But then again, I remember everyone fighting with Francine. Still, with what Peter did…killing himself. Peter was a bit of a strange man with intense religious beliefs. He also had a temper, which usually came out as a lot of screaming and boiled down to angry muttering. It wasn't hard to believe that he had gone into a rage and dragged her out to the History Tree—and then been horrified by what he had done and regretted his action. Committed suicide."

"That's what was assumed. Never proved," Brock told her. "He was stabbed in the gut, something someone else could have done. Wipe the knife...put it in his hand. Leave him in the freezer. Easy to believe he might have done it himself. Especially when there were no other solid suspects. Just as easy to believe he was stabbed—and that the scene was staged."

He took a slight step back—almost as if he needed a little space. "Well, I'm in room three. I guess we should call it a night. I...uh... Well, you look great. And congratulations. I understand that you're doing brilliantly with your career. But I guess we all knew that you would. You're a natural storyteller—easy to see how that extends to directing people, to making them look great on video."

"Thanks. And you're exactly what you wanted to be—an FBI agent." She paused and took a deep breath. "And... Brock, I never received any of your messages. I don't know if my parents thought they were protecting me... They're good people, but... I am so sorry. I really had it in for you for years—I thought you just walked away."

He shook his head. Shrugged.

"Well, where are you?"

"I'm the last down the hallway, in five," she said.

"I'll watch you through your door," he said with a half smile. "I mean, I'm here—might as well see it through to perfect safety."

"Okay, okay, I'm going. I... I assume I'll see you," she murmured.

"You will," he assured her.

She turned and headed down the short hallway to the end. There, she dug out her key, opened her door, waved and went in.

Finally alone and in the sanctuary of her room, she leaned against the door, shaking.

How could time be erased so easily? How could the truth hurt so badly…and mean so very much at the same time? What would have happened if she had received his messages? Would they have been together all these years with, perhaps, a little one now, or two little ones…

She could have turned to him, laughed, slipped her arms around him. She knew what it would feel like, knew how he held her, cupped her nape when he kissed her, knew the feel of his lips…

Time had gone by. She hadn't received his messages.

She hadn't known he'd tried to reach her; she should have. As soon as she was home, her parents had gotten her a new phone with a new, unlisted number. They'd insisted that she change her email and delete all her social media accounts—not referencing Brock specifically, so much as the situation and the danger that could possibly still come from it.

Maybe she should have tried harder to get in touch with him. But when she'd never heard from him, she'd given up. Tried to move on.

Now they were living different lives.

She pushed away from the door. It had been a long day. She was hot and tired and suddenly living in a land of confusion. A shower was in order.

Maybe a cold shower.

She doffed her clothing, letting it lie where it fell, and headed into the bathroom. And it was while the water was pouring over her that she felt a strange prickle of unease.

It was like a perfect storm.

She was here. Brock was here…

Nils and Mark Hartford were here. Donald and Marie Glass… Fred Bentley…

And then, today her and Angie in St. Augustine, Brock in St. Augustine.

In the same restaurant. At the same time.

She turned off the water, dried quickly and stepped back out to the bedroom. She knew that Brock was working—that they all needed to be concerned. One poor woman was beyond help. Three were still missing, and maybe, just maybe…

There was nothing that she could do except, of course, be smart, as Brock had warned. And suddenly she couldn't help herself. She was thinking like Angie.

A night, just a night.

As Angie had made sure they all knew at dinner, Brock wasn't sleeping with anyone now in his life. There was no reason that the two of them shouldn't re-live the past, if only for a night, for a few hours, for…

Memory's sake. If Maura just revisited the past, she might realize that it hadn't been so perfect, so very wonderful, that Brock wasn't the only man in the world who was so perfect…for her.

She knew his room number. It was wild, but…

Yes. It was too wild. She forced herself to don a long cotton nightgown and slip into bed.

And lay there, wide-awake, staring at the ceiling, remembering the contours of his body.

Chapter Five

Brock closed and locked his door, set his gun on the nightstand, and his phone and wallet on the desk by his computer. He shrugged out of his jacket and sat at the desk, opened his computer, keyed in his password and went to his notes.

He quickly filled in what he had learned that afternoon.

The most interesting had not been his conversation with the manager at Saint.

It had been earlier, when he had visited the offices of SAMM.

The event Lydia Merkel had played had been a social for members of the society. It hadn't been a mere boat, but the yacht *Majestic*, and fifty-seven members of SAMM had been invited.

Donald Glass and his wife had been among them.

The contact at SAMM had known that Maureen Rodriguez—or her sad remains at any rate—had been discovered. Every hotel, motel, inn and bed-and-breakfast that used the laundry facility had been questioned upon that finding. But no evidence had led to any one property.

Donald Glass knew about the women who had disappeared. He had never mentioned that he had met any of them.

To be fair, he might not have known that he had met Lydia Merkel. She had been working under her performance moniker—Lyrical Lee.

And, of course, the proprietors of many of the properties that used the laundry service were among those who had been on the yacht.

It was still a sea of confusion.

Except that Frampton Ranch and Resort was the location where the missing girls had been—or been headed to.

Brock filled in his notes, then stood, cast aside the remainder of his clothing and got into his shower. He needed to shake some of the day off. His puzzle pieces were still there, but he was missing something that was incredibly important.

Hard evidence.

And back to the old question—what the hell could something that had happened twelve years ago have to do with the now?

And why, in the middle of trying to work all the angles of the crimes, concentrating on detail and logic, did he keep seeing Maura's face as she stood before him in the hallway?

He knew her so well. He smiled, thinking that she hadn't really changed at all.

She'd been polite, always caring, never wanting to hurt another person.

She'd been so stunned to see him in the restaurant and stopped short and then...

He smiled again, remembering her face. So mortified.

And then trying to clean up the mess herself because she'd caused it. When they had spoken…

She'd obviously been stricken, hearing that he had tried to reach her. He'd seen the pull of her emotions—she had to be angry with her parents, but they were good people and she did love them, and now, with the passage of time, she surely knew that they had thought they were doing what was best, as well.

He showered, thinking that washing away the day would help; sleep would be good, too, of course. He felt that learning about Lydia Merkel and her aspirations to be a full-time musician were another piece of the puzzle—not because she entertained, but because of who she had done entertaining for: the hospitality industry—including the Frampton Ranch and Resort.

Brock and Maura had once been part of that. And they had intended to work part-time through college. His future had been planned out—he'd known what he was going to do with his life. And he had done it.

But Maura had always been part of his vision for his life, and maybe the most important part, the part where human emotion created beauty in good times and sustained a man through the bad.

He wasn't sure he ever made the conscious decision to go to her. He threw on a pair of jeans and left his room, years of training causing him to take his weapon and lock the door as he departed.

Which made him look rather ridiculous as he knocked softly on her door. When she opened it—he hoped and assumed she'd looked through the peephole before doing so—she stared at him wide-eyed for a minute, a slight smile teasing her lips—and a look of abject confusion covering her features.

"Um—you came to shoot me?"

She backed into the room. He entered, shaking his head, also smiling.

"Can't leave a gun behind," he told her.

"I see," she said.

For a moment, they stood awkwardly, just looking at each other, maybe searching for the right words. But words weren't necessary.

He set his holster and Glock down, fumbling blindly to find the dresser beside the door. He wasn't sure if she stepped into his arms or if he drew her in. But she was there. And time and distance did nothing except heighten each sensation, make the taste of her lips sweeter than ever. Their kiss deepened into something incredible. He felt her hand on his face, her fingers a gentle touch, a feathery brush, something unique and arousing, incredible and just a beginning.

His hands slid beneath the soft cotton of her gown and their lips broke long enough for him to rid her of it. He felt her fingers, teasing now along the waistband of his jeans. A thunderous beat of longing seemed to pound between them; it was his own heart, his pulse, instinctive human need and so much more.

Her fingers found the buttons on his jeans.

He couldn't remember ever before stepping from denim so quickly or easily.

Nor did he remember needing the feel of flesh against flesh ever quite so urgently.

They kissed again, his hands sliding down her spine, hers curving from his shoulders and down to his buttocks. They kissed and fell to the bed, and as his lips found her throat and collarbone, she whispered, "I was on my way to you."

He found her mouth again. Tenderness mixed with urgency, a longing to hold the moment, desire to press ever further.

It had been so long. And it was incredibly beautiful just to touch her again, hear her voice, bask in the scent of her...

Love her.

Familiar but new.

Their hands and lips traveled each other. He loved the feel of her skin, the curves of her body, loved touching her, feeling her arch and writhe to his touch.

Feeling what her touch did to him, hands traveling over his shoulders and his back; hot, wet kisses falling here and there upon him; that touch, ever more intimate.

As his was upon her. The taste and feel of her breasts and the sleekness of her abdomen, the length and sweet grace of her limbs.

And finally moving into her, moving together, feeling the rush of sweet intimacy and the raw eroticism of spiraling ever upward together, instinct and emotion bursting upon them with something akin to violence in their power, and yet so sweetly beautiful even then.

They lay together in silence, and once again he heard the beat, the pulse, his heart and hers, as they lay entwined, savoring the aftermath.

At last, he kissed her forehead, smoothing hair from her face.

She smiled up at him. "Twelve years," she said. And her eyes had both a soft and a teasing cast. "Worth waiting for, I'd judge."

"How kind. May I say the same?"

"Indeed, you may," she said, curling tighter against him. "You may say all kinds of things. Good things, of course. My hair is glorious—okay, so it's a sodden, tangled mass right now. My eyes are magnificent... Well, they are open. And, of course, you've waited all your life for me."

"I have," he said gravely.

She grinned at that. "You joined the FBI monastery?"

"I didn't say that. And I'm doubting you joined the Directors Guild nunnery."

She smiled, but she was serious, looking up at him. "I—I knew some good people."

"I would expect no less," he said softly.

"None as good as you," she whispered.

"Now, that can be taken many ways."

"But you know what I mean."

"I do. And don't go putting me on a pedestal. I wasn't so good—I was...a bit lost. The best way I had to battle it was to plunge head-on into all the plans I had made. Most of the plans I had made," he added softly.

"I am so sorry."

"Neither of us can be sorry," he assured her.

She kissed him again. For a while, their touching was soft and tender and slow.

But it had been so many years.

Somewhere in the wee hours, they slept. And when morning came, he awoke, and he saw her face on the pillow next to his. Saw her eyes open and saw her smile, and he pulled her to him, just grateful to wake with her by his side.

"Perfect storm," she murmured. "And I'm so sorry for the cause of it. So grateful for...you."

"We can't change what happened then. Now it's all right to be glad that we've...connected."

She nodded thoughtfully. "I keep thinking...there's something in history, something in the books, something that has to give us a clue as to what is going on."

"You need to stay out of it all," he told her firmly.

She rolled on an elbow and stared at him. "How? How would I ever really stay out of it? I was here when Francine was killed. That in itself...it's most horrible that a woman was so cruelly murdered, but, Brock...it changed everything. Changed us. And you do believe that what is happening now is related."

"There is really no solid evidence to suggest that," he said. "In fact, as far as profiling and evidence go, there is little reason to suppose that a killer might have hanged Francine—and then stuck around for over a decade to murder one young woman and kidnap three more. Really, the best thing would be for you to head to Alaska—as quickly as possible."

She smiled. "I would love to see Alaska one day. I haven't been. I'd love to see it—with you."

He was certain that, physically possible or not, his heart and soul trembled. They had just come together—tonight. And, well, thanks to Angie, they were both aware that nothing else had ever really worked for either of them in the years that had been lost between them.

He had never found *her* again. And she had never found him.

He grinned, afraid to let the extent of his emotion show.

"I don't think I have vacation coming anytime soon. But how about Iceland? What an incredible place for you to do legends and stories."

She was next to him, the length of her body close, and she touched his forehead, moving back a lock of his hair. "I don't work for myself—well, I do, but I'm a vendor hiring out my services. We need to be realistic. This is your work and more than your work. And now I'm working here, too. And I can help. I'm not stupid, Brock, you know that. I lock doors. I stay where there are other people. Whoever is doing this—be it a new thing or a crime associated with the past—they're smart enough to work in the shadows. No one is going to be hurt in the resort. You're in room three, and I'm in room five, and I'm not worried at all about the nights. Brock, I'm all grown-up. Quite a bit older than the last time, remember."

"And around the same age—"

"The missing women weren't wary or suspicious. They were just leading normal lives, trying to work and survive and simply enjoy their lives. Brock, most people are wonderful. They will lend others a helping hand. They just want the same things. Maureen Rodriguez was probably a lovely person—simply expecting others to be like that, too. From the little I know, the three missing women were probably similar—expecting human beings to act as human beings, having no idea that a very sick person was out there. I know that there's a predator. I won't be led astray, into any darkness—or off alone anywhere with anyone."

"Okay," he said quietly. "But if we're apart, I'll be calling you on the hour. Oh, screw the hour. Every five minutes, maybe."

"That will be fine. But unlikely. I think most of your interviews and investigations will take more than five minutes. And you really don't need to worry about me today—we'll be videoing out at the pool, in the restaurants—and I'm sure Angie would like to show herself speaking with Marie Glass—maybe Donald, too."

He heard a buzzing from the floor and leaped up. Luckily—he hadn't thought about it when he had left his room with just pants and his Glock—his cell phone was in the pocket of his jeans.

He dug for his phone.

"Yeah, Mike," he answered, having seen the detective's name on his caller ID.

"I'd like you to come with me to the Gainesville County morgue," Flannery said.

Brock gritted his teeth; the morgue meant a body. A body meant that his actions thus far had failed to save anyone.

"One of the missing girls?"

"I don't think so—I believe—or the ME there has suggested—that the remains are much older. But… Well, I'll fill you in. How soon can you be ready?"

"Ten minutes," Brock said.

"Better than me. Meet you downstairs in fifteen. We can grab coffee and head out."

"I'll be there."

"First man to arrive orders the coffee. Never mind—Rachel will beat us both. She'll order it."

"I'll be down."

He hung up and slipped into his jeans, looking back at the bed. Maura was up, staring at him, her face knit into a worried frown.

"I have to go… Not sure when I'll be back. Keep in touch, please. And stick with Angie and Marie Glass—and don't go walking into any old spooky woods, huh, okay?" he asked.

She smiled. "I promise," she told him. "But—"

"Old bones—we have to see what they are. And no—not one of our three missing girls. You'll be here all day?"

She smiled back at him.

"I'll be here all day," she assured him.

He hurried out of her room, heading to his own, hoping he wouldn't run into anyone while he was clad in his jeans only—but not really caring.

He would shower, dress and be ready in ten minutes. He wasn't worried about that.

He did hate that he was leaving.

And hoped it was something he was going to have to get used to doing.

MAURA WAS HAPPY—and determined. No, she wasn't an agent. Or a cop of any kind. No—she wasn't even particularly equipped to defend herself should she need to do so.

But she was smart and wary and everything else that she had told Brock.

Like it or not, she had been at the ranch when Francine was killed. And she was here now, and she was a Floridian and these horrible things were happening in her state. Today she would be filming around the estate with Angie and Marie, and she'd be speaking with all those here as much as possible—especially Fred, Marie, maybe Donald and Nils and Mark.

Her reasoning might be way off. Just because they had all been here twelve years ago and were here now didn't mean a thing. The solution to Francine's murder and answers about the girls who were dead and missing now might be elusive. It was sad but true that an alarming percentage of murders went unsolved. She'd read the statistics one time—nearly 40 percent of all homicides in the US went unsolved each year.

Except on this, while it was in his power, she knew that Brock wouldn't let go.

So, in her small way, she would do her best. And maybe that meant going through the library again— finding out everything she could about the Frampton Ranch and Resort—and the people who were here.

Maura showered, dressed and set out to edit some of her video from the day before. At nine she decided to go down to breakfast; Angie, she knew, would wake up when she was ready and come down seeking coffee.

Maura took her computer with her, curious to see what various search engines brought up on the ranch. As with most commercial properties, the results showed every travel site on the planet first. And the history of North Central Florida didn't provide any better results. She didn't find much that was particularly helpful— nothing she didn't know already.

Frustrated, she was about to click over into her email when she noticed a site with the less-than-austere title of Extremely Weird Shit That Might Have Happened.

Once there, she read about a strange organization that had sprung up in the area in the 1930s. Various local boarding schools and colleges had provided the members—usually rich young men with a proclivity for hedonistic lifestyles. They had created a secret society known as the Sons of Supreme Being, and considered themselves above others, apparently siding with the Nazi cause during World War II, dissolving after the war, but supposedly surfacing now and then in the decades that followed.

They had been suspected of the disappearance of a

young woman in the 1950s, but it had been as difficult for police to prove their complicity as it had been to prove their existence. Members were sworn to secrecy unto death, and in the one case when a young man had admitted to the existence of the society and the possible guilt of the society in the disappearance of the girl, that young man had been found floating in the Saint Johns River.

"My dear Maura, but you are involved in your work!"

Startled, Maura looked up. Marie Glass had come to her table. She was standing slightly behind her.

Maura quickly closed her computer, wondering if Marie had seen what she'd been reading.

"I'm so sorry," she said. "Have you been waiting on me long?"

"No, dear, I just saw the fascination with which you were reading!" Marie said, sliding into the seat across from her. "Today is still a go, right? You and Angie will shoot some of the finer aspects of the resort?"

"Oh, yes, we're all set," Maura said. "Or we will be, once Angie is down."

"That's lovely. I thought we'd start with the pool and patio area, maybe scan the gym so that people can see just how much the resort offers? I know that Angie's forte lies in a different sort of content—as does yours—but she does have such an appeal online. She reaches a big audience. I can't help but think it'd be good exposure."

"Of course. Whatever you'd like."

"It's lovely that Angie Parsons will use her video channel for us."

"She couldn't wait to come here. She's fascinated with the resort."

"Well, her fascination was with the History Tree—" She paused a bit abruptly, then smiled. "I've seen some of Angie's videos and heard her podcasts and I even saw her speak at a bookstore once. The tree does seem right up her alley. And, of course, since it does seem to draw much of our clientele, I do appreciate the tree. Or trees. But… Well, those of us who knew Francine can't help but take that all with a grain of salt. Anyway…when do you think we'll be able to get started?"

"I imagine Angie will be down anytime," Maura told her. "I don't want to see you held up, though. Do you want me to call you when she's had her coffee?"

"Well, dear, this is my plan for the day, but if you could… Oh, there she is now," Marie said with pleasure.

Maura turned toward the entry to the coffee shop. Angie was walking in with Nils Hartford. She was her smiling, bubbling, charming self, talking excitedly.

She saw Maura sitting with Marie and waved, excused herself to Nils and came over. "Good morning. Mrs. Glass, you are bright and early."

Marie slowly arched a silver brow. "If one can call ten in the morning early, Angie, yes, I am bright and early." Apparently in case her words had been too sharp, she added, "But I'm certainly grateful for your work and ready whenever you are."

"Right after one coffee," Angie said. "One giant coffee!"

"Wonderful. I'll just check on the patio area and make sure someone's darling little rug rat hasn't made a mess of the place."

Marie rose and smiled again, perhaps trying to take the sting from her comment. "At your leisure," she said and sailed out of the coffee shop.

Angie made a face and sat. "If America had royalty, she'd be among it. If she hadn't been born into it, she would have married into it. Oy!"

"She is a bit…"

"Snooty?" Angie said.

Maura shrugged.

"Kind of strange, don't you think?"

"What's that?"

"Donald doesn't seem to be as…well, snooty. Best word I can come up with."

"To be honest, I don't know either of them that well. I mean, I worked for them before, but I was among the young staff—they hardly bothered with us. Fred was our main supervisor at the time."

"Along with Francine Renault?" Angie asked.

"Yep."

"And wasn't your beau kind of like the ranking student employee here?"

"Yes."

Angie smiled and leaned toward her. "And?"

"And what?"

"What about last night?"

"What about it?"

"Oh, you are no fun. Details. Ouch! You can feel the air when you two are close together. I'll admit—well, I don't need to admit anything, I frankly told you that I was deeply into him."

"Angie, you're deeply into a lot of people."

"True. So I've turned my attention to Nils. He is a cutie, too. Maybe even more classically handsome. Not as ruggedly cool—not like fierce, grim law enforcement. But damned cute. And, hmm, we are here a few more days. I do intend to have some fun."

"Angie—"

"Yes, I mean get laid!" Angie laughed at Maura's reaction. "Too graphic and frank for you? Oh, come on, Maura, you know me."

"And I wish you luck in your pursuits. I'm sure you'll do fine."

"Ah, you see, I shall do as I choose, which is much better than fine." Angie frowned suddenly. "Where is your law-and-order man?"

"He's here working, Angie. He went off—to work."

"Well, I suppose we should work, too. Let me grab my coffee."

"Great. I'll run my computer up and grab the camera."

Angie didn't need to get up for her coffee; Nils arrived at their table with a large paper cup.

"Two sugars, a dash of cream, American coffee with a shot of espresso," he said, delivering the cup to Angie. Her fingers lingered over his as she accepted the drink.

"Thank you so much," Angie said, smiling at him brilliantly. "When we talk about the restaurants, you will be in the video with me, won't you?"

"My absolute pleasure," Nils assured her. He smiled over at Maura. "Morning. I saw you earlier, but you were so involved, I didn't want to interrupt."

"You can interrupt anytime," Maura told him. "I was really just web browsing."

"Anything in the news—or have Brock or that Detective Flannery made any progress on the missing girls? Or, wow, I keep forgetting—Rachel?"

"Not that I know about."

"Something is going on this morning. There was a discovery just south of the Devil's Millhopper," Nils said. "I saw it on the news. Human remains were found. A Scout troop discovered them during a campout."

"I—I probably should have started with the news," Maura said. "I didn't." She didn't tell him that she knew something had been found because Brock had taken off early with Detectives Flannery and Lawrence to investigate. "More human remains. How sad."

Angie didn't seem concerned. "The Devil's Millhopper?" she asked. "That's…a cool name. What the hell is it?"

"A sinkhole," Maura told her. "Devil's Millhopper Geological State Park—it's in Gainesville. It's a really beautiful place, a limestone sinkhole about 120 feet deep. The park has steps all the way down, a boardwalk—sometimes torn up by storms—and beautiful nature plants and trees and all that."

"We need to go there," Angie said. "How did I miss a sinkhole?"

"I don't think it's haunted. But, hey, who knows? Anything can be haunted, right?" Nils asked. "It's not all that far from here—a cool place. Hey, I'd love to take you. I have a day off coming up, if you want to go."

"I'd love it if you could go with me… We'll need Maura, of course, for the video," Angie said.

"I'd love to go with both of you," Nils said.

While Angie smiled back at him, Maura found herself remembering the Nils she had known before—the young man who had thrived on being so superior. She tried to remember if she had noted any of his interactions with Francine. Francine most probably wouldn't have reacted to any of his behavior.

Could Francine have angered Nils…and could he, at eighteen, have been capable of murder?

Ridiculous. He'd been the same age as Brock; they'd all just been kids.

"Seriously, I love the park, too," Nils said, looking at Angie and then flashing a quick smile at Maura. "It's really a pretty place."

"Isn't Florida at sea level? Doesn't it flood?" Angie asked.

Nils looked at Maura again and shrugged. For a moment, he just looked like a nice—and attractive—man. One with a sense of humility—something he had once been lacking.

"Hey, we even have hill country in this area. But honestly, I don't know. It's a sinkhole. It has something to do with the earth's limestone crust or whatever. Geology was never my forte. Hey, we really do have hills in the state—not just giant Mount Trashmores, as we call them. And we have incredible caverns and all kinds of things. Most tourists just want warm water and the beaches, but it's a peninsula with all kinds of cool stuff. I'll find a ghost there for you if you want!"

Angie laughed and even Maura smiled.

"Great—we'll set it up," Angie said.

Maura quickly stood. "Meet you by the pool," she told Angie.

She clutched her computer and ran up both flights of stairs to her room. Housekeeping had already been into her room, she saw.

It seemed so pristine now. Cold.

Maybe just because Brock was no longer there.

She shook her head, impatient with herself. And for a moment, she paused. Being with him again had been so easy, so wonderful, so…perfect.

And she was, perhaps, wrong to dwell so much on one night. Things had torn them apart before.

She was suddenly afraid that events might just tear them apart again.

"WHEN REMAINS ARE down to what we have here," Dr. Rita Morgan told them, "it's almost impossible to pinpoint death to months, much less days and weeks. The bones were found just south of the Devil's Millhopper, as you know, deep in a pine forest. The area was just outside a clearing where the Scouts set up often, but not in the clearing, and it was only because a boy went out in the middle of the night to avail himself of a tree—no facilities out there, camping is rugged—that he came across them. Of course, the kid screamed and went running back for his leader or one of the dads along on the trip, and the dad called the police and... Well, here we are. The bones were scattered and we're still missing a few. I believe that all kinds of creatures have been gnawing upon them, but...there are marks—here, there—" she pointed to her findings "—that were not made by teeth. This young woman—we did find the pelvis, so we can say she was female—was stabbed to death. Oh, these are rib bones I'm showing you with the knife marks. I guess you figured that."

Brock nodded, as did Michael Flannery and Rachel Lawrence.

They were all familiar with the human skeletal system.

"But you think that she was killed sometime in the last year?" Brock asked.

"The integrity of the bone suggests a year—and a few teeth were left in the skull," Dr. Morgan explained.

"I'm going to say that she was killed sometime between six and twelve months ago. She was most probably buried in a very shallow grave in an area where the constant moisture and soil composition would have caused very quick decay of the soft tissue, and insects and the wildlife would have finished off the rest. We're still missing a femur and a few small bones. And I'm afraid so many teeth are missing I doubt we'll ever be able to make an identification. We can pull DNA from the bones and compare to missing persons, but as you know, that will take some time."

"She's not one of the three recently missing women, though, right? We are talking at least six months?" Brock asked.

"At least six months," Dr. Morgan agreed. She indicated the pile of bones that were all that was left of a young life, shaking her head sadly. "I wish I could tell you more. She was somewhere between the ages of eighteen and thirty, I'd say. Again—the pelvis is intact enough to know that. We'll keep trying—we'll do everything that we can forensically."

They thanked the doctor and left the morgue.

Outside, Michael Flannery spoke up. "I think that whoever killed Francine Renault twelve years ago got a taste for murder—and liked it. I think that whoever it is has been killing all these years. Maybe slowly at first, fewer victims. I'm not a profiler, but I've taken plenty of classes with the FBI—and I'm sure that you have, too. He's speeding up—for years, he was fine killing once a year. Now—or in the last year—he's felt the need becoming greater and greater."

"It is a possibility," Brock said. "Michael, it is possible, too, that whoever killed Francine did so because she was really unlikable and made someone crack—and that these two dead women we've found have nothing to do with Francine's death. And that the kidnappings aren't associated, either."

Rachel shook her head. "You're playing devil's advocate, Brock."

He was. Brock didn't know why—maybe just too much pointed to the Frampton Ranch and Resort, and he didn't really want it to be involved. Despite what had happened, he had a lot of good memories from his time there.

They now had the bones of two women killed within the past year. Three women were still missing. He'd barely had a chance to scratch the surface of what was going on.

"Come on, Brock. I've been chasing this for twelve years," Flannery said. "I did something I came to learn the hard way simply wasn't right—and now I'm chasing the results of my mistake."

"It wasn't your mistake. You weren't high enough on the food chain back then to insist that the case not just remain open, but that it continue to be investigated with intensity," Brock said. "But say your theory is right. If the killer is at large, then the killer hanged Francine and stabbed Peter Moore to death to make it appear like a suicide and provide a fall guy. That may have been where the killer decided stabbing afforded a greater satisfaction than watching someone strangle to death."

"Where they got a taste for blood," Flannery agreed.

"And you think it's someone who was or is still involved with the Frampton ranch," Brock said.

Rachel watched them both. "Honestly, Nils Hartford was a bona fide jerk—but I don't believe he was a killer," she said, though neither of them had accused Nils. "He... I mean, he and I were never going to make it, but we did become friends. When his family lost all their money, he admitted to me that he loved restaurants and he loved the ranch and that he believed Fred might give him a chance. And as to Mark... Mark was just a kid."

"Kids have been known to be lethal," Flannery reminded her.

"Fred Bentley?" Brock asked, looking at Rachel. "He wasn't a bad guy to work for—and I think he was well liked by the guests. He's still holding on to his position."

"And he'd oversee any laundry sent out by the hotel," Rachel said.

"If not Bentley...and you're right about the Hartford boys..."

"That leaves Donald Glass himself," Brock said.

Donald Glass—who was married. Who, it had been rumored, had been indulging in an affair with Francine Renault.

A man who had acquired quite a reputation for womanizing through the years.

But would a man brilliant enough to have doubled a significant family fortune have been foolish enough to commit murder on his own property—and leave clues that could lead back to him?

"Time to head back," Brock said. "I say we casually interview all of our suspects. Let them in a little on our fear that the three missing women are dead—and that there is, indeed, a serial killer on the loose."

"Can you get someone at your headquarters tracing the movements of our key possible suspects at the ranch?" Flannery asked Brock. "FDLE is good—but your people have the nation covered."

"Of course," Brock said. He hesitated. "I haven't spoken with Glass that much, but he expressed pleasure that we chose his place as a base. Of course, it's possible that such a man thinks of himself as invincible. Above the rest. But still, I'd say there's another major question that needs to be answered."

"What's that?" Flannery asked.

"Where are the missing women? There are no bodies. Of course, it's difficult for police when adults disappear—they have the right to do so, and often they have just gone off. But the woods were searched. Bodies weren't found. If it's Glass committing these crimes—or someone else at the Frampton property or someone not involved there at all—he might be taking the women somewhere. Keeping them—until he kills them. If we can find that place…maybe we can still save a few lives."

"And maybe we're all barking up the wrong tree," Rachel said. "And if we concentrate too hard in the wrong direction…well, there go our careers."

"We have to put that thought on hold—big thing now is to find the truth and hope that we can find the missing women. Alive," Brock said. "Agreed?"

Rachel winced. "Right, right. Agreed."

"Agreed. Oh, hell, yeah, agreed," Flannery said.

Brock didn't like what he was coming to believe more and more as a certainty.

A killer was thriving at the Frampton Ranch and Resort.

And Maura was there.

A beautiful young woman who had a history with the ranch.

A perfect possible victim.

Ripe for the taking.

Except that he wouldn't allow it. God help him, he'd never allow it.

He had found her again; he would die before he lost her this time.

Chapter Six

Maura and Angie wrapped up at the pool. Out in the back of the main house and nestled by the two wing additions, the pool was surrounded by a redbrick patio. While the many umbrellas and lounge chairs placed about the pool were modern and offered comfort and convenience, the brick that had been set artfully around managed somehow to add a historic touch that made it an exceptional area.

Maura didn't have to appear on camera; she took several videos of the pool itself and then several with Angie and Marie Glass seated together, sipping cold cocktails, with Marie talking about the installation of the pool twenty years earlier and how carefully they had thought about the comfort of their guests.

A young couple had come out while Maura was filming the water with the palms and other foliage in the background. They'd been happy to sign waivers and be part of the video—laughing as they splashed each other in the water.

When Maura's cell rang, she was so absorbed in detail that she almost ignored it—then she remembered that she and Brock had made a pact and quickly excused herself to answer the phone, leaving Angie and Marie to sit together chatting—just enjoying the loveliness of the pool and one another's company. It was evident that Marie did admire Angie very much. The two women almost looked like a pair of sisters or cousins sitting there, chatting away about the adults around them.

Maura turned her back and gave her attention to the call.

Brock sounded tense—he reminded her to stay with Angie and in a group at all times.

"I won't be leaving here," she assured him. "I'm with Angie and Marie. We're going to go film the restaurants and then the library. We'll probably record in Angie's suite. Are you heading back?"

He was, he told her.

She smiled and set her phone down and looked at Angie and Marie, who were watching her, waiting politely for her to finish her call.

"Onward—to the restaurant," she said.

"Perfect. They won't open for lunch for another twenty minutes," Marie said. "We can show all the tables and will let Nils describe some of our special culinary achievements."

"Yes. Perfect," Maura said.

"Oh, yes, that will be wonderful—we'll have the daily specials, and Nils can serve them. First, Maura can take the restaurant empty, and then some of the food—it's going to be great!" Angie said, always enthusiastic.

Angie and Marie went ahead of Maura; she collected her bag and the camera and expressed her appreciation to the young couple again.

They thanked her—they couldn't wait to send their friends to Angie's web channel when the video was posted.

Maura hurried after Marie and Angie.

The restaurant was pristine when they went in—set for lunch with shimmering water glasses and wineglasses and snowy white tablecloths. The old mantel and fireplace and the large paned windows created a charming atmosphere along with all that glitter. Angie did a voice-over while she scanned the restaurant.

Nils stood just behind Maura; that made her uneasy, but she wasn't alone in the restaurant, she was with Marie and Angie, and a dozen cooks and waitstaff lingered just in the kitchen. She knew that she was fine.

She wondered if Nils made her nervous because she did suspect him of something, or…

If she was just nervous because she didn't like anyone at her back.

When Nils touched her on the shoulder, she almost jumped. "Sorry, sorry!" he said quickly. "I don't want to mess this up—if I do something wrong, you'll tell me, right? You'll give me a chance to do it over?"

"Nils, this is digital. We can do things as many times as you want, but I believe what we're trying for is very spontaneous, natural—just an easy appreciation for what the resort offers."

"Okay, okay—thank you, Maura," he said.

She smiled. "Sure."

Marie was going to sit with Angie. Before she could, there was a tap on the still-locked door. "Let me just tell them we'll open in a few minutes, right at twelve," Nils said.

Angie and Marie took a seat at a circular table for two right by a side window.

But Nils didn't come back alone.

Donald Glass, elegantly dressed in one of his typical suits and tall and dignified—as always—arrived with him.

"I'd thought it would be good if I popped into one of these videos Marie thinks will be such a thing. If you don't mind. Darling," he told Marie, "would you mind? I think I speak about our wine list with the most enthusiasm."

"No, darling, of course, you must sit in," Marie said.

She rose, giving up her seat. "I'd have thought you might want to do the library," she said. "You do love the library so."

He grinned. "Yes, I'm proud of my libraries. But even then…good wine is a passion."

"Okay, dear."

Maura thought that Marie seemed hurt, but she really didn't show anything at all. She smiled graciously, telling Nils, "They'll need the menus and wine lists."

"Already there, Mrs. Glass, already there," Nils said.

"Okay, then," Maura said. "In five, four…" She finished the count silently with her fingers.

"Angie Parsons here, and I'm still at the Frampton Ranch and Resort. After a day at the oh-so-beautiful pool—and before a night at the incredible historic walk—there's nothing like a truly world-class dinner. And I'm thrilled to be here with Donald Glass, owner of this property and many more, and—perhaps naturally—a magnificent wine connoisseur, as well."

"Thank you so much, Angie. Marie and I are delighted to have you here. I do love wine, and while we have Mr. Fred Bentley, one of finest hotel managers in the state, and Nils Hartford, an extraordinary restaurateur, manning the helm, no wine is purchased or served without my approval." He went on to produce the list, explaining his choices—and certainly saying more in a few words than Maura would ever know, or even understand, about wine.

But the video was perfect on the first take.

Nils came in as they discussed the menu. He spoke about the excellence of their broad range of menu choices. He suggested that Angie enjoy one of their fresh mahi-mahi preparations, and that Donald order the beef Wellington. That way they could indulge in bites of each other's food.

He might have been nervous, but he did perfectly.

"And now we really have to open the restaurant," he said.

Donald Glass smiled and nodded. "No special stops—we run a tight ship. But, of course, that will be fine, right, Maura?"

"That will be fine. I can avoid other tables, not to worry," she said.

But people were excited when they noted that something was going on.

Many had been at the campfire when she had filmed. They wanted to be involved.

As she spoke to other diners pouring in, Maura knew that Marie Glass was watching her. She turned to her.

"Is that okay?" she asked.

"Yes, yes, lovely," Marie said. She glanced back at Donald, chatting away still with Angie at the table.

They were laughing together. Angie was her ever-charming self—flirtatious. She basically couldn't help it. Glass was enamored of her.

Marie looked back at Maura, her eyes impassive. "Indeed, please, if others wish to sign your waivers, it will certainly add on. Hopefully the food will come out quickly for my husband and Miss Parsons, and we'll be moving on. I can lock down the library, though, of course, Donald will want to be on the video then, too, as I suggested earlier."

"Thank you," Maura told her.

Marie was at her side as she chose a table close by to chat with the guests and diners who arrived—wanting to be on video.

She was startled when she accepted the last waiver and Marie spoke.

But not to her...

Not per se.

She spoke out loud, but it was as if she believed that her words were in her mind.

"And I have always vouched for him. Always," she murmured.

"Pardon?" Maura said.

"What? Oh, I'm so sorry, dear. I must be thinking out loud."

She walked away; Maura went to work.

The head chef himself, a new man, but well respected and winner of a cable cook-off show, came out to explain his fusions of herbs and spices with fresh ingredients.

The videos were coming out exceptionally well, Maura thought.

But she couldn't help remembering the way Donald Glass had sat with Angie—and the way Marie reacted to her husband.

BROCK WAS PARKING the car when he received a message from his headquarters. He hadn't contacted Egan. He had gotten in touch with their technical assistance unit and had reported on the remains that had been found, but it was Egan who called.

Egan wanted to know about the body that they had seen that morning; Brock told him their working theory, thinking that Egan might warn them against it.

He didn't.

Then he put Marty Kim, the support analyst who had been doing extra research for Brock's case, on the phone.

"I did some deep dives this morning," Marty told him. "Before coming to the Frampton Ranch and Resort, Nils Hartford was working at a restaurant in Jacksonville, Hatter and Rabbit. Trendy place. He left there for the Frampton resort, but there was a gap between jobs. I found one of the managers willing to talk. Nils resigned—but if he hadn't, he would have been fired. There was a coworker who complained about sexual harassment. Hartford was managing. The young woman was a waitress. She told the owner that she was afraid of Nils Hartford."

"Interesting. And do we know if the waitress is still alive and well?"

"Checking that out now," Marty told him. "I can't find anything much on Mark Hartford. He went to a state university, majored in history and social sciences, came out and went straight to work for Donald Glass."

"Fred Bentley?"

"He's been with Glass for nearly twenty years—at the Frampton Ranch and Resort for fifteen of them. Before that, he was working at a big spread that Glass has in Colorado."

"Anything on Donald Glass himself?"

"Nothing—and volumes. If you believe all the gossip rags, some more reliable than others, Glass has had many affairs through the years. Some of the women kept silent, some of them did not. He has been married to Marie for twenty-five years, and if I were that woman—I'd divorce his ass." Marty was silent for a minute. Then he added quickly, "Sorry, that wasn't terribly professional."

"You're fine. So…he's still playing the dog, eh?"

"One suspected affair he enjoyed was reportedly with Francine Renault. That hit a few of the outlets that speculate on celebrities without using their names— avoiding legal consequences. Over the years, he did pay off several women. One accused him of sexual assault—except, when it came to it, she withdrew all charges. There was a settlement. But most of these are confidential legal matters, and without due process and warrants, I can only go so far."

"Thanks. He's been spending most of his time and effort down at his property in Florida, right?"

"Oh, he travels. London, New York, Colorado and LA. But yes, most of the time he is in Florida. His trips to other properties tend to be weekends, just twice a year or so."

"Does Marie go with him?"

"It seems he does those trips alone. But, of course, paper trails can only lead you so far," Marty reminded him. "I'll keep searching. I'll naturally get back to you if I find anything else that might be pertinent to your investigation."

He'd parked the car. Detectives Flannery and Lawrence had waited for him.

He reported what he'd just learned to them.

Flannery shook his head. "A man with all that Glass has... Could it be possible?"

"We have nothing as yet, so let's not go getting ourselves thrown out of the resort before we have something tangible, okay?" Brock said.

"Of course not," Flannery said, and he looked at Rachel, frowning. "You should try to get some talk time in with Donald Glass," he said.

"Are you pimping me out?" she asked him.

"Never," Flannery said. "But maybe he'll respond more easily to you on many levels."

"You mean that you doubt that he takes me seriously," Rachel said.

"Rachel, Rachel, you have a chip on your shoulder," he told her.

Brock groaned slightly.

Rachel looked at Brock and he shrugged. "You never know."

"Yes, Rachel, I'm pimping you out—whatever works," Flannery told her. "He might still think of you as the teenager who spent summers at the resort, instead of the whip-smart detective you are now. You might catch him off guard."

She grinned. "Okay, just so I know what I'm doing."

"Let's get lunch," Flannery said. "Oh, and feel free to flirt with your old beau, if need be. I'm sure you've got enough wiles to go around."

Rachel paused before they reached the house, looking at Brock. "Maybe Brock could get Maura on that one," she said.

"Maura is a civilian," he said, hoping he hadn't snapped out the words.

"Yes, but..." Rachel hesitated, glancing at Flannery,

who nodded. "Everyone around here always had kind of a thing for Maura. I know that I'd be with Nils—and see him look after her longingly, even though she was a summer hire. And I'd see Glass looking at her, too, and I even think that Francine Renault was hard on her because the others seemed so crazy about her. If she could just draw Nils into conversation—with us around, of course, and see where that leads."

"We do remember that we are professionals, that we play by the book," Flannery said. "But come on, Brock, what led you to law enforcement was the knowledge that you had instincts along with drive. What made me follow your career as you moved on was…well, hell, like I said. You obviously have the instincts for it. Sometimes lines get a little blurred. I am not suggesting that we really use Maura—I'm just suggesting that she could help us chat some of these people up—with one of us right there."

Brock stared at the two of them. He didn't agree, and he didn't disagree. He was surprised by Rachel's words, but he'd been mostly oblivious to others back then. He shouldn't have been surprised by Michael Flannery's passion; he'd always known that Flannery was like a dog with a bone on this case.

Brock would never use Maura. Never.

But on the other hand she was in there interacting with all the persons of interest right now.

Twelve years ago, Maura had been with him; he had been with her. No room for doubt, and certainly, they had never thought to mistrust each other.

Now she had grown into an admirable professional—and a courteous and caring human being. And she was with him once again, although he reminded himself that they had been together just a night. There had been no promises. In the end, whether there was or wasn't a future for them didn't matter in the least. She was a civilian, and that was that.

He raised a finger in an unintentional scold. "She's never alone—never, ever, alone with any of them. With Fred Bentley, either of the Hartford brothers or Donald Glass."

"Right," Flannery said.

At his side, Rachel nodded grimly. He turned and they followed him.

"I'm starving," Rachel murmured as they entered the lobby and tempting aromas subtly made their way out and around them from the restaurant.

"Yeah, it's lunchtime," Flannery said.

"I'll join you soon," Brock told them. He headed to the desk; there was a clerk there he hadn't seen before.

"Good afternoon, sir. How can I help you?" he asked.

"You're new," Brock said.

"I am, sir."

"What happened to the young lady who was working?"

"I don't know, sir, and I don't know which young lady you might mean. Mr. Bentley gives us our schedules, sir. I'm doing split shifts, morning and night now, if I can be of assistance."

"Yes, I understand Angie Parsons is doing some filming here at the resort today. Can you direct me to where they're working now?"

"They're in the library, but they don't wish to be disturbed, sir. Sir!"

Brock turned and headed for the library.

"Sir! I shouldn't have told you. They don't want to be disturbed. Please, I have just been hired on—sir!"

Brock paused to turn back. "It's all right. I'm FBI," he said.

His being FBI didn't really mean a damned thing in this scenario. But he felt he had to say something reassuring to the clerk.

He went through the lobby and down the hallway that led to the library, in back of the café.

The door was closed.

There was a sign on it that clearly said Do Not Disturb.

Well, he was disturbed himself, so he was going to do some disturbing. He knocked on the door.

To his surprise, it opened immediately.

Marie Glass stood before him, bringing a finger to her lips. He nodded. She closed the door behind him.

Angie was holding the camera. He had arrived just before they were to begin a segment. While she loved being the director and videographer, Maura was also a natural before the camera. She smiled right into the lens and said that she was in her favorite area of the resort—the library. She was with Donald Glass, who kept the library stocked, not just here, but at all of his properties, and that he bought and developed places specifically because of unique or colorful histories.

"A true taste of life, the good, the bad and the evil," Maura said, smiling.

"Exactly, for such is life, indeed, and history can be nothing less," Glass said.

Maura knew what she was doing; Glass had been interviewed so many times in his rich life that he was apparently well aware of a good ending.

"Cut! Perfect!" Angie said. "Marie, what do you think?"

Marie smiled—her usual smile. One that maintained her dignity—and gave away nothing of her real thoughts. "Excellent. If we can just do an opening at the entry…perhaps have Fred giving the guests a welcome along with Angie." She turned and looked at Brock. "Oh, would you like to appear in a video, Brock? This was once a home away from home for you."

"No, thank you—though I would enjoy watching," he said. He looked at Maura, who was looking at him then, too. He couldn't read what she was thinking, but she had that look in her eyes that indicated there were things she had to say—but to him alone.

He glanced at Marie. "Not sure my bosses now would like it," he explained.

"Well, we can finish up then," Marie said. "Donald, dear, would you like to find Fred? He has been our general manager now for over fifteen years. He should be shown greeting Angie."

"Good thinking, my dear," Glass told his wife. "Meet you out front."

Donald left. Brock smiled, excused himself and hurried after Glass.

"Sir!"

Glass stopped and turned around with surprise. "Oh, Brock, yes, what can I do for you?" He frowned. "Have you learned anything? I caught a 'breaking news flash' about thirty minutes ago. More remains have been discovered, but those over south of Gainesville. It wasn't… Did they find one of the missing girls?"

He seemed truly concerned.

"No, sir. Whoever they found has been missing much longer. They don't have an ID yet."

"You never know if that's true, or if it's what the media was told to say."

"It's true. They have no identity on the remains yet. Indulge my concern for a moment—there was a young woman working at the front desk here. She might have been just on nights, and I may be a bit overly cautious, but I noticed you have a new hire on the desk."

"We do?"

He appeared genuinely surprised. "You'd have to ask Fred about that. I must admit, I don't concern myself much with the clerks. I worry more about the restaurants and our entertainment staff. But Fred will be able to tell you."

"Thank you."

"Have you seen Fred?"

"No, I haven't, but—"

"He's probably at lunch. I'll take a look in the restaurant. Excuse me."

Brock watched him as he went on by. The man was polite to him—always had been. But he couldn't imagine that dozens of reports were all false—the man evidently had an eye for women and an appetite for affairs.

Did he leave for tours of his other properties because he just needed to work alone, or because he needed space for casual affairs?

Or maybe he didn't really leave every time he said that he was doing so, or go exactly when and where he said that he was going.

Power and money.

Maybe Glass lured young women with those assets.

Brock hurried out front.

Maura wasn't alone. She was with Marie Glass and Angie, and they were standing in broad daylight.

He was still anxious to be with her.

More anxious to hear what it was she might have to say to him alone.

IT WASN'T THAT her work was hard, but Maura was weary—ready to be done.

Most of the videos had gone very smoothly.

Angie spoke spontaneously, and they had needed no more than three takes on any one scene that day. Maura had known what she'd wanted to say—she truly loved any library, especially one as focused and unique as the library at the Frampton Ranch and Resort.

And still, she was tired.

The idea made her smile. She was happy to be tired—because she was happy that she hadn't spent much of the previous night sleeping.

She didn't want to be overly tired that night, though!

Brock appeared on the steps of the porch before Donald Glass got there. He had an easy smile as he joined them and waited for Donald to appear with Fred Bentley.

"The Devil's Millhopper! Sounds like a place I have to see!" Angie said, smiling and looking at Brock.

He shrugged. "It's geographically fascinating—and has great displays on how our earth is always changing, how the elements and organic matter often combine to make things like sinkholes and other phenomena work. Sure—I love it out there." He laughed. "I love our mermaids, too. Weeki Wachee Springs and Weeki Wachee State Park. Absolutely beautiful—crystal clear water."

"Mermaids, eh?"

"Mermaids," he agreed politely and turned away; Glass was coming down the steps with Bentley. The stocky manager was beaming.

"I get to be in a video!" he announced.

"You do," Angie said.

"With the famous Angie Parsons," Fred said. He paused, frowning. "Or with our beautiful Maura—which is fine, too. Love our beautiful Maura."

Maura smiled. "No, sir—thank you for the compliment. You get to be with our famous and beautiful Angie."

"What do I say?" Fred asked.

Maura already knew exactly where she wanted them to stand for the afternoon light—and how she wanted them walking up the steps to the porch and the entry for the finale of the little segment.

"If you could give a welcome to the Frampton Ranch and Resort—and tell us how you've been here for fifteen years," Maura said. "Naturally, in your own words, and you can add in any bit of history you like."

She probably should have expected that something would go badly.

First, Fred froze and mumbled.

Maura smiled and coaxed him.

Then he went blank.

Then he forgot to follow Angie up the stairs at the end.

He apologized and said that he should be fired—from the video, not the property. He tried to laugh.

Maura encouraged him one more time, and they were able to get a decent video.

Brock stood nearby through the whole painful process, as did Donald and Marie. The owners—the married pair—did not stand next to each other.

Nor did they speak with each other.

And when they were done, Marie thanked Angie and Maura, bade the others good-afternoon and said that she was heading out for some shopping.

Donald thanked everyone and said that he'd be in his office.

Fred thanked Angie—then Maura.

"I was horrible. You fixed me. I guess that's what a good director does. Anyway, back to work for me. See you."

He lifted a hand and started up the steps.

"Fred," Brock said, calling him back.

"Yeah?"

"I noticed you have a new hire on the front desk."

"I do," Fred Bentley told him. "Remember when I was night clerk—well, I don't like being night clerk. Heidi didn't show up at all—and didn't call with an excuse. That's grounds for dismissal, and everyone knows it, so I left a message telling her not to come back."

"You never spoke with her?" Brock asked.

Bentley frowned. "No, I got her voice mail. She must have heard it. She never came back in."

"What's Heidi's last name and where does she live?"

"Heidi Juniper. She lives between here and Gainesville," Bentley told him. His frown deepened. "You don't think that—"

"I'll need her address and contact information," Brock said. "We'll just make sure that Heidi is irresponsible—and not among the missing."

"Of course, of course, I'll get it for you right away," Bentley told him.

When Fred was gone, Angie turned to Brock, repeating Bentley's concern. "You don't really think—"

"I don't know. I think we'll just check on her, that's all," Brock said. He looked at the two of them. "Lunch?"

"Are they still serving lunch?" Maura asked. "They do close for an hour, I think, between lunch and dinner."

"I bet they'll serve us," Angie said. She smiled broadly. "Oh, I do love it when people feel that they owe you."

She started up the steps. Maura was glad; she wanted a few minutes with Brock alone.

She believed that she'd have all night, but she needed a moment now.

But Angie stopped, looked back and sighed impatiently. "Come on! Let's not push our luck too hard, okay? I want them to keep owing me."

She was waiting.

No chance to talk.

Maura started up the stairs to the porch, grateful, at least, that Brock was with her.

Grateful, in fact, that he was simply in the world—and in her part of the world once again.

Chapter Seven

Brock saw that Michael Flannery and Rachel Lawrence were still in the restaurant when he arrived—they had taken a four top, expecting him to join them.

They hadn't expected Maura and Angie, but Michael quickly grabbed another chair and beckoned them all on over.

Angie was happy to greet them both, offering to film some of the campfire fun again with them in it. She hadn't quite figured out that law enforcement officers didn't often want their faces on video that went around to the masses—especially when they worked in plain clothes.

Both politely turned her down.

"I feel like a terrible person," Angie said. "I mean, I'd seen the news. I knew that women had been kidnapped and one had been found dead…or her remains had been found. I just didn't associate it with worrying about the central and northern areas of Florida. And the state has a huge population… Not that having a huge population makes terrible things any better, but statistically, they are bound to happen. I had no idea that the FBI and the FDLE would be staked out at the resort. But I can't tell you how glad I am. Though we did finish here today. And we went to St. Augustine yesterday. I want to see this Devil's Millhopper—the big sinkhole. But I'm not sure if Nils can go right away, and he did say that he wanted to."

Nils must have been close; as if summoned, he was suddenly behind Angie's chair. "While you're waiting to go to the Devil's Millhopper, there's some other cool stuff for Maura's cameras not far from here. Cassadaga—it's a spiritualist community, and the hotel there and a few other areas are said to be haunted. There's a tavern in Rockledge that's haunted, a theater in Tampa... It goes on and on. We can find you all manner of places."

"You need permits for some of them, advance arrangements and all," Maura reminded him.

Nils grinned. "Well, there's more here, too. Hey, I know what we have—and near here! Caves. Yes, believe it or not, bunches of caves in Florida. Up in Marianna, but closer to us—not really far at all—Dames Cave. It's in Withlacoochee State Park, but...outside the state park, on the city edge, there's an area that's not part of any park system. Not sure who owns the land but you can trek through that area and find all kinds of caves."

Maura glanced at Brock; he knew from that look that she definitely didn't want to go off exploring caves alone with Angie.

"Caves! Cool—haunted caves? Weird caves?" Angie asked.

"Oh, yes, there's an area called Satan's Playground. Not in a state park, and not official in any way. I know that Maura and Brock know it—they used to love to go off exploring when they were working here and they had a day off," Nils said. He smiled at Angie. "I'd truly love to explore the Devil's Millhopper with you, if you don't mind waiting."

Angie leaned toward him, smiling. "I don't mind at all. We'd intended to spend several days here."

Nils nodded, apparently smitten; they might have been a match made in heaven.

"Well, hey, Nils, can we still get lunch?" Maura asked.

"No," he said. "But yes, for you. Order quickly, if you don't mind. Chef saw you come in and he said that you're going to help make him more famous, so he'll wait. But he did have a few hours off before dinner, so…"

"I ate," Angie said, smiling. "Two of Chef's lunches would be great, but I just don't think I could manage to eat a second. I suggest the mahi-mahi."

Brock looked at Nils and then Maura. "Two hamburgers?" he asked.

Rachel cast Nils a weary gaze. "Mike and I had the hamburger plate. Chef makes a great hamburger."

"Yes, hamburgers sound good," Maura said.

"Done deal," Nils told them.

When he had walked away, Flannery leaned toward Angie. "I know how important your books and your videos are to you, but for the time being, please don't go off to lonely places on your own."

"I would never go on my own," Angie said.

"Good," Rachel murmured.

"I wouldn't be alone. Maura would be with me," Angie said. She turned to watch Nils. The chef had come out of the kitchen and they were speaking.

"Good-looking man," she murmured.

"So he is. Many women think so," Rachel said, studying something on her hand. "Anyway, the point is…"

"Don't go off anywhere alone as just two young women," Flannery said.

Angie smiled at him. "Detective Flannery, did you want to come along with us? Brock? It could be fun."

"Actually, if you want to see the caves, sure," Brock said.

Maura stared at him, surprised. She quickly looked away.

She knew that if he wanted to head out to the caves, there had to be a reason. And yes, he did have a reason.

Remains had been found not far from the caves.

And there were areas where more remains might be found, or where, with any piece of luck, the living just might be found, as well.

"Nice!" Angie said. "Great—it will be a date. Well, a weird threesome date," she added, giggling. "Unless, of course, Detective Flannery, Detective Lawrence, you two could make it?"

"We're working," Rachel reminded her sharply.

"Yes, of course," Angie said.

"And," Rachel added, "we don't want to be picking up your remains, you know."

Angie stared back at her, smiling sweetly. "Not to worry on my account. Brock will be with us, and when we go to the Devil's Millhopper, we'll be with Nils. Anyway! If you all will excuse me, I just popped in for a few minutes of the great company. We did such a good job with the video this morning that I'm dying to get into the pool."

She stood, motioning that Brock and Flannery didn't need to stand to see her go. "If you take work breaks other than food, join me when you're done."

Angie left them. When she was gone, Rachel stared at Maura.

"You *like* working with her?" Rachel asked.

"She's usually just optimistic about everything," Maura said. "And I guess she has that same feeling that most of us do, most of the time—it can't happen to me."

"Until it does," Brock murmured.

Maura glanced at Brock uncertainly. She had things to say that she hadn't been about to say in front of Angie.

"What is it?" Brock asked her. "We're working a joint investigation here—Rachel and Mike and I are on the same team."

"You want to go to the caves—really?" she asked.

She hoped he would just tell her the truth. "I want to go out to the area south of the Devil's Millhopper we talked about before. The remains today were found between the Millhopper and the caves. I think it might be a good thing to explore around there some more, though it could so easily be a futile effort," Brock told her. "People tend to think of Florida with the lights and fantasy of the beaches—people everywhere. There are really vast wildernesses up here. Remains could be… anywhere."

"It's so frustrating. Nothing makes sense, and maybe we're just creating a theory that we want to be true because we don't want more dead women, and we're all a little broken by Francine's murder. Maybe these cases are all different," Rachel said, looking over at Flannery. "One set of remains in a laundry, another in a forest where a Scout had to trip over them trying to pee. The one suggests a killer who wants to hide his victims. The other suggests a killer who likes attention and wanted to create a display. I mean, it's the saddest thing in the world, the way these last remains were discovered, by a kid…out on his night toilet rounds. Oh, sorry—you guys didn't get your food yet."

Brock waved a hand in the air and Maura smiled, looking down. She hadn't been offended.

But their hamburgers had arrived. And it wasn't how the remains had been discovered that was so disturbing—it was simply that now a second set had been found.

Rachel was looking at Brock with curiosity. "Do you think that the killer could be hiding kidnap victims in a cave or a cavern? Wouldn't that be too dangerous?"

"The better-known tourist caverns?" Brock asked. "Yes. The lesser-known caverns that are just kind of randomly outside the scope of the parks? Maybe. I don't know. He'd keeping them somewhere for days, maybe even weeks. Then there are also hundreds of thousands of warehouses, abandoned factories, paper mills…" He broke off. "I just know that there are three missing women somewhere, and I'd sure as hell like to find them while they're still just missing."

"And not dead," Flannery said grimly. He turned slightly, looking at Maura. "Do you remember anything, anything at all, from back then that might suggest anyone as being…guilty? Of killing Francine Renault."

Maura shook her head, then hesitated, glancing at Brock. He nodded slightly, and she said, "I was stunned—completely shocked—when we came upon Francine's body. When the news came out that Peter Moore had killed himself, I was already far away, and we were young and… I didn't know what else to believe. I—I was exploring on the internet today, though, and came across something that might—or might not—

have bearing on this. It's a bit strange, so stick with me. There was a society in this area, decades ago, called the Sons of Supreme Being. They were suspected of the disappearance and possible death of a woman in the 1950s. That's why it struck me as maybe relevant. One of their members was supposed to testify in court—he died before he could. Now, I got this information from a random site—I haven't verified it in any way, but..."

Brock looked over at Flannery. "Have you ever heard anything about this group—this Sons of Supreme Being society or club or whatever?"

Flannery shook his head and then frowned. "Maybe, yes, years ago. I'm not sure I remember the name... When I joined the force, some of the old-timers were wondering during a murder investigation if the group might have raised its head again—a girl had been found in a creek off the Saint Johns River. She was in sad shape, as if she'd been used and tossed about like trash. But her murderer was caught—and eventually executed. Talk of rich kids picking up the throwaways died down. But as far as I know, nothing like that has been going on."

Maura was still looking at Brock.

"You have something else," he said.

She nodded and lowered her voice. "I don't think that Marie Glass realized that she was standing by me or that she was speaking aloud, but...she was watching her husband with Angie. And she said something to the effect that she shouldn't...cover for him. And she acted as if she hadn't said anything at all when she caught me looking at her. But in all fairness... Glass has always been decent to the people who worked for him, even if..."

"He's paid off a number of women through the years," Rachel said. "He was always decent to me. But there were rumors about him and Francine."

Glancing over at Maura, Brock said, "I want to find out if a young lady named Heidi Juniper is all right."

"Heidi Juniper?" Flannery asked him.

"She was working here. She didn't show up and Bentley left her a message that she was fired. He's supposed to be getting me contact information for her. Under the circumstances, I think it's important to know why Heidi didn't show up for work."

They had all finished eating. Flannery stood first. "Rachel and I will get to work finding out about Heidi Juniper. I was thinking you might want to talk to your old friends Donald and Marie Glass."

"Hardly my old friends," Brock said.

"I'm going to go to the library," Maura said. She paused, looking at them all. "It really wouldn't make sense. Donald Glass may be a philandering jerk, since he is a married man. But he is so complete with his libraries, with his campfire stories…he included Francine's murder in the collection. Would he be so open if he was hiding something?"

"Being so open may be the best way of hiding things," Flannery said. He hesitated, glancing from Brock to Maura.

"Young lady, you are a civilian. You be careful."

"Not many people think that reading in a library is living on the edge," she said, smiling. "Brock will be near, and reading is what a civilian might do to help."

"We thank you," Flannery said. "Rachel…"

She rose and the two of them headed out.

"I'm going to the library with you," Brock told Maura.

"But I thought you wanted to speak with Marie and Donald," she said.

"What do you want to bet that they both show up while we're there—separately, but…"

"You're on," she said softly, standing.

MAURA KNEW WHAT she was looking for—anything that mentioned the Sons of Supreme Being. She delved into the scrapbooks that held newspaper clippings through the decades, aiming for the 1950s. Brock was across the room, seated in one of the big easy chairs, reading a book on the different Native American tribes who had inhabited the area. It was oddly comfortable to be there with him, even though she did find her mind wandering now and then, wishing that they could forget it all—and go far from here, someplace with warm ocean breezes and hours upon hours to lie together, doing nothing but breathing in salt air and each other.

Gritting her teeth, she concentrated on her research.

After going through two of the scrapbooks that went through the 1950s, she came upon what she was seeking.

The first article was on the disappearance.

In 1953, Chrissie Barnhart, a college freshman, had disappeared. She had last been seen leaving the school library. Friends had expected her to meet up with them at the college coffee shop to attend a musical event.

She had not returned to her room.

There was a picture of Chrissie; she had been light haired and bright eyed with soft bangs and feathery tresses that surrounded her face.

The next article picked up ten days later.

In a college dorm, a young man had awakened to hear his roommate tossing and turning and mumbling aloud, apparently in the grips of a nightmare. Before he had wakened his friend, he had heard him saying, "I didn't know we were going to kill her. I didn't know we were going to kill her."

The event was reported to the police and an officer brought the student who had the nightmare in for questioning; his name had been Alfred Mansfield. At first, Mansfield had denied doing anything wrong. He'd had a nightmare, nothing more. But the police had put the fear of God into him, and in exchange for immunity, he had told them about a society called the Sons of Supreme Being. Their fathers had been supportive of Hitler's rise to power in Germany. After the war, they had made their existence a very dark secret. Only the truly elite were asked to join—elite, apparently, being the very rich.

Alfred Mansfield hadn't known who he had been with, but he was certain he could help bring those who had killed Chrissie to justice. He had simply accepted a flattering invitation, donned the garments sent to him late one night and joined with a small group, also clad in Klan-like masks, in the clearing.

All were anonymous—but he thought that their leader might have been Martin Smith, the son of a wealthy industrialist.

They hadn't killed Chrissie on the day she had been taken; Alfred didn't know where she had been kept. He only knew that he was in the clearing with the double tree when she had been dragged out, naked and screaming, and that the leader had spoken to the group about their need to make America great with the honor of those who rose above the others; to that end, they sacrificed.

Alfred had tried not to weep as he watched what was done to her and how she died. He didn't want to be supreme in any way. He wanted to forget what had happened.

He wanted the nightmares to stop.

He would serve as an informant for the police.

He was released, both he and the police believing that they had taken him in for questioning quietly and that he was safe out in the world. He'd done the right thing by letting the police know, and they would take it from there.

Alfred's body had been dragged out of the Saint Johns River twenty-four hours after his release. He had been repeatedly stabbed before being thrown into the water to drown.

The body of Chrissie Barnhart had never been found.

Maura turned a page to see an artist's rendering of Alfred's description of the murder of the young woman.

She gasped aloud.

It was a sketch created by a police artist. But it might have been the clearing by the History Tree, looking almost exactly as it did today.

Minus the masked men.

And the naked, screaming woman, appropriately hidden behind the sweeping cloaks of the men.

"Brock… Brock…"

Maura said his name, beckoning to him, only to hear him clear his throat.

She spun around. As they had both expected to happen, a Glass had come into the room.

Marie. Brock had risen and was blocking the path between Maura and Marie.

"Mrs. Glass," Maura said, rising. She felt guilty for some reason—and she must have looked guilty. Of something. She quickly smiled and made her voice anxious as she asked, "Did we miss something? I know that Angie will be more than happy to start up again with anything else you'd like."

"Oh, no, dear, I think we did a great job today. I just heard that someone was in the library—I should have known that it was you two! My bookworms. Still, in my memory, the best young people we ever hired for our summer program," Marie said.

"Thank you," Maura said.

Marie was looking at Brock. "Such a shame," she said. "And I'm so sorry. What happened… Well, the mistake cost all of us, I'm afraid."

She did appear as if the memory caused her a great deal of pain.

"Marie, it's long over, in the past—and as far as things went, my life hardly had a ripple," Brock told her. Maura looked at him; he was so much taller than Marie that she could clearly see his face. His look might as well have been words.

She'd been much more than a ripple; losing her had been everything.

She lowered her head quickly, not wanting Marie to see her smile.

"It wasn't your fault," Maura assured her.

Marie was silent for a minute, and then said, "Maybe, maybe I could have… Um, I'm sorry. I didn't mean to disturb you. Get back to it—I have to…have to…do something. Excuse me."

She fled from the library.

"See?" Maura whispered to Brock. "See? There's something bothering her. She has, I think, been telling law enforcement that Donald was with her—*when he wasn't*. Brock, you have to come read this. Donald Glass didn't go to school here, but…if there was ever a candidate for the Sons of Supreme Being, he is one! Do you think that he could be resurrecting some old ideal? And look—look at the police sketch. Well, you have to read!"

Brock sat down where she had been. She set a hand on his shoulder, waiting while he went quickly through the clippings.

He was silent as he studied the pictures.

He turned back to her, rising, and as he did so, his phone began to ring. He pulled it from his pocket, glanced at the ID and answered. "Flannery. What did you find?"

His face seemed to grow dark as he listened. Then he hung up and looked at her.

"What is it?" she asked.

"I think we have another missing woman. Which frightens me. I just don't know how many this killer of ours keeps alive at one time."

"I'LL BE FINE. I'll stay right next to Angie—and the group. We saw Mark Hartford in the hallway—he said that he had twenty people signed up for tonight. Oh, yeah—and Detectives Flannery and Lawrence are staying behind," Maura told Brock.

"I wish you'd just lock yourself in this room until I got back," he said, smoothing his fingers through her hair.

They hadn't slept; they weren't waking up. But they

were in bed, and he was still in love with her face on the pillow next to his.

They'd left the library, making plans. But while talking, they'd headed across the lobby, to the elevator, up to her room.

And then talking had stopped, and they were kissing madly, tearing at each other's clothing, falling onto the bed, kissing each other's bodies frantically—very much like a pair of teenagers again, exploring their searing infatuation.

"Reminds me of staff bunk, Wing Room 11," she had told him breathlessly, her eyes on his as they came together at last, as he thrust into her, feeling again as he had then, as if he had found the greatest high in the world, as if nothing would ever again be as it was being with her, in her, feeling her touch and looking into her eyes.

And it never had been.

"I wonder if Mr. and Mrs. Glass ever knew how much the staff appreciated the staff room?" he'd asked later when, damp, cooling and breathing normally again, they had lain together, just touching.

Their current conversation had started with, "We have to get up. You have to go and see Heidi's family, and I'm taking my camera out for the campfire and ghost walk again."

"No. You're locking yourself in this room."

"No, that would be ridiculous. I'll be with about two dozen witnesses. No one would try anything."

The argument had been done; she did have logic in her favor. And so they dressed, reluctant to part, knowing that they must.

The evening had been decided.

Brock hesitated. "Do you think that Angie knows we're together again?"

"Probably, but…"

"But?"

"I'm not so sure she'd care. Angie is—Angie. Unabashed. Men are dogs—adorable dogs, and she loves them. But one of her great sayings is that if men are dogs, women definitely get to be bitches."

He frowned, thinking about Angie's behavior at lunch. "Does she know anything about Rachel and Nils having once been hot and heavy?"

"I don't think so. Why would she? She wasn't around way back then. Angie does like Nils. She likes you better, but…"

"I'm spoken for?"

"She might actually think that you're more interested in me—and that wouldn't sit well with her ego. She did tell me that if I wasn't interested, she'd move in."

He laughed. "Well, honesty is a beautiful thing."

"It can be—it can be awkward, too," Maura assured him. "So, are you leaving?"

"Not until I see you gathered with a large group of guests and Angie to head out to the campfire."

"Okay, then, we should go down."

He opened the door for her. They headed for the lobby. It was busy—people were gathering. One was a family, including a mom and a dad and three children: older boys and a girl of about five. The couple from the pool was going to be at the campfire that night; they greeted Maura warmly. A few people seemed to be alone. There were two more families, one with a little girl, one with twin boys who appeared to be about fourteen.

Angie was there already, chatting with Mark.

"Hey—are you coming out tonight?" Mark asked Brock. He seemed pleased with the prospect.

"No, duty calls," Brock said. "But hopefully I'll catch up by the end."

"You have to go?" Angie asked.

"I do."

"You can't send that other cop?"

"No—because Mike Flannery and Rachel Lawrence are coming here tonight. Rachel knows all about the campfire and the walk and the stories, but Mike has never had a chance to go. And there are things I like to do myself," Brock said.

"Ah, yeah, every guy thinks he's got to do everything himself," Angie said.

"Just on this. Mike and Rachel have really been taking on the brunt of the load. My turn for an initial investigation," he said pleasantly.

He saw that Mike and Rachel had arrived.

"I'll just have a word with Mike—maybe I'll see you later."

He walked over to join Flannery and Rachel, aware that they'd be heading to the campfire any minute.

"Thanks for doing the interview tonight," Flannery said. "Really. I know you don't want to leave. I swear, we'll watch her like a pair of parental lions."

"I think male lions just lie around," Rachel said.

"I'll be a good male lion," Flannery said. "I feel that I do need to do this. Everyone really knows the stories and the tree—or trees—but me."

Brock didn't want to admit that he really wanted to interview Heidi's parents himself; there were often little things that could be said but lost in retelling. It was always better to have several interviews with family, witnesses and more. And he did owe this one to Mike.

"I'll be back as soon as possible," Brock told them.

"And really, we don't know that you need to be worried."

"I don't know. Glass is looking like a more viable suspect all the time," Brock said.

"Glass won't be out here. No need to fear," Rachel said. "And I may be small, but trust me—I am one fierce lioness."

Brock smiled. "I know," he told her.

He turned. Mark Hartford was deep in conversation with Maura. She wasn't looking Brock's way— she was listening.

He turned and headed out to the parking lot and his car. He knew he couldn't be ridiculous—he'd never keep his job that way.

It was a twenty-minute drive east to Heidi's home in a quiet neighborhood just south of St. Augustine. He noted that the girl lived in a gated estate.

The houses were about twenty years old and reflected an upper-working-class and family atmosphere.

Heidi's parents were eagerly waiting for him. Her mother, Eileen, a slim woman with curly gray hair and dark, tearstained eyes—was frantic. Heidi's father, Carl, bald and equally slim, kept trying to calm her.

"The police didn't even want to start a report until today—they said that she hadn't really been missing. I know my daughter—when she says she's coming home, she's coming home!" Eileen said and started to cry.

"When was the last time you spoke with her?" Brock asked gently.

"She was at work. She said she was leaving soon.

It was right at the end of her shift—for that day. Shifts could change, and she didn't care at all. She sometimes worked double shifts, but she said that she wasn't going to work double that day. She was tired. She was coming home. But she never arrived. I waited up. I woke Carl. We drove all up and down the highway. I mean, nothing happened to her here—our community is very secure."

"Did you call her work—talk to anyone there?"

"Some man answered the phone—he just sounded irate. He said that they weren't a babysitting service and she wasn't even with the summer program. That she probably ran off with some friends!"

"You don't know the man's name?"

"He just answered the phone, 'Front desk, how can I help you?'" Eileen said.

"Rude. If I'd known how rude… You'll investigate, right? The detective who called us—Flannery—he was the first one who seemed concerned," Carl said.

Brock nodded. "We'll take this very seriously, I swear," he assured them, taking Eileen's folded hands. "This is important. Did she say anything else? Had she been having any trouble with anyone there? Had any of the other employees or guests been ugly to her—or come on to her inappropriately?"

"She loved her job," Carl said. "Loved it." He looked at his wife. "She said that Mr. Glass was nice, but she hardly saw him. Or Mrs. Glass. Fred Bentley was her supervisor, and he seemed to be fine. She said he was a stickler for time and the rules, but she was always on time, and she never broke the rules, so they got on fine. Oh, she loved the guy who was like a social director— and she was welcome to use the pool and the gym and go on the walks—as long as she wasn't disturbing or taking anything away from the guests. There wasn't anything she told you that she wouldn't have told me, right?" Carl asked his wife. "As far as I know, she simply loved her job."

"Yes, she did," Eileen agreed. "But…"

She frowned and broke off.

"Please, tell me what you're thinking," Brock said. "Even if it seems unimportant."

Eileen's frown deepened as she exhaled a long sigh before speaking. "Something odd… She was muttering beneath her breath. She said…"

"Yes?"

"Well, I think… I'm not even sure I heard her right. The last time I talked to her on the phone—before she left work and disappeared—she said something like… 'Supreme Being, my ass!' Yes, that was what she was muttering. I didn't pay that much attention—I thought she was talking about a guest—someone acting all superior. I didn't think much of it—people can act that way, when they think they're superior to those who are working. And my daughter would deal with it—and mutter beneath her breath. Yes. I'm almost positive, and honestly, I'm not sure what it can mean, if anything, but… Yes. She murmured, 'Supreme Being, my ass.'"

Chapter Eight

"The beautiful Gyselle," Mark Hartford said, "is sometimes seen in the woods near the History Tree. Running from it. A ghost forced to live where she saw the end of her life. Or, as a spirit, does she remember better times? Is she running to the tree—where she would meet her lover and dream of the things that might have been in life?"

He told the tales well, Maura thought. And even after they had finished at the campfire, he spoke as they moved along the trails into the woods, and finally, to the History Tree.

Mark had asked her to speak twice and she'd obliged; she'd had the camera rolling again, too—she might as well since they were out there. Angie could decide later which night's footage she liked best.

Maura noted with a bit of humor that Mike and Rachel were being true to whatever promises they had certainly given Brock—they hadn't been ten full feet away from her all night.

But at the tree, she found that she wanted it on video from every angle. She kept picturing the police artist's rendering she had seen that day.

Creepy figures surrounding the tree, unidentifiable.

The victim from the 1950s, Chrissie, caught in the arms of one of her attackers.

Were the current victims being held—as she had been held? And if so, how in the hell were they being hidden so well…until their remains were left to rot in the elements?

"You are getting carried away," Angie whispered to her.

"Just a little," Maura agreed.

"Questions—anything else?" Mark asked his group pleasantly.

Maura wondered if she should or shouldn't speak, but her mouth opened before her mind really worked through the thought.

"Yes, hey, Mark, have you ever heard of a group called the Sons of Supreme Being?" she asked.

He looked at her, a brow arching slowly.

His entire tour group had gone silent, all curious at her question.

"Yeah," he said. "I—yeah. I thought it was kind of a rumored thing." He lifted a hand. "No facts here, folks, just stuff I heard at college. They say they existed once. They were a pack of snobs—thought they were better than anyone else. They were never sanctioned by any of the state schools—in fact, I heard you got your butt kicked out if you were suspected of being one of them. They were like an early Nazi-supporter group—seemed they watched what Hitler was doing in the 1930s. But, hey, nothing like that exists now, trust me!" He grinned at his crowd. "I'm a people person. Someone would have told me. Where did you hear about them?"

"Oh, I read something," Maura said. "I was just curious if it had been real or not."

"I can't guarantee it, but I heard that they did exist.

No one I know has anything on who the members might have been or anything like that," Mark told her. "Although I did hear that while the rumors of the group started in the 1930s, it really went further back—like way, way back. It was the rich elite even in the 1850s— dudes who came to Florida from the north and all, and built plantations and homes and ranches after Florida became a territory and then a state. They considered themselves to be above everyone else—everyone! If you ask me—a theory I've never spoken aloud before— I have a feeling that Gyselle's death might have been helped along by members—even way back then. Those dudes would have thought that this tree was a sacred spot. And Julie Frampton could have easily whispered into someone's ear. Gotten them to do the deed."

"There is an idea for you," Maura murmured. "Thanks, Mark."

She felt Detective Flannery take a step closer to her.

"Okay, time to head on back, folks. No stragglers— no stragglers. We don't know what's up, but we're asking people to stay close." Mark pointed to the way out.

His group obediently headed back along the trail.

As they came out of the woods, she saw that Brock was walking from the parking lot toward them. "Brock!" Angie called. "You missed new stuff—the beautiful Gyselle might have been killed by a secret society. Wild, huh?"

Brock frowned and glanced past her at Maura, Mike and Rachel.

"I asked Mark if he'd ever heard of the group," Maura said.

"Oh," he said. "Well, you got something new and fresh on a tour. Great."

He wasn't going to talk, not there, not then—not with others around them. She thought, too, that he seemed tense.

Maybe even with her.

Because, perhaps, she shouldn't have spoken.

But the day was done at last; she wanted nothing more than to get back and close out the world—except for Brock.

She knew that he'd meet first with Mike and Rachel. And, she knew, he'd probably had a rough last few hours—talking to the parents of another girl who had disappeared.

She yawned. "Long, long day—I'm going up to bed," she said. "Angie, we can head out to those caverns tomorrow—at least, I think we can. Brock, can you take the time?"

"Yes. In fact, I think that maybe Detectives Flannery and Lawrence can join us."

Flannery might have been taken by surprise; if so, he didn't show it.

"Yes, we'll all go. Search those woods—close to where the last remains were discovered. You okay with that, Angie?"

"You bet—that will be perfect. Oh, I do hope we find something!" she said enthusiastically. "Oh, lord, that sounded terrible. Terrible. I mean, I didn't mean it that way. Except, of course, it would be cool to find a lair, a hideout—save someone!"

"That would be something exceptional," Maura said, looking at Brock. He still seemed disturbed. "So," she added, "Angie, an excursion tomorrow means you have to wake up fairly early."

"Oh, I will, I will. Meet in the coffee shop at 8:30 a.m.?" she asked.

"Sounds good," Brock said.

"Adventure day—nice break," Rachel murmured.

"You're really going to be there at eight thirty?" Maura asked skeptically.

"Ah, and I even have plans tonight! But yes, I'll be there," Angie said.

"You have plans tonight?" Brock asked her.

"Not to worry—I'm not leaving the property. I'm just meeting up with a new friend in the coffee shop— or not the actual coffee shop, you know, the little kiosk part that stays open 24/7. We'll be fine."

Maura wanted to get away from everyone.

"Okay," Maura said. "I am for bed." She didn't wait for more; she hurried past them and straight for the resort, anxious to get to her room.

And more anxious for Brock to join her.

BROCK REMAINED OUTSIDE, just at the base of the porch steps, with Mike and Rachel—waving as Angie at last left them, smiling and hurrying on up the steps to meet her date.

He quickly filled them in on what Heidi's parents had told him.

Flannery shook his head. "It just gets more mired in some kind of muck all the time. I can see a serial kidnapper and killer, but... You think that there's some idiot Nazi society that has been going on for years— oh, wait, even before there were Nazis?"

"I know, I never heard of it before today—and then that's all that I've heard about. So there is a cult—or someone wants us all to believe that there is," Brock said.

"That could mean all kinds of people are involved," Rachel mused. She frowned. "I never heard what Mark was saying tonight before—that a really narcissistic group being 'supreme' might have existed as far back as the end of the Seminole Wars. Seriously, come on, think about it—and let's all be honest about humanity. At that time, males were superior, no hint of color was acceptable and no one had to say they were or weren't supreme. Society and laws dictated who was what."

"Okay, historically, we know that Gyselle was dragged out of the house to the hanging tree and basically executed there. History never told us just who did the dragging," Brock said. "I do believe that Heidi was taken by the same people who took the other girls— and I don't believe that she's dead yet, and we can only really pray—and get our asses moving—to find them."

"Brock, we have had officers going into any abandoned shack or shed, getting warrants for anything that was suspicious in the least. The state has been moving, but yeah, we need to get going on the whole instinct thing. You think that the caverns might yield something?"

"I think that remains were found very close to them," Brock said. "Anyway, I'm going up for the night. I'll see you in the morning."

"Yep. We'll say good-night and see you in the morning," Flannery said.

By then, the group from the campfire tales and walk had apparently retired for the night. The lobby was quiet as Brock walked across it.

The young man he'd met the night before was on the desk. Brock waved and headed for the elevator, but then noted that he didn't see Angie or the date she was meeting.

He headed to the desk.

"Yes, sir, how may I help you?" the young clerk asked.

"Miss Parsons was down here, I believe. I think she was meeting up with someone in that little twenty-four-hour nook by the entrance to the coffee shop. I don't see her."

"She was down here... I guess she went up."

"Was she alone?"

"I... I said hello, and then I was going through the reservations for tomorrow and okaying a few late departures. I didn't really notice."

Angie's room was on his way to the attic floor. Brock could knock on her door and check on her.

According to what he had seen and learned from Maura, Angie might well have cut to the chase with whomever she had met.

She might be in her room—occupied.

Well, hell, too bad. He was going to have to check on her—whether he interrupted something intimate or not.

MAURA WASN'T SURE what was taking Brock so long, except that he'd be filling Mike and Rachel in on whatever had gone on with Heidi's parents.

She paced her room for a few minutes, then paused as her phone rang.

She answered quickly, thinking it was Brock.

It was not.

It was Angie.

"Maura," Angie said. "You've got to come out—find Tall, Dark and Very Studly, and come on out here."

"Come on out here? Angie, where are you?"

Angie giggled. "Almost getting lucky!" she said in a whisper. "You need to come out here—first. I've found something. Or rather, my own Studly found something for me. Come on, quickly, just grab Brock and get out here."

"Out here where?"

"The History Tree. I have something for you!"

Maura heard a strange little yelping sound—excitement or a scream? She dropped the phone and hurried out into the hallway, just in time to see Brock coming up the stairs at the end.

"Brock, come on. We have to go." Maura said.

"I tried to check on Angie because I didn't see her in the lobby, but she's not answering her door," he told her.

"She isn't there. She's out at the History Tree. Brock—she said that she's found something. She was excited, but then, it was strange—come on!"

She didn't wait for the elevator—she headed straight for the stairs. He followed behind her, calling her name.

"You shouldn't go. I should go alone. Maura!"

He didn't catch up with her until they were out on the lawn, halfway out to the campfire and the trail. He caught her by the arm. "Let me go—you get back in the resort, up in your room—locked in."

"I don't think there's anything wrong," Maura said. "She wanted me to see something. Brock, you're armed and she said to bring you. She just wanted us both to come."

He shook his head, staring at her, determined.

"It could be a trap."

"Angie sounded like Angie. What kind of a trap would that be? Come on."

"No! You don't know—go back into the resort, into your room and lock the door."

She stared back at him.

"Please, Maura, if we're to go on…"

"But, Brock, I just talked to her. This is silly. I'm with you, and… Please, let's just hurry!"

She broke away from him, but he overtook her quickly. "Maura!"

"What?"

"You can't put yourself in danger," he told her. "Let me do my job."

"Oh, all right!"

"Go!"

She did. And since she knew that he'd wait until he saw her heading back into the resort, she turned and headed for the steps.

Something was bugging her about Angie's call. There had been that strange little noise. And then Angie hadn't spoken again. The line had gone dead.

Irritated but resolved, she hurried back into the resort. She waved to the night clerk and headed to the elevator—too tired and antsy for the stairs.

She walked down the hallway, feeling for her phone to try calling Angie again. She remembered that she'd dropped her phone on her bed.

That was all right; she was almost there.

She walked down the hallway to her room and pushed open the door.

The room was dark.

She hadn't left the lights out.

And neither had she thought to lock the door.

She had no idea what hit her; something came over

her head, smothering any cry for help she might have made, and then she hit the floor.

And darkness was complete.

BROCK WALKED CAREFULLY through the woods, swiftly following the trail to the History Tree but hugging the foliage and staying in the shadows.

Long before he reached the tree, he heard the cries for help and the sobs. He quickened his pace, but continued to move stealthily.

When he reached the clearing, he saw that Angie was tied to the tree.

She hadn't been hanged as the long-ago Gyselle had been; she was bound to the massive trunk of the conjoined trees, sobbing, crying out.

Brock didn't rush straight to her; he surveilled the clearing and the surrounding areas the best he could in the darkness. The moon was only half-full, offering little help.

There seemed to be no one near Angie. Still, he didn't trust the scene. It made no sense. Girls disappeared. Months later, remains were found.

None had been tied to the History Tree.

He pulled his phone out and called Flannery. "History Tree—backup," he said quietly.

And then, with his Glock at the ready, he made his way forward, still waiting for a surprise ambush from the bushes.

"Brock, Brock! Be careful, he knows you're coming... He knows... He could be here, here somewhere..."

"I'm watching, Angie," he said, reaching her. He

found his pocketknife to start sawing on the ropes that bound her to the tree.

When she was free, she threw herself into his arms. "You saved me. Thank God I called Maura. He might have come back. He might have... He would have killed me. Oh, Brock, thank you, thank you."

Mike and Rachel came bursting into the clearing.

Angie jerked back, frightened by their arrival.

"It's all right, Angie. It's all right—who brought you here? Who the hell brought you here?" Brock demanded.

She began to shake. "I don't believe it! I still don't believe it!" she said, and she began to sob.

MAURA AWOKE TO DARKNESS. For a moment, the darkness confused her.

At first she had no recollection of what had happened. When she did start to remember—it wasn't much. Someone had attacked her when she'd walked into her room.

She touched her head. No blood, but she had one hell of a headache.

Brock had been right. The call had been a trap.

Angie had called...and there had been that little yelp, and then the phone had gone dead. But Brock hadn't allowed her to go with him.

Whoever had done this knew how Brock would react. Knew that he would never allow Maura to chance her own life.

She didn't know who it was. Mark or Nils Hartford? Bentley?

Donald Glass himself?

She tried to move and was surprised that she could.

She struggled her way out of the covering that all but encased her. It was a comforter—the comforter from her bed at the resort.

She struggled to sit up and realized the earth around her was cold—as if she were in the ground. Struggling, she sat up—but she couldn't stand. The space was too tight. She could see nothing at all.

On her hands and knees, she began to crawl, blinking, trying to adjust to the absolute darkness. Where was Angie—had they taken her, too? Had Brock raced out to the clearing—to find nothing?

If so…

He'd wake the very dead to get every cop in the state out to start looking.

Maura began to shake, terrified. Then, wincing at the pain in her head, she moved forward again.

Brock would search for her, she knew.

She also needed to do her damned best to save herself.

She paused for a minute, listening. Nothing—but it was night. Late at night. She breathed in.

Earth. Earth and…

She paused, and suddenly she knew where she was— well, not where she was, but what she was in. There was earth, but she'd also touched something hard, a bit porous.

And native to a nearby area. Coquina. A sedimentary rock made of fossilized coquina shells that had been used in the building of the great fort in St. Augustine, that still graced walkways and garden paths and all manner of other projects. But to the best of her knowledge, there hadn't been any at the Frampton Ranch and Resort, unless it had been long, long ago.

Maybe she was no longer near the resort. She didn't know how long she had been unconscious.

She kept crawling, not even afraid of what night creatures might be sharing this strange underground space with her.

And then, suddenly, she touched flesh.

"Who, Angie? Who did this to you?" Brock demanded, his arm around her still-shaking body as they headed back toward the resort. Flannery and Rachel had searched the area, a call had been put out for a forensic team and cops would soon be flooding the place.

"It was—it was Donald Glass!" she said, still sounding incredulous. "He was so polite, so gracious, and he said that he wanted me to see something very special. It was him!"

Flannery, right behind them, pushed forward. "Let's see if the old bastard is at the house. Supreme Being. I'll bet he sure as hell thinks that he's one. What the hell was he going to do? Did he think that Angie would die by herself by morning? Or was he coming back to finish the deed—right where he probably murdered Francine years ago?"

As they neared the house, Brock called to Rachel. "Stay with Angie, will you? I've got to go and bring Maura down."

"Don't leave me!" Angie begged, grabbing his arm.

He freed himself. "I have to get Maura."

Rachel had gotten strong; she managed to help Brock disengage a terrified Angie.

Brock raced up the stairs to Maura's room. He could tell the door to her room was open from halfway down the hall. He sprinted into it.

Empty.

The comforter was gone from the bed; her phone lay on the floor.

The breath seemed to be sucked out of him. His heart missed a beat, and for a split second, he froze.

It had been a trap. And he'd been such an ass, he hadn't seen it.

By the time he raced downstairs, the terrified desk clerk was hovering against the wall and Flannery had Donald Glass—in a smoking jacket—in handcuffs.

"No, no, this is wrong—I've been in my room. Ask my wife! Angie! Why the hell would you say these things, accuse me? I did nothing to you. I opened my resort to you. I… Why?"

Angie was shaking and crying, but Donald Glass was agitated, too. He appeared wild-eyed and confused.

"You meant to kill me!" Angie cried.

"I've been in my room all night!" Glass bellowed. "Ask my wife!"

Marie Glass was coming down the stairs, her appearance that of a woman who was stunned and stricken. Her hands shook on the newel post of the grand stairway as she reached the landing.

"Marie, tell them!" Glass bellowed.

Marie began to stutter. Tears stung her eyes. "I—I can't lie for you anymore, Donald."

"What?" he roared.

Brock strode up to him, face-to-face, his voice harsh, his tension more than apparent. "Where's Maura?" he demanded.

"Maura?" Glass asked, puzzled. Then he cried out, "Sleeping with you, most probably!"

"She's gone—she was taken. Where the hell is she?"

Donald Glass began to sob. He shook his white head, far less than dignified then. "I didn't take Maura. I didn't hurt Angie. I swear, I was in my room. I was in my room. I was in my room—"

"Get every cop you can. We have to search everywhere. Maura is with those other girls, I'm certain, and they're near here," Brock said.

A siren sounded, and then a cacophony of sirens filled the night.

"We'll get him to jail—you can join the hunt," Flannery told Brock.

"I'll get out to the car with him. By God, he's going to talk." Brock said. He set a hand hard on Donald Glass's shoulder, following him and Flannery out to the police cruiser.

A uniformed officer jumped out of the driver's seat and opened the back door for them.

"He's not going to talk, Brock, get on the search—" Flannery began. "Or don't," he said as Brock shoved Glass into the rear of the car and then crawled into the seat next to him.

"I don't have her. I don't have her. I don't have her!" Donald Glass screamed. "Don't kill me. Please, don't kill me!"

"I'm not going to kill you," Brock said. "What I need to know from you is anything I don't. Where around here could someone hide women?"

"But I swear, I didn't—"

"You—or anyone else. Dammit, man, I'm trying to believe you! Talk to me."

"WATER...PLEASE... Don't kill me... Water..."
The flesh Maura had encountered spoke.

"I don't have water. I'm not going to kill you," Maura assured the voice she heard. "I'm Maura Antrim. Who are you?"

"Maura!"

The person struggled in the darkness. Maura felt hands grab for her. "I know you... I know you... I'm Heidi... I'm so scared! I stopped because a car had flashing lights and... I went out to help and there was no one to help, and someone hit me, and... I'm dying, I'm sure. I'm going to die down here. I'm so scared. It's so dark. I don't know... Did they take you, too?"

"Yes, they hit me over the head in my hotel room. You don't have any idea of who did this to you?"

Maura felt the girl shake her head.

"We're not far from the resort—I know that. Not far at all."

"But where...?"

"I think we're in a bit of a sinkhole—covered up years and years ago—but someone used it as something. They shored up the sides with coquina. But they got us in here—there has to be a way out. Can you still move?"

"Barely."

"Okay, so stay still. I'm going to try to find a way to escape."

"No! Don't leave me!" Heidi begged, clinging to her.

"Then you have to come with me," Maura said firmly.

She began to crawl again, and she felt the earth grow wetter.

They were in a drainage culvert. They were probably right off the main highway, and if she could just find the grating...

Her mind was numb, and it was also racing a hundred miles an hour. Angie had called her because she had been meeting someone. That someone had lured Angie out and let her lure Brock out and, of course…

That someone had known Brock. Yes, she'd thought that right away. Known that he would make her go back, that he'd consider himself trained, ready to meet danger.

Brock would want Maura safe.

Whoever it had been walked easily and freely through the resort, knew where to go—how to avoid the eyes of the desk clerk and the cameras that kept watch on the lobby.

Thoughts began to tumble in her mind. One stuck.

It couldn't be. And, of course, it was just one someone…

It wasn't a society or an organization—but rather someone who had known about it.

She suddenly found herself thinking about the long-lost Gyselle, the beautiful woman running from her pursuers, those who would hang her from the History Tree until dead.

Maybe they had been part of a society. Maybe they hadn't. Maybe they had just…

She saw a light! A tiny, tiny piece of light…

THE NIGHT WAS ALIVE. Police were searching everywhere.

Dogs were out, each having been given a whiff of Maura's scent. But while they searched the woods and the house and the gardens and the pool, Brock headed off toward the road.

Donald Glass had spilled everything he knew. No, there had never been a basement; there were foundations, of course, but barely wide enough for one maintenance man. There had been a well, yes, filled in years and years ago.

Outbuildings had been torn down. The wings on the resort were new. There were no hidden houses; the one little nearby cemetery had no mausoleums or vaults…

Where to hide someone?

Warehouses aplenty on the highway. And the drainage tank off the road, ready to absorb excess water when hurricanes came tearing through.

A perfect place for a body to deteriorate quickly.

Donald Glass had been taken off to jail.

That didn't matter to Brock right now. Nothing mattered.

Except that he find Maura.

He reached the road and raced alongside the highway, seeking any entrance to the sunken areas along the pavement.

He ran and ran, and then ran back again, and then noted an area where foliage had been tossed over the drain.

He raced for it.

And as he neared, he heard her. Crying out, thundering against the metal grate.

"Maura!"

He cried her name, surged to the grate and fell to his knees. His pocketknife made easy work of the metal joints. He pulled her out and into his arms, and for a long moment, she clung to him.

And then he heard another cry.

"Heidi—she says there are other women down there… Dead or alive, I don't know."

He pulled Heidi from the drain. She crushed him so hard in a hug that he fell back, and several long seconds passed in which it seemed they were all laughing and crying.

Then, in the distance, he heard the baying of a dog. He shouted, "Over here!" Soon, there were many officers there, many dogs, and he was free to take Maura into his arms and hold her and not let go.

Epilogue

"You know," Maura said, probably confusing everyone gathered in the lobby of the Frampton Ranch and Resort by being the one to speak first. "Sometimes, really, I can still see her—or imagine her—the beautiful Gyselle, running in the moonlight, desperate to live. Legends are hard to shake. And I'm telling you this, and starting the explanation because, in one way, it's my story. And because Gyselle's life has meaning, and legends have meaning, and sometimes we don't see the truth because what we see is the legend."

She saw interest on the faces before her. The employees knew by now that Donald Glass had been taken away. They knew that horrible things had happened the night before, that Angie had been attacked by her host and that Maura had been attacked—but found, and found along with Heidi and the other three missing girls. Heidi was already fine and home with her parents. The other girls were still hospitalized. For Lily Sylvester it would be a long haul. She'd been in the dark, barely fed and given dirty water for months—and it had taken a toll on her internal organs. Lydia Merkel would most probably be allowed to go home that afternoon, and for Amy Bonham the hospital stay would be about a week.

There was hope for all of them. They'd lived.

The resort guests had all gone. They had been asked to vacate by the police and Marie Glass until the tragedy had been appropriately handled.

The resort was empty except for the staff, Detectives Flannery and Lawrence, and Angie and Maura.

Donald Glass remained gone—biding his time in jail before arraignment. But if things tonight went the way Maura thought they would, that arraignment would never come.

"Thinking about Gyselle brings to mind—to many of us—what happened to Francine Renault. Well, I don't really see her in a long gown running through the forest, but she, too, met her demise on this ranch. And through the years, we suspect, so did many other young women. They didn't all come to the tree. After Francine they were stabbed. Yes, by the same killer. Brutally stabbed to death. As Peter Moore, a cook here back then, was stabbed. It doesn't sound as if it should all relate. One killer, two killers, working independently—or together? All compelled by just one driving motive—revenge."

Blank faces still greeted her. She wasn't a cop or FBI. They were curious, but confused.

"I thought they were random kidnappings," someone murmured.

"Yes and no," Maura said.

Brock stepped forward. "We discovered a longtime association or society. It was called Sons of Supreme Being. They don't—we believe—really exist anymore. So legend gave way to what might be revamped—and imitated."

"I thought the police were going to explain what really went on here," Nils Hartford said.

"I guess Donald Glass did consider himself a supreme being," his brother added sadly.

"Well, he might have," Maura said. "But...there you go. I'm back to beautiful Gyselle, running through the forest. Her sin being that of a love affair with the owner of the plantation."

"I'm letting Maura do the explaining," Brock said. "She's always been a great storyteller."

Maura turned and looked at Marie Glass. "Donald didn't kill Francine, Marie. You did."

"What?" Marie stared at her indignantly. "I did not kill Francine. My husband killed Francine."

"No, no, he didn't. He didn't kill Francine. Nor did he kill Maureen Rodriguez or the other woman whose remains have been found. Donald loved history—and kept it alive. He loved women. You found your way to take revenge on those who led him astray—and, of course, on Donald himself. Oh, and you killed Peter Moore—that's when you discovered just how much you enjoyed wielding a knife."

"This is insane! How do you think that I—" Marie gestured to herself, demonstrating that she was indeed a tiny woman "—could manage such acts? Oh, you ungrateful little whore!"

"No need to be rude," Brock said. "Marie, you were good—but we have you on camera."

"Really? How did I tie up Angie and get back and..."

"Oh, you didn't tie up Angie."

"Of course not!"

"Angie tied herself up," Brock said calmly.

Angie sprang to her feet. "No! I wasn't even around when Francine Renault was killed. Or the cook. Why on earth do you think that I could be involved?"

"I still don't know why you were involved, Angie," Brock said. "But you were. There was no one else in the woods. We've found sound alibis for everyone else here. Oh, both Mark and Nils Hartford were sleeping with guests that night—a no-no. But you weren't one of those guests. And there's video—the security camera picked it up—of Fred Bentley talking to the night clerk right when it was all going on. What? Did you two think that we were getting close? That we'd figure it out— that Marie's hints about her husband were a little too well planted? Then, of course, there was you—wanting to see where the bones had been discovered. Strange, right? But I'm thinking that the bones washed out in the drainage system somehow—and Marie panicked and wrapped them in hotel sheets, thinking she could dispose of the remains with the laundry. And maybe you were hoping that you hadn't messed up somehow. Maybe you didn't know. But for whatever reason, you and Marie have been kidnapping and killing people. Marie getting her rage out—certain she could frame her husband if it came to it. But you…"

"That's absurd!" Angie cried.

"No, no, it's not. We checked your phone records— you talked to Marie over and over again during the last year. Long conversations. She chose the victims. You helped bring them down."

The hotel staff had all frozen, watching—as if they were caught in a strange tableau.

"You're being ridiculous!" Angie raged. She looked like a chicken, jumping up, arms waving at her sides in fury. "No, it was Marie! I didn't—"

"Oh, shut up!" Marie cried. "I'm not going down alone. I can tell you why—she wanted to hurt Donald as badly as I did. We were willing to wait and watch and eventually find a way to create proof that made the system certain that it was Donald. And those women... Whores! They deserved to suffer. We could have seen that Donald rotted for years before he got the death penalty. There's no record of it—her mother was one of my husband's whores. He paid her off very nicely to have an abortion. The woman took the money—she didn't abort." She looked at Angie. "You should have been an abortion!"

"Oh, Marie, you lie, you horrible bitch!"

Angie tore toward her in a fury.

Rachel stepped up, catching her smoothly and easily, swinging an arm across her shoulders.

She then snapped cuffs on Angie.

And Marie—dignified Marie—was taken by Mike.

She spit at him. She called him every vile name Maura had ever heard.

And then some.

They were taken out. The employees stood in silence, gaping.

Then, suddenly, everyone burst into conversation, some expressing disbelief, some arguing that they were surprised.

"No," Fred Bentley said simply, staring after them. "No."

"Yes. You saw," Brock told him.

"So, what do we do now?" Mark asked.

"Well, Donald Glass is being released. Right now he's sick and horrified at what has happened. He believed that he caused Marie to be cruel. He never knew he had an illegitimate child, and now he's left with the fact that his child...became a killer. He needs time. He's the one who has to make the decisions," Brock said. "For now, he has said to let you know that you don't need to worry while he regroups—everyone will be paid for the next month, no matter what."

There was a murmur of approval, and then slowly the group began to break up.

Fred stared at Brock and Maura for a long time. "Well," he said. "I will be here. I will keep the place in order. Until I know what Donald wants. I'll see that the staff maintain it. I'll be here for—for anything anyone may need." He started to walk away, and then he came back. "I'm… I can't believe it. Imagine, that cute little Angie. Who could figure…? But thank you, Brock. Yeah, thank you so much."

He turned and left, heading behind the restaurant toward the office.

Brock and Maura stood alone in the center of the lobby.

"Shall we go?" he asked her.

"We shall, but…"

"But where, you ask?" Brock teased. "An island. Somewhere with a beautiful beach. Somewhere we can lie on the sand and make up for lost time, hurt for those who died and be grateful for those who lived. You are packed and ready to leave?"

"I am," she told him.

They drove away.

MAURA COULD FEEL the deliciousness of the sea breeze. It swept over her flesh, filtering through the soft gauze curtains that surrounded the bungalow. She could hear the lap of the waves, so close that she could easily run out on the sand and wade into the water.

It was beautiful. Brock had found the perfect place in the Bahamas. It was a private piece of heaven, and no one came near them unless they summoned food or drink with the push of a button. The next bungalow was down the beach, and they were separated by palms and sea grapes and other oceanfront foliage.

It was divine.

Though nothing was more divine than sleeping beside Brock so easily, flesh touching, sometimes just lying together and talking about the years gone by, and sometimes, starting with just the slightest brush against each other, making love.

There would be four days of this particular heaven, but…

"You did talk to your parents, right?" Brock asked Maura.

"Of course! If news about what happened had reached them and they hadn't heard from me…they would have been a bit crazy," Maura assured him. She inched closer to him. "I almost feel bad for my mother—she's so horrified, and she admitted all the messages she'd gotten from you and kept from me… poor thing. And then, I have myself to blame, too. I was hurt that I didn't hear from you—and so I never tried to contact you myself. I thought I was part of your past— a past you wanted closed."

"Never. Never you," he said with a husky voice. Then he smiled again. "But your mom… She is coming to the wedding."

Maura laughed. "Oh, yes. She didn't even try telling me that we were rushing things when I said we were in the Bahamas but coming home to a small wedding in New York at an Irish pub called Finnegan's. And my dad… Well, he thinks that's great. Why wait after all this time? Now or never, in his mind. It's nice, by the way, for your friend to arrange a wedding and reception in one at his place—his place? Her place?"

"Kieran and Craig have been together a long time. Craig is a great coworker and friend. Kieran owns Finnegan's with her brothers—they're thrilled to provide for a small wedding and reception. And you...you don't mind living in New York? For now? Maybe one day, we'll be snowbirds, heading south for the winter. And maybe, when we're old and gray, we'll come home for good. Or, hell, maybe I'll get a transfer. But for now..."

She leaned over and kissed him. "I lost you for twelve years. I'm going to say those vows and move to New York without blinking," she promised. "Besides... Hmm. I'm going to be looking for some new clients— New York seems like a good place to find them."

He smiled, and then he rolled more tightly to her, his face close as he said, "It's amazing. I knew I loved you then. And I never stopped loving you—and I swear, I will love you all the rest of my years, as well. With or without you, I knew I loved you."

"That's beautiful," she whispered. "I love you, too. Always have, always will." She smoothed back his hair.

He caught her hand and kissed it.

Then the kissing continued.

And the ocean breeze continued to caress them both as the sun rose higher in the sky.

Later, much later, Maura knew that the ocean breeze wouldn't be there every morning. They wouldn't be sleeping in an oceanfront bungalow with the sea and sand just beyond them.

And it wouldn't matter in the least.

Because his face would be on the pillow next to hers, every morning, forever after.

* * * * *

SUSPICIOUS

To the Miccosukee tribe of Florida.

Prologue

The eyes stared across the water.

They were soulless eyes, the eyes of a cold-blooded predator, an animal equipped throughout millions of years of existence to hunt and kill.

Just visible over the water's surface, the eyes appeared as innately evil as a pair of black pits in hell.

The prehistoric monster watched. It waited.

From the center seat of his beat-to-shit motorboat, Billy Ray Hare lifted his beer can to the creature. He squinted as he tried to make out the size of the beast, an estimation at best, since the bulk of the body was hidden by the water. Big boy, he thought. Didn't see too many of the really big boys down here anymore. He'd even read some article about the Everglades alligators being kind of thin and scrawny these days, since they were surviving on insects and small prey. But every once in a while now, he'd still see a big beast sunning along the banks of the canals in the deep swamp.

He heard a slithering sound from the canal bank and turned. A smaller gator, maybe five feet long, was moving. Despite the ugly and awkward appearance of the creature, it was swift, fluid and graceful. Uncannily fast. The smaller crocodilian eased down the damp embankment and into the water. Billy watched. He knew the canals, and he knew gators, and he knew that the long-legged, hapless crane fishing for shiners near the shore was a goner.

"Hey, birdie, birdie," Billy Ray crooned. "Ain't you seen the sun? It's dinnertime, baby, dinnertime."

The gator slid into the water, only its eyes visible as the body swiftly disappeared.

A split second later, the beast burst from the water with a spray of power and gaping jaws. The bird let out a screech; its white wings frantically, pathetically, beat the water. But the huge jaws were clamped. The gator slung its head back and forth, shaking its prey near death, then slid back into the water to issue the coup de grâce, drowning its victim.

"It's a damned dog-eat-dog world, ain't it?" Billy murmured dryly aloud. He finished his beer, groped for another, and realized that he'd finished the last of his twelve-pack. Swearing, he noticed that the big gator across the canal hadn't moved. Black reptilian eyes, evil as Satan's own, continued to survey him. He threw his beer can in the direction of the creature. "Eat that, ugly whoreson!" he croaked, and began to laugh. Then he sobered, looking around, thinking for a minute that Jesse Crane might be behind him, ready to haul him in for desecrating his precious muck hole. But Billy Ray was alone in the swamp. Alone with the bugs and birds and reptiles, with no more beer and no fish biting. "Bang-bang, you're dead! I'm hungry, and it's dinnertime. Damned environmentalists." Once upon a time, he could have shot the gator. Now the damn things were

protected. You had to wait for gator season to kill the
suckers, and then you had to play by all kinds of rules.
You could only kill the wretched things according to
certain regulations. Too bad. Once upon a time, a big
gator like that could have meant some big money....

Big money. What the heck.

They made big money out at that gator farm. Old
Harry and his scientist fellow, Dr. Michael, the stinking
Australian who thought he was Crocodile Dundee, and
Jack Pine, the Seminole, and hell, that whole lot. They
made money on alligators. Damn Jesse and his reeking
white man's law. Now he was the frigging tribal police.

Billy Ray shook his head. The hell with Jesse Crane
and his whole bleeding-heart crowd. What did Jesse
know? Tall and dark and too damned good-looking,
and all powerful, one foot in the swamp, the other foot
firmly planted in the white world. College education,
plenty of money now—his late *wife's* money, at that.
The hell with him, the hell with all the environmentalists, the hell with the whites all the way. They'd been the
ones who screwed up the swamp to begin with. While
the whole country was running around screaming about
rights—equal pay for women, real justice for blacks,
food stamps for refugees—Jesse Crane didn't see that
the Indians—the *Native Americans*—were still rotting
in the swamps. Jesse had a habit of just leaning back,
shrugging, and staring at him with those cool green—
white-blooded—eyes of his and saying that no white
man was making old Billy Ray be a mean, dirty alcoholic who liked to beat up on his wife. Jesse wanted
him in jail. But Ginny, bless her fat, ugly butt, Ginny

wouldn't file charges against him. Ginny knew where a wife's place was supposed to be.

Alcoholic, hell. He wasn't no alcoholic. God, he wanted another beer. Screw Jesse Crane.

"And screw you," he said aloud, staring at the gator. Those black eyes hadn't moved; the creature was still staring at him like some prehistoric sentinel. Maybe it was already dead. He squinted, staring hard. Tough now to see, because it was growing late. Dinnertime.

Sunset. It was almost night. He didn't know what he wanted more, something to eat or another beer. He had neither. No fish, and he'd used up his government money.

The sky was orange and red, the beautiful shades that came right before the sun pitched into the horizon. But now the dying orb was creating a beautiful but eerie mantle of color on the water, the trees that draped their branches over it, and the seemingly endless "river of grass" that made up the Everglades. With sunset, everything took on a different hue; white birds were cast in pink and gold, and even the killer heat took a brief holiday. Jesse would sit out here like a lump on a log himself, just thinking that the place—with its thick carpet of mosquitoes and frequent smell of rot—was only a small step from heaven. Their land. Hell, he had news for Jesse. They hadn't been the first Indians—Native Americans—here. The first ones who'd been here had been wiped out far worse than animals ever had. But Jesse seemed to think that being half Indian made him Lord Protector of the realm or something.

Billy smiled. Screw Jesse. It gave him great pleasure just to think nasty thoughts about the man.

A crane called overhead, swooped and soared low, making a sudden catch in the shimmering water, flying away with a fish dangling from its beak. Smart bird— caught his fish, flew away, didn't wait around to become bait himself. In fact, it was a darned great scene, Billy thought sourly. Right out of *National Geographic*. It was all just one rosy-hued, beautiful picture. The damn crane had captured his dinner, the five-foot gator had captured *his* dinner, and all Billy Ray had caught himself was a deeper burn and a beer headache.

And that other gator. The big one. Big enough to gulp up the five-footer. Hell, it was big enough, maybe, to be well over ten feet long. Maybe it was way more than that, even. Son of a bitch, he didn't know. He couldn't tell its size; it was just one big mother, that was all. It was still staring at him. Eyes like glittering onyx as the sun set. Not looking, not moving. The creature didn't seem to blink.

Maybe the big ole gator staring at him was dead. Maybe he could haul the monster in, skin and eat it before any of the sappy-eyed ecologists got wind of the situation.

Ginny always knew what to do with gator meat. She'd "gourmeted" it long before fashionable restaurants had started putting it on their menus. Hell, with that gator, they could eat for weeks....

"Hey, there, you butt-ugly thing!" Billy Ray called. He stood up; the boat rocked. Better sit down. The beer had gotten to him more than he'd realized. He picked up an oar and started slowly toward the big gator. It still didn't move. He lifted his oar from the water. Damn, but he was one asshole himself, he realized. Gator had to be alive, the way it was just sitting there in the water, eyes above the surface.

Watching him.

Watching him, just like the smaller gator had watched the crane.

"Oh, no, you big ugly asshole!" Billy Ray called out. "Don't you get any ideas. It's *my* dinnertime."

As if duly challenged, the gator suddenly began to move. Billy Ray saw more of its length. More and more…ten feet, twelve, fifteen…hell more, maybe…it was the biggest damned gator he'd seen in his whole life. Maybe it was a stray croc—no, he knew a croc, and he knew a gator. This fellow had a broad snout and clearly separated nostrils, it was just one big mother…cruising. Cruising smoothly toward him, massive body just gliding through the water. Coming fast, fast, faster…

He frowned, shaking his head, realizing he really was in something of a beer fog. Gators didn't come after boats and ram them. They might swim along and take a bite at a hand trailing in the water, but he'd only seen a gator make a run at a boat once, and that was a mother protecting her nest, and she only charged the boat, she didn't ram it.

This one was just warning him away. Hell, where was his gun? He had his shotgun in the boat somewhere….

Unable to tear his eyes from the creature's menacing black orbs, he groped in the boat for his shotgun. His hand gripped the weapon; the creature was still coming. He half stood again, taking aim.

He fired.

He hit the sucker; he knew he hit it.

But the gator kept coming with a sudden ferocious speed.

The animal rammed the boat.

Billy Ray pitched over.

Sunset.

The water had grown dark. He couldn't see a damned thing. He began to kick madly, aiming for the bank. He swam. He had hit the gator with a shotgun. Surely he had pierced the creature's tough hide; it had just taken the stupid monster a long time to die. He'd been an idiot. His rifle was at the bottom of the muck now; his boat was wrecked, and the water was cool and sobering.

Sober...yeah, dammit, all of a sudden he was just too damned sober.

He twisted around and was just in time to see the monster. Like the others of its kind, it stalked him smoothly. Gracefully. He saw the eyes again, briefly. Cold, brutal, merciless, the eyes of a hell-spawned predator. He saw the head, the long jaws. Biggest damn head he'd ever seen. Couldn't be real.

The eyes slipped beneath the surface.

Billy Ray started to scream. He felt more sober than he had ever felt in his life. Felt everything perfectly clearly.

Felt the movement in the water, the rush beneath him...

He screamed and screamed and screamed. Until the giant jaws snapped shut on him. He felt the excruciating, piercing pain. Then he ceased to scream as the razor-sharp teeth pierced his rib cage, lungs and windpipe.

The creature began to toss its massive head, literally shaking its prey into more easily digestible pieces.

The giant gator sank beneath the surface.
And more of Billy Ray's bones began to crunch....
Billy Ray had been right all along.
It was dinnertime.

Chapter One

At first it seemed that the sound of the siren wasn't even penetrating the driver's mind.

Either that, or the Lexus intended to race him all the way across the lower portion of the state to the city of Naples, Jesse Crane thought irritably.

It was natural to speed out here—it felt like one of the world's longest, strangest drives, with mile after mile of grass and muck and canal, interspersed by a gas station or tackle shop here or there, the airboat rides, and the Miccosukee camps.

But after you passed the casino, heading west, traces of civilization became few and far between. Despite that, the road was a treacherous one. Impatient drivers trying to pass had caused many a traffic fatality.

He overlooked it when someone seemed competent and was going a rational number of miles over the limit.

But this Lexus…

At last the driver seemed to become aware that he was trailing, the siren blazing. The Lexus pulled over on the embankment.

As Jesse pulled his cruiser off on the shoulder, he saw a blond head dipping—the occupant was obviously searching for the registration. *Or a gun?* There were plenty of toughs who made it out to this section of the world, because there was enough godforsaken space out here for all manner of things to go on. He trod carefully. He was a man who always trod carefully.

As he approached the car, the window came down and a blond head appeared. He was startled, faltering for a fraction of a second.

The woman was stunning. Not just attractive. Stunning. She had the kind of golden beauty that was almost spellbinding. Blond hair that caught the daylight. Delicate features. Huge eyes that reflected a multitude of colors: green, brown, rimmed with gray. Sweeping lashes. Full lips, colored in shell-pink gloss. Perfect for her light complexion and hair.

"Was I speeding?" She sounded as if he were merely a distraction in her important life.

Yeah, the kind of beauty that was almost *spellbinding. But there was also something about her that was irritating as hell!*

The soft sound of a splash drew his attention. Her head jerked around, and she shuddered as they both looked toward the canal. A small alligator had left its sunning spot on the high mud and slipped into the water.

Then she turned back to him and gave him her full attention. She studied him for a moment. "Is this…a joke?"

"No, ma'am. No joke," he said curtly. "License and registration, please."

"Was I speeding?" she asked again, and her seriousness was well done, especially after her earlier remark.

"Speeding? Oh, yeah," he said. "License and registration, please."

"Surely I wasn't going that fast," she said. She was

staring at him, not distracted anymore, and frowning. "Are you really a cop?" she demanded suddenly.

"Yes."

She twisted around. "That's not a Metro-Dade car."

"No, I'm not Metro-Dade."

"Then—"

"Miccosukee. Indian police," he said curtly.

"Indian police?" she said, and looked back to him. His temper rose. He felt as if he might as well have said *play* police, or *pretend* police.

"This is my jurisdiction," he said curtly. "One more time. License and registration."

She gritted her teeth, staring at him, antagonism replacing the curiosity in her eyes. Then, every movement irate, she dug into the glove compartment. "Registration," she snapped, handing him the document.

"And license," he said politely.

"Yes, of course. I need to get it."

"Do you know how fast you were going?"

"Um…not that far over the speed limit, surely?"

"Way over," he told her. "See that sign? It says fifty-five. You were topping that by thirty miles an hour."

"I'm sorry," she said. "It didn't feel like I was going that fast."

She dug in her handbag, which was tightly packed and jumbled, in contrast to the businesslike appearance of the pale blue jacket she wore over a tailored shirt. He began writing the ticket. She produced her license. He kept writing. Her fingers, long, elegant, curled tightly around the steering wheel. "I don't know what's waiting for you in Naples, Miss Fortier, but it's not worth dying for. And if you're not worried about killing yourself, try to remember that you could kill someone else. Slow down on this road."

"I still don't believe I was going that fast," she murmured.

"Trust me, you were," he assured her curtly. He didn't know why she was getting beneath his skin to such a degree. She was passing through. Lots of people tried to speed their way through, east to west, west to east, completely careless of their surroundings, immune to the fact that the populations of Seminoles and Miccosukees in the area might be small, but they existed.

And their lives were as important as any others.

"Fine, then," she murmured, as if barely aware of him, just anxious to be on her way.

"Hey!" He demanded her attention.

She blinked, staring at him. She definitely seemed distracted. And yet, when she stared at him, it was with a strange interest. As if she wanted to listen but somehow couldn't.

"Slow down," he repeated softly and firmly.

She nodded curtly and reached out, accepting her license and registration back, along with the ticket he had written.

Then she shook her head slightly, trying to control her temper. "Thanks," she muttered.

"I'm a real cop, and it's a real ticket, Ms. Fortier."

"Yes, thank you. I'll pay it, with real money," she said sweetly.

He forced a grim smile in return. *Spoiled little rich girl, heading from the playgrounds of Miami Beach to the playgrounds of the western coast of the state.*

He tipped his hat, grateful that she couldn't know what he was thinking. His sunglasses were darkly tinted, well able to hide his thoughts. "Good day, Miss Fortier."

He turned to leave.

"Jerk!" he heard her mutter.

He stiffened, straightened, turned back.

"Pardon? Did you say something?" he asked politely.

She forced a smile. "I said good day to you, too, Officer."

"That's what I thought you said," he told her, turning to go. "Bitch," he murmured beneath his breath.

Or, at least, he thought he'd murmured beneath his breath.

"What did you say?" she demanded sharply.

He turned back. "I said we should both have a lovely day. One big old wonderful, lovely day. Take care, Ms. Fortier."

He proceeded back to his car.

The Lexus slid back onto the road.

He followed it for a good twenty miles. And she knew it. She drove the speed limit.

Not a mile under.

Not a mile over.

The dash phone buzzed softly. He hit the answer button. "Hey, Chief. What's up? Some good ol' boy beating up on his wife again?" He spoke evenly, hoping that was all it was. Too often, out here, it was something else. Something that seldom had to do with his people, his work. The Everglades was a beautiful place for those who loved nature, but pure temptation for those who chose to commit certain crimes.

Over the distance, Emmy sighed. "Nope, just a call from Lars. He wants you to have lunch with him at the new fish place just east of the casino next Friday."

"Tell him sure," Jesse said. "See you soon. Time for me to call it a day."

Clayton Harrison's place was just up ahead. The driveway wasn't easily discernible from the trail, but Jesse knew right where it was. He took a sharp left, turned around and headed back.

He was certain that, as he did so, the Lexus once again picked up speed.

LORENA FORTIER SET down her pen, sighed, stood and stretched. She left her desk and walked to the door that led out to the hallway in the staff quarters of Harry's Alligator Farm and Museum. She hesitated, looked both ways, then walked down the shadowy hallway. Dim night-lights showed the signs on the various doors she passed.

Her second full day on the job. And her second day of living a deception. She thought about Naples and Marco Island. If only one of those lovely beach communities had been her destination.

She felt herself bristling again as she remembered being stopped the day before by the Miccosukee officer. She had been speeding, and she should have slowed down. It was just that her mind had been racing, and her foot had apparently gone along with it.

And the man who had stopped her...

She felt an odd little tremor shoot through her. He'd just been so startling, and then even a little frightening. For the good or bad, she couldn't remember anyone who had made such an impression on her in a long time. His appearance had been so striking, not at all what she expected from a police officer.

She had apparently made an impression on him, as well. *Rich bitch, no care for anything local...*

She gave herself a shake. Forget it! Move on. Concentrate on the matter at hand!

Large letters on the third door down read Dr. Michael Preston, Research.

She hesitated, then tried the knob. The door, as she had expected, was locked. She slipped her hand into the pocket of her lab coat, curling her fingers around the small lock pick she carried. She was about to work the door open when she heard voices coming from the far end of the hallway.

"So how are the tours going, Michael?" It was her new boss, Harry Rogers, speaking. He was a huge man, with a smile as wide as his belly.

Dr. Michael Preston replied with forced enthusiasm. "Great!"

"I know that you're a researcher, Michael, but part of my dream here is to educate people about reptiles."

"I don't mind the tours. I think I'm pretty good at conveying what we're doing."

Okay, so what did she do now? Lorena wondered. She was new at this whole secret-investigation thing. Should she run back down the hall and into her own office? Or should she bluff it out, walk on down the hall to meet the two of them and ask some kind of lame question?

Running would be insane. They might see her. She would have to bluff.

"Harry, Dr. Preston!" she called, smiling and starting toward them.

"You're the boss, but she calls you 'Harry,' while I'm 'Dr. Preston,'" Michael said to Harry with a groan.

"She knows she can trust me," Harry said, grinning. "She's the new girl on the block—she can't tell yet if you're a dangerously handsome devil, or simply an innocent charmer, a true bookworm."

Lorena laughed softly. "Which is it, Dr. Preston? Are you a devil in disguise? Or a man who is totally trustworthy?" she asked. He was a striking man, not bookish in appearance in the least, considering his reputation as a dedicated researcher, completely passionate about his work. The man was actually the epitome of "tall, dark and handsome," with a wicked grin that could easily seduce a woman into trusting him.

She didn't like the sound of her own laugh, or her question. She tended to be forthright; she wasn't a flirt or a tease, and acting like a coquette felt ridiculous.

But, as she was learning, Dr. Preston was aware of his looks, and more than willing to make use of his natural charm.

He turned it on her now, smiling in her direction, even though he directed his questions to their boss. "What about the lovely Ms. Fortier? Our mystery woman, a glorious golden-haired beauty suddenly landing in this small oasis in the middle of a swamp. Can she be totally trustworthy?" he asked Harry. "Or has she come to seduce our secrets out of us?"

"Well, whatever secrets I have aren't too fascinating, son," Harry said apologetically.

"And I'm afraid my mystery life is rather dull, as well," Lorena said sweetly.

"Were you looking for me?" Harry asked.

"Um…yes. You told me that you had a small gym for the employees. I thought I would take a look at it. If you could just direct me…"

"The gym is just past the holding pens. Be careful in the dark. The pens are walled, but you don't want to go getting curious, try to bend over the walls and fall in, you know. My gators are well fed, but they're wild animals, after all. And even though I've got security out there, the guards patrol, and with gators, help can never come fast enough."

"I know to be careful, Harry. Thanks." She flashed them both a smile and turned away, feeling frustrated. Did Preston sleep in his lab?

She returned to her room and changed into bike shorts and a tank top. When she left her room again, she could still hear Harry and Michael talking. They were in Preston's lab.

Maybe the gym wasn't such a bad idea, after all.

She left the staff area and started across the huge compound. There were hundreds of gators here, in various stages of growth. Then there was the special pen with Old Elijah. He was huge, a good fifteen feet. He was never part of any show; he was just there for visitors to look at. Next to him were Pat and Darien, both of them adolescents, five feet in length, the gators that were wrestled for the amusement of the crowds.

Jack Pine, a tall, well-muscled Seminole, was standing by the pens with Hugh Humphrey, a wiry blond handler from Australia. Hugh had experience with Outback crocs, and Harry valued having him. When she walked over, the two men were talking quietly with a tall, white-haired man and a veritable giant.

The white-haired man said goodbye, starting away before Lorena got close enough to be introduced to him.

The big man followed. He seemed to grunt, kind of

like the alligators, but she assumed that was his way of saying goodbye.

"Ms. Fortier!" Hugh called to her, seeing her as he turned away from the pair who were leaving.

"Hi there!" she called back as she crossed over to the western arc of the building complex. "Who was that?" she asked.

"Who was who?" Hugh asked.

"The men who just left. Do they work here?"

"No, no. They do work for Harry now and then, but they're totally independent. The old guy is Dr. Thiessen, a local vet, and the Neanderthal is the doc's assistant, John Smith. I should have had Doc stay to meet you, but I didn't see you, and he's always busy. He just checks in with us now and then. Doc Thiessen is a hero among the local kids—he's the only guy out there who can really treat a sick turtle or a ball python. You'll meet him soon enough, I wager. He's something. Also knows cattle, gators—and dogs and cats."

"Ah," she murmured. "The big guy is kind of…big."

"Creepy, is that what you mean?" Hugh asked with a laugh.

"No, just…big."

"And dumb. But he's a good worker. Thiessen needs someone like that. He works with some big animals."

"That's certainly understandable. You guys work with some big animals, too," she reminded them.

Hugh offered a grin. "But we're fit and muscled—perfect specimens of manhood. You're supposed to notice that."

She laughed. "You're both in great shape."

"Thanks," Jack Pine offered. "You're welcome to

go on about us if you want, but…how are you enjoying the work so far?"

"So far, things have been quite easy. I know you need a nurse on staff, but I haven't even had to deal with a skinned knee yet."

"But you like the place all right?" Hugh asked.

"Yes, just fine."

"A lot of women would find it incredibly weird," Jack told her, inclining his head in a way that made her feel special. Like Preston, he was an intriguing man. Unlike Preston, there didn't seem to be anything cerebral about the attraction. His hair was dark and slick, his eyes nearly as black as his hair; he was bronzed and built—just as he had said. She had liked him instantly—but warily, as well.

He had proudly shown her when they'd met that he'd lost the pinkie finger on his left hand to a gator when he'd learned to wrestle the big reptiles as a boy growing up at Big Cypress Reservation. He seemed to be fearless.

"I like animals," she said.

"These guys are hardly cute and cuddly," Hugh remarked. As if they'd heard him, a number of the alligators set up a racket. They made the strangest noise, as if they were pigs grunting. The cacophony was eerie. She shivered, then thought about the animal's deadly jaws.

She thought about her reasons for being here. Whether she liked the guys who worked here or not, she had to remember to be wary.

She shivered again, suddenly uneasy about being with either man around the prehistoric predators.

Come to think of it, she thought, *she didn't want to be here at all, not at all.*

But she had to be. It was that simple. She had to be.

"You both seem to like gators a lot," she said.

Hugh shrugged. "Well, I made a good living off crocs, so I figure I can make a good living off their cousins, too."

"Like 'em? Hell, no. Respect 'em? Hell, yes," Jack said with a shrug. "But if you're going to work with them, you need to know them. And I can definitely say I know them. I was born and bred in the swamp, so I knew about gators long before I knew about lions, tigers and bears." He grinned and shrugged. "But you, young lady, need to remember a few things that will be important if you ever get in trouble down here. Never get closer than fifteen feet to one of these suckers. And if he's hissing, back away slowly and get the hell away."

"And if you can't get away, make sure you get your weight on its back and push down hard on the nose. It's the top jaw that exerts the pressure. The lower jaw is pretty much worthless," Hugh said.

"I don't intend to get that close to any of them," she assured the men. "You're right—alligators definitely aren't cuddly, but so far, I like this place a lot. I seem to be working with great people," she said, forcing herself to sound nonchalant. They were giving her friendly warnings, nothing more. Despite the grunts from the creatures, which seemed more eerie and foreboding by the moment, she couldn't scream and run away.

"Why, shucks, thanks, ma'am," Hugh teased.

"Thank you both, and good night. See you guys in the morning."

She walked away. She could have sworn she heard the man whisper in her wake. Her skin crawled as she wondered what they were saying.

She entered the gym feeling winded, gasping for breath, though she hadn't walked far at all. She didn't want to work out; she wanted to lock herself into her room. Still, in case she was being followed or watched, she had to act normal. She'd come here to work out, so that was what she would do. She walked to a stationary bike, crawled on and pedaled away.

Fifteen minutes was enough for the night.

She exited the employee gym, more tired from feeling nervous than from her workout. She opened the door a crack, then paused, looking out.

There was a man in the compound. He was standing between two of the alligator pens, hands on hips. At first he was very still, nothing but a dark silhouette in the moonlight. He was tall, broad-shouldered, yet lithe-looking, somehow exuding energy, even in his stillness. He stood in plain view; then he walked around one of the pens, and she noticed that he moved with a sure, fluid stride that was both graceful and, somehow, menacing. Dangerous.

And oddly familiar.

It was her mind tonight, she thought. Everyone she saw seemed furtive, dangerous.

He might just be the security guard. There were several of them, she knew. And, she had been assured, their backgrounds had been checked out by the same careful procedures that casinos used.

No. This man wasn't a security guard. Somehow she knew it.

As he moved and her eyes became more accustomed to the shadows, she could see him more clearly.

He was in black jeans and a black T-shirt. The short sleeves were rolled, and in the moonlight, she could see the bulge of his arm muscles beneath the rolled cotton. His hair was on the long side, sleek, touching his shoulders. Very dark.

The cop! It was the jerk who had given her the ticket!

He turned toward the gym suddenly, as if he knew he was being watched. He couldn't, of course. The light was out. He had no way to know the door was open even a crack.

She continued to study him from her safe distance, trying to determine just what made him so imposing and unique.

His features were compelling. Hardened, fascinating. He was a combination of Native, white and God knew what else. His skin was bronzed, his cheekbones broad, his chin square, like that of a man who knew where he was going—and where he had been. His nose was slightly crooked, as if it might have been broken at some time. She couldn't make out the color of his eyes against the darkness of his hair and the bronze of his flesh. He couldn't possibly see her; still, she felt as if he was staring right through her. She almost stepped back, feeling as if she had been physically touched, as if a rush of smoke and fire had swept through her.

"Jesse," a soft feminine voice said from behind her.

She gasped, then spun around. Sally Dickerson, the head cashier and bookkeeper, was standing behind her. In her early thirties, she was an attractive redhead. Harry said she had a temper, a way with men, and one heck of a way with numbers that had dollar signs attached to them.

"Sorry, you startled me," Lorena said.

Sally glanced at her, and she realized the woman

hadn't even heard her gasp. Her attention had been on the man in the moonlight.

"No, *I'm* sorry—I came in the back way, and I didn't realize you hadn't heard me." She was still staring at the man and didn't offer anything more.

"Jesse?" Lorena pressed lightly.

Sally's eyes flicked her way, and the woman smiled broadly. "Yeah, Jesse. He's a cop. A local cop. On the Miccosukee force. He hasn't been back long."

"Oh, I realize that he's a cop," Lorena murmured, wondering if Sally could hear the slight note of bitterness in her tone. "But…he's back from where?"

"Oh…the city. He's something, huh?"

Lorena turned back to study the man in question. Sally didn't need an answer.

Yes, something. He seemed to be both pure grace and pure menace. Powerful, smooth. Sensual, she thought, with some embarrassment. In a thousand years, she never would have admitted that she understood exactly what Sally meant.

No, no, no, no. He was definitely a man with an attitude, and that attitude definitely contained an element of disdain for her. She shook her head slightly, mentally emitting an oath. It now seemed likely that she would meet him again.

Apparently, he hung out around here. And that made him…suspicious.

Cops had been known to be dirty, dirtier even than other men. Sometimes they needed money. Sometimes even good men went bad, seeing how the rich could buy good lawyers and get away with all kinds of things. They had more chance to abuse power, to sneak around, to bribe…

To threaten.
To kill?

"Interesting. We have security guards. Why is he here?" Lorena asked, looking at Sally once again.

"He checks in now and then, makes sure everything is running smoothly."

"Why did he come back?" she asked.

"Oh," Sally said slowly, "his wife was murdered. He was devastated."

"How horrible."

"I know. Damn, I have a busy night ahead of me… but still… Jesse. Excuse me, will you, honey? I want to talk to the man."

"Sure…friends help when you're devastated," Lorena said pleasantly.

Sally shot her a quick glance. "Honey, I said he was devastated, not dead. Take another look at the man, will you?" She opened the door fully and exited the gym. With a sway of her hips, she approached him, calling his name. He turned to her, arching a brow, acknowledging her presence. Sally went straight to him, placing her hands on his chest. She said something softly. He lowered his head, grinning, and the two turned to walk toward the staff quarters.

When they were gone, Lorena left the gym and hurried back across the compound. The alligators began to grunt in a wild, staccato song.

She let herself into her own room, closed and locked the door. She was breathing too heavily once again.

Maybe she was the wrong woman for this job.

No, there was no maybe about it, but that didn't matter. She had to become the right woman, and she would.

She showered, slipped into a nightgown, and assured

herself once again that her door was securely locked. Even then, she also checked once more on the small Smith & Wesson she carried. It was loaded, safety on, but close at hand in the top drawer of the nightstand next to the bed. She took one last look at it before she lay down to sleep.

Despite that, she dreamed.

She didn't want to have nightmares; she didn't want to toss and turn. She dreamed far too often of horrible things. She knew that dreams were often extensions of the day's worries, and she *was* constantly worried.

But that night, she didn't dream horrible things. She dreamed about him. The cop. The world was all foggy, and people were screaming all around her, but he was walking toward her, and she was waiting, heedless of whatever danger might be threatening her because he was watching her, coming for her....

She awoke, drenched with sweat, shaking.

She was definitely the wrong woman for this job. She was losing her mind.

No, she had to toughen up. What the hell was wrong with her? She had to be here.

Had to.

Because she, of all people, had to know the truth.

EAST OF THE deep swamp, Maria Hernandez plucked the last of her wash from the clothesline. The darkness had come; night dampness had set it. She pressed her clean sheets to her nose, deciding that they still smelled of the sunshine, even if she had cleaned up dinner late and gotten the clothes down even later. Sometimes it seemed that darkness came slowly. Sometimes it descended like a curtain, swift and complete.

But tonight…

Tonight was different.

There were lights. Strange lights appearing erratically down by the canal.

"Hector! Come see!" she called to her husband. He'd been picking all day. He picked their own crops, then rented his labor out like a migrant worker. This was the land of opportunity; and indeed, she had her nice little house, even if it was on the verge of the swamps, but one had to work very hard for opportunity.

"Maria, let me be!" Hector shouted back to her.

"But you must see."

"What is it?"

"Lights."

Hector appeared at the back of the house, a beer in his hand. He was a good man. One beer. Just one beer when he came in at night. He loved his children. They had grown quickly in this land of opportunity, and they had their own homes now. He was a hardworking and very good man. He had provided them with a dream.

But now he was tired.

"Lights?" He had spoken in English. Now he swore in Spanish, waving a hand in the air. "Maria, it's a plane. It's boys out in an airboat. It's poachers. What do I care? Come inside."

But the lights were so strange that Maria found herself walking toward them. The farther she got from the house, the stranger it seemed that there should be lights. What would children be doing out here? Or poachers? Yes, she was on the edge of the swamp, land just grasped from it, but…

Then she heard the noises.

Strange noises…

There was a big lump on the earth. She walked toward it, then paused. Instinctively, she knew she should go back. There were stories about things that needed to be watched out for—things that came from the swamp. Snakes…bad snakes. And there were reports of alligators snatching foolish dogs from the banks of the canal.

She started to back away from the lump on the ground, but then, just as she had instinctively felt that she was facing danger, she suddenly knew that the lump was a dead thing. She kept walking to it.

Clouds drifted against the dark sky, freeing the moon for a brief moment.

It was an alligator, but a dead one.

She didn't know much about alligators. Oh, yes, she lived out here; she had driven along the Trail, seen them basking in the sun. They came in close—the canals were theirs, really, this close to the Glades. But she didn't do foolish things. She didn't try to feed them, heaven forbid! She knew enough to stay away, and little else. But this one was dead, harmless, so she moved closer. And closer.

Because this one seemed very strange.

It had been big, very big. It lay on its back, and it looked almost as if it had been stuffed, and as if all the stuffing had been pulled out of it. There was a strange hole in the center of its chest, as if a fire had burned a perfect circle in the center of the white underbelly. Toes were missing. The jaw gaped open in death.

The lights started flickering again. Maria lifted a hand to her eyes so that they would not blind her.

Her heart quickened.

UFOs! Aliens, spacemen. She was proud of her English; she read all the papers in line at the grocery store.

They came down to study earth creatures; they abducted men and women.

She'd seen lights before. Strange lights, late at night. In fact, she'd told her daughter, Julie, about them not so long ago, laughing at her own silliness, because of course Maria had never believed in aliens until now, and Hector scoffed at such silliness. But the lights…

And the alligator…

If they were UFOs, then her initial instinct to run had been right. She had to get back to the house and ask Hector to call the police. Maybe the tall Indian policeman was close by and could help them quickly, far more quickly than the white policemen from the city would make it.

She started to back away. At first it had seemed that the lights were coming from the sky. But now…

They were coming from the brush. From the foliage where the swampland that had not been reclaimed started, just feet from where her lawn began.

Suddenly she was very afraid. She looked at the alligator. A hole in its underbelly. Toes cut off. Eyes…

Eyes cut out.

She turned and started to run.

"Hector!"

A single bullet killed her. A rifle shot straight through her back, tearing through the anterior region of her heart.

Hector heard his wife's scream. He came running out.

The shot that killed him was square between his eyes. He dropped dead still wondering why his wife had called him.

Chapter Two

It had already been one hell of a bad morning.

It had started out with Ginny Hare calling first thing, before it had even begun to be light outside. Jesse was an early riser, but hell, Ginny's hysterical voice before coffee was not a good way to start off the morning.

Billy Ray hadn't come home.

He'd tried to calm Ginny. Lots of times Billy Ray would crash out wherever he'd been and find his way home the next morning.

This was different—Ginny was insistent. He'd gone out fishing with a twelve-pack of beer. And he hadn't come in the morning, the afternoon or the night, and now it was morning again and Billy Ray still wasn't back.

Jesse had tried to soothe her.

"Ginny, I'll get out there looking for him, but you quit worrying. A twelve-pack of beer, Ginny, think about it."

"But, Jesse, he's stayed out two nights!"

"Ginny, I'll look for him, I promise. But he probably got himself as drunk as a skunk and he's sleeping it off somewhere—or, he woke up and knew he'd be in major trouble, and he's trying to figure out how to come home."

When he'd hung up, he'd wondered about the power of love. Billy Ray Hare was the worst loser he'd ever met—white, Native, Hispanic or black. He hit Ginny all the time, though he denied it, as Ginny did herself. He was her man, and in Ginny's eyes, whatever he did, he was hers, and she was going to stand up for him.

Jesse knew that Billy Ray hated him. That was all right. He had no use whatsoever for Billy Ray. Billy Ray liked to call him "white boy," which was all right, because yes, his father had been white. But his mother could trace her lineage back to Billy, Old King Micanopy, back before the start of the Seminole Wars, back before the government had even recognized the Miccosukee as an independent tribe, speaking a different language from the Seminoles with whom they had intermarried and fought throughout the years. Billy Ray never understood that Jesse was proud of being Native American—and furious when men like Billy Ray fell into stereotypes and became lazy-ass alcoholics.

So Billy Ray was useless. But despite the fact that she loved Billy Ray, there was something very special about Ginny. And for her, Jesse would spend half his day in the sweltering heat of summer looking for her no-good husband.

But he hadn't had a chance to look for Billy Ray yet.

Before he'd gotten out of the house, he'd gotten the call about Hector and Maria Hernandez.

Their property was on the county line, so the Metro Police were already on the scene. The homicide detective in charge of the case was Lars Garcia, a man with whom Jesse had gone to college up at the University of

Florida. His Cuban refugee father had married a Danish model, thus his ink-dark hair, slim, athletic build and bright powder-blue eyes. The media liked to make it sound as if the Indian—or Native American cops— were half-wits who were given only a small measure of authority and who hated their ever-present big brothers, the Metro cops. Jesse resented the media for that, because it simply wasn't true. The Metro-Dade force had suffered through some rough years, with rogue cops and accusations of corruption and drug abuse. But they'd cleaned house, and they weren't out to make fools of the Miccosukee policing their own.

Besides which, he'd been a Metro homicide cop himself before making the decision to join the Miccosukee police force.

He felt lucky wherever he got to work with Lars when a body was discovered. Unfortunately, that wasn't a rare happening.

A swamp was a good place to dump a body. There had been the bizarre—body pieces dredged up in suitcases—and there had been the historical: bodies discovered that had lain in the muck and mud for more than a century. Man's inhumanity to man was not a new thing. Sad as it might be, he was accustomed to the cruel and vicious.

Homicides happened.

But the unfairness of homicide happening to good people never ceased to upset him.

Jesse had known Hector and Maria. Known and liked them. They were as homespun as cotton jeans, without guile or cunning. She always wanted to bring him in and feed him; Hector always wanted him to taste a fresh strawberry or tomato. They had loved their small home, loved their land more. It was theirs. He'd never seen two people appreciate the simple things in life with such pure and humble gratitude and pleasure.

Uniformed cops were cordoning off the crime scene as he arrived; Lars had been talking with the fingerprint expert but excused himself and walked over to Jesse as soon as he saw him. "Terrible thing, huh? It's technically outside your jurisdiction, but the killers must have come from somewhere. Maybe they were hiding in the swamp, maybe…" His voice trailed off.

"The bodies?" Jesse said.

"You don't have to see them."

"Yeah, I do."

Hector's body was covered when they walked to it; Lars hunkered down and pulled back the blanket. Hector looked oddly at peace. His eyes were closed; he just lay there—normal-looking except for the bullet hole in his forehead. Nothing had been done to the body; the killer probably hadn't even come near him.

"Tracks?" Jesse asked.

Lars shook his head. "None so far. The lawn is all grassy…then there's foliage, and the canal. No tracks yet."

Jimmy Page from the medical examiner's office was still bending over Maria when they reached her. She lay facedown, her head twisted. Her eyes were still open.

She had seen something terrible.

There was a hole through her back.

"Hi, Jesse," Jimmy said, making notes. "I'm sorry as hell, I heard you knew them."

"Yeah. Nice couple. Really good people. Have the children been notified?"

"The son is in the navy, on active duty—they're trying to reach him. The daughter will be here this afternoon."

He winced. Julie was going to come home alone to see her murdered parents. He would have to make a point of being available later.

"Know when she's coming in?"

"American Airlines, two-thirty flight from LaGuardia. Want to meet her with me?" Lars asked.

"Yeah."

"Thanks. I wasn't looking forward to talking to her on my own."

"Have you got anything, Jimmy?" Jesse asked. "I mean…" He looked down into Maria's eyes, thinking he would remember the way she looked for a very long time to come. "This is no drug hit. These people were as clean as they came."

Jimmy shook his head. "Jesse… I've got to admit, about all we're going to know is the caliber of bullet that hit them, maybe the weapon that fired it, an approximate time of death and maybe a trajectory. They were shot," he said, sounding angry. "As to why they were shot… Jesus, you're right. Who can tell?"

"Mind if I take a look around?" Jesse asked Lars.

"Be my guest. We think the killers must have been to the southwest, from the way Maria fell. She was running. Hector was coming to help her."

Jesse nodded, surveying the expanse of lawn. The neat yard the couple had tended so lovingly reached a point where it became long, thick grasses. Back in the grass, the water table began to rise and mangroves grew. Beyond that lay the canal.

He walked carefully to where the thick grass began to grow, studying the lawn. Although his relations with

the Metro police were good, he wondered if any of the
beat cops were cracking jokes about an Indian being
better at finding footprints than they were.

Hell. He was going to look for them, anyway. He was
going to look for anything.

He turned, calling back to Lars, "I think an airboat
came through here. See the flattening?"

"Yeah."

"And..." Jesse began, then trailed off. He walked a
little further, seeing something in the grass. He moved
closer. Bent over. Frowned.

"What is it?" Lars asked.

"Got a glove and an evidence bag?"

"Yeah."

Lars came over to him, slipping his hand into a glove.
Jesse pointed to the grass. Lars reached for what appeared to be a branch.

"That?" he inquired. "Jesse, it's just a tree limb."

"No, it isn't."

"Then, what the hell...?"

"It's a gator arm," Jesse said. "From one damn big
gator."

"A gator arm? What the hell do I want with a gator
arm?"

"I don't know, but where's the rest of the body?"

"It looks like it was sliced off."

"I think the rest of the body was moved, and then
this arm tore off."

"But..." Lars began.

"But why? And just where the hell is the rest of the
body?"

Lars shook his head. "Maybe..."

"Maybe a dead gator and the murder have nothing to do with each other," Jesse said. "And maybe they do."

"Well, they shouldn't have anything to do with each other," Lars said. "Hell. I can't believe that someone out alligator-poaching would murder two people in cold blood just because he was seen. I mean, it's not as if we execute people for killing gators out of season without a license."

"No, it's not," Jesse agreed. He looked at Lars and shrugged. "But what else is there? Like Jimmy said, there are bullets, there's a time of death…but where the hell is a motive? You're not going to get prints, no fluids for DNA…that's all you've got—an alligator arm."

"I've got nothing," Lars said hollowly.

"Maybe. Maybe not. Send the gator limb to Dr. Thiessen. See what you can get, if anything."

"Of course we'll get it to the vet," Lars said impatiently. "Because you're right. I haven't got anything else. And I'm damned sorry that I may have to tell a young woman who loved her parents that I can't begin to explain why they're dead, except that maybe her mother saw an alligator poacher in the backyard!"

"Lars, you tell me. What else is there?" Jesse said. "This kind of killing looks like an execution, as if it were connected to drugs. But it wasn't. I'd bet my life on that. I'm telling you, Lars, I knew these people. They were bone clean."

"They must have seen something, then. They must have known something, but…you're sure? I mean, sometimes we think we know people, but they're living double lives."

"No. I knew them, Lars."

"All right. Maybe the daughter can help us."

"I doubt it. But I'll go with you. I'll talk to her with you. But, Lars, after today…you'll keep me informed on this one all the way, right?"

"Yes."

"No matter what goes on in Homicide?"

"Yes!"

"Swear it?"

Lars looked at him, arching a brow. "We're already blood brothers," he reminded him with a rueful grimace.

Jesse stared at him, shaking his head. Yeah. Forever ago, when they had been young and going to college.

Strangely, or so it seemed now, their college mascot had been an alligator.

They had both pledged the same fraternity. It had been during that period that they'd been out drinking together and Lars had gotten into the blood brother thing, having seen one too many John Wayne movies, Jesse decided.

"Yeah, blood brothers," Jesse returned, surprised that he could almost smile, even if that smile was grim.

"Jesse, the only thing—"

"I won't go off half cocked to shoot to kill if I find out who did it. I'm a cop. I'll bring them in."

Lars watched him for a moment. Jesse locked his jaw, staring back at his friend. Maybe Lars had the right to doubt him. When Connie had died…

Fate had kept him from killing the man who had murdered her. But there had been no question in his mind that, given the chance, he might well have committed murder himself in turn, so great had been his rage.

"I'm telling you, I'll be a by-the-book lawman." He

shook his head, sobering. "They didn't deserve this, Lars."

"I swear, I will keep you up on what's happening. I'll have to—the killer or killers probably came from the swamp and maybe ran back that way. We'll have lots of our guys in your territory."

"I'll brief my men, as well."

"Get a warning out to them right away."

"Will do."

"You want to take this piece of gator over to Doc Thiessen?" Lars asked him. "You're more familiar with the damn things than I am." He didn't add, Jesse noticed, that he was probably also far more convinced than Lars was that the alligator remains might have something to do with the case.

They started back toward the house. Jesse found himself pausing by Maria's body. The forensic photographers were still at work. He looked into her eyes. In Metro Homicide, he'd seen a lot. A bullet was a fairly quick, clean way to die. He'd seen mutilations that had turned even his strong stomach.

But this...

He'd seen her face alight and beautiful when she'd smiled.

"Jesse, quit looking at her," Lars said.

"Yeah. Well, I'll inform the office, then get out there looking for Billy Ray Hare."

"Billy Ray? You don't think—"

"That Billy Ray killed these two? Not on your life. Billy Ray may be a drunk, and he may not be a prime husband, but he keeps to himself and wouldn't step outside the area he's accustomed to. And he'd also be too damned drunk to make it this far by that time of night.

I've got work to do, and so do you. I'll meet you at two so we can get to the airport. Where?"

"The restaurant at the turnpike entrance."

"I'll be there," Jesse said.

When he left, his first stop was the vet's. Dr. Thorne Thiessen was a rare man, pleased to live deep in the Everglades, and fascinated more by birds and reptiles than the more cuddly creatures customarily kept as pets. He was such an expert with snakes that people traveled down from Palm Beach County, a good hour or so away, to bring him their pythons and boas, king snakes, rat snakes and more.

He was in his early fifties, both blond and bronzed, almost as weathered as some of the creatures he tended with such keen interest. He was just finishing with a little boy and his turtle when Jesse arrived, bearing the alligator limb.

He looked at Jesse with surprise. "People usually call on me with living creatures, you know."

"Yeah, but Metro-Dade and I both think you can help on this one. You *are* the reptile expert. You can make some preliminary findings, then pass some samples upstate. Hopefully, someone will figure something out."

Thiessen had been smiling; now he frowned. "What have you got?"

"What do you think?"

"I think it's a piece of an alligator."

"Great."

"No, no, I can do tissue and blood samples, do a profile…and get samples upstate, just like you suggested, but why?"

Jesse explained. Thiessen stared at him for long moments. "And you found this at the scene?"

"Yes."

"Jesse…"

Jesse sighed. "They weren't into drugs."

"Still, they might have witnessed an exchange in the Everglades, or, hell, God forbid, another murder."

"They might have. But this is what we've got for now."

Thiessen shrugged. "Big sucker," he said.

"Yep," Jesse agreed.

"I'll do what I can," Thiessen promised.

Jesse thanked him. In the waiting room, he looked for Jim Hidalgo, who worked for the vet, but then he remembered that Jim worked nights.

The man at the desk was a big guy, John Smith. He was so big, in fact, that he was almost apelike. Jesse didn't remember when he hadn't been with the vet.

Good man to have on, Jesse thought. Big enough to cope with any animal out there.

At least, almost any animal out there.

He grunted to Jesse in a combination of hello and goodbye.

Come to think of it, a grunt was the only conversation Jesse had ever shared with the man.

He waved and went out.

"Look into the eyes of death! Stare into the burning pits of monster hell. See what it would have been like to face the hunger and rage of a carnivore older than the mighty *Tyrannosaurus rex!* Ah, but, believe it or not, once upon a Triassic age, this was an even more ferocious and terrifying creature, in fact, one that made minced meat of the mighty dinosaurs themselves." Michael Preston paused for effect as he talked to the small, wriggling creature he held in his right hand.

The week-old hatchling let out a strange little squeaking sound, its jaws opening, then snapping shut. The eyes were yellow with central stripes of black. It was small, almost cute in a weird sort of way, but the mouth shut with a pressure that was chilling, despite its size.

The hatchling began squealing and wriggling again.

"Loudmouth," Michael said, shrugging. He liked the fact that the American alligator made noise. Noise was good. Noise was warning. "But you *are* being awfully dramatic here," he told the hatchling. "Okay, so I'm a little dramatic myself. Because I *hate* tour groups," he grumbled.

Even as he slipped the hatchling back into its tank, the door to his lab opened and Lorena entered.

"Watch out—the monsters are coming," she warned.

Michael arched a brow. "Monsters," she whispered, emphasizing the warning. Then she turned, a beautiful smile plastered on her face as she allowed room for the tour group to enter. Ten in all, a full tour: two young couples, perhaps on their way to register for college, maybe on honeymoon. They looked like ecology-minded types, surveying the wonder of the Everglades. There was an attractive, elderly woman, probably a widow, seeing the Sunshine State now that old Harvey or whoever had finally bitten the dust. Then there was a harried-looking couple with three boys who looked to be about twelve. The woman had once been pretty. The man had a good smile and looked like a decent father. The boys seemed to be the monsters. They walked right up to his lab table, barged against it, then leaned on it, peering into his tanks and petri dishes.

"Uh, uh, uh—back now," Michael said, frowning at Lorena as if she might have forgotten to warn her group that the tour was hands-off. She shrugged innocently and grinned back with a combination of mischief and amusement. No doubt the boys had been a handful since they'd started their tour. Actually, Lorena wasn't responsible for leading tours. She was a trouper, though. She seemed to like to be in the middle of things; when there were no injuries or sniffles to attend to, her work was probably boring. And it wasn't as if there were a dozen malls or movie theaters in the area to keep her busy.

"Back, boys," he repeated. "Even hatchlings can be dangerous."

"Those little things? What can they do?" demanded the biggest boy as he stuck his hand into the tank with the week-old hatchlings.

Michael grabbed his hand with a no-nonsense grip that seemed to surprise the boy.

"They can bite," Michael said firmly.

"Mark Henson, stand back and behave, now," the boy's obviously stressed mother said, stepping forward to set a hand on Mark's shoulders. "We're guests here. The doctor has asked you—"

"He ain't no doctor—are you?" the boy demanded.

The woman shot Michael an apologetic look. "I'm so sorry. Mark is my son Ben's cousin, and I don't think he gets out very often."

"It's all right," Michael said. He was lying. Mark was a brat. "Mark seems to be very curious. Yes, Mark, I *am* a doctor. I have a doctorate in marine science. Salt- and freshwater reptiles are my specialty. I also studied biochemistry, animal behavior and psychology, so trust me, hatchlings can give you a nasty bite. Especially these hatchlings."

"Why *those* hatchlings?" Mark demanded immediately.

Because we breed them especially to chew up nasty little rugrats like you! he was tempted to say. But Lorena was already answering for him.

"Because they're tough little critters, survivors," Lorena said flatly. "Ladies and gentlemen, Dr. Preston is in charge of our selective-breeding department. He knows a tremendous amount about crocodilians, past and present. He'll tell you all about his work now—for those interested in hearing," she finished with just the slightest edge of warning in her voice for the boys. They stared at her as she spoke, surveying her intently. No wonder she was glad to let the group heckle *him* now. Lorena was an exceptionally attractive woman with lush hair, brilliant eyes, and a build that not even a lab coat could hide.

The two older boys were at that age when they were just going into adolescence, a state when squeaky sopranos erupted every ten minutes, and sexual fantasies began. And they were obviously having a few of those over Lorena. She made a face at Michael, surprised him by slipping quickly from his lab. Well, she didn't have to be here, he told himself. It wasn't her job. But she'd seemed fascinated by everything here ever since she'd arrived.

Even him.

Not that he minded.

Except that...

She was bright. And really beautiful. So what was she doing out here?

She was good with people, he would definitely give her that. The complete opposite of the way he felt. He hated having to deal with people.

He gave the boys a sudden, ever-so-slightly malicious smile. "Well, gentlemen, let me introduce you more fully to these hatchlings. Alligators, as you might have heard already, date back to prehistoric times. They didn't descend from the dinosaurs. They were actually cousins to them. They shared common ancestors known as thecodonts. And way back in the late Cretaceous period, there was a creature called Deinosuchus—a distant relative of these guys—with a head that was six feet in length. Imagine that fellow opening his jaws on you. True crocodilians have been around for about two million years. They're fantastic survivors. They have no natural enemies—"

"That's not true!" Mark announced. "I saw a program on alligators and crocs. An anaconda can eat an alligator, I saw it. You could see the shape of the alligator in the snake. Man, it was cool—"

"We don't have anacondas in the Everglades," Michael said, gritting his teeth hard before he could continue. "Birds, snakes and small mammals eat alligator eggs, and it's easy for hatchlings to be picked off, but once it's reached a certain size, an alligator really only has one enemy here. And that's…?"

He let the question trail off, arching a brow toward Mark. He looked like a jock. Probably played football or basketball, at the very least. He liked to talk, but he didn't seem to have the answer to this one.

"Man," said one of the boys. He was thinner than his companion, with enormous dark eyes and long hair that fell over his forehead. Nice-looking kid. Shy, maybe, more of a bookish type than Mark. "Man is the only enemy of a grown alligator in the Everglades."

"That's right," Michael said, an honest smile curving his lips. He could tell that this kid had a real interest in learning. "You're Ben?" Michael asked.

The boy nodded. He pulled the third kid up beside him. "This is my other cousin, Josh."

"Josh, Ben and Mark."

"Do we get to see the alligators eat a deer or something?" Mark asked.

"Sorry, you don't get to see them eat any living creatures here, kid. The juveniles and adults out in the pools and pens are fed chicken."

"They're so cool," Ben said, his brown eyes wide on Michael.

Michael nodded. "Yep, they're incredible. Alligators were near extinction here when I was young, but then they became protected. The alligator has made one of the most incredible comebacks in the world, mainly because of farms like this, but also in the wild. They look ugly, and they certainly can be fearsome creatures, but they have their place in the scheme of life, as well, keeping down the populations of other animals, often weeding out the sick and injured because they're easy prey."

"I think they're horrible creatures," Ben's mother said with a shudder.

"Some people hate spiders—but spiders keep down insect populations. And lots of people hate snakes, but snakes are largely responsible for controlling rodent populations," Michael said.

"What's that mean?" Mark asked.

"It means we'd be overrun by rats if it weren't for snakes," Ben answered, then flushed, staring at Michael.

"That's exactly what it means," Michael said.

"What do you do here, Dr. Preston?" the third kid, cousin Josh, asked.

"That's easy. He's a baby doctor for the alligators," Mark insisted.

"I study the growth patterns of alligators," Michael said. "We raise alligators here, but this is far from a petting zoo. We farm alligators just like some people farm beef cattle. We bring tourists in—and other scientists, by the way, to learn from the work we do here—but the owners are in this for the same reason other farmers work with animals. For the money. Alligators are valuable for their skins, and, more and more, for their meat."

"Tastes like chicken," Mark said.

"That's what some people say," Michael agreed, bristling inside at the boy's know-it-all attitude. "They're a good food source. The meat is nutritious, and little of the animal goes to waste. We're always working on methods to make the skin more resilient, the meat tastier and even more nutritious. By selective breeding and using the scientific method, we can create skins that improve upon what nature made nearly perfect to begin with."

"Perfect?" Ben's mother said with a shudder. Her husband slipped an arm around her.

"They make great boots," he said cheerfully.

"Belts, purses and other stuff, too," Ben supplied.

"You'll see more of that as your tour progresses," Michael said. "I'll tell you a bit more about what goes on in here, then you can watch them eat, Mark, and at the end, guess what?"

"We can all buy boots, belts and purses made out of

alligator skin?" one of the young women inquired with a pleasant smile.

"That's right," Michael agreed.

"And we really get to see them chomp on chickens?" Mark demanded, as if that were the only possible reason for coming on the tour.

"Yeah, you can see them chomp on chickens," Michael agreed. He pointed at Ben. "Come back here, Ben, and you can help me." Michael looked up at the adults in the crowd. He never brought a kid back behind his workstation, but for some reason, it seemed important to let Ben lord it over Mark. He was sure that life usually went the other way around. "One of the most incredible things we're able to do in working with crocodilians is studying the growth of the embryo in the egg. Ben, lift that tray, so they can see what I mean."

"Wow!" Mark gasped, stepping forward again. Even he was impressed.

"It's possible to crack and remove the top of the alligators' eggs to study the growth of the embryos without killing them. It's also possible to cause changes and mutations in the growing embryos by introducing different drugs, genetic materials or even stimuli such as heat or cold. Here…in this egg, you'll see a naturally occurring mutation. This creature cannot survive even if it does reach the stage of hatching. You see, it's missing a lower jaw. Can you imagine an alligator incapable of using its jaws? Everywhere in nature, there are mishaps and imperfections. Over here, in this egg, you have an albino alligator. They have tremendous difficulty surviving because—"

"Because they sunburn!" Mark interrupted, laughing as if he'd made a joke.

"Actually, that's true. They have trouble coping with the intense sun that their relatives need to survive. They also lack the element of surprise in their attacks—they're easily seen in greenish or muddy waters where their relatives are camouflaged by their surroundings."

"He's a goner," Mark said.

"Well, not here," Michael told him. "He'll hatch and grow, and he'll have a nice home at the farm, and we'll feed him and take care of him—you know why?"

"Why?"

"Because he's unusual, and our visitors will like looking at him, that's why," Michael said, pleased with himself because he seemed to be growing a little more tolerant of Mark.

"So that's what you do—you try to make white alligators?" Mark asked.

Michael shook his head. "Selective breeding...well, it's what makes collies furry or Siamese cats Siamese. We find the alligators with the best skins and we breed them, and then we breed their offspring until we create a line of animals with incredibly hardy skins that make the very best boots and bags and purses. We also find the alligators that give the most meat with the most nutritional value—"

"Because it's a farm, and it's out to make money," Ben's mother said, and she shuddered again. "Thank God!"

"She thinks you should kill them all," Ben's father said.

Michael shrugged. "Like I said—"

"They should all be killed," the attractive older woman said, speaking out at last. She had keen blue eyes, and she stared at Michael, somehow giving him the creeps. "They eat people."

"They *do* eat people, right?" Mark demanded with a morbid determination.

"There have been instances, yes."

"A friend of mine was eaten!" the elderly woman said, and she kept staring at Michael, as if it was all his fault.

"Anytime man cohabits with nature, there can be a certain danger," he said gently. He looked at the others. "It's dangerous to feed alligators. The alligators are repopulating Florida, and they do get into residential canals, especially during mating season. I know of one incident in particular when a woman was feeding the alligators…and, well, to the alligator, there is no distinction between food and a hand offering food."

"And children," the woman said, growing shrill. "Children! It's happened. It's horrible, and they should all be destroyed. Little children, just walking by lakes, looking at flowers—these monsters need to be killed! All of them! How can you people do this, how can you!" Her voice had risen; she was shouting.

There was a buzzer beneath his workstation; all Michael had to do was hit it and the security people would come. Sign of the times. But Michael didn't touch the button; the older woman had stunned him by suddenly going so ballistic, and he just stared at her.

She pointed a finger at him. "Tell them. Tell them the truth. Tell them about the attacks."

"Yes, there have been attacks, and of course that's horrible. But we need to live sensibly with nature. In Africa, along the river, the Nile crocodiles are far more ferocious, but they're a part of the environment. We can't just eliminate animal populations because the animals are predators. We're predators ourselves, ma'am."

She shook her finger at him, and her voice grew more strident. "They're going to eat you. They're going to eat you all. Rise up and tear you to pieces, rip you to shreds—that's how they do it, you know, little boy!" she said, suddenly gripping Mark by the shoulders. She stared at him with her wild eyes. "They clamp down on your body, and they shake you, and they break you and rip you, and your bones crunch and your veins burst. Your blood streams into the water, and you're dying already while they drown you."

"Oh, my God, please!" Ben's mother cried, trying to pull Mark from the woman's grip.

"Hey now!" Michael said, and he came around his station, setting an arm around the woman's shoulders to hold her while Ben's mother, pale as a shadow, pulled Mark to her.

"You!" the elderly woman said, turning on him again. "You! They'll eat *you*. You made them, and they'll eat you. They'll tear you to bits, and your own mother won't be able to find enough bloody pieces to bury you!"

"Now, really, I didn't invent alligators, ma'am—"

"You'll die!" she screeched.

He reached for her again, aware that he had to take control of the situation before it became a monumental disaster. He could see her going completely insane and destroying his lab. Then the cops would be called in, and soon reporters would be crawling everywhere, and then...

"Please, now—" he began.

The door suddenly opened. Security hadn't come;

Lorena had, presumably drawn by the noise. She stared reproachfully at Michael.

"What happened?"

"That lady is telling Dr. Preston that the alligators should eat him!" Mark said excitedly.

"We have a problem," Michael agreed. "I think I should call Security—" he began.

"No, no, we're all right." Lorena—who, he had been told, had a degree in psychology and another in public relations, as well as being an RN—assessed the situation quickly and took charge. "Mrs. Manning, right? Come along and tell me about it. We'll get you something cold to drink. It can be so hot here, even with the air-conditioning on the heat can get to you and—"

"Young woman, I am not suffering from the heat!" the elderly woman proclaimed. But her shoulders sank, and she suddenly seemed to deflate. "I'm sorry, I'm sorry. I'm not a lunatic, I don't usually behave this way.... I shouldn't have come. Yes, young woman, you may get me something cold to drink."

Lorena led her quickly toward the door, but once there, the woman stopped and turned back, staring at Michael. She pointed at him again. "I hope they don't eat you, young man," she said. Then she smiled, but it wasn't a pleasant expression, and despite himself, he felt the strangest chill snake along his spine.

Then she was gone, as Lorena whisked her out the door.

Michael, with the nine remaining members of the tour group, was dead silent as seconds ticked by.

He suddenly felt a small hand slipping into his. He looked down. Ben was staring up at him. "Don't worry. She was just crazy. She probably had a friend who got eaten, and she probably misses her. I'm sure you're not going to get eaten, Dr. Preston."

Michael smiled; the chill dissipated.

"All right, everyone. I have a question for you. What animal is most dangerous to Americans?"

There was silence for a moment, then Mark cried out, "I know, I know! Bees!"

"Bees are up there in the top ten, but they're not in the number-one slot."

"I know what it is." A young man, one of the two who looked like a newlywed, was speaking for the first time. He held his wife tightly against him, and seemed pale himself, probably shaken by the older woman's display. "The deer."

"The deer?" Ben protested.

"That's right," Michael said.

"The deer? You mean like Bambi?" Josh asked.

"More Americans are killed each year due to accidents involving deer than are killed by any rattler, spider, shark or reptile out there. So we have to remember to always be careful in any animal's environment," Michael said.

His door opened again; Peggy Martin, one of the guides, stepped in. "Well, ladies and gentlemen, it's time to move on to the pens, or straight into either the gift or coffee shop, if you'd rather," she said cheerfully.

"Mark, you get to see the gators eat chickens," Josh said.

Mark looked at Ben's parents. "I'm really hungry. Maybe we could just get a hamburger. Please?" he said politely.

"Sure, sure," Ben's father said. He looked at Michael. "Thank you for the information, Dr. Preston."

"Yeah, it was great," one of the pretty young women Michael had pegged as a newlywed agreed.

"Thanks," Michael said. "Thanks very much, you were, er, a great group."

He leaned back against his workstation, strangely exhausted. The old woman had given him the creeps. He kept a false smile plastered to his face as the group filed out, the boys in the rear.

Mark was the last. Before he exited, he turned back, looking uneasy.

"Dr. Preston?"

"Yes?"

The boy seemed about to say something, but then he shook his head. "Thanks. You were all right."

Michael nodded.

"Come back sometime," he told Mark, wondering if he meant it or not.

"Yeah."

The door closed behind Mark.

The hatchlings began to squeak.

Chapter Three

In the gift shop, Josh began to play with a two-foot-long plastic alligator. "I've got five dollars," he told Ben. "Think this looks real?"

"Yeah, it's cool," Ben told him.

Mark walked up to the pair in the corner of the shop. He still looked a little pale—they had all been kind of spooked, the old lady had been *really, really* creepy, scarier than the alligators—but he was kind of swaggering again, which Ben was sure meant that Mark was all right.

"That don't look real, Josh. Not compared to this!"

Reaching into the pocket of his baggy, oversize jeans, he pulled out one of the hatchlings. The little creature's mouth was opened wide. Tiny teeth were already chillingly visible.

"Mark! You stole one of the hatchlings—" Josh began.

"Shh," Mark protested.

"Oh, man, you've got to give that back," Ben said.

"No way," Mark said. "Look at him!"

The jaw opened, snapped.

Mark shoved the hatchling toward Josh, who jumped back. "Don't do that, Mark."

"He's going to eat you all up," Mark said, laughing as he started to stuff the creature back into his pocket.

But suddenly he cried out, his hand still in his pocket.

"Oh, shut up," Ben commanded. His cousin was big stuff around school; he had looked up to Mark, and he'd wanted to be like him. But Ben had never been on an outing like this with Mark before. Mark was always on, like maybe there were always girls watching or something. Now the way people were staring was just embarrassing. "Come on, Mark, stop it. People are looking—"

Mark jerked his hand from his pocket. "Get it off! Get it off!" he screamed. The hatchling had his forefinger in its mouth. To Ben's amazement, there was a trail of blood dripping down his cousin's finger.

Instinctively, he reached for the hatchling. But Mark started screaming again. "No, no, don't pull. You'll tear my whole finger off!"

People were beginning to stare. Ben pushed Mark toward a rear door. It read No Admittance: Staff Only, but Ben ignored that; the way the buildings were set up, he could tell that the door led back into the hallway where the labs were housed.

"What are we doing? Where are we going?" Mark cried frantically. "Oh, my God, it hurts! He's eating me!"

"Shut up, shut up, we're taking him back!" Ben said. He moved Mark faster and faster down the hall, pushing back into Dr. Preston's lab without knocking at the door.

Dr. Preston was there, thankfully, standing almost where they had left him. He started when they entered, standing taller in his lab coat. He wasn't very old for a doctor; he was tall and nice-looking, with sandy hair and green eyes, and if Mark hadn't been such a jerk—

and if the old lady hadn't freaked out—he might have spent more time with them and told them a lot more neat stuff.

"What the—" Dr. Preston began.

"Mark took one of the babies, but it bit him and we can't get it off and we're real sorry, honest to God, we're real sorry, but can you help—"

Preston helped. Right away, he knew where to pinch the hatchling so that it let go rather than ripping. He dropped the hatchling back into a tank. By then there were tears in Mark's eyes, ready to spill down his face.

"Come over here," Preston said to Mark, taking him back behind his workstation, washing the wound at a sterile-looking sink, then covering it with some slimy cream. "We'll have to take you to the nurse and tell your folks—"

"No, please, no!" Mark protested. "I'm here with Ben's parents. If my parents ever found out I—that I tried to steal from this place, they'd..."

Preston stared at Mark, then at Ben, and then at Josh, who had followed them, silent and so white that his freckles stood out on his face.

"Mark, you were bitten—"

"It's a tiny hole. Look, you can barely see it."

"Yes, but—"

"I've had a tetanus shot, honest."

"Mark, there's always a rare chance that reptiles can carry disease—"

"Not alligator-farm reptiles!" Mark said. "Please, please, please don't say anything. You don't know my dad."

Preston hesitated.

"Please," Mark whispered. "Please."

Ben held his breath. Preston was staring at Mark, studying his face.

The door behind them quietly opened and closed. Ben jumped, turning around. It was their first guide, the really pretty lady with the dark hair and bright blue eyes.

She didn't say anything, just leaned against the door, watching the situation. Dr. Preston looked at her. He lifted Mark's fingers. "They were trying to leave with a souvenir."

"Ah…" she murmured to the boys. "What were you going to do? Drop him in your hotel swimming pool?" She turned to Dr. Preston. "I need to look at that, and then we need to file a report."

Mark went pale.

"I was thinking about letting him go. I think he already paid enough of a price," Dr. Preston said.

Ben was surprised to see that the beautiful nurse was the one who seemed to think they needed the authorities. She was staring at Dr. Preston. "We really shouldn't take the chance. Just in case there are consequences, an infection…"

Dr. Preston stared back at her. "This is one of the cleanest labs you're ever going to find." He sounded indignant.

The nurse, however, wasn't backing down. "I don't know…."

"Please," Mark begged.

"Hey, I'd never let anything happen to a kid," Dr. Preston swore. "Though this one…all right. Call in the authorities."

"No, please," Mark begged.

The woman stared at Dr. Preston for a moment longer.

Then she looked at the boys. They were staring at her with downright prayers glittering in their eyes.

She nodded, a smile twitching at her lips; then she walked over to look at Mark's finger. Her glance at Michael assured him that it was a minor injury. "We have some antibacterial medicine to put on that."

Preston stared at Mark. "You know, Ms. Fortier has a point. This is against my better judgment. I could lose my job. I could be sued. Who knows, maybe I could go to jail. Lorena, could I go to jail for this?"

"I don't know, but there's a cop outside. Jesse Crane." She made a tsking sound. "I've heard that he feels passionately about people messing with things like this. The Everglades, well, this place is his passion. So I've heard."

"I'll never say a word, never, even if my finger drops off—even if my whole hand explodes!" Mark swore.

Lorena pulled a tube of cream from her pocket and dabbed some of the contents on the injured finger.

She took a bandage from another pocket and covered the bite. When she was finished, though, she was in a real hurry. "I've got to get back to the office. I just came by to make sure everyone was okay. That poor woman is still…well, in bad shape."

"This is just a tiny bite," Mark said apologetically. He gulped. "Thank you, Nurse," he murmured.

She took off. Preston watched her go.

Ben was surprised and pleased to see that Dr. Preston was actually smiling when he said, "Mark, you take this as a lesson. And if your hand swells up, don't keep it a secret. Tell the doctor you stuck your hand in the tank and got bitten by a hatchling, and then you have them call me right away, got it?"

"Yes, sir," Mark swore.

He turned, flying for the door. Ben ran after him. At the door, Mark stopped. Ben crashed into him. Josh, always close, crashed into Ben.

Mark didn't notice the pileup. He was staring back at Dr. Preston. "Thanks, Doc. Honest. I'll make it up to you one day."

Preston nodded at him.

"Okay. I'll hold you to your word."

The boys hurried back out to the gift shop. Ben plowed right into his mother.

"There you are! Thank God. If you're buying anything, do it now. I can't wait to leave this place. Honestly, Howard," she said to his father, "couldn't we have taken them on an overnighter to Disney World? I can't believe we're going from here to an airboat ride and a night in one of those open-air chickee things!"

"It will be fine, dear," Ben's father said. He winked at Ben.

"I knew I should have gone with Sally and the Girl Scouts," she said.

Ben flashed a quick smile to Mark. Mark smiled back. It was going to be all right.

No one was in trouble. The alligator farm wasn't going to call the police or Mark's parents; Ben's folks weren't even any the wiser.

The day was saved.

The airboat ride was next.

JESSE HAD PULLED into the parking lot at the alligator farm already tired. He hadn't found Billy Ray. Where the hell the man had crawled off to, he didn't know. He

would need lots more time to comb the swamp to find
Billy Ray.

Just what he needed to be doing when two friends
had been shot down in their own yard for no apparent
reason.

And now this.

A call because a woman had gone into a fit while
visiting the alligator farm.

Lots of tourists, he noticed. That was good. Along
the Tamiami Trail, a lot of the Miccosukee Indians depended on the tourist trade for a living. Along Alligator Alley, stretching from Broward westward across
the state in a slightly more northerly route, a lot of the
state's Seminole families depended on the tourist trade,
as well. The big alligator farms pulled people in, and
then they stayed and paid good tourist dollars for airboat rides, canoe treks along the endless canals at sunset, and even camping in traditional chickees. The locals
made money, which was good, because they needed it.

Of course, the biggest earner in the area was the casino. Still, there were a lot of other good ways to make
a living from tourists. Either way, it was money honestly earned, and to Jesse, the setting alone was worth
the price of admission. The Everglades was a unique
environment, and though civilization was steadily en-
croaching on the rare, semitropical wilderness, it was
still just that: a wilderness. Deep in the "river of grass,"
a man could be so entirely alone with God and nature
that civilization itself might not exist. There were miles
and miles, acres and acres, where no one had as yet
managed to lay a single cable or wire; there were places
where even cell phones were no use. There were dangerous snakes and at times the insects were thick in the

air. But it was also a place of peace unlike anything else he'd ever experienced. Every once in a while he thought of himself as a rare individual indeed—a man finally at peace with himself, satisfied with his job, and certain, most of the time, that he was the best man for it.

At least, he usually felt at peace with himself and as if he could make a difference in his work.

Today…

Today the world didn't make sense. That a couple as fine and hardworking as Maria and her husband could meet such a fate…hell, what good were the police then? Even if they solved the crime, his friends were still dead.

But thanks to his work, he wasn't powerless. He would find the killers and see justice done. That was his job, and it was one worth doing.

He wasn't making a fortune or knocking the world dead, but he didn't need money. He needed solitude, and the opportunity to be alone when he chose. And he needed to feel that he had some control over his own life and destiny, and this job certainly gave him that. Sometimes, he was very much alone, but that was a choice he had made, consciously or perhaps subconsciously, when he had lost Connie.

"Jesse!"

Harry Rogers, major stockholder and acting president and supervisor of Harry's Alligator Farm and Museum, hurried toward Jesse, who got out of his car. Harry was a big man, six foot two by what sometimes appeared to be six foot two of girth. He'd been born in a Deep South section of northern Florida, and he was proud of being a "Cracker," even if he'd gone on to acquire a degree in business administration from none other than such a prestigious Yankee institution as Harvard.

"Thank God!" Harry exclaimed, clapping him on the back. "We got a lady went berserk in the middle of Michael's speech, started screaming that he was going to get eaten up, and going on and on about how dangerous the gators were. I didn't want the Metro cops coming in here with their sirens blazing and all...and God knows, we don't need the community up in arms about the gators any worse than they already are, but..."

"Where is she?"

"My office, and is she a loose cannon or what? I'm telling you, she's downright scary. I've got Lorena, the new nurse, with her. We made her some tea, Lorena's talking to her, but she's still going off every few minutes or so."

Harry stopped talking and looked at Jesse closely. "Hey, what's the matter? You look grim."

"I am. An old Cuban couple in that new development east of here was murdered."

"How?"

"Shot."

"That your jurisdiction?" Harry asked, scratching his head.

"No, but they were friends."

"I'm sorry. Real sorry. Were they into drugs?"

That was the usual question, especially in a shooting. "No, it had nothing to do with drugs."

"You sure?" Harry asked skeptically.

Jesse gritted his teeth. "Yes, I'm sure."

"Well, if I can help...but at the moment, you've got to be a cop here for me, since this is your jurisdiction."

"All right. I'll see what I can do, but if this lady has

really lost her mind, we may need some professionals out here, and we may have to call in the county boys."

"I hate the county boys."

"Hell, I like to settle our own problems, too, Harry. You know that."

"Sure do," Harry said. "'Course, you're the only man among us I've seen put those boys down."

"There are good county cops, Harry. We're a small community out here."

"We're an Indian community," Harry said dryly.

"Doesn't matter. We're small. You have to have the big boys around when you need real help. Hopefully, we don't need it now. Do you know where this woman is from? Has she said?"

Harry shook his head. "Every time we ask her, she goes on about her friend who was eaten. She's got to live near a lake somewhere, but that could be half the state. Don't that just beat all? The old broad has a friend eaten by a gator—so she comes to visit a gator farm. Folks are weird as hell, huh?"

"Folks are weird," Jesse agreed without elaborating. The whole thing was weird, he thought. The woman here had a friend who'd been eaten by an alligator.

A piece of an alligator had been found where two innocent people had been murdered.

He followed Harry in through a side entrance to the administrative buildings and down a long hallway.

The place might be an alligator farm out in the swamp, but Harry knew how to furnish an office. It was at the end of a long hallway. A single door opened onto a room with a massive oak desk surrounded by the best in leather sofas and chairs. To the rear were more seats, a large-screen TV, and state-of-the-art speakers for his elaborate sound system. Harry loved the Everglades; he even loved reptiles. He was part Creek, not Seminole or Miccosukee, but he'd worked his way up from cotton picking at the age of three to millionaire businessman, and he liked his creature comforts. His office might have been on Park Avenue.

Jesse could hear the woman as he followed Harry in. She was speaking in a shrill voice, talking about how nothing had been found of "Matty" other than a hand with a little flesh left on the fingers. Jesse glanced at Harry, then walked over to the woman, who was standing in a corner, flattened against the wall. Her hair was silver, her eyes a soft powder blue. She was trim and very attractive, except that now the flesh around her eyes was puffy from crying, and she gazed around with a hunted, trapped look of panic on her face.

In front of her, trying to calm her, was a young woman in a nurse's standard white uniform. Jesse couldn't see her face because a fall of sleek, honey-colored hair hid her features, but before she turned, he knew that he'd already met her.

And she was certainly the last person he'd expected to see at Harry's.

A woman who looked like that and drove a car like that, pedal to the metal...

To get *here?*

She stared back at him for a fleeting moment, instantly hostile—or defensive?

"You're going to get eaten!" the woman was shrieking, pointing at the nurse. "You've got to get out of here. Don't help these people breed monsters. They'll kill you, too. Crush you, drown you... Oh my God, a hand, a hand was all that was left...some flesh, just bits and pieces of flesh...."

"Hey, now, ma'am," Jesse said, stepping forward, trying to remember what he had learned in Psychology 101. "It's going to be all right, honest. Calm down. The alligators here are being raised as food. They're no danger to anyone on the outside—"

"They'll get loose!" the woman protested. But she had given Jesse her attention. He had kept his voice low, deep and calm—Psychology 101—and his firm tone seemed to be working with her. He stepped closer to her, reaching out a hand.

"They're not going to get loose. No one's going to let them get loose." He smiled. "Besides, Harry here is a charter member of the National Rifle Association. He and his staff wouldn't hesitate to shoot any gator that moved in the wrong direction. He's not out to save the gators, ma'am, he's out to make money off them."

She took his hand, staring into his eyes.

Next to him, Jesse heard a deep sigh of relief. He glanced at the woman standing by him, Harry's new nurse. Despite himself, he felt a little electric tremor.

Nature, simple biology, kicking in.

She was probably one of the most beautiful women he had ever seen.

Harry had a habit of finding pretty girls. Strange that a fat old man who owned an alligator farm could convince any young woman to come work in the middle of a swamp. Not that Harry was a lecher; he was as faithful as could be to Mathilda, his equally round and cheerful wife of thirty-odd years. But he did like attractive young people, and he had managed to fill the place with them, so this new nurse shouldn't have been too much of a surprise. Still, Jesse felt himself pause, as he hadn't in a very long time, staring at her.

Maybe it was just the day he'd had so far.

She looked back at him gravely, studying him with the same intensity as he had studied her. Then she looked down, biting her lower lip, embarrassed. In a moment she looked up again, straightening her shoulders and inclining her head, an acknowledgment that he had defused an uncomfortable situation. Her eyes were a dark-rimmed light hazel, startling against the classical, pure cream perfection of her face. Her hair was like a halo of crowning glory; she looked almost fragile in her blond beauty, yet he sensed that there was a lot of substance to her, as well.

He felt the warmth of the older woman's hand and, with a start, looked back to the gray-haired visitor—his current objective. He gave himself a little shake, surprised that Harry's new nurse had so impressed him, and continued to talk to the older woman. "It's okay. We're going to get you home. Except you're going to have to give us a bit of a hand to do that," he continued. "I'm Jesse Crane, a police officer out here. I'd like—"

"Oh!" the woman cried. "So now you're going to arrest me for telling the truth about these monsters and the horrible people purposely breeding them."

"No, ma'am, I just want to get you home and make sure you're going to be all right."

"Oh, like hell. You're just trying to shut me up!"

Jesse smiled at her. He couldn't help it. She was a tough old broad. She might be going over the edge, but she was going with passion and style.

"What's your name?"

"Theresa Manning."

"How do you do, Mrs. Manning? You're free to call the newspapers, or buy a banner ad and have a plane drag it through the sky. We guarantee freedom of speech in this country. But you're hot and miserable, and if you lost a friend to an alligator, this is not a good place for you to be. Let me take you home."

Theresa Manning hesitated, then sighed deeply.

"Where is your home?" he prodded.

"The Redlands."

"All right." He glanced at his watch. It was important to him that he meet Lars to go to the airport and pick up Julie Hernandez. "Let's go. Let me take you home now."

She nodded, looking at him. But as she rose, she suddenly gripped the nurse's hand.

"You, too. Please."

"But, Mrs. Manning—" the nurse protested.

"Please," Theresa Manning insisted.

"Go with her," Harry said softly to the nurse.

"Harry, I won't be able to bring her back for a while," Jesse said.

"Oh, please," Theresa Manning said, starting to grow hysterical again.

"Lorena, just go with him. When you get back, you get back!" Harry said impatiently.

Lorena's startling eyes fixed on Jesse's, and she said, "All right. If Mrs. Manning wants me with her, I'll be with her, and whatever you have to do, Officer, I'll wait until you're able to get me back. Shall we go?"

Jesse lifted his hands in surrender. He almost smiled. Maybe she felt this was her way of getting back at him for what had happened yesterday.

Fine. If she wanted to wind up involved in a murder

investigation and not get back until the wee hours of the morning, so be it.

"Yeah. Sure. Let's go," he said flatly. "Mrs. Manning?" He smiled, taking the older woman's arm. She actually smiled back.

He let Lorena follow behind as he escorted Theresa Manning from the office to his car.

Damn, this was one hell of a day.

Chapter Four

Lorena sat in the back of the car, while Theresa Manning sat in the front with Jesse Crane.

She felt somewhat useless being there, but the woman had been insistent. And though Lorena felt a twinge of guilt, aware that she had been eager to come not so much to help out—which she certainly was willing to do—but because she wanted the time with Jesse Crane.

As Sally had pointed out, the man was something special. But that wasn't why she was interested in him.

Despite the heavy traffic, he drove smoothly and adeptly. They left the Trail and headed south. He kept up a casual stream of conversation with Mrs. Manning, pointing out birds, asking about her home and family. By the time they neared her neighborhood, she seemed relaxed, even apologetic. Jesse told her not to be sorry, then suggested that she not take any more tours in the Everglades for a while.

At her house, she asked them in. Jesse very respectfully declined, but he gave her a card, telling her to call him if she needed him.

When they got back in the car, Lorena told him, "That was impressive."

He shrugged. "The woman isn't a maniac, just really upset. And maybe feeling that kind of rage we all do when something horrible has happened and we're powerless to change it." He glanced at his watch, then at her. "Sorry, I have to get to the airport, and it's not going to be pleasant."

"I told you...whatever you need to do...do it. I'll hang in the background," Lorena said.

He nodded, and after a few minutes she realized that he was heading for the turnpike. He glanced over at her, a curious smile tugging at his lips. "What brought you to our neck of the woods?" he asked her.

She shrugged, looking out the window. Then she looked at him sharply. "Well, I thought you'd already figured that out. I was racing out to one of the resorts. A spa. To be pampered."

"I'm sure you'll find time to slip out and hit some of the prime places," he said dryly.

"Really?" she murmured.

He couldn't resist a taunting smile. "You do your own hair and nails?" he asked.

"As a matter of fact, I do," she told him.

He shook his head. "You don't look the type," he said.

"You have to look a type to work out here?"

"You'll burn like a tomato in a matter of minutes," he warned her.

"They do make sunscreen," she returned.

"So... I repeat, what are you doing out here?"

"The job at Harry's," she said simply.

"There are nursing jobs all over the state. And most of them not in the Everglades."

She gazed over at him, surprised to realize that she was telling the truth when she said, "I like it out here."

"You're fond of mosquitoes the size of hippos and reptiles that grunt through the night?"

"I think the sunsets out here are some of the most beautiful I've ever seen. As to the alligators…well, they're just part of the environment, really. The birds are glorious. And the pay's exceptional."

"I see. Well, it's still a lonely existence."

It was her turn to smile. "Okay, so it may take an hour to get anywhere, but…it's a straight shot east to Miami and a straight shot west to Naples. Not so bad."

"I guess not. But in bad weather, you can be stuck out here and feel as if you're living in the Twilight Zone."

"You came back out here to work," she said softly.

There was silence for a minute. "This is home for me," he said.

"It's not so far off from home for me," she said.

"It's pretty far."

She glanced at him sharply.

"Jacksonville. I took your license, remember? And now that I know you were flying like a bat out of hell to reach Harry's, I'm more stunned than ever."

"I was starting a new job," she said defensively. "And however far it might be, I *am* from this state." Great. Now he was curious. What if *he* decided to investigate *her*?

She noticed that they had left the turnpike and were following the signs for the airport. He glanced at her again. "I'm meeting with a Metro-Dade detective. We're meeting a detective named Lars Garcia and picking up an old friend of mine." He hesitated just slightly. "That's why I didn't want you along. It's not going to be pleasant. Julie's parents were murdered last night."

"Oh, my God! I'm so sorry."

"I warned you."

"What happened?"

"They were shot," he said flatly.

She decided not to ask any questions for the next few minutes. He'd obviously been deeply affected by the murders.

They parked at the airport. Jesse knew where he was going and walked quickly. Lorena followed him. Outside the North Terminal, he walked over to a man in a plain suit, a man with light brown hair and green eyes, but dark brows and lashes. Even before she was introduced, Lorena knew that this was Lars Garcia.

She felt the keen assessment he gave her. Part of his job, she imagined. Summing people up quickly.

"So you're working out at Harry's?" he murmured.

She didn't have time to answer.

"There she is," Jesse said softly, spotting his old friend, Julie.

"I'll go," Lars Garcia offered.

But Jesse shook his head.

He left Lars and Lorena, and walked toward the dark-haired, exotic-looking Latin beauty who was coming their way. She was wearing glasses, apparently to hide the redness in her eyes, which was apparent when she saw Jesse and took them off. Then she dropped the overnight bag she'd been carrying and went into his arms, sobbing.

Lorena looked down, feeling like an intruder. "It's all right," Lars Garcia said softly.

She looked up at him.

"They're just good friends."

Lorena felt her cheeks flush hotly. "No, no, don't get

the wrong impression. I'm just here…by accident, really. I barely know Officer Crane."

Lars Garcia continued to assess her as Jesse, an arm around Julie, led her to where Lorena and Lars stood waiting.

"Julie, this is Detective Lars Garcia. He's in charge of the case," Jesse said. "And this is… Lorena. Lars, Lorena, Julie Hernandez."

Julie offered Lorena a teary, distraught but somehow still warm smile.

"Julie, I'm so sorry," Lorena murmured, feeling totally inadequate and wrenched by the girl's pain. She could all too easily remember the feelings of agony, frustration and fury, and always the question of why?

And after that, the *who?*

And now?

And now the gut-deep fury and determination that the truth would be known.

"Thank you." Julie looked at her for a long moment, as if sensing Lorena's sincerity. Then she turned to Garcia. "Whoever did this…why? My parents never hurt a soul in their entire lives."

"We're going to find out why," Lars vowed softly. "We need your help, though. We need anything you can give us."

Julie visibly toughened then, summoning her anger and determination from deep within, her inner reserves rising over the natural agony she was feeling. "I was just telling Jesse… I have no idea. They had no enemies. But I promise you, I'll help you in any way I can."

"Are you up to coming to the station with me now?" Lars asked. "It can wait, if you'd rather."

"No. No, I'll go now," Julie said, and swallowed. She looked at Jesse. "Jesse…?"

"Call me when you're done."

She nodded, trying to smile.

Lars took Julie's arm and cast a grateful glance over her dark head at Jesse.

The two walked off.

"I'm so sorry," Lorena said. She had never met the couple, but the sense of loss had seemed to envelop her. Impossible to see Julie and not feel it. She felt horrible, like an intruder, again. "I…wish there were something I could say, do."

Jesse nodded, then said only, "I can get you back now."

The silence, growing awkward between them, lasted as they left the airport, taking the expressway to the Trail, then heading straight down the road that stretched the width of the southern tip of the peninsula.

They passed homes and developments, and then the casino. After that, houses and businesses became few and far between.

She was startled when Jesse suddenly said, "Can you give me another half hour?" He turned and looked at her with those startling eyes of his. She wondered if he had decided he didn't feel quite so much contempt for her, or if he was merely so distracted he'd barely even been aware till then that she was there with him.

"I…of course. Of course. Harry said it was no problem," she murmured.

They pulled off onto something she wasn't sure she would have categorized as a road. As they proceeded along a winding trail, she realized that they were on farmland.

A minute later, she saw the crime tape. Jesse Crane pulled off the road.

"Excuse me. Stay here—I'll be just a minute," he said.

He exited the car, leaving her in the passenger's seat. Lorena hesitated for the briefest fraction of a second, then followed him.

She wasn't about to stay.

Jesse wasn't in the area enclosed by the tape. He was standing just outside of it, talking to a uniformed officer and a man in street clothes who had an ease in being there that suggested he was also a cop.

As she walked up, she could hear the man in street clothes talking. "Yeah, Doc Thiessen has the gator arm…the leg, whatever, that you discovered. I really don't see how it's going to help us. The Hernandezes were killed by bullets, not wildlife run amok!" He saw Lorena approaching before Jesse did, and he watched her, curiously and appreciatively, as she walked up to the scene.

Jesse turned to look at her with annoyance, a serious frown furrowing his brow.

"I told you to wait in the car," he said coldly.

"Hello, ma'am," the young uniformed officer said.

"Yes, hello," the man in plainclothes said. "How do you do? I'm Abe Hershall."

"Officer Gene Valley, ma'am," the uniform said.

"How do you do?" She shook hands with the tall, slender, dark-eyed man who was obviously a detective, and the uniformed officer. Jesse stood by silently, waiting, not apologizing for his rudeness, and certainly not offering any information about her.

"I'm working at Harry's," she said herself.

"The new nurse," Gene Valley said. "Well, welcome to the area."

"Thanks," she said softly.

"Working for old Harry, huh?" Abe Hershall said, shaking his head ruefully. "Well, good for Harry."

"This is a crime scene," Jesse reminded them all. "Ms. Fortier, now that you've met everyone, I believe it's time for me to get you back."

Taking Lorena by an elbow, he steered her forcefully back to the car.

"I can walk on my own," she said.

"I told you to stay in the car."

"It's a million degrees in there." She looked him in the eye. "Who was that?" she asked. "Abe…is he Lars's partner?"

"Yes."

He forced her determinedly back into the car. The door slammed. She gritted her teeth.

"You found a piece of a gator out there?" she asked when he was in the driver's seat.

"This is the Everglades. There are lots of alligators, and naturally, some die." He put the car in gear and started driving, his eyes straight ahead.

"But you found a *piece* of one."

Jesse slammed on the brakes, turned and stared at her, angry. Whether with her, or with himself, she wasn't sure. "Look, we found a piece of an alligator, yes. And I'd appreciate it if you would just shut up about it. I'm trying to keep that bit of information out of the press. You see, I'd really like to know if there's a connection between that and a murder. Damn! This is all my fault. I shouldn't have brought you out here, and I sure as hell shouldn't have counted on you staying in the car just because *I told you to!*"

Lorena looked straight ahead. "I have no intention of leaking any information," she said.

He stared at her. "Really? And should I ask for that as a guarantee, written in stone? After all, I don't know anything about you."

She grated her teeth. "Do I look like someone who would shoot an innocent couple?"

"No. But you don't look like someone who'd be working at Harry's, either," he said sharply.

She let out an explosion of exasperation. "I don't suppose you'd believe I actually like it out here?"

"Right. Nothing like being a nurse at an alligator farm," he murmured.

"Maybe it's just an easy gig," she said.

He didn't reply. Her heart sank. She had a feeling that he was going to know everything there was to know about her within the next forty-eight hours.

Maybe she should just tell him.

Maybe not. He obviously thought of her as some kind of fragile cream puff. Maybe a rich brat playing games. She shouldn't have brought her own car, she thought, hindsight bringing sudden brilliance.

If he found out anything about what she was doing, he might well find a way to get her out of Harry's— fast. Even that evening.

Could he do such a thing? Was he good friends with Harry—or whoever was involved?

She kept silent.

A few minutes later, they drove back into the complex that comprised Harry's Alligator Farm and Museum.

"Thanks," Lorena murmured, getting ready to hop out of the car as quickly as possible.

He caught her hand lightly. She held still, not meeting his eyes, but careful not to make any attempt to jerk free. She realized that he frightened her. Not because she thought he would hurt her, but because he aroused something in her, something emotional. She found herself waiting to tell him everything, wanting just to be with him.

"Be careful," he warned softly.

"Of...?" she murmured.

"Well, an elderly couple was just shot," he said impatiently.

"I'll be all right," she said. Then she pulled free. There was something far too unnerving about his touch. She didn't like the fact that though she barely knew him, she respected him already. Admired him. Even *liked* him. "Thanks."

"I'll be seeing you," he said pleasantly.

"Of course," she said, and then, at last, she managed to flee.

THERE WASN'T MUCH daylight left, but since Ginny had called in to the station several times saying that Billy Ray hadn't yet come home, Jesse decided it was time to check out his fishing spots.

Billy Ray was lazy, a creature of habit, and Jesse wasn't surprised when he found the man's beat-up old boat at his first stop in the vast grounds off the Trail.

The boat had been floating in the middle of the canal—already suspicious—and there was no sign of Billy Ray.

Jesse began walking along the embankment. At

first he let his mind wander, mentally reminding himself that he had a record of Lorena Fortier's driver's license, enough to find out something about the woman. Frankly, he admitted to himself, he was worried about her. He could hardly say that he knew her from their two encounters, but there was something about her eyes, about the very real compassion she had shown the elderly woman, that made him feel she was—despite his original assessment—a decent human being.

There was something about her that made him feel a lot more, as well. Now that he'd gotten closer to her, it was far more than the simple fact that she was stunning, though that was good for a swift, hot rise of the libido. She was quick to show empathy, and in the right way. She seemed to sense pain and use her warmth to heal it. Her energy was electric.

Sensual.

He swore out loud, reminding himself that he was here trying to determine what had happened to Billy Ray Hare.

Still…

She had roused not just his senses, but thoughts that he had kept at bay for a long time. There was nothing casual about her. She evoked real interest—and very real desire. But, he realized, not the kind that could be easily sated, then forgotten.

What was it about her?

Her eyes? Her behavior? Or the way she looked? Like a blond goddess, tempting in the extreme.

He mentally shook his head, reminding himself again that this wasn't the time to discover that there was life not just in his limbs, but in his soul. Two good people had been murdered, and Billy Ray was missing. This definitely wasn't the time to be feeling a stab of desire just because a woman had walked into his neck of the woods.

Still, even as he concentrated his attention on the wet ground, the endless saw grass and the canal, he felt a strange sense of tension regarding *her*.

She was involved. Somehow, she was involved.

Just as that thought came to his mind, he found Billy Ray.

What was left of him.

SALLY FINISHED UP with the day's entrance receipts, locked her strongbox and papers in the safe, and smoothed back her hair. Quite a day. All the commotion.

So much going on. Admittedly, most of the time so little went on here. That was why she had to make things happen. With that in mind, she started humming.

She was done for the day.

She walked determinedly down the hallway. News, any little bit of it, spread like wildfire around here. She loved to be the first to know any little tidbit.

She headed across the center of the complex.

"Hey, Sally!"

She smiled at the man leaning against one of the support poles.

"Hey, yourself," she said softly. Teasingly. It got boring out here, after all.

"Got anything for me?" he asked softly, since there were still both tourists and co-workers around.

She walked up to him, smiled, placed a hand lightly on his chest. "Maybe," she murmured seductively.

"Maybe?"

"Well, it depends."

"On what?"

"On what *you've* got for *me*," she whispered.

She let her hand linger for a moment. A promise, just like her whisper. Then she walked away.

She could be warm; she could give.

But she fully intended to receive in return. After all, there was pleasure.

And then there was business.

THE GATES HAD CLOSED; the last of the tourists were flooding out as Lorena returned. She headed straight for her room, a quick shower and a change of clothes.

Though she wasn't accustomed to choosing her wardrobe for the purpose of seduction, she did so that night. A soft, pale blue halter dress seemed the right thing—cool enough for the summer heat, a garment that molded over the human form. She brushed her hair until it shone, then played with different ways to part it. She found a few of the effects amusing, but decided to go back to a simple side part and a sleek look. A touch of makeup, and she was off.

She found Dr. Michael Preston in the company cafeteria. The kitchen was centrally located between the employee dining area/lounge and the massive buffet area where visitors were welcome. During the day, a head chef worked with two assistants and three buffet hostesses. By night, only the offerings of the day and two cafeteria workers remained.

Alligator—sautéed, fried and even barbecued—was always on the menu. Lorena had dined on it in the past, but tonight she didn't want it, not in any form.

As she'd expected, she saw Michael Preston—who hadn't ordered gator, either—sitting with the keepers, the blond Australian, Hugh Humphrey, and the tall, striking Seminole, Jack Pine.

The three men rose as she approached. Jack whistled softly. "Wow! And welcome. Are you joining us?"

"If you don't mind."

"Are you kidding?" Hugh demanded pleasantly.

"You're definitely a breath of beautiful fresh air around this place," Jack assured her.

"Please," Michael Preston said, pulling out a chair. She smiled, thanked him and sat down.

"I heard we had a bit of a freak-out today, and that you went with Jesse to take the woman home," Jack said. "Bizarre, huh?"

"Her friend was...eaten," Lorena said softly. "Why she was out here after that, I don't know."

Michael made an impatient sound. "Do you know what happens most of the time when gators kill? Some idiot thinks you can feed them like you feed the ducks at a pond." He shook his head. "First we destroy their natural habitat. Every year, development spreads farther west, into the Everglades. Naturally there are waterways. Then people wonder what the alligators are doing in their canals."

"Well, trust me," Jack said ruefully, his tone light and teasing, "you're not going to stop progress."

Hugh looked at Lorena seriously. "You're not afraid of being eaten, are you?"

She shook her head. "Trust me, I have no intention of feeding the gators. I'll leave that to you guys."

"Man is not the alligator's natural prey," Michael said. "Go out to Shark Valley. You can walk those trails, and, trust me, there are hundreds of gators around, but they don't bother anyone."

"It really is unusual, and there's always a reason, when a human is attacked," Jack explained. "Most of the time Hugh and I get called because a gator has strayed into a heavily populated area. We catch it and bring it back out to the wilds. The end."

"Do you ever keep the ones you 'rescue'?" Lorena asked.

"No. We breed our own alligators here," Michael said. "Harry's been here a long time now. He started up with a small place when they were still really endangered, so a couple were captured. But now all our gators are farm raised, because they do make good eating. And their hides make spectacular leather. Farms like this one are an important part of the state's economy. They're much more than just tourist attractions."

Lorena smiled. "They really are fascinating creatures," she told Michael. "I'm absolutely intrigued by your work."

"Cool," Jack said, folding his arms over his chest and leaning back. "We get a nurse who not only patches up our scrapes, she's into the entire operation. I hear that you don't mind working with the tour groups, either."

She shrugged. "I'd die of boredom here if I weren't interested."

"Hey, did you want something to eat?" Jack asked her.

She turned slightly to see that one of the remaining kitchen workers was standing by her side.

"Mary, have you met Lorena yet?" Jack continued, speaking to the heavyset woman at his side.

Mary shook her head, then pointed across the room to where Harry was sitting, engaged in conversation with Sally.

"The boss said to check on you," Mary said, looking

at Lorena. "Usually people come up to the buffet. So are you hungry? You'd better eat now. We break down in half an hour, then there's nothing except the vending machines until morning—unless you want to drive for an hour to find something open." She shrugged. "You go into Miami, you got some places open twenty-four hours a day. But you want to drive back here in the middle of the night?" Mary shuddered. She'd been looking grim, but then she smiled. "You want some alligator?"

"Um, actually, no, thank you," Lorena said. "Is there another choice?"

"There's always chicken," Michael offered, grinning at last.

"How about a salad?" Lorena asked. She wasn't a vegetarian; she just didn't think that at the moment she wanted meat of any sort. Especially crocodilian.

"Caesar?" Mary suggested.

"Lovely."

"Of course, we do offer the caesar with a choice of chicken, sirloin or alligator," Mary said.

"A plain caesar would be perfect," Lorena said.

Mary shrugged, as if a plain caesar was probably the least appetizing thing in the world. "Something to drink?"

Lorena ordered iced tea and thanked Mary, assuring her that she would know to go to the buffet herself from then on.

When Mary was gone, Jack Pine nudged Lorena, his dark eyes dancing with amusement. "She's all right, really. Just a bit grim."

"She doesn't like alligators at all," Michael said.

"Why does she work out here?" Lorena asked.

"Harry pays well," Michael said. He leaned forward

suddenly. "The guys and I were going to head to the casino for a few hours. Want to come?"

"We'd love to have you," Jack said.

"You look far too lovely to hang around here," Hugh said, grinning.

If they were all leaving, this might well be her best chance to get into Michael's laboratory. She yawned. "Actually, I'd love to take you guys up on that, but at a later date? I'm just getting accustomed to my new surroundings, and I'm feeling pretty tired."

"You really should come," Michael said, placing a hand over hers.

She smiled at him, as if enjoying the contact. "I will. Next time," she said sweetly.

Mary arrived with her salad. The men remained politely waiting for her to eat, then rose together when she was done. Lorena said that she would walk them out to the parking lot, then head for her room.

The three men climbed into Jack Pine's Range Rover, and she waved.

As soon as they were gone, she headed for the inner workings of the museum.

And Dr. Michael Preston's lab.

LARS AND ABE stood by Jesse on the embankment, watching as the M.E. bagged the remnants of Billy Ray.

At the moment, Jesse felt the weight of the world on his shoulders.

There was no one else who could go to see Ginny. This was going to be his responsibility, and with the Metro-Dade force on the scene, that meant he could go to her now.

But he hesitated, seeing the floodlights illuminate

the immediate darkness and feeling the oppressive heat of the ebony beyond.

"I don't believe it," Lars said, staring in the direction of the M.E., shaking his head.

"I'm not quite sure I do, either," Jesse said. He pointed. "The best I can figure it, Billy Ray was in his boat. His shotgun was still in it, and it had been fired. It looks as if an alligator actually rammed the boat, Billy fell out, and…well, you know how they kill, shaking their prey, then drowning it."

"Alligators don't ram boats," Lars said.

"Looks like this one did," Jesse said.

Abe frowned, staring at Jesse. "Alligators may follow a boat, looking for a hand out—literally." He smiled grimly. "But they don't ram boats. I'd say maybe someone was out here with Billy Ray. Maybe they fought. Maybe Billy Ray even shot at him. Then the fight sent him overboard, and a hungry old male might have been around. A really hungry old male, since we all know gators don't choose humans."

"Gentlemen, this is my neck of the woods, and God knows, I want tourists out here as much as anyone, but I'd say it was time we get some kind of warning out," Jesse said.

"Warning?" Abe protested. "Like what? Don't head into the Everglades? Killer alligators on the loose?"

"Yeah, something like that," Jesse said flatly.

Abe shook his head. "Jesse, you're nuts. What do you want to do, destroy the entire economy out here?"

"I'll tell you this, I intend to issue a warning," Jesse said.

"Hey, you do what you want," Abe said.

"What the hell are you saying?" Jesse demanded,

his temper rising. "We all know that Billy Ray was killed by a gator."

"How do we know that?" Abe demanded. "Seriously. You do an autopsy I don't know about?"

Jesse stared at him, incredulous. "What?"

"We have a ripped-up body. You said yourself that Billy Ray's gun had been shot. Maybe someone shot back at him, he wound up in the water, bleeding, and then the gator attacked him. That's a far more likely scenario."

"Stop it," Lars protested. "Both of you. We've got a bad situation here."

"Yeah, we do. A couple shot to death—with the remains of an alligator found nearby. Now a fellow who knew this place better than any living human being, killed by an alligator. If that isn't enough—" Jesse said.

"That couple were killed because they saw something going on in the swamp—I'd lay odds on it. And alligators don't shoot people," Lars argued. "These incidents are totally unrelated."

Jesse just stared at him, so irritated he longed to take a jab at Abe's out-thrust, obstinate jaw. Instead, he turned and walked away. "You do what you want. So will I."

"Hey!" Lars called after him.

Jesse turned back.

"Jesse...you may want to be on the lookout for a... well, I don't know. A rogue alligator. A big one," Lars suggested.

"Yeah. Are you going to contact the rangers, or should I?" Jesse asked.

"I'll see that they're notified," Lars assured him grimly.

Abe snorted. "Yeah. We'll handle this one by the book. This is your neck of the woods, Jesse. Billy Ray was one of yours. Homicide only comes in when we've got a murder. We'll see that the site is investigated, and then we'll sign off on it. This is your ball game."

"And I'll get warnings out on Indian land. And I also intend to arrange a hunt."

"It ain't season, Jesse," Abe said.

Jesse crossed his arms over his chest. "Maybe not, but it *is* tribal land. Like you said, it's my call. At the least, we're talking about a nuisance animal. I'll be taking steps."

Abe threw up his hands.

"This one is your call, Jesse," Lars told him.

"Fine. And you know the call I've made. You put out the warnings in your territory."

"Because of one alligator?"

"How do we know it's just one?" Jesse demanded.

"And how do we know Billy Ray didn't just drink himself silly, then irritate the creature—a normal, everyday predator that happens to live out here—and make the mistake of going in right where a big boy was hungry?"

"What was an alligator limb doing out where Hector and Maria were killed?" Jesse demanded.

Abe shook his head. "People murdered with big guns—and a natural predator attack. There's no damned connection!"

"Hey," Lars said. "The matter will be under investigation."

"Abe, I'm warning you, there could be a lot more trouble," Jesse said.

"Great. I'm warned," Abe said.

"Jesse, no one is going at this with a closed mind," Lars assured him. "Hell, I'm a cop, not a kindergarten teacher. We're professionals. We'll complete our investigation of the scene and sign this one over to you. Abe, dammit—you know as well as I do that anything is possible. All right, children?"

"Sure," Abe said.

"Yeah," Jesse said. "You're right. And now I have to go talk to a woman about the fact that her husband is dead."

Abe snorted. "She should be relieved."

Lars exploded, swearing.

Jesse turned away.

He couldn't put it off any longer. He had to go to see Ginny.

And then...

Then he would have to talk to Julie.

The night ahead seemed bleak indeed.

Chapter Five

Since she was carrying a lock pick in her purse, Lorena had no problem waving with a smile as the car drove away, then heading straight back inside and down the hall to Dr. Michael Preston's lab.

She stood for several seconds in the hallway, but the place was entirely empty.

There were guards on duty, of course. But they were outside, protecting the alligator farm. She had made a point in the beginning of seeing whether there were cameras in the hallways, but there weren't—not unless they were exceptionally well hidden.

She headed for the door, reaching into her purse.

"Lorena!"

Stunned, she spun around. Michael was there in the hallway, right behind her.

"Hey!" she said cheerfully, approaching him quickly.

"I thought you were going to get some rest tonight?" he said, frowning.

"I changed my mind. I was hoping to find you."

"In the hallway? You just waved goodbye to us."

"I don't know—sixth sense, maybe. You're back, and I'm so glad. I can still go with you. If you're still going."

He nodded. "I forgot my cell phone, so I came back to get it."

"Great. I'll wait for you."

He nodded, still appearing puzzled, but she kept her smile in place, following him into the lab.

The hatchlings squeaked from their terrariums.

Lorena stood politely by the door, waiting. As she had before, she inventoried what she could see of the lab.

The file cabinets. Michael's desk. The pharmaceutical shelves. The computer.

He took his cell phone from the desktop, then joined her. She linked arms with him, and felt the tension in him ease.

"Are you a poker player?" he asked her.

"Not really," she admitted.

"There's not too much else," he warned.

"I love slot machines," she assured him.

He smiled back at her. Apparently her attempt at flirtation was working. He slipped an arm around her shoulders. He was a good-looking man, with a sense of humor, and though it seemed he sometimes wondered if he were too much of an egghead in comparison with the rugged handlers, he apparently also had faith in his own charisma. "Let's head out, then, shall we?" he asked, and there was a husky note in his voice. If she was happy in his company, it apparently wasn't too big a surprise to him.

Then again, she'd been trying to keep the right balance. Flirt just the right amount with the bunch of them.

"Let's head out," she agreed, and she fell into step with him, aware of his arm around her shoulder—and also aware that the lab was where she really needed to be.

JESSE HAD A feeling that Ms. Lorena Fortier from Jacksonville would be quite surprised when she learned that the Miccosukee police department currently consisted of a staff of twenty-seven, nine of them civilian employees, the other eighteen officers deployed throughout the community in three main areas: north of the Everglades in Broward County; the Krome Avenue area, encompassing the casino and environs; and the largest center of tribal operations, on the Tamiami Trail. The pay was good, and the Miccosukee cops were a respected group. The department had been created in '76, because most of the tribal areas were so remote that a specific force was necessary to protect the community, and to work with both the state and federal agencies in tracking down crime.

Jesse wondered if Lorena was under the impression that he was working as the Lone Ranger.

Before he made his dreaded trip to Ginny's place, he returned to the station. His crews were up on everything that happened in the jurisdiction, but he hadn't been back in himself yet, and he disliked being in a situation where communication wasn't tight as a drum.

The night crew was coming on, but he was in time to catch the nine-to-fivers and give everyone his personal briefing on both the double homicide and the death of Billy Ray.

He liked being at the office; he wasn't a one-man show, but the department was still small enough that every officer and civilian employee knew that they mattered, and that their opinions were respected. He got the different departments researching activities in the area, possible drug connections, the backgrounds of Hector and Maria, and anything that might strike their minds as unusual, or any kind of connection.

Barry Silverstein, one of the night patrolmen, was especially interested in the alligator limb that had been brought to the veterinarian for examination. "Strange that you found only a piece," he said. "Think maybe we're looking for a poacher?" he asked.

"Could be," Jesse said. "But it's not likely. We have an alligator season, and a license is easy enough to obtain. Besides, the alligator farms have pretty much taken the profit out of poaching."

"Kids?" Brenda Hardy, the one woman on night duty, inquired. "You know, teenagers, maybe. Or college students. Say that the piece of the alligator has nothing to do with the murders. Maybe some kids pledging a fraternity or just making ridiculous dares to one another."

"I sure hope it's not a trend," Barry said. "They may have gotten that gator, but you start playing around with some of the big boys out there...well, hell, we know what they're capable of."

"Poor Billy Ray," Brenda said sadly, shaking her head. She was a pretty woman, tall and slim, and all business. She was light-skinned and light-haired, probably of Germanic or Nordic descent. You didn't have to be Native American to be on the force. Barry, who was Jewish and had had ancestors in the States so long he didn't know where they'd originally come from, always liked to tease her that she was an Indian wannabe. Brenda had once gravely shut him up by assuring him that she had been a Native American in her previous life.

"I'll tell you frankly that this situation scares the hell out of me. These people are brutal and ruthless. Everyone has to be alert," Jesse warned.

George Osceola, one of the Native officers on the force, a tall man with huge shoulders and a calm, controlled way of speaking that made him even more imposing, had been watching the entire time. He spoke then. "Jesse, you think these incidents are related, don't you. How?"

"That's what I can't figure. Murders that cold-blooded are usually drug related. And we're not ruling that out," Jesse said.

"Could we be dealing with some kind of cult?" George asked.

"I don't know. What I do believe is that we've got to get to the bottom of it fast. George, ask questions, see if anyone has seen anything out of the ordinary. People coming through who aren't out to enjoy nature or a day at the village. Strangers who hang around. Anything out of the ordinary. *Anything.* Metro-Dade homicide is working the murders. I'm afraid we may find the killers closer to home."

"We'll all be on it," Brenda said.

Jesse nodded. "Brenda, do me a favor. Get background investigations busy for me, will you?"

"On the Hernandez family?" Brenda asked, sounding puzzled.

"No. On a woman named Lorena Fortier. I just wrote her a ticket, so we'll have her driver's license information. Find out more about where she comes from, what she's been doing."

"Lorena Fortier?"

"She just started working at Harry's."

"All right," Brenda said, still puzzled, but asking no more questions.

"You going out to Ginny's now?" Barry asked.

"Yeah," Jesse said. "And then to see Julie."

No one replied. No one offered to take on the responsibility. He didn't want them to, and they knew it. These were things he had to do.

He left to see Ginny, and it was rough. As rough as he had expected.

Eventually he left Ginny with her sister and niece, both of whom apparently thought that Billy Ray had come by accident to an end that he deserved. Thankfully, they weren't saying that to Ginny, though; they were just holding her and soothing her. Anne, Ginny's niece, had told him that as soon as possible, she was going to take her aunt away for a while. For the moment, they had called the doctor, who had prescribed a sedative for her.

Before he left, Ginny had gripped his hand. Her large dark eyes had touched his.

"Help me, Jesse—please. Find out...find out what happened."

"Ginny, he met with a mean gator," her sister said.

But Ginny shook her head. "Billy Ray knew gators. Jesse, you have to help. I have to know...*why.* Oh, God, oh, God... Jesse I need to know, and you're the only one who can help."

With her words ringing in his ears, he had gone on to meet Julie.

Hell of a night.

So now he sat with his old friend in the upstairs bar of the casino hotel where she had chosen to stay. Julie had told him that she appreciated his offer to let her stay at his place, but she had wanted to be closer to the city and couldn't quite bring herself to stay in her parents' house.

He agreed that she shouldn't stay at her folks' house—certainly not alone. Neither he nor the Metro-Dade police had any idea what had happened, and the houses in that area were way too few and far between for him to feel safe with her there.

"I'm telling you, Jesse, there's no way my folks were connected to anything criminal," Julie said, at a loss. "I'd give my eyeteeth to help. In fact... I think I could kill with my own bare hands, if I knew who did this. But they were as honest as the day is long."

"I know that, Julie."

She sighed, running a finger around the glass of wine she had ordered. "I'm glad you're on this, Jesse. The other guys...they didn't know my folks."

"Lars is a good man. So is Abe. A bit of an ass, but a good detective."

That brought a hint of a smile to her lips. "Still, no matter what you tell people...everybody seems certain that my dad had turned a blind eye to some drug deal, at the very least. The thing is, you and I both know that there was no such thing going on."

"Of course." He patted her hand. "Did your mom or dad ever say anything to you about anything strange going on out there?"

Julie shook her head. "No." She hesitated, frowning. "Actually, once..." She fell silent, shrugging.

"Once what?"

"Oh, something silly. It can't have anything to do with what happened," Julie said.

Jesse touched her hand. "Julie, I don't care how silly you may think something sounds. Tell me what it is."

"Um, well, I lose track of time, but a few days ago, maybe a week, when I was talking to my mom, she was getting into talking about ETs. You know, extra-terrestrials."

"Oh?"

"She said there were weird lights. I'm sure it was just someone out in an airboat, but…"

"But?"

"Well, my mom was getting on in years, but her vision was good. She thought the lights were coming from the sky. That's why she got it into her head that aliens were searching the Everglades."

"A lot of planes come in that way," Jesse pointed out.

"The lights from planes don't stay still."

"Helicopters," Jesse said.

Julie shrugged. Then her face crumpled and she began to cry. Jesse didn't try to tell her that it would be okay. He just came around the table and held her.

Helicopters. If anything big had been going on—the police searching for someone, for instance—he would have known about it.

Maria had had fine eyesight, no more fanciful than the next person. And she had seen lights.

Jesse knew that there had been an airboat behind the house the night Julie's parents had been killed. That wasn't surprising. Airboats abounded. But helicopters…

They were uncommon, especially in that area. Not unless someone was looking for something.

But in the middle of the night?

"Jesse, what could it have been?" Julie whispered, as if she had been reading his thoughts.

"I don't know. But I swear, Julie, I will find out."

THE CASINO DIDN'T compare with a place in Las Vegas or Atlantic City—there were no roulette tables and no craps—but it was nice, and it was apparently quite convenient for people in Miami with a free night but not the time to really get away.

It was thriving when they arrived.

The three men tried to encourage Lorena to try her hand at one of the poker tables, but she managed to convince them that she preferred slots and would be happy wandering around, just getting to know the place. There were several restaurants, and though there were tables offering free coffee, she opted for café con leche at the twenty-four-hour deli. She noted the numerous security officers and stopped to chat with one young man. His name was Bob Walker, and he had bright blue eyes, thanks to a dad who had come to the States from the Canary Islands, and superb bone structure, thanks to a Seminole mom. He told her that casino security departments and the Miccosukee Police were two separate entities, but of course they worked together, just as Security would work with the Metro-Dade police or any other law enforcement agency. He'd sounded a little touchy at first, but as they spoke, he explained with a grin, "Too many gamblers drink, lose and get belligerent. And they think we can't take care of them. We do. We have the authority."

She grinned. "I don't intend to get rowdy," she assured him.

He flushed, and she thanked him and went on.

The place was big, and she wandered a while before finding a slot machine that looked like fun. It had a little mouse, and a round where you got points for picking the right cheese. She liked the game—it might be stealing her money, but it was entertaining.

Out twenty bucks, she left to walk around some more.

It was fascinating, she thought. The crowd was truly representative of the area, running the entire ethnic gamut. Miccosukee, Hispanic, Afro-American, and whatever the blend was that ended up as Caucasian on a census form.

She could see the poker tables and was aware that, from their separate poker games, the guys were also keeping an eye on her.

She was frustrated, throwing away quarters when she should have thought of a better lie when she had run into Michael in the hallway. This would have been the perfect time to have gotten into the lab. Still, since the mouse game was diverting, she went back to it. She was just choosing her cheese bonus when she was startled by an already familiar voice.

"What are you doing here?"

She looked up to see Jesse Crane, leaning casually against her machine. It made her uneasy to realize that his scent was provocative, and that he looked even better in his tailored shirt, khakis and sport jacket. When she glanced up, the bright green of his eyes against the bronze of his face was intense. She wouldn't want to face him at an inquiry, that was certain.

She wondered what it was about certain people that made them instantly attractive. About certain *men,* she corrected herself, and the thought was even more disturbing. Michael Preston was definitely good-looking; Hugh was charming; Jack Pine exuded a quiet strength. But Jesse Crane…just the sound of his voice seemed like a sexual stimulant. The least brush of his fingers spoke erotically to her innermost recesses. She was tempted to touch him, because just the feel of crisp fabric over muscled flesh would be arousing.

A blush was rising to her cheeks. She looked away from his eyes, but her gaze fell on his chest. And then below.

She closed her eyes.

"Hello?" he said softly.

What *was* she doing here? She forced herself to focus. To shake off the ridiculous sensation of instant seduction and sensuality.

Nothing, frankly, accomplishing nothing. "Um… gambling," she murmured.

She arched a brow, shrugging as she looked at him and hit the button on the machine again. "Losing money. What about you?"

He shrugged. "I live in the area."

"So do I, remember?"

"Who did you come with?"

"A group from Harry's."

"And who would that group be?"

"Michael, Jack and Hugh." She stared at the machine, trying not to let him see her mind working. "Are you out for a night on the town? Or just passing through?" Her machine did some binging and banging—three cheeses in a row. She had a return of ten dollars. Not bad.

"Why?" he asked.

"Just curious. Well, actually, if you're heading out…" She yawned, moving away from the machine. "I'm not much of a gambler. I was thinking of going back, but I came with the guys."

"I'll give you a ride," he told her. "Who should we tell you're leaving? Michael?"

"Um…any of them, I guess," she murmured. *Not Michael. He might get suspicious.* "Hugh is right there—we'll just tell him."

She slid off the stool, ready to head for Hugh's poker table.

"Aren't you forgetting something?" Jesse asked.

"What?"

"Your money."

"Oh. I didn't lose it all?"

"No. There's more than a hundred dollars there."

"Oh. Of course I want it," she said.

His eyes seemed to drill right through her. "Do you?" he inquired lightly. "I didn't think money means a thing to you."

She ignored him and gave her attention to the machine, hitting the "cash out" button.

"You have to wait for an attendant," he told her. "I'll let Hugh know you're leaving."

"Sure. Thanks."

The place was busy, the wait for an attendant long. She was ready to leave her winnings for some lucky stranger, she was so antsy, but she didn't know whether she was being watched. By the time they actually left, she fumed silently, the men might well be right behind them.

Finally, money stuffed into her bag, Lorena hurried past the slots and found Jesse waiting for her at the end of the row.

She quickly checked to make sure that the three men from the alligator farm were still at their tables.

They were.

"Sure you want to go?" Jesse inquired.

"Yes, thank you."

As they turned to leave, he set his palm against the small of her back, nothing more than a polite gesture.

Even so, she felt that touch as if she had connected with a live electric current.

Outside, Jesse didn't speak as he politely seated her on the passenger side and slid behind the wheel.

She felt the silence.

"Thanks for taking me back," she said nervously.

"Not a problem."

Again there was silence. Uncomfortable silence. It should have been a casual drive. It wasn't. It felt as if the air between them was combustible.

"Is our casino a little too tame for you?" he asked at last.

"No. Honestly, I liked it a lot. All I ever play is slots, anyway. I don't understand craps, so it doesn't matter to me if there's a table or not. I guess I'm just not that much of a gambler."

"I'd say you were."

"Pardon?"

He glanced at her sharply. "Oh, you take chances. Racing out here like the wind. Working at Harry's. Going out with three men you've barely met. Especially when there have just been two truly gruesome murders in the area." His tone was amazingly matter-of-fact.

"I hardly think I'm in danger with my co-workers."

He didn't say any more until they had taken the turn into Harry's. She was digging in her purse for the pass that would open the door after hours when he startled her by leaning over and gripping her shoulder. The force was electric, and when she looked at him, she was certain she had guilt written all over her features.

"I really don't understand why you're lying to me. Or what makes you think I'm such a fool that I believe you. What are you doing here?" he demanded roughly.

"Working!"

"You know I'll have you checked out by morning," he said.

She prayed that he couldn't feel the trembling that was suddenly racing through her.

"Go right ahead. Check me out. I'm an RN. You'll find that to be a fact." She reached for the door handle.

"You're playing with fire."

"I'm working. Earning a living."

"Two people, shot. I'd bet everything I have that the killer or killers didn't even know them. It was cold-blooded murder, as cold as it gets."

"Look, I know you're going to check me out. Believe me, you won't find a criminal record. I'm out here to work."

"Right." The green of his eyes was sharp, even in the dim light. "You've come down here to start over, start a new life, that's all."

"May I get out of the car now?"

He released her. The sudden loss of his touch created a chill.

Tell him the truth!

But she couldn't. She had nothing to go on. And he couldn't help, not if she couldn't offer him some kind of proof. And, anyway, could she be certain, absolutely certain, that he wasn't in any way involved?

Actually, yes. Somewhere deep inside, based on instinct, she simply knew the man was completely ethical.

But she didn't dare speak. He would send her packing.

"I'll tell you what you're not," he said softly.

"Oh?"

"A very good liar. So whatever you're up to, God help you."

She stared straight at him. "I am a registered nurse."

"And what else?"

"I dabbled in psychology, but a lot of those classes went toward the nursing degree."

"So you came down here to bandage knees and psychoanalyze the great American alligator?" he inquired dryly. "What else should I know about you?"

"There's this—I'm really tired," she told him.

"And stubborn as hell. You've barely arrived and everything has gone insane. So I'm going to hope that you're not dangerously stupid—or carelessly reckless."

She wondered how he could simply look at her and be able to read everything about her. Or was she that transparent to everyone?

It's just him, she thought with annoyance. Even when he wasn't touching her, it somehow felt as if he was. And even when he grilled her, she was tempted to lean closer to him, to do anything just to touch him, feel a sense of warmth. Even with so much at stake, no matter how she tried to control her mind, it kept running to thoughts of what it would be like just to lie beside him....

"May I get out of the car now?" she asked again, once more feeling drawn to tell him that she actually wanted to stay. Put her head on his shoulders. Tell him the whole truth. But she didn't dare.

"Well, I can't arrest you. At the moment." He turned away from her, shaking his dark head. "Good night, Ms. Fortier. And lock your door," he said.

"I intend to," she assured him, then exited the car as

quickly as she could. Her fingers slipped on the little plastic ID entry card. She had to work it three times.

At last the door opened.

Jesse waited until she was inside, then drove away.

When he was gone, she didn't bother heading toward her own room. She walked straight to Michael Preston's lab. With no one around, she surprised herself with her ability to quickly pick the lock.

She knew it was dangerously stupid as she checked the big wall clock over the door, but she didn't stop. The hatchlings began to squeal the minute she entered the room.

Almost as if they sensed prey.

She ignored the sound and started with the desk drawers, then the computer. She knew that she would need a password to access his important files, but she hoped to study his general entries and discover whether he was involved or not.

The clock ticked as she worked. She read and read, keeping an eye on the clock.

Almost an hour since she had left the casino.

Regretfully, she turned off the computer and made a last survey to assure herself she'd left nothing out of order.

Then she left the room, quietly closing the door behind her. She listened for the lock to automatically slip into place.

Just in time. As she hurried down the hall, she heard voices. She quickly turned the corner, out of sight.

"If you're not bright enough to ask that woman out on a real date, I will."

Lorena recognized the voice. It was Hugh.

Michael answered, laughing dryly, "Yeah, well, I

kind of thought that she was interested. But she lit out like a bat out of hell once Jesse arrived."

"She's not a poker player. One of us should have stayed with her."

"Is that it?" Michael said dryly. "Women *have* been known to find Jesse appealing."

"Yeah, and then they find out that they're lusting after the unobtainable."

"He won't be grieving forever," Michael said. "And either she went with him because she wanted to, or..."

"Or what?" Hugh demanded sharply.

"Or she wanted to get back here without the three of us."

She heard the rattle of the lab doorknob then. "Locked," he murmured.

"I'm asking her out," Hugh said. "For an airboat ride. That's innocent enough."

"Hey, every man for himself, huh?" Michael said.

Hugh laughed. "Yep, every man for himself."

She heard the lab door open and shut. Not knowing if Hugh had joined Michael or would be heading on down the hallway, Lorena fled.

As soon as she reached her own room, she thought of Jesse's warning and made sure her own door was locked.

Then she dragged a chair in front of it, wedging it tightly beneath the knob.

Still, it was a long time before she slept.

JESSE SAT OUTSIDE the alligator farm complex, watching.

He'd left, parked on the embankment, and waited.

Once he'd seen Preston's car return, he'd counted

the seconds carefully, then slipped his car back into gear to follow.

Just in the shadows, off the drive near the main entrance, he parked.

He spent the night in the car, his senses on alert.

The grunts of the gators, loud in the night, sounded now and then, sometimes just one or two, sometimes a cacophony.

Strange creatures. He'd been around them all his life. They were an amazing species, having survived longer than almost any other creature to have walked the earth.

Their calls and cries could be eerie, though.

He stayed until daybreak, waiting, though for what, he wasn't certain. Something. Some sign of danger.

Dawn broke. Light came softly, filling the horizon with pastels. There was a breeze. Birds cried and soared overhead.

He began to feel like a fool.

Then he heard the scream.

Chapter Six

Lorena bolted out of the bed, stunned and disoriented. The first sharp, staccato shriek that had awakened her had been followed by other screams and cries.

She threw on a robe and went flying out of her room, down the hall, and then burst out back to the ponds, the area from which the sounds of distress were still coming.

Then she heard the distant sound of sirens.

It was far too early for the gates to have opened to tourists, and she couldn't imagine what had happened. Her heart was thundering as she saw that most of the employees had gathered around the deep trench pond where Old Elijah was kept.

The biggest, meanest alligator in the place.

At first she stood on the periphery of the crowd, trying to ascertain what had happened, listening to the shouts that rose around her.

"How in hell did *he* fall in?" one of the waitresses asked, incredulous.

"Roger has been a guard here from the beginning... what would make him lean far enough over to fall in?" asked one of the ticket-takers.

"Jesse's in there now. He'll get him out," a feminine voice said.

Lorena swung around to see that Sally Dickerson was there, threading her fingers through her long red hair. She turned to stare at Lorena. Where everyone else seemed to have eyes filled with concern, Sally's had a gleam. She was enjoying the excitement.

"What?" Lorena said.

"Jesse's gone in. He'll get Roger out."

Lorena wasn't sure who she pushed out of the way then, but she rushed to the concrete rim of the great dipped pond and natural habitat that held Old Elijah.

There was a man on the ground, next to the concrete wall. Jack Pine and Hugh Humphrey were there at the side of the wall, maneuvering some kind of rope-rigged gurney down to the fallen guard, who was apparently unconscious.

There was Jesse.

And there was Old Elijah.

The way the habitat was set up, there was the concrete wall and rim, a pond area, and then a re-creation of a wetland hummock.

The great alligator had so far remained on the other side of the water. He watched with ancient black eyes as Jesse Crane moved with care to manipulate the body of the fallen guard with the greatest care possible onto the gurney.

Jesse was no fool. He kept his eye on the alligator the whole time.

"Where the hell is Harry with that tranq gun?" Jack demanded hoarsely.

"Got him!" Jesse shouted. "Haul him up, haul him up!"

Tense, giving directions to one another as they

brought up the gurney, the men were careful to raise it without unbalancing the unconscious figure held in place by buckled straps. Jesse helped guide the gurney until it was over his head.

And all the time, Old Elijah watched.

Motionless, still as death, only the eyes alive.

Others jumped in to help as the gurney rose. Jesse reached for the rope ladder that he'd come down and started up.

And then Old Elijah moved.

He was like a bullet, a streak of lightning. Someone screamed.

The massive jaws opened.

They snapped shut.

They caught the tail end of the rope ladder, and the great head of the beast began to thrash back and forth.

Jesse, nearing the top, teetered dangerously. A collective cry rose; then he caught the rim of the concrete barrier and hauled himself over.

At the same time, they heard the whistle of a shot.

Harry had arrived, holding a huge tranquilizer gun on his shoulder.

The dart struck Old Elijah on the shoulder.

At first, it was as if a fly had landed on his back, nothing more.

The gator backed away, drawing the remnants of the rope ladder with him. Then, as if he were some type of blow-up toy with the air seeping from him, Old Elijah fell. The eyes that had blazed with such an ancient predatory fervor went blank.

The crowd was cheering Jesse; med techs were racing up, and more officers had arrived to control the space and let the emergency techs work.

Jack slammed a hand on Jesse's shoulder. Hugh shook his head and fell back against the barrier, relieved.

Jesse looked down into the enclosure, shaking his head as he stared at Old Elijah. Then his gaze rose, almost instinctively, and met Lorena's.

She stared back, oddly frightened to see the way his eyes narrowed as he regarded her, filled with suspicion. His mouth was hard. She flushed; he didn't look away.

Someone caught his attention, and he turned.

"Damn, Harry, it took you long enough to get that gun," Jack called, shaking his head.

"Jack Pine, you're the damned handler, so get a handle on what happened here," Harry shouted back.

"Calm down. We're going to have an inquiry," Jesse said.

"Inquiry?" Harry snorted. "Roger was out here by himself. What the fool was doing leaning over the concrete, I don't know. We'll just have to wait until he's regained consciousness to find out."

"Yeah, *if* he regains consciousness," Jack snorted. He was tense, and his features were hard as he stared at Harry.

"Hell of a thing—" Harry began, and then realized that he had an audience, more than a dozen employees hanging around. He stopped speaking and shook his head again. "This show's over, folks. Back to work, everybody back to work." Then he turned to Jesse. "Hell, Jesse, what kind of questions could anybody have?"

"That will come later. I'm getting in the ambulance copter with Roger," Jesse said, brushing past Harry.

He stared at Lorena again then. His features remained taut and grim, and his eyes now held...

A warning?

He hesitated, speaking to a couple of officers who had arrived along with the med techs, then hurried after the stretcher.

A man in one of the Miccosukee force uniforms spoke up, his voice calm and reassuring, yet filled with authority. "Go ahead, folks, get going. We'll be speaking with you all one by one."

The crowd slowly began to disperse. Harry was complaining to the officer. "I don't get it. What could your questions be? For some fool reason, Roger got stupid and leaned too far over the barrier. No one else was out here. Security was his job."

"Harry, we have to ask questions," the officer said. "Hey, if there were an outsider in here, giving Roger or anyone a problem, you'd want to know, right?"

"Well, yeah," Harry said, as if the idea had just occurred to him. "You boys go right ahead. Question everyone. Damned right, I'd want to know."

He turned to walk away, then saw that several of his employees hadn't left.

"Get going, folks. It's a workday, and this isn't a charity. So get to work. And everyone, give these officers your fullest cooperation." Then he walked away himself, followed by one of the officers.

Lorena nearly jumped a mile when she felt a hand on her shoulder. She swung around. Michael was there, looking sleepy, concerned but foggy, also clad in a robe.

"What the hell happened?"

She explained.

He shook his head. "Well, that's about as weird as it gets. Roger has been here forever. He should have known better."

"Would that alligator… Old Elijah…would he have eaten the man, do you think?" Lorena queried softly.

"He's really well fed, so…who knows," Michael said. "Eaten him? Maybe. More likely he just would have gotten angry, taken a bite, tossed him around, drowned him. Who knows. I don't question Old Elijah. There's only one thing I can say with certainty about alligators."

"And that is?"

Michael's eyes met hers directly. "That you'll never really know anything about them," he said flatly. "You'll never know what goes on behind the evil in those eyes."

JESSE SAT IN the back of the emergency helicopter, doing his best to keep out of the way of the men desperately working to save Roger's life. He didn't need to ask questions, not that they would be heard above the roar of the blades, not from where he sat. A glance at the med tech who had taken the man's vitals and affixed his IV line told him that Roger had not regained consciousness.

As soon as they reached the hospital, Jesse paced the emergency room waiting lounge. Hell of a place. He knew the hospital was good; one of the best in the nation for trauma. But it was also the place where those without insurance came for help, and the place was thick with the ill, the injured and those who had brought them.

He wasn't the only law enforcement officer there. As he waited, two drug overdoses and a man with a knife in his back were rushed in, escorted by cops. Strange place, he thought. Stranger here, in the heart of the city, than out in the Glades. The wealth to be found in the area was astounding; movie stars, rock stars and celebrities of all kinds had multimillion-dollar mansions out on the islands, in the Gables and scattered throughout the county. At the same time, refugees from Central and South America abounded, many who slept under bridges, or lived in the crack houses that could be found not so far from the million-dollar mansions.

At length, one of the doctors came out. "Well, we've got him stabilized. But he's in a coma. He's not going to be talking."

"Will he come out of it?" Jesse asked.

"I don't know," the doctor told him honestly.

Jesse nodded, and handed the doctor his business card.

"I'll call you first thing, and I mean first thing, if there's any change at all," the doctor promised.

Jesse thanked him. There was a Florida Highway Patrol officer in the waiting room who had just finished with an accident victim. He offered to drive Jesse back. It was a long way, and Jesse thanked him for the offer.

"Heard you've been having some bad business around here," the officer, Tom Hennesy, said as they drove. "Anything new on those shootings?"

"No. Metro-Dade Homicide is handling that case, though."

Hennesy nodded. "You had a fatal gator attack, too." Jesse nodded.

"Strange, huh?" Hennesy said. "Usually that kind of thing only happens when someone wanders into the wrong place." He shrugged. "Of course, the 'wrong' place is getting harder to avoid these days, what with developers eating up the Everglades. Still, it's usually only the big gators that will attack an adult. It's usually toddlers. Or pets." He cast a sideways glance at Jesse and flushed slightly. "I was reading up after the attack the other day. Since 1948, there have been fewer than 350 attacks on humans in this state, and the number of fatal attacks is only in the teens." He laughed. "I remember when the creatures were endangered, and when the first alligator farm opened in 1985. My uncle used to come out to the Glades, sit in a cabin and drink beer, and go out and hunt gators—till they made the endangered list. And now…my wife wanted to move close to the water. Now, after the latest incident, she wants to move out of state and up into the mountains somewhere."

Jesse smiled at the man, offering what he hoped was polite empathy.

"Hell, you're down here all the time," Hennesy said. "Think about it. How many attacks have you seen?"

Jesse looked at him. "Well, my uncle Pete lost a thumb, but he was one of the best wrestlers the village down there ever had. He was proud of it, actually. I don't think you can call that an attack, though."

When they at last reached the alligator farm, Jesse was disturbed to realize that more than half the day was gone.

The place was full of tourists, as if nothing had happened. A discreet inquiry assured him that Lorena was busy, helping out with Michael Preston's hatchling speeches.

He took a glance into the lab and saw that there were at least twenty people on the current tour. Lorena didn't see him. He watched her, watched the way she smiled, seemingly at ease. But in reality she was moving around the lab looking for something, he realized. She was subtle, leaning against a cabinet, a desk, casually assessing the contents, but she was definitely searching for something.

He was tempted to shout at her. *Stupid!*

Was she stupid, or dangerously reckless? Why? What was driving her?

A little while later, when he drove away from the farm, he realized that he'd been afraid to leave, afraid to head home for a shower. He was tired as hell, but the shower was necessary. Sleep would have to wait.

LORENA HEARD THAT Jesse had returned to Harry's. That he had spoken with a number of people.

Just not her.

The next morning she met Thorne Thiessen, the veterinarian. He had come to take a look at Old Elijah.

He was a distinguished-looking man, weather-worn, with a pleasant disposition, very tall, very fit. He had his assistant with him, a huge guy named John Smith. They both looked like extremely powerful men, in exceptional shape.

Maybe that was a requirement for survival in the swamp. Or else something in the genetics of the men in the area.

Watching Thiessen examine Old Elijah had been a real education. They had pulled out a lot of equipment— Elijah was one big beast—and they had snared him, something that had taken Jack Pine, Hugh, John Smith and two part-time wranglers to manage. The gator had thrashed, even when caught, and sent several of the handlers flying. Between them, however, they got the creature still, with Jack making the leap to the animal's back, shutting the great jaw and taping it closed.

Only then did Thiessen go into the pit. He took blood samples, checked the crocodilian's eyes, did some kind of a temperature reading and checked out his hide.

Despite the time she'd spent in school, Lorena really didn't know how the vet was determining if the ancient creature was in good health or not. Personally, she thought that the way he had been able to toss grown men around as if they were weightless seemed to prove that he was doing okay.

Jesse showed up right when Thiessen was leaving. Lorena, who had been watching from the pit area, did her best to eavesdrop. The men greeted each other cordially enough, but then Jesse pressed the vet, who in turn became defensive.

"I'm working on it, Jesse. But come on, Homicide doesn't see any connection between the alligator limb and the murders. Something ate the rest of the thing, that's all. Poachers don't kill people with high-powered rifles."

Jesse shrugged. "I can see where this may not be at the top of your priority list, but it *is* high on mine. If you don't want to deal with the responsibility, I can just take it to the FBI lab."

Thorne frowned, even more indignant. "No one knows reptiles the way that I do!"

"That's why I brought the specimen to you. Another day or so, Thorne, then I'm going to have to go for second best."

As he finished speaking, Lorena realized that he'd noticed she was there. She had forgotten to eavesdrop discreetly.

But there were others around, too. Jack and Hugh were speaking together, just a few feet away. Sally was standing politely to the rear, obviously waiting for a chance to have a word with Jesse.

Even Harry was still by the pit, calling out orders to

the two wary part-time handlers, who had been left to free Old Elijah from the tape on his snout.

Michael Preston was there, too, sipping coffee with a thoughtful frown as he watched all the activity.

Jesse, however, was gazing thoughtfully at *her*.

"Ms. Fortier," he murmured. "I need to see you later," he said.

He turned to leave. Sally tapped him on the arm, asking a question that Lorena couldn't hear. As Jesse walked away, Sally was still at his side.

"Hey!" Harry called. "Doors are opening."

LORENA REALIZED THAT although she was always distracted when she brought visitors through Michael's lab, she actually enjoyed his talks. He had a nice flair for the dramatic. That morning, though, she felt the frustration of not being able to find anything out of the ordinary. Except for the eggs with the cracked shells. That was where changes—or *enhancements*—might take place. But they were out in the open. Part of the show.

In the afternoon, she watched as Jack and Hugh both put on their own demonstrations. Jack wrestled a six-foot gator to the amusement of the crowd. Hugh brought out gators in various stages of growth, thrilling the children, who were allowed to touch the animals. After the last show, Hugh approached her.

"How about an airboat ride? See some of the scenery up close and personal?" he suggested, his grin charming and hopeful.

She agreed, and soon, they were out in the Glades. She had been afraid, at first, when it had looked as if they were trying to take off over solid ground. But it wasn't ground at all.

The river of grass. That was what it was and exactly the way it looked. As they traveled, Hugh educated her about their environs, shouting to be heard over the motor. The Everglades really wasn't a swamp but a constantly moving river; it was simply that the rate at which the water moved was so slow that it wasn't discernible to the naked eye.

Hugh obviously loved the area. Before they started out, he had explained that he was an Aussie, would always be an Aussie at heart, but that he had come to love this place as home.

Trees on hummocks seemed to rush by with tremendous speed. Ahead of them, brilliantly colored birds, large and small, burst out of the water and into the sky. At last Hugh cut the motor, and the airboat came to rest in the middle of what seemed like a strange and forgotten expanse of endless water, space and humid heat.

"So how do you like the airboat?" Hugh asked. He had a cooler in the rear of the boat and edged around carefully to open it. He produced two bottles of beer.

She accepted one.

"The feel of the wind is great," she told him.

He took a seat again, grinning as he looked at her. "You like it out here?"

"It's strange. A bit to get used to. But yes. I don't think I've ever seen more magnificent birds. Not even in a zoo."

"Around the early 1900s, some of them were hunted into extinction. Their feathers were needed for every stylish hat," Hugh said, leaning back. "But they *are* fabulous, aren't they?"

She nodded. "So, Hugh, were you a croc hunter back home in the Outback?"

He laughed. "Actually, I was born and raised in Sydney, but I always wanted to find out about the wilds. We've got some beautiful country at home, but there's just something here…the loneliness, the trees, the birds, the… I don't know. Some people simply fall in love with the land. Despite the SST-size mosquitoes, the venomous snakes and the alligators."

"Have you been a handler ever since you got here?" she asked. "I mean, did you ever help with the research side of things?"

He laughed. "Research?" He shook his head. "I know enough about gators without that. I know when they mate, know that a mother gator is one of the fiercest creatures known to man. And I know about the jaws, and that's what counts."

He sat back easily, adjusting his hat. He was attentive and clearly glad to be with her. In fact, he really seemed like a nice guy.

And he knew nothing about research.

Or so he claimed.

But here they were, in the middle of nowhere, and if he had wanted to cause her any harm…

"Damn!" he said suddenly.

"What?" she asked.

He lifted his beer, indicating something west of them. She peered in that direction, squinting, trying to see what he was seeing.

She realized that there was an embankment, and that they were in a canal. Trees grew at the water's edge, and it seemed that there was a small hummock in the direction he was pointing.

Limbs were down here and there, no doubt a result

of the early summer rainstorms she had heard came frequently here.

"There… They really are amazing creatures. They blend perfectly with their environment," Hugh said, his voice a whisper touched with awe. "See him?"

Suddenly she did. Just the eyes and a hint of the nose were visible above the water. And then, way behind the head, she could see the slight rise of the back.

"He's huge!" Hugh continued softly. "I've never seen one that big. I've never even seen a croc that big."

"How can you tell his size?" she asked, whispering, too, though she didn't know why. Actually, she did, she realized. She didn't want to attract the creature's attention.

"Well," Hugh said, "if you look at the water—"

"The water looks black," she protested.

He laughed softly. "It's not the water, it's the vegetation. But look closely. You can see the length of the body. We're talking huge. Maybe twenty-something feet."

"They don't get that big here!" she heard herself protest.

As they watched, the alligator suddenly submerged. Lorena felt a sharp stab of fear, sudden and primitive. She was certain that the creature was coming for them.

The airboat was small and built for two, with both seats at the rear. The nose of the vehicle offered only a small bit of space for supplies. The boat was fairly flat-bottomed, and it would be hard to knock over, but…

How much could a creature like that weigh?

"Man, I would have liked to see him up close," Hugh marveled.

Lorena couldn't speak. She was certain that Hugh

was going to get his wish, that the gator would be there, beneath them, in a matter of seconds.

Frowning, Hugh rose. Despite the rocking of the airboat, he moved easily and confidently. She was about to scream to him to sit down, that he needed his gun, that...

She heard it then. The motor of another airboat.

Just then something brushed by their boat. Just touching it. Nosing it.

Testing it?

Then the other airboat came into the picture, whipping over the water. It was a much larger vehicle, with the motor and giant fan far in the rear, and with more storage space and six seats in front of the helm. She noticed that it bore a tribal insignia.

Then she saw Jesse.

She released a long breath, aware that she wasn't afraid anymore, that even his airboat seemed to shout of authority.

The creature had disappeared; it was no longer touching their airboat.

"Hey!" Jesse shouted, cutting his motor as his vehicle drew next to theirs.

"Hey, Jesse," Hugh said dryly. It was apparent that his romantic plans had just been shattered.

"What are you two doing out here?" Jesse asked with a frown.

Hugh cocked his head, his hands on his hips. "I asked the lady out, and she agreed."

Jesse looked impatient. "Hugh, I don't know how you missed my notice. We've got a man-eater out here. We're going to get a group of hunting guides out here and go after it. The medical examiner says that Billy

Ray was bushwhacked by one big son of a bitch. We're going after it. It's not safe out here right now."

Hugh snorted. "Jesse, I've been dealing with gators for half my life. I'm armed, and I can take care of Lorena. I carry more than one big gun."

Jesse shook his head. "Hugh, you're one of the best. But Billy Ray knew alligators, too. Take your airboat on back. Lorena, step over here."

"Now, wait a minute!" Hugh protested. "Lorena is with me."

"She's coming in for questioning," Jesse said.

"What?" she and Hugh asked simultaneously.

Those startling green eyes leveled upon her hard. "Lorena needs to answer some questions about an incident at the alligator farm the other day."

"Jesse, you are crazy—" Lorena began.

"I can put the cuffs on you," he assured her.

"What the hell are you talking about?" Hugh demanded.

Jesse leveled his eyes on Lorena as he answered Hugh's question. "Something to do with a little kid getting a bite. I'm sure Harry wants it kept quiet. Therefore, I need a few answers."

Hugh frowned, staring at Lorena. "You don't have to go with him. What are you trying to pull here, Jesse Crane?" Hugh demanded.

"I think that Lorena wants to come with me," Jesse said, staring at her meaningfully.

Her skin prickled. It wasn't with the kind of panic she had felt when she believed that a monster gator was stalking her, but with an overwhelming sense of unease. *He knew.*

And maybe he was giving her a chance to talk to him before he blew the whistle on her.

She sighed, rising. The boat rocked.

"There was a bit of a problem with one of the children the other morning, Hugh. Easily taken care of. I'll just go with Jesse now," she said smoothly.

Panic seized her once again when she was ready to step from boat to boat. Where had the gator gone?

Whatever ruffled male feathers had begun to fly, the situation was suddenly eased as Hugh, holding her arm as she moved to join Jesse, said, "I think we just saw your alligator."

"Here?" Jesse asked.

There was about a foot and a half of empty space between the boats as they rocked gently in the water. Lorena looked down.

Her heart slammed into her throat.

There it was. Submerged, and moving in fluid silence, just beneath the surface.

She nearly threw herself into Jesse's arms.

"There!" she said. "Underneath us."

He frowned at her, dark brows drawn, eyes narrowed. He forced her into a seat and strode back to the edge of the airboat. "Where? Hugh, you see it?"

Hugh was also searching the water. He had a shotgun in the back of the airboat. He reached for it and stood still, watching.

Time passed.

It felt like an eternity to Lorena, who heard the drone of a mosquito but was afraid to move, too frozen even to swat at the creature.

At last Jesse sighed.

"It might have been here, but I don't see it now," he

said. "But this might well be its territory, so we'll start here tomorrow."

"Sunset?" Hugh asked.

"Right before. You gonna join us?"

"Yeah," Hugh said. "I travel around here all the time, though. I haven't seen that gator before."

"What was left of Billy Ray's body was tangled in the trees not too far from here. You know, right around the bend, where he had his favorite fishing spot. Yes, this is its territory. I'll pick you up at Harry's, six o'clock sharp tomorrow evening."

Jesse started up his motor.

The sound was like the sudden whirr of a thousand birds, rising from the swamp.

She gripped her chair, still feeling cold. Hugh waved.

She couldn't wave back.

The wind lashed around her, whipping her hair around her face. She closed her eyes.

She was startled when the motor died, along with the forward motion of the boat.

She opened her eyes. They still seemed to be in the middle of nowhere.

There was a hummock where they had come to rest, land that wasn't covered in the deceptive saw grass that grew where the water ran, making a person believe that there was terra firma beneath.

And yet in all directions, she still saw only wilderness.

There was no sound, except for the cries of birds, the rustle of foliage.

She swallowed, frowned, and stared at Jesse uneasily. "Where are we?"

"My place," he said. "And you can talk to me here,

tell me the truth, or we'll just head downtown, to the FBI office. Here's your chance, Lorena. Truth or dare. What do you know, and what the hell are you really doing here?"

Chapter Seven

Despite the fact that there was a well-maintained dock, Jesse could see that Lorena was more than a bit concerned about where they were going when he helped her out of the airboat.

His house had been built on a hummock and, he thought, combined the best of tradition and the modern world. There were still members of his tribe who made their homes in chickees, but for the most part, beyond the village and the other tourist stops, tribal members lived in normal houses, concrete block and stucco, sturdy structures that offered the same comforts as those enjoyed by everyone else.

He was lucky to own the land, which had been his father's. And it was a good stretch of hummock, rich with trees and foliage, and high enough to keep it from flooding during hurricanes or the rainy season. As they came in from the rear, winding along the path from the canal, the first sight was a chickee. Chickees had first come into being when various tribes—once grouped together under the term "Seminoles"—had moved deep into the Everglades to escape persecution and the white determination to export every last Native American to the western reservations. High above the ground, the chickee offered protection from snakes and gators. The open sides allowed the breezes to pass through continually, keeping the inhabitants cool year round.

Lorena gave the chickee a nervous glance, and he saw the relief on her face when they rounded a bend and she saw the house.

There was a screened-in patio with a pool, and sliding glass doors that led from it into the house. He owned a fairly typical ranch-style dwelling, with the large rear, "Florida room" extending the width of the back. He had a good entertainment center and comfortable sofas and chairs, which often led to him being the one to host Sunday football get-togethers. His home probably differed from some in that it was filled with Indian artifacts: Miccosukee, Seminole and others, including South American and Inuit. He had totem poles, lances, spears, shields and buffalo skulls, all artistically—at least in his mind—arranged, and he had come to love the feeling that he was surrounded by both past and present, tradition and the need for all Americans to be aware of the modern world. He considered education the most necessary tool for any Native American, and finding the path between prosperity and ethnicity was not an easy one.

"Thank God for bingo," he murmured aloud.

"What?"

Her eyes were wide; he could tell that she was decidedly uncomfortable, yet apparently relieved at the same time.

"Coffee? Tea? Soda? Beer or wine?" he asked. "Sorry, that's all I keep around." He left her standing in the Florida room and walked through the hall, hanging a quick left into the kitchen, where a bypass over the counter opened to allow him to keep an eye on her.

She shook her head uneasily. "I'm fine."

"Then I'll have coffee."

He reached into the cupboards for the paraphernalia he needed, watching her as he did so.

Some of the trepidation in her face had eased. She was walking around, studying the various pieces on the walls. She turned suddenly, as if feeling him watching her.

"Have you always lived here?" she asked, trying to sound casual.

"In the general area, yes. This house is new, though."

"Ah."

"And, let's see…you were raised in Jacksonville. Attended the University of Florida. Where you did indeed earn a nursing degree."

"Yes," she murmured, looking away.

"And a law degree."

Her eyes flew to his again. Belligerent, defensive.

"All right, so I've spent the last few years with a law firm. My nursing credentials are still good. You seem to know everything, so you must know that, too."

"I do," he assured her grimly. "Sure you don't want a cup of coffee?"

"All right," she murmured.

She walked around to join him in the kitchen. He wondered how she could have spent the late afternoon in an airboat in the swamp and still manage to retain such an alluring scent.

"Sugar…cream," he said, indicating the containers.

She added a touch of cream to her cup, not looking at him. Her fingers were shaking as she stirred, but she quickly returned to the Florida room, taking a seat on one of the sofas that looked out over the pool.

"All right," he said, taking a seat next to her. "We need to start communicating here. This is serious. Shall I continue, or do you just want to talk to me?"

"You're going to try to get me out of here," she said, not looking at him. Then her eyes shot to his. "And I'm not inept. Actually, I'm a crack shot."

"Your life seems filled with accomplishments," he said with obvious irony.

She blushed, looking away. "I thought I wanted to go into nursing…but then I wound up taking some legal courses related to medical ethics and I found out that I liked the law. I was able to work part-time in a hospital while I went back to college. I was lucky. My dad was associated with a firm that was known for going to bat for the underdog. They hired me right out of law school."

"Which has nothing to do with why you're here," he said softly.

"Actually, in a way it does," she murmured, staring down again. Then she looked up at him. "One thing about studying the law is that you learn you need proof to go to court."

He shook his head, looking at her, then taking the cup from her and setting it on the coffee table. He took both her hands. "All right, here's the rest of what I know. You're going under the name Fortier because that was your mother's maiden name. Your father was Dr. Eugene Duval, working for Eco-smart, a company that, among other facilities, ran an alligator farm. He died last year after a fall down a stairway. So why does that bring you here?"

She shook her head. "He didn't fall."

"Lorena, I've read the police reports. He was alone in the building at the time."

"No. He did *not* just fall."

Jesse sighed, squeezing her hands. "Lorena, I know what it's like to desperately seek something behind the obvious. Your father fell down a stairway. He broke his neck."

"No," she said stubbornly.

"Why are you so convinced it wasn't an accident?"

"Because he had something. Something that his killer wanted."

"And that was?" Jesse persisted.

She hesitated, realizing that he didn't know everything.

He squeezed her hands more tightly. The lingering scent of her cologne wafted around him, seemed to permeate his system. He realized that his own heart was pounding, that the blood was rushing in a hot wave through his system. He was torn between the desire to gently touch her face and the equally strong desire to draw her into his arms, shake her, tell her none of this was worth her life.

He desperately wanted to hold her. And more. The texture of her skin was suddenly so fascinating that he longed to explore it with the tips of his fingers. Her features were so delicate, elegant and determined that he was tempted to test them with the palm of his hand.

He fought the desire that had begun to build in his system the first time he had seen her. She was angry, lost, determined…and trusting. He knew he should pull his hands away. He didn't. He couldn't. He had to get answers from her—now.

"Lorena, what did your father have?" he demanded.

She stared back at him, clenching her teeth; then she shook her head. "You mean you don't know? It's obvious. He had a formula."

"A formula for what?"

"Well, basically, steroids," she said flatly. "There were other ingredients, but the formula was based on steroids." She inhaled, exhaled, looking away but not drawing away. "My father was a great man. He wanted to feed the world. He worked with all kinds of animals, trying to find a way to improve the amount and quality of their meat without creating the chemical dangers you so often find in farmed meats. He saw alligators as the wave of the future. A creature that had been endangered—nearly wiped off the face of the earth—then raised in captivity to return with a vengeance. In his mind, we were going to be looking to a number of basically new food sources, new to the American public, at least. Emu. Beefalo. Different fish. Eels. And alligators. He thought they were magnificent creatures, with hides that could be used for all kinds of things and meat that could be improved in taste, quality and quantity. So he began working on a formula. Now he's dead and someone else has it—and I think Harry's place may be involved."

Jesse stared at her blankly, wondering why something like this hadn't occurred to him. *Because it was right out of a science fiction novel, that was why.*

"Lots of people work with alligators," he said, his tone sharper than he had intended. "Lots of scientists work with formulas to improve breeding and supply."

"Maybe, but my father had found one that improved

the creatures' size to such an extent that…that he destroyed his own specimens."

Jesse felt frozen for a moment. It was all beginning to make sense. Too much sense. He was accustomed to drug-related crimes in the Everglades, or illegal immigrants, and the big money and guns that came with both. He knew the tragedy of greed, gangs, and the jealousy and fury behind domestic violence, and the tribulations brought on by the abuse of alcohol. And now industrial espionage might well be exactly what they were looking for. *A formula that was dangerous, but that could take a business to the top of the heap?* It made way too much sense. A couple killed for what appeared to be nothing had probably seen something they shouldn't see. A man who knew the Glades like the back of his hand, dead, killed by an alligator. But what kind of an alligator? Perhaps one scientifically induced to grow bigger—and more dangerous?

"All right, your father was working on a formula, but he's been dead for more than a year. There are all kinds of establishments working with alligators, all through Florida, Georgia, Texas and more. What brought you here?" he asked.

She hesitated. "I finally cleaned out all my dad's business communications. An old e-mail I found from Harry's Alligator Farm and Museum seemed to point in this direction."

"Was Harry Rogers ever in Jacksonville? Did he know your father?"

She shook her head. "Not that I know of."

"I assume your father communicated with a lot of other institutions."

"Yes, but…none of the others were…well, located

in such a wilderness. A place where it's possible to hide so much."

"Exactly what did the e-mail say, and who was it from?"

"I don't know. It wasn't signed. It was just a query, but there was something off about it. Something greedy. My father wrote back that he couldn't help."

"Then…?"

"It came right after there had been an article about my dad that mentioned the kind of research he was doing. So I came here, and…that couple got killed, and you found a piece of an alligator there, and then that poor man was…eaten."

"Still…"

"Jesse, I'm telling you, there was nothing else to go on, nothing."

"What about the other employees where your dad worked? What did they say?"

She shook her head in disgust. "According to everyone, my father had destroyed his research, the formula and his specimens. He worked for a very aboveboard corporation. When he said his research had taken a dangerous turn, they gave him the freedom to start over. So now they're all sorry, and they all understand that I'm upset. But as far as they're concerned, it was an accident."

She stared at him, then grasped his hands. "But it *wasn't* an accident. I know it. Harry—or someone here—got my father's formula, and they killed him to do it. You have to believe me! And now they've lost a few of their specimens, and those gators are running around the Glades killing people. They're trying to track them down, but they don't want to get caught, and I think that's why your friends were killed. Whoever was out there picking up the specimen decided that Hector and Maria had seen too much. But what really scares me is that I think they're still trying to use the formula. Jesse, please, think about it. You said that Hector and Maria were wonderful people, that they couldn't have been drug-running. So you have to go to the next conclusion—that they were killed for something they saw, for what they might know. Come on! Why else would anyone kill your friends? They were shot because they saw the alligator. And the killers dared to murder them because they knew everyone would just assume it had something to do with drugs. Jesse, I'm right, and you know it."

He drew away from her at last, then stood and walked to the glass doors, looking out at the pool and the deep, rich green of the hummock beyond, not seeing. "Lorena, your dad has been dead more than a year, right?" he said softly.

"Right."

"And his research went back several years. But alligators, even pampered hatchlings, only grow about a foot a year. To get a creature big enough to kill a man would take well over a decade."

"Jesse, you don't understand just what can be done once man starts messing with nature. My father began his studies about five years ago, and with the alterations he could create, a gator could grow as much as four feet in a year. You figure it out. Do the math. See where we'd be right now," she said softly.

"I don't believe it," he said, but he wondered, *Was it possible?*

"You've got to get out of here," he said flatly. "This is

about the wildest theory I've heard in my entire life, but if there's any truth in it whatsoever, someone is going to find out who you are. You've got to get away." He spun on her. "And another thing. Why the hell didn't you tell me about this when you arrived down here?"

"Hey! The second time I ever saw you, you were *at* Harry's. Sally told me you come there all the time. How could I know for certain that you weren't involved somehow?"

He sighed, looking down. "I'm a cop, Lorena. And just like I said at the beginning—a real one."

She rose, staring back at him. "And you're going to tell me that there haven't been dirty cops?"

He lifted his hands; then his eyes narrowed, and he strode over to her, taking her by the shoulders, ready to shake her for real. His fingers tensed where he held her, his teeth locked. He fought both his temper and his fears for her. At last he said, "You couldn't tell? You couldn't tell by *getting to know me* that I wasn't crooked?"

She inhaled, staring at him, eyes wide. She parted her lips, ready to speak, but words didn't come. She moistened her lips, ready to speak again, then just shook her head and, to his surprise, leaned it against him.

He wrapped his arms around her. Time ticked away as they stood there and he felt the soft force of her body against his, his own emotions washing through him with the force of a tidal wave. Heat began to fill him. He was torn, ready to rush out and pound his fist into anyone who would so coldly kill and let loose such a danger. But he was a police officer, sworn to uphold the law. He'd been a detective, trained to find out the truth before ripping into something like a maniac.

But he was also simply a man.

And here *she* was, in his arms. She had elicited emotion and longing in him from the first time he had seen the green-and-gold magic in her eyes, heard the tone of her voice. He'd been irritated, angered, enchanted. He'd seen the empathy in her eyes for others, the spark of fire when she was angry.

This wasn't the time.

He had taken her away from Hugh, and Hugh would be angry now, telling the tale to everyone.

And at Harry's, they might be suspicious....

"You can't go back there," he said, and he lifted her chin, his thumb playing over the flesh of her cheek.

Her eyes met his. Her fingers moved down his back, dancing lightly along the length of his spine. "I *have* to go back," she whispered.

"No," he said. And he brought his lips to hers. She didn't protest or hesitate for a second. It was as if they had both been simmering, awaiting the boiling point, and when they touched at last...

She melted into his arms, breasts and hips fitting neatly into his form. Her fingers threaded into his hair; her mouth tasted of mint and fire.

They broke apart. "I have to..." she said, and her meaning was unclear, because they fused together again, and her hands worked down to his hips, then below, cupping his buttocks, drawing him closer.

At last he caressed her face as he had longed to, exploring texture and shape. Then his fingers fell to the buttons of her shirt, and the fabric obediently parted. His fingers slid along the flesh of her throat, stroked, then careered down the length of her neck. Beneath the cotton of her shirt, he found her bra strap, slipped it away, and his lips dropped to her shoulder, while his fingers continued to disrobe her, baring more flesh for the eager whisper of his tongue. He felt her hands at his belt, then realized his gun was there. He released her long enough to discard his gun belt, then drew her back quickly, fevered, heedless of anything then but the wanting and the heady knowledge that she was just as hungry as he was.

Her skirt and delicate lace bra fell to the floor, and the sleek length of her back was available to be savored by the touch of his fingers, while his lips found the hollows at her collarbone, then moved steadily down, finding her breasts. He felt the quickening of her breath, and that, too, was an aphrodisiac. She was smooth and soft, erotic, hot, vibrant. Her lips and teeth on his shoulders, bathing, biting, aroused him. Her hands, deft and seductive, were at the waistband of his trousers. It was then he realized that, remote as his house might be, the glass panes opened to the glory of the Everglades—and the eyes of anyone who might wander by. He caught her up into his arms, heedless of the clothing they left scattered behind, and strode down the hallway to his bedroom. As he did so, her eyes met his, dazed and mercurial, fascinating, poignant pools. And then her fingers swept back a dark lock of his hair, touching his face as he had so tenderly touched hers.

Night was coming to the Everglades. Coming in hues of crimson and purple, red and gold. The light shone dimly into the room, illuminating them as they fell onto the bed and came together again in a fury of naked flesh. Every little nuance of her seemed to touch and awaken and arouse him. Whispers and soft moans escaped her lips, a siren's song, as he reveled in the discovery of her, the tautness of her abdomen, the length of her legs, the firm fullness of her breasts. And in return…her hands were on him, touching without restraint, fingers no more than a whisper, and then a tease that brought the blood thundering through his veins again, his own breath a drumbeat, the tension in him unbearable.

And yet the anguish was sweet. As if the moment would not come again and had to be cherished, savored. He felt he died a thousand little deaths, not willing to allow it to end, hands upon her everywhere, lips tasting, teasing, giving homage, demanding response. He held himself above her, found her mouth, his tongue thrusting within, gentle at first, then almost angry. Finally he allowed his body to slide slowly against hers as he eased himself lower, again finding the fullness of her breasts, the rose-tipped peaks of her nipples, and below, his tongue stroking a rib, delving into her naval, the lean, low skin of her midriff, then…a kneecap, outer thigh, inner thigh, and the crux of her sex.

He heard the anxious, heady sound of her whispers and moans, protest, encouragement. She writhed against him and into him, and he felt the pulse of her body, until at last he rose above her again and thrust into her, his eyes locked with hers, his soul needing to encompass the length and breadth and being of her with the same searing need that ruled his body. The world rocked in the colors of the sunset, soaring, shooting reds, golds that burned into heart and mind. He moved, and she moved with him, a fit as sweet as it was erotic. Fever seized him, and the rhythm of their union became staccato and desperate. The sounds of their breathing rose to storm pitch, hearts attuned in physical cacophony. Searing lava seemed to rip through his veins, and he fought it, until he felt her surge against him, and then his own climax seized him with violence and majesty.

He moved to her side, and felt the thundering in his chest decrease to a steady beat, the pulse slow, the air move. The colors of sunset faded. Mauve darkness settled over them as she curled against him. He touched her hair in wonder, but his voice rang harsh again when he spoke. "You can't go back there."

The wrong words. She pushed away from him.

"I have to."

"No."

"Jesse..."

"Shh."

"I have to go back. And I have to go back soon."

"Not now."

"They'll know I'm with you."

"It's early."

"But..."

"Shh."

"Jesse, you can work with me or against me," she whispered.

He didn't reply. He was fascinated by the color of her hair against his sheets in the dying light. She went rigid beside him, so he smoothed her hair, then her brow. Then he kissed her forehead, her lips.

And then it began all over again, and this time, when the final thunder came, the black of night had descended fully.

They didn't speak, just held each other for the longest time, her head on his chest, their legs entwined. At last she pushed away from him, rose and found the shower.

He found her there. And in the spray of heat and

steam, he found himself exploring anew, touching, tasting, licking tiny water drops from her flesh....

Feeling them licked from his own skin, feeling himself touched, taken, stroked.

Soap upon flesh, flesh upon flesh, a night in which he found he could not be sated, in which he soared, in which he was afraid. And he didn't want it to end, because, when it did...

Eventually they managed an actual shower. The lights on, they moved in silence, finding all the scattered pieces of their clothing. And then, a new cup of coffee in his hand, Jesse told her firmly, "You can't go back."

She was rigid and determined; he could see that immediately. She regally smoothed back a piece of wet hair and said, "I told you, you can work with me and keep me safe, if that's what you feel you have to do. But I *am* going back."

"I can stop you," he told her.

She lifted her chin. "You'd really arrest me?" she demanded. "For what?"

His teeth grated.

"I can tell Harry that you're acting suspiciously. That I think you're dangerous." He lifted his hands in frustration. "Lorena, your being there is pure insanity. You've told me that someone killed your father. An innocent couple was shot down in cold blood. A man was eaten by a gator. If someone at Harry's is involved, that someone is ruthless."

She set her hands on her hips, indignant, eyes narrowing dangerously. "What? I'm a woman, and that means I have to be incompetent?"

"I didn't say that. But I'm not letting you go back there."

"Then you'll never find the killers you're after!" she told him.

He stared back at her, feeling anger rise in him again.

"I need to go back. And I need to go back now. I'm already going to have to think of something to say when everyone wants to know why you detained me."

"I told both you and Hugh that I was going to talk to you about the incident at the farm," he said flatly. He shook his head in disgust. "You're playing a dangerous game. You haven't just entered a pit of vipers, you're asking them to bite."

"What?"

"Oh, come on. You're flirting with the pack of them."

"I went for a ride in an airboat," she said. "So what?" But there was no conviction in her tone.

He stared at her, torn, impotent, and furious because he knew that, on the one hand, she was right.

He had no proof of anything. So…what? Wait until something else terrible happened and hope he was there to save her? Find some reason for a search warrant, a legal way to get into Harry's, and rip the place apart?

"No one was suspicious of me except you," she reminded him. "Honestly, Jesse, I told you I'm a crack shot. I carry a gun, and I'm licensed."

"Great. And do you walk around armed all day?"

She let out a sigh. "Do you really think anyone is going to hurt me in front of dozens of witnesses?"

"Two days," he said.

"What?" she asked him, frowning.

"Two more days. That's what I'll give you. And you have to swear to me that you'll go nowhere alone with any of those men. When it's night, you lock yourself in. When it's morning, you get where you need to be—fast."

"I need to get back into the lab," she said.

"You can do that when I'm there."

She cocked her head to the side, wary. "And we'll manage that how?"

"Easy. I'm around enough."

She hesitated. "Jesse—"

"That's the deal. Take it or leave it." He shook his head angrily. "You toe the line, and I mean it. It's going to be busy as hell right now, too, because I have to arrange hunting parties to find your scientifically mutated alligators—assuming they even exist. Every one of them has to be caught and killed. God knows how many people could die if some super race of huge, aggressive gators starts breeding out there."

"Two days, then," she said softly. "But, Jesse…that's my point, don't you see? I have to find the truth. I have to find out what they know and just how they've altered the alligators, not to mention just how many of them are out there."

"I need enough evidence to get a search warrant, nothing more," he said.

She nodded, then said softly, "I really have to go back now."

"I need a minute to get a few things," he told her.

"For what?"

"For the morning."

"You can't stay out there," she protested.

"Yes, I can."

"They'll know! Someone will definitely get suspicious if you start staying out there."

"No one is going to know."

"And how can that be?"

He smiled grimly. "Because you're going to sneak me into your room at night."

Her breath seemed to catch in her throat as she stared at him.

"Jesse, I've told you, I'm a crack shot."

"So was my wife," he informed her softly.

Then he turned away.

Chapter Eight

Harry was beside the canal, looking both anxious and edgy, when they returned in the airboat.

Lorena cast Jesse a quick frown to warn him that they had clearly made the man suspicious.

"What are you two doing out this late at night?" he demanded.

Jesse managed to look a little sheepish as he tied up the airboat and helped Lorena to the embankment. She was surprised that he bothered, and that he could sound so casual as he said, "Just trying to avoid a problem."

"Maybe you want to let me in on it?" Harry said.

"We had a complaint, Harry," Jesse said. "But don't worry, it's all been nipped in the bud."

"What do you mean, don't worry? I thought I owned this place!"

"Just some kid said he'd been bitten by a hatchling. Turns out, it was the kid's fault. He was trying to steal it," Jesse explained.

"Steal one of my hatchlings?" Harry looked enraged.

"Yep, and that's why the parents have dropped the whole thing. I just needed Lorena's account of the prob-lem. There's nothing to worry about, Harry. I thought it would be a minor thing, and it was. If there had been anything to worry about, naturally I would have spoken with you immediately."

"This could mean a lawsuit," Harry protested.

"It might have, but it isn't going to," Jesse said.

Harry was still glowering. "It's my place. I need to be apprised of everything that happens here."

"Harry, chill. The complaint has been dropped. Lorena told me everything I needed to know. There was no reason to upset you."

Harry stared hard at Lorena. She tried to decide if he looked worried or not. Mostly he just seemed concerned about his place. And angry with Jesse. "You're not doing your job right, Jesse Crane," Harry said angrily. "Cutting corners, kidnapping my nurse."

Lorena was instantly aware that Harry had said the wrong thing. Jesse stiffened, and the look in his eyes turned chilling. "Harry, two good people have been shot to death, a tribal member has been killed by an alligator, and you've got a security guard in the hospital, hovering between life and death. Drop it," he said icily.

Harry backed down, instantly. "I, uh, I just checked on Roger. He's still in a coma," he said gruffly. "You found out anything else on the murders?" he asked.

"No," Jesse said simply. "Nor can I tell you anything else about Billy Ray. But we're going out gator-hunting from here tomorrow evening around six. The office will set things up with the guys who run the licensed hunts. I'll be needing Jack Pine and Hugh. We know we've got a man-eater out there, and it's got to be put down."

"Now you're going to take my handlers?" Harry said incredulously. "Like hell! This is a business."

"And you can do business tomorrow. You'll just be minus a couple of handlers come six o'clock."

"Dammit, Jesse—"

"How many tourists do you think you're going to have if this rogue gator attacks more people?" Jesse demanded.

Harry waved a dismissive hand. "Are you going to need my nurse again, too?" he demanded.

"Hopefully not," Jesse said calmly, not raising his own voice to meet Harry's indignant tone.

"You coming in for dinner?" Harry asked Jesse, clearly changing the subject to avoid an argument.

Jesse glanced at Lorena. "If there's still dinner, might as well," he murmured.

Harry made an unhappy snorting sound, and they walked together toward the main building. As they went, they could hear the bellowing of the alligators in their ponds.

Soon they reached the cafeteria. "I've eaten," Harry said curtly. "You two go on."

Lorena murmured, "Thank you," and stepped in ahead of Jesse.

Sally was seated at one of the tables, with Jack Pine and Hugh.

Hugh rose when he saw them enter.

"Well, that took a while," he said dryly.

"We got to talking, that's all," Jesse said.

Sally set a hand on his arm. "Jesse, how are you doing?" she asked, real concern in her voice.

Jesse frowned at her. "I'm worried," he said flatly.

Jack Pine waved a hand in the air. "Jesse, there may be one big gator out there, but face it, Billy Ray was a drunk. Do we really want to cause a panic out there when for all we know he passed out, fell in the water and drowned, and *then* got eaten by that gator?"

"No panic. Just a hunt," Jesse said.

"Let me get you all some food," Sally said sweetly, flashing a smile at Jesse, then Lorena. "It's late, they're closing down, so I'll just make sure you two get to eat."

"Thanks, Sally," Jesse said, smiling back at her.

Lorena found herself remembering how Sally had talked about Jesse earlier. *Devastated, but not dead!* She felt at a loss for a moment, realizing that she knew so little about him. The night had been strange. Intimacy had been sudden and yet…she felt as if it had been something that, unbeknownst to herself, she had actually been awaiting. But she didn't know anything about whatever might have gone on with him—and Sally?— before she got here. She did know that he'd had a wife, and that she was dead.…

And that she'd been a crack shot.

"Harry teed off about the hunt?" Hugh asked.

Jesse shrugged.

"Harry's all about the bottom line," Jack said. "He doesn't even give a damn about Michael's research. He just wants to please the tourists, grow the gators, harvest the meat and hides."

"Yeah, but if we catch the rogue that killed Billy Ray, he'll want it on display, don't you think?" Sally said, returning to the table. One of the waiters was behind her, carrying two plates piled with something Lorena couldn't identify.

"Jesse won't be letting Harry have that old gator, will you, Jess?" Jack said.

"Why not?" Harry asked.

"It should go to the village, to the Miccosukee," Jack said flatly.

"Let's catch the thing first," Jesse said.

"Hey…you're not going soft, are you? Thinking it's just a good ol' predator doing what comes naturally, and planning to transplant it somewhere deeper in the Glades?" Hugh asked.

Jesse shook his head. "No. It's dangerous. We have to put it down. There's one thing I'm really hoping, though."

"What's that?" Sally asked.

"That it *is* an 'it.' That we're not searching for more than one really dangerous alligator."

"There's one thing *I'm* wondering," Jack said.

"And what's that?" Lorena asked.

He stared at her. "Where the hell did a bugger that big and vicious come from?"

There was silence at the table. Lorena found herself intensely interested in her meal.

The conversation never really recovered after that.

Jack left the table first, a few minutes later. Then Hugh. Sally didn't seem to want to leave, though.

But finally Jesse stood. "Ladies, I've still got some work to do, so I'll bid you good night."

Sally watched him go, obviously appreciating the view.

Lorena cleared her throat. Sally glanced at her, her eyes sparkling with amusement. "Well, I see that you're coming to enjoy our local…wildlife, shall I say?"

Lorena ignored the other woman's teasing tone. "What happened to his wife?" she asked.

Sally didn't seem to mind dispensing information. "She was a cop, too. Some coked-up prostitute she was trying to help walked up to the back of her car one night and—on the order of her pimp—put a bullet into the back of her head."

Lorena let out a long breath. There was really nothing to say except "Oh."

"She was something, I'll tell you. An heiress determined to make the world better through law enforcement." Sally assessed Lorena carefully. "Don't go getting any ideas. He'll never marry again."

Lorena forced a smile. "Sally, I barely know the man."

"But you know enough, don't you?"

Lorena rose. "Like I said, I barely know the man. Thank you for making sure we could eat."

"He's interested in one thing, and one thing only. So you'd better play like a big girl, if you intend to play."

"Thanks for the advice," Lorena said lightly. "Good night."

As Lorena started walking away, Sally called softly after her, "Be careful."

Lorena spun back around. "Why?"

"Well, hell!" Sally laughed. "Old Billy Ray—eaten. And Roger... Just goes to show, you can never trust a gator. Believe me, I'm going to be very careful myself."

"Are you suggesting that Roger was helped into that pit?"

"Good God, no! He must have thought he heard something. Then leaned too far over the edge."

"So you think he fell in?" Lorena asked.

"Of course. Who would have pushed him?" Sally demanded.

"Hey, you're the one who warned *me*," Lorena said lightly, then smiled and left.

On her way to her room, she paused at the door to Michael Preston's lab and started to test the knob. Then she heard his voice from inside and stopped, listening.

She thought maybe he was on the phone. His voice was low but intense.

She tried desperately to eavesdrop, but she couldn't make out his words. Nothing other than *giant* and *hunt*. There was nothing suspicious about that. By now everyone knew that Billy Ray had been killed by an alligator, a big one, and that it had to be hunted down and destroyed.

Still, she lingered, listening, until the sound of footsteps down the hallway warned her that she'd better get going. Worried that he might eventually have said something useful and now she was going to miss it, she gave up and hurried on to her own room.

JESSE TOOK THE airboat back to headquarters and checked in with his staff.

Brenda Hardy was there, doing paperwork. She perched on the edge of Jesse's desk. "I don't care what anyone says. There's more going on here than just some big gator. Billy Ray had a shotgun with him, he could shoot dead drunk. I'd bet cash money you're thinking what I'm thinking. All this happening at one time is too much to be coincidence."

Jesse nodded to her, then excused himself as his cell phone rang. It was Julie.

"Jesse."

"Julie. You all right?"

"Yeah…yeah. You know what I've been doing? Playing bingo out at the casino. I bought about a million cards. You can't think when you're trying to put little dots on a zillion numbers at once."

"Good, Julie. I'm glad. Anything that works for you is what you need to be doing."

"Right, I know. I had to tell you, Jesse. I drove out by the house before, and…and I drove back here as quickly as I could. I didn't go in. I didn't even get out of my car. But I saw the lights. I saw lights…like my mother said. I know why she thought aliens were landing. It was creepy…the way they seemed to come out of the swamp and the sky at the same time."

"Julie, don't go back there. Stay at the casino, stay in the bingo hall, at the machines, or locked in your room, all right? And don't tell anyone you drove by the house."

"All right, Jesse. I just thought you should know."

"I should, and I'm glad you called me. But you have to keep yourself safe. You understand?"

"I will, Jesse. I guess I thought I needed to go back to believe it. But I'll stay away."

"Promise?"

"I swear."

Jesse hung up. As he did, George Osceola walked over to his desk. Jesse looked up.

"You're not going to like this," George warned.

"What?"

"Dr. Thiessen, the vet, just called," George said.

"And?"

"He went back into his office tonight to get some notes. He'd decided to send the specimen and his samples to the FBI lab."

"And?"

When he got there, his night security man slash animal sitter was out cold in the kennel area."

"And let me guess. The alligator specimen and all the tissue and blood samples were gone?" Jesse said.

George nodded. "I'm meeting some of the fellows from the county out there now."

"I've got a drive to make," Jesse said. "Then I'll meet you there."

He got in his car and started speeding along the Trail, only slowing as he neared Julie's parents' house. He turned off his lights before he entered the drive, knowing that, even for him, that was foolhardy, considering the terrain.

He parked on the embankment that bordered the property. The crime tape still hung limply around the house itself and the place where Maria had died. The whole area seemed forlorn, desolate.

Whatever Julie had seen, Jesse realized after about twenty minutes of watching from the front seat, it was gone now. Tomorrow night, if Lars couldn't send a man to keep watch, he would send one of his own men, or even keep watch himself.

He got out of the car, carrying his large flashlight, and walked toward the water. As he reached the wet saw grass area that fell away from the hummock toward the water, he saw that the long razor-edged blades were pushed down. Once again, someone had been through with an airboat. He looked around but didn't see anything else suspicious.

When he got back to his car, he put a call through to Lars Garcia, despite the time. Lars already knew about the break-in at the vet's and was on his way out there.

When Jesse arrived at Doc Thiessen's, he found that the CSI team were already working, dusting for fingerprints, looking for footprints, searching for tire tracks, seeking any small piece of evidence.

Doc Thiessen had been born into a family of fruit-and-vegetable farmers in Homestead. He'd earned his veterinary degree at Florida State University and determined to come back to his own area to work. Now he had a head full of snow-white hair and a gentle, lined face. He worked with domestic as well as farm animals, and was known in several counties for his abilities to help with pet turtles, snakes, lizards, birds and commercial reptiles.

He was standing with Lars and the uniforms who had apparently been first on the scene when Jesse arrived. He shook his head as Jesse approached. "Jesse, I'm damned sorry. I was trying to prepare my samples properly, study them myself... I should have sent them straight out."

Jesse placed a hand on his shoulder. "It's not your fault. You couldn't have known this was going to happen. What about your night man? Jim? Did he see anything?"

"He's over there," Lars said, pointing. "Go on. I've already spoken with him."

Doc's night guard was a man named Jim Hidalgo, half Peruvian, half Miccosukee. He and Jesse were distantly related. They shook hands, and Jim looked at him, wincing. "Jesse, I didn't even see it coming. We've got a few dogs in the kennels, you know, belonging to folks on vacation. I heard something, went to check on the pups. One little beagle was going wild, and I walked over to it and...that's the last thing I remember until Doc was standing over me, taking my pulse."

"Thanks, Jim." The man had a bump the size of Kansas on the back of his head. Jesse stared at it and whistled softly. "You're lucky you're alive."

"They're insisting I go to the hospital," Jim said.

"Yeah, well...that's quite a bump. Let them keep an eye on you, at least overnight."

Jim sighed. "All right. If you say so."

Jesse walked back to Lars, who was waiting for him. He told him about Julie's call and his trip out to the house.

"I had officers out there last night," Lars said with a sigh. "It's just that the department only stretches so far. But I'll send some men out again, twenty-four-hour watch. Anything else? You find your rogue gator?"

"Not yet. We're doing an organized hunt tomorrow night." He hesitated. "We may be on to something, though."

"What?"

"I need someone else to explain it to you."

Lars's partner, Abe, walked up then. "You know something, Jesse? If so—"

"Know something? Let's see. A couple is murdered, and there's an alligator limb at the scene. A man is attacked and killed by an alligator. A guard falls or is pushed into an alligator pit, and now the vet's guard has been attacked and specimens have been stolen. Gee. Think anything might be related here? Does the word 'gator' mean anything to you?"

"Go to hell, Jesse," Abe snapped. "I want to know what you've got to go on. I'm Homicide. I look for human killers. You're the alligator wrestler."

"An alligator is a natural predator, Abe."

"My point. I can hardly arrest one."

"If an animal is trained to kill, that makes the trainer a murderer, doesn't it?" Jesse asked dryly.

"I just said that if you've got something—"

Jesse ignored Abe and turned to Lars. "How about lunch tomorrow? The Miccosukee restaurant? On me."

"Yeah, we can make it," Abe answered for Lars.

Jesse shook his head. "I have someone who may know something. But she won't talk if we make this too big a party. Abe, just let Lars handle it."

"Who is she?" Abe said angrily. "We can just bring her in."

"And do what? Issue a lot of threats and get nothing back?" Jesse asked angrily.

Lars set a hand on Abe's shoulder. "Partner, whatever I get, you know we share. So…"

Abe glared at Jesse. Jesse glared back. "Dammit, Abe, I'm not asking Lars to hide anything from you, and I'm not trying to hide anything myself. Hell, I'd invite anyone who could bring justice for Hector and Maria. But, Abe, you're not a guy with a gentle touch. Let Lars take this one. He can call you the minute he leaves."

"Fine," Abe grated.

With the crime-scene people busy at the vet's, Jesse knew there was nothing he could do there for the night. "I'm going to have a last word with Jim," Jesse said. "Lars, see you tomorrow."

They were almost ready to take Jim to the hospital for observation. He was being laid out on a stretcher.

"Jim?"

"Yeah, Jess?"

"You walked back to the beagle. You were hit on the head. Then nothing, nothing at all until Doc was there?"

"Nothing, Jesse. I'm sorry."

"That's all right."

"Does Doc usually come in at night?"

"No, but he'd been worrying about finishing up the work you wanted, 'cuz he hasn't been able to get to it during the day. We've been really busy lately. It's a bitch, huh?"

"Yeah, it's a bitch."

Then the med tech gave Jesse a thumbs-up and rolled Jim into the vehicle.

Jesse waved and headed out.

LORENA SHOULD HAVE been dog-tired, but she was nervous. Television couldn't hold her attention. She found herself prowling the room as the hour grew later.

He had said he would be here.

Irritated with herself, she sat down and tried staring at the television again. She thought she was just blanking on the screen, since she didn't understand a word that was being said.

Then she realized she was on a Spanish-language channel.

Insane.

She should work, she told herself.

Work, and not wonder if Jesse was really coming.

Work, and not feel on fire with such breathless anxiety, both physical and emotional....

What she'd told Sally was true: she barely knew the man.

It was also true that she needed to work. She hadn't managed much of her "real job" since she had come here. But then she had happened to arrive just when there had been terrible murders, and when a Native American who knew the canals better than his own features had met with his fate in those waters. There should have been time. Time to become trusted. Time to flirt, if necessary.

She needed to get into that lab.

She was convinced there were answers to be found there. She was usually so organized and analytical. But she was afraid to make notes, afraid that her room might be searched and her real purpose discovered.

She showered more to hear the sound of the water and feel the pounding of it against her flesh than anything else. Then she slipped into a cotton nightshirt and lay on her bed, but she still felt ridiculously keyed up.

Had he been serious? Was Jesse really coming back here?

Forget Jesse, she told herself.

She tried to fathom the truth from what she had been able to glean from Michael's files. As yet, nothing that was proof positive. He was experimenting with gator eggs, of course. The temperature at which they were hatched determined the sex of an alligator; that kind of manipulation was easy. Breeding was basic biology. And here, at an alligator farm, it made sense to weed out characteristics one didn't like and fine-tune those features that were favorable to farming. Sex, size, the quality of the meat and hide.

But selective breeding hadn't created the monster she had seen today. Steroids and a formula—one that her father had known was too dangerous to exist—were behind what she had seen. Still, even if she got back into Preston's lab and found out what he was working on, how could she prove he had stolen her father's work?

Two days. Jesse had given her two days.

Just as she thought of the man, she heard a soft rapping at her door. She glanced at her glow-in-the-dark Mickey Mouse watch. It was after 1:00 a.m. She leapt from the bed, her heart thundering, and angry because of it.

The tapping sounded again. Then, softly, "Lorena, will you open the door?"

She hurried over, threw it open. "It's after one in the morning," she informed him.

He closed the door. "Shh."

"I actually do sleep at night. I have a job to do here. I wake up and start early. I—"

He drew her into his arms. "Shh."

"Jesse, I have to tell you—"

"Shh."

There was warmth in the depth of his eyes as well as amusement. There was something possessive in his hold, and she felt him slipping into her heart even as he inflamed her desires.

He's devastated, not dead. He'll never marry again. He's interested in one thing, and one thing only, so you'd better play like a big girl, if you intend to play.

He started to frown, staring into her eyes. "What's wrong? Has something happened?"

Lorena placed her fingers against his lips. "Shh," she said, and moved closer to him. His flesh was rich and warm, burnt copper, vibrant, vital.

He groaned softly, pulling her to him, and his lips found hers, pure fire. When they broke, she heard his whisper against her forehead, felt the power of his touch against her. "Lorena."

Fumbling, she found the light switch. And once again she said very softly, "Shh…"

Then she was in his arms. And the hour of the day or night didn't matter in the least.

When the alarm rang, rudely indicating that morning had come and it was time for the workday to begin, he was gone.

Chapter Nine

It seemed to be business as usual at the alligator farm.

Lorena went through greeting the tourists and taking them to their first stop: Michael Preston's lab.

While working with a group of children, she tried to get a good look at the hatchlings and at the cracked eggs.

They appeared normal, as far as she could tell. She wished she had been more interested in her father's work at the time he'd been doing it, but she had simply never liked alligators.

It was the eyes, she was certain.

Two more groups of tourists came through. Michael was his usual self, valiantly trying to give a good speech, but obviously uncomfortable. Or maybe he only seemed so to Lorena because she knew he loved research and hated tourists. He did seem happy, however, to have her come through with the groups.

Happy to have her stay.

At eleven, her cell phone rang. It was Jesse. "I'm coming to get you for lunch," he told her.

"I'm not sure I'm supposed to leave during the day," she said.

"Everyone gets lunch. You won't even be ten miles away," he assured her.

At noon, he picked her up in front of the farm. He was in uniform. "Where are we going?" she asked.

He grinned. "A restaurant."

"Okay."

She had passed the place on her way out to Harry's she realized when they got there. It was directly across from the Miccosukee village.

Jesse glanced her way dryly. "Don't worry. You won't have to eat grilled gator or anything."

"I never thought I would," she responded. "You have a chip on your shoulder."

"I do not," he said indignantly, and she had to smile.

She balked when they reached the place and she saw that Lars Garcia was standing out front.

"What is this?" she demanded heatedly.

"You have to tell him what you think is going on."

"You gave me two days!" she said.

"There's been a complication. The vet's office was broken into. Another man was attacked. Thankfully, we have hard heads out here. He survived."

Jesse was grim, but she was still furious. She had nothing, no evidence at all, really, and he had brought her here to tell her story to another policeman. She was stiff and still angry when they went in.

Lars was as polite and decent as ever. He chatted about the weather while they waited for their food, and he and Jesse talked about an upcoming musical festival put on by the Miccosukee tribe in the Glades. "People come by the hundreds. It's great," Lars said.

When their food came—she'd ordered a very boring meal: hamburger, fries and an iced tea—Lars lowered his voice and said, "Jesse says I need to know why you're here."

She'd thought she was tense already, but now her muscles constricted to an even greater degree, and she shot Jesse a furious glance.

"Lorena, it's important I know."

"Then I'm surprised Jesse didn't tell you," she said.

"I need to hear it from you."

She clenched her teeth, set her hamburger down, shot Jesse one last filthy stare, and explained what she knew and feared to Lars. He listened without mocking or doubting her, though he glanced at Jesse several times, as if Jesse might have put him in the middle of a science fiction tale, but when she finished, he sighed and asked, "Your father's death was ruled an accident?"

"Yes. But I know it wasn't."

"That's going to be very difficult to prove."

"Maybe not now, when other people are dying," she said.

That caused a glance between Lars and Jesse.

"What was in the e-mail from the alligator farm?" Lars asked.

She shrugged. "It was vague. They were interested, of course, in learning about any developments to increase quality and efficiency. They suggested that they could pay well."

"What was your father's reply?" Lars asked.

"That he had nothing ready as of yet. And he explained that research was difficult, that all genetic scientists had to take the greatest care when playing with the makeup of any life form."

"Did other alligator farms contact your father?" Lars asked.

She shrugged. "Yes."

"So why are you concentrating on this one?"

"Every other e-mail was signed by a specific person. At Harry's, the same e-mail account can be used by almost anyone who works there."

"We can trace the computer," Lars said.

"If so, what will that prove?" Lorena asked.

"Whether it was in the office, in the lab or somewhere else," Lars said.

"Preston would have to be involved, wouldn't he?" Jesse asked.

"There are no 'have-tos,' Jesse. We both know that," Lars said. He looked at Lorena. "You need to get out of that place."

She tensed again, staring at Jesse. "I can't see how I can be in any personal danger. I had nothing to do with my father's work."

"Anyone can be in danger," Lars said softly.

Lars sat back, wiped his mouth and stared at Lorena. "I'll have to talk to the D.A.'s office about a search warrant. In the meantime, you shouldn't go back."

Lorena leaned forward, speaking heatedly. "My father is dead. A local couple have been killed. You don't know how many enhanced alligators you might have running around the Everglades. You need me, and you need my help."

"There's something I don't understand here," Lars said, and he glanced at Jesse, frowning. "This research has to be fairly new. Alligators take time to mature and grow. How could this one have gotten so big so fast?"

Lorena shook her head. "The formula causes an increase in the growth rate. Take people. Better diets, rich in protein, make for taller, stronger teens. Body builders bulk up with steroids. You'd be amazed at what chemicals can do to the body. That's why it's so important not only that we find out who was doing what but to just how many specimens."

"We need a search warrant," Lars said simply.

"Do you think you can get one?" Lorena asked anxiously.

He shrugged. "If I can argue well enough. And prove just cause. Well, I should get moving." He lifted a hand to ask for the check. Jesse caught his arm.

"I told you yesterday. This one is on the tribe."

"Thanks." He rose. Lorena and Jesse did the same.

When Lars had walked out, Lorena turned on Jesse. "You told me that I had two days."

"Lorena, what do you think you're going to find in two days?" Jesse demanded.

"More than anyone else?"

"Is biochemistry another of your degrees?"

She gritted her teeth, staring at him. "No. But I know what might have been stolen from my father."

"Lorena, face it, you're not going to be able to do anything if you're dead!"

She turned away from him and headed toward the door, clearly indicating that lunch was over for her, as well.

He followed. As soon as he came out, she got into the car. There was no possibility that she was going to walk back to work.

He didn't pull straight back onto the road but instead drove almost directly across the street. She gazed at him with hostility. "You have a few minutes left. I thought you might want to see the village."

She didn't have a chance to refuse. He had already gotten out of the car.

They entered the gift shop first. It offered Indian goods from around the country. There were a number of the exquisite colorful shirts, skirts and jackets for which both the Seminoles and Miccosukees had become famous, along with dream catchers, posters, T-shirts, postcards, drums, hand-carved "totem" recorders and jewelry. Some of the unique beadwork designs on the jewelry might well have attracted Lorena's attention, but Jesse was already headed straight out the back. There was an entry fee, but Jesse just smiled at the girl, and he, with Lorena trailing behind him, walked on through. She offered the girl an awkward smile, as well.

Out back, there were a number of chickees, along with more items for sale. Women were there working on intricate basketry, sewing the beautiful colored clothing and designing jewelry.

Lorena, fascinated, would have paused, but Jesse was again moving on to one of the huge pits where alligators lived with a colony of turtles.

Looking into the pit, Lorena noted that a number of the gators were large, very large. But not one of them was more than ten feet.

"Jesse, what's up?"

A man with ink-dark hair and Native American features, wearing a T-shirt that advertised a popular rock band, walked up to them.

Jesse nodded to him. "Mike. This is Lorena Fortier. She's working at Harry's."

The man studied her with a smile. "Welcome."

"I thought she might want to see the village."

Mike smiled and shrugged. "Well, there's the museum, the pits, we do some wrestling, give a few history lessons."

"She's on lunch break. I just thought she should come look around. And I wanted to make sure you'd seen the notice."

"About the hunt tonight? I'll be there," Mike said grimly. He shook his head. "Billy Ray...well, he wasn't the kind of man that gave us a lot of pride, but hell, I wouldn't have wanted my worst enemy to go that way."

"Right. Make sure everyone knows we're hunting something big, really big. Close to twenty feet, maybe even more."

Mike whistled softly. "We do know what we're doing, Jesse," he said. "But it's good to be warned."

"See you later, then. And extend my thanks to everyone showing up from the tribe."

Mike nodded. "See you then."

Jesse turned and headed toward the exit without a word to Lorena. She had been angry, but now he was the one who seemed irritated. They reached the car, where, despite his apparent anger, he opened her door.

"You're the one who betrayed me," she reminded him.

He shot her a scowling glance. "I'm trying to get you out of what might be a dangerous situation. But you know what? I don't usually have a chip on my shoulder, but today, I do. Chemists, biochemists, biologists! They're playing with life. Interesting, sure. Let's see how we can improve what God made. But, the thing is, people play God, and things can happen. Billy Ray was no prize specimen of humanity. But you heard it in Mike's voice. He was one of ours. We're a small tribe. We were forced down to this land, and we learned how to live on it. Billy Ray had every right in the world to be fishing. Hell, if he wanted to drink himself silly, that was his choice, too. He shouldn't have been attacked by an animal that was only there because someone decided to play God."

Lorena gasped. "My father wanted to help people," she insisted angrily. "And when he was afraid he might be on to something dangerous, he was willing to destroy years of research!"

"Too bad you couldn't have explained that to Billy Ray while he was being eaten," Jesse said.

Lorena stared at him incredulously. "Evil people come in all colors and nationalities, you know!"

The drive from the village to the alligator farm was short. Jesse pulled in just as Lorena finished her tirade, and she was out the door before the engine could die. She walked around to his window. "Thank you for your concern for my safety, but since you've turned things over to Metro-Dade now, I'm sure I'll be just fine. You can feel secure in the fact that I'll be safe without your assistance."

She spun around, her feet crunching on the gravel path, heedless as to whether he called her back or not.

Lunch was over. It was time to get back to work.

She did so, energetically, talking to the tourists, helping Michael, even going with the tours to the pits and watching while Jack wrestled one of the six-foot alligators.

It didn't matter what she did, as long as she did something. With Michael in his lab, she certainly wasn't going to get anywhere there, so she put her heart into the business of people. Anything at all to keep busy.

To keep from thinking.

She shouldn't have gotten so close so fast. Getting intimate with someone so unique, so unusual, so very much…everything she might have wanted in life…had been more than foolhardy. She had let herself become far too emotionally involved, and then…

She'd felt that wretched knife in her back. His bitterness against her father had been unexpected and deeply painful.

That afternoon, she actually put her nursing skills to the test. A little girl fell on one of the paths.

Nothing like a registered nurse to apply disinfectant and a bandage.

As she tended the child, Lorena suddenly wondered why Harry had decided that he needed a nurse on the premises. It had made sense at first. The alligator farm was in an isolated location. But she had seen the local services in action. Help had arrived almost instantly when Roger had been found in the pit. Helicopters provided a swift transport to the emergency room.

Of course, nothing so drastic was necessary for little scrapes and bruises, but still…

Still, the question gave her pause. She forced herself to concentrate on it. It was good—no, it was *necessary*—to think about something—anything—other than Jesse Crane and the startling color of his eyes, the sleek bronze warmth of his flesh, the sound of his voice, the way he touched her, the structure of his face and the way she just wanted to be with him…

No! She had to think of something else.

He would be back at the end of the day, there to organize the hunt. As it veered toward five o'clock and closing, she determined to spend some quality time with Dr. Michael Preston.

BY THE TIME Lorena stalked off, Jesse had already cooled down and realized that he'd been a fool, taking his frustration over what had happened out on her.

What was it about the woman? She made him forget everything the moment he was with her, even though she wasn't his type at all.

And why not?

Because she was blond?

Elegant, feminine…a powder puff, or so he had assumed at first.

But she wasn't. She was determined. Reckless, maybe, but determined and fierce, and she had told him that she was a crack shot. Not a powder puff at all.

But also not the kind to spend a lifetime in the wilds. Then he reminded himself ruefully that his "wilds" were just a forty-five-minute drive from an urban Mecca with clubs, malls, theaters and more.

What was he doing, arguing with himself, convincing himself that his lifestyle was a good one? Because…?

Because he hadn't felt the way he felt about her in a very long time. In fact, he'd thought he'd buried those feelings along with Connie, that as long as he threw himself back into his passion for the land and the tribe, he could learn to live without all they had shared, the tenderness and sense of being one, loving, laughing, waking together, sleeping each night entwined. There was the chemistry that brought people together, and, if you were lucky, the chemistry, excitement and hunger that remained. And more. The longing to see someone's eyes opening to the new day, the times when no words were necessary, the nights when life was good just because the world could be shared.

He lowered his head, wincing, feeling as if the scars that had covered his wounds were ripping open. As if they were raw and bleeding, all because of the promise of something, some*one,* else. But that promise brought with it the one emotion he dreaded more than anything. Fear. No wonder he'd pushed her away.

He clenched and unclenched his fists. This wasn't the right time. In fact, it was idiotic. And, anyway, she was furious with him, probably regretting the very fact that they'd touched.

He forced his mind onto the case.

He felt that they were closing in, that Lars would be able to get the search warrant after what he had learned from Lorena. There were, however, other alligator farms in the area. It might be tough for him to convince the D.A.'s office, without concrete proof, not only that there really were "enhanced" alligators in the Everglades, but that Harry's Alligator Farm and Museum was responsible, and that whoever had gone to the extremes of biochemical manipulation was also willing to kill for it.

He hesitated, then decided to take another drive out to Dr. Thiessen's place to see if the Metro-Dade cops had missed anything, though he doubted it. They were good.

Then again, this was a world he knew far better than anyone else, a world that could not be taught in any lab or classroom.

In her room, Lorena found herself amazed to be carefully considering her wardrobe for the evening.

She hadn't been asked on the hunt, which made sense. Only experienced alligator trappers were going, and that definitely did not include her.

Nor, she suspected, did it include Michael Preston.

Which was good, because she wanted to spend some time with Michael. She didn't want to appear as if she had dressed to seduce, but she *did* want to look attractive.

Not in an aggressive way. Just enough to be compelling, so she could conduct her own hunt this evening.

She opted for casual slacks and a soft silk halter top. When she was dressed, she headed for his lab, listened, and heard movement. She tapped on the door.

"Yes?"

Lorena slipped in. "Hey. Are you going on that hunt this evening?" she asked him.

He arched a brow, grimaced and shook his head. "I'm a scientist. The brains, not the brawn."

"Ah."

"I guess you're into brawn."

"I am?"

"Well…" He perched on the edge of his desk, still in his lab coat. "You've been spending a lot of time with our bronzed-and-buff policeman, Ms. Fortier."

She shrugged casually. "Not really. I wound up driving with him when that poor woman freaked out over her friend having been killed. And I probably shouldn't have headed out to the casino to begin with, the night I left with him. Too tired. And then someone told him about the incident with the hatchlings, so he wanted to talk to me."

"Not me."

"Did you tell anyone here?" Lorena asked.

He lifted his shoulders. "I don't think so. Maybe the kid complained in the end, I don't know. Maybe we shouldn't have let the little brat off the hook."

"Maybe not," she agreed. She walked closer, then sat on the other corner of his desk. She frowned. "Michael, did you ever believe any of those stories about kids buying baby alligators and then their parents flushing them down the toilet, so they wound up in the sewers of New York, that kind of thing?"

He waved a hand in the air. "Science fiction," he assured her. "Alligators, even in a sewer, wouldn't last long in New York. They need the sun, the heat. You know that."

"Right," she mused. "But...down here, I wonder how many alligators wind up free after they've been lifted from a place like this one by a kid like that brat. I mean it's possible. We both know that."

He slipped from his position on the desk and approached her, a smile on his face. She was a bit unnerved when he came very close, leaning toward her, resting his hands on the desktop on either side of her. "Possible," he said softly, his face just a whisper away. "But no kid is going to steal a hatchling from here, then let it loose in the New York sewers to grow into a monster."

"But there's at least one monster alligator out in the canals right now," she said. "That's what they're hunting tonight."

She saw a pulse ticking in his cheek. He didn't move. "Just what are you suggesting, Ms. Fortier?" he asked very softly.

"What else could it be?" she asked innocently. "I think that alligator escaped or was stolen from a lab," she said, and shrugged.

"From here?" he asked.

"From somewhere," she breathed. He was close. So

close. And he might be the brains and not the brawn, but he still had quite an impressive build, and she just might have taken things too far.

"If I could create a super-gator, I'd be rich," he said, sounding surprisingly disgusted.

But she could see the tension in his face, feel it in his muscles. Her recklessness could prove dangerous. This, however, had been the time to take chances. Dozens of men from around the area would be arriving shortly. If he came any closer...

If she felt a deeper surge of unease...

All she had to do was scream.

He was staring at her intently. Searching her eyes.

He started to raise a hand toward her face, smiling.

"Michael?"

The call and a fierce knocking were followed by the door simply opening.

Lorena slipped from the edge of the desk as Michael turned.

Harry was there.

"Michael, can you get out here and help with the equipment? This is insane, if you ask me. Half the guys have no supplies. Damn Jesse. Leave it to him to get the full cooperation of the Florida Wildlife and Game Commission for a wild-goose chase."

If Harry had noticed that he had interrupted something, he gave no sign. But maybe he hadn't noticed, she thought. He seemed much more upset about the hunt than that a man had been killed by a gator.

Lorena grimaced as she caught Michael's eye, then escaped in Harry's wake.

Hurrying out back to the canal, she saw an unbelievable lineup of airboats and canoes. Jesse was up on some kind of a huge tackle box, giving instructions. "Remember, folks, we're looking for something really large—not indiscriminately killing off a population for trophies."

"How big, Jesse?" a man shouted from one of the canoes.

"Bigger than the norm," Michael Preston answered for him, hurrying forward. "The biggest gator ever recorded in Florida was seventeen feet, five inches long. The biggest gator recorded in Louisiana was nineteen feet, two inches. So if you find anything smaller than that—wrong gator."

"Ah, hell!" the same fellow snorted. "We have to have something real to go by."

"You heard the man. We're looking for fifteen feet or over. All right?" Jesse asked.

"We get to harvest what we get?"

She saw Jesse defer to a man who looked like he was about to go on safari, in khakis and a straw hat. He was tall and lean.

Jesse reached a hand down and helped the man up on the box. "This is Steven Bear, Florida Wildlife and Game Commission."

"We can harvest the fellas, huh?" another man called.

"Gentlemen, the important thing is this—we're not out on a regular hunt. Make sure your quarry is over fifteen feet. Then the meat is yours. Nothing small is to be taken. Understood?"

She saw both Steven Bear and Jesse jump down from the box. Someone asked Jesse a question, and he answered, then headed for an airboat with a number of men already aboard.

Michael came up behind her. "Half those guys see this as a free-for-all," he murmured.

She turned to him, frowning herself. "I don't get it. I mean, there are so many boats. Are they going to try to sneak up on it with all those lights, all that noise?"

"You'll see," Michael said.

And she did. It had seemed like chaos, but when the airboats took off, they headed in all different directions. Once again, she had forgotten that what appeared like solid ground in this area most often wasn't.

River of grass.

They were taking off over that river in a dozen different directions.

"Well, they'll be gone awhile," Michael said. "Why don't we have some dinner?"

"Sure."

They ambled to the cafeteria together, chose pork chops for their meals, and sat together.

The place was almost eerily empty. "Did Sally go on the hunt?" Lorena asked, curious that the outspoken, sexy redhead was nowhere to be seen.

"I didn't see her," Michael said.

"Does she help with the research here at all?" Lorena asked.

Michael laughed. "There's only one green thing that Sally would research—money," he told her.

"Oh?"

"Um."

Lorena smiled, smoothing back a lock of hair. "I don't get it then. Why is she working out here?"

"I think she's trying to be so indispensable to Harry that he makes her a partner. He owns land all over the place. And we're doing well here…but I think he'd like to open another facility, closer down by the Keys. He's already opened a few shops in Key Largo."

She frowned again. "Michael, this is a totally dumb question. But Harry raises gators for their meat and hides, right? So where does he—"

"Lorena!" Michael said, grinning. "You don't 'harvest' animals where you show them off to the tourists! I told you—Harry owns a lot of land closer to the Keys, down in the Florida City–Homestead area."

"Ah."

"You really are interested, aren't you?" When she nodded, he said, "I can show you a few things, then. Are you done?"

"Um, yes," she murmured.

He wiggled his eyebrows in a manner suggestive of a hunched Igor in a horror movie. "Come, my dear, I'll show you my lab," he growled jokingly.

Lorena froze for a moment. She'd been doing everything in her power to sneak into the lab, and now he was making this offer.

While anyone who might have come to her rescue was off hunting for a rogue alligator.

No. There were more live-ins around the compound. And Harry hadn't gone on the hunt; he was around somewhere.

Besides, she had waited far too long for this opportunity. She could take care of herself.

And she was going in.

"Let's see what you've got to show me," she said with a smile.

He flashed her a smile in return, showing very white teeth. They rose and walked across the compound. She noted that there was another guard on duty.

She noted as well that he was spooked. When he heard their footsteps, his hand flew to the hilt of his gun, buckled at his hip.

"Just Ms. Fortier and me," Michael said.

"Evenin'," the guard replied.

When they reached the door to the lab, Michael drew out his keys and opened it, pressing the small of Lorena's back lightly to get her to proceed inside.

He followed, closed the door, then locked it.

Then he turned and stared at her. "I don't know why I bother. Someone picked it open the other day."

"Oh?"

He shook his head, approaching her. She cocked her head, looking at him. The guard had just seen the two of them together. He couldn't possibly be planning anything…evil.

Not unless he meant to go back out and kill the guard as well!

He was still smiling, as if his intent was to seduce, but she knew it wasn't. She found herself backed against the desk.

He was the brain, he had said, not the brawn. But he was a liar. She could feel the heat and strength of his muscles.

And his anger.

His menace…

"You picked the lock, Lorena, didn't you?" he asked softly.

"What?"

"Ah, the innocence. Like hell, Ms. Fortier. You're flirting madly with me, while it's more than obvious that it's Jesse Crane who's really stirred your senses. And yet you're charming as hell to Jack and Hugh, too.

Are you just a little vamp, Ms. Fortier? I don't think
so. I think you're up to something. You want something in this lab. Tell me what it is. Here we are, you
and me, alone, finally. So…it's time. You want to see
what's going on in here? You might as well. I think you
should see exactly what you've been wanting to see.
Now. *Right now.*"

Chapter Ten

Nighttime in the Everglades, and it was eerie.

No matter how well a man knew the place, the near-total darkness hid the predators haunting the swamp and made this a dangerous place.

When light touched the gators' eyes, they glowed, as if they were demons from hell, not of this world at all.

Jesse was accustomed to the glowing eyes, and yet even he found them chilling in the dark of the night.

Despite his familiarity with the creatures, it was difficult for him to determine the size of one with only the eyes to go on. Sometimes, he knew instantly when he was looking at an animal of no more than five to eight feet, but with just the eyes above the water to go by, more often than not it was a crap shoot.

Twice they snared a creature only to realize that the specimen they had in their loops was no more than nine feet, ten tops.

Each time they released their catch. Enraged, the alligators made swift departures from the area once they had been freed.

The rest of the group on the airboat, Jack, Leo and Sam Tiger, were soaked and exasperated, but no one suggested giving up as they moved closer to the location where Billy Ray had been attacked and killed.

They had been out a few hours and had just cut the motor, and only the noises of the night were echoing in the air around them, when Jack Pine said softly, "There," and pointed.

Jesse looked in the direction Jack was indicating.

The alligator wasn't completely submerged. The length of the head was incredible. He focused hard and saw the length of the animal as it floated just beneath the surface.

And he knew they had found the beast they were searching for.

Sam whistled softly. "I have never seen anything remotely near that size before," he said.

"Let's bait it," Jesse murmured.

Their bait was chicken. He tied several pieces on the line.

The alligator watched them as they approached. It didn't move; it showed no fear.

When the line was cast in the water, the animal moved at last.

It went for the bait. They were ready with their snares.

A massive snap of the mighty jaws severed the lines as well as securing the meat, but Jack managed to get a noose around the neck.

The alligator made one swing of that massive head. Jack went flying off the airboat, a shout of surprise escaping his lips. The animal instantly began to close in on him.

Sam quickly started the engine and headed in for a rescue. Jesse went for one of the high-powered revolvers. He aimed and fired, aimed and fired, as they neared Jack.

Sam swore, shouting to Jack.

In a frenzy, Jack moved toward the airboat.

Jesse, taking care to miss the man, fired again and again.

Ten bullets into the gator.

It kept coming, heedless of the men, heedless of the bullets that had pierced its hide.

They reached Jack. Sam and Leo instantly reached for him, and he reached back, grabbing their hands, the muscles bulging in his forearms and a look of dread in his eyes.

They were just dragging Jack over the edge of the airboat platform when the gator's head emerged, mammoth jaws wide with their shocking power.

Jesse aimed again, dead into one of the eyes.

The explosion ripped through the night.

The eye and part of the head evaporated.

And at last, with Jack's feet just clearing the water, the creature began to fall back.

Jesse fired again and again, aiming at what was left of the disappearing head.

He felt a hand on his arm. Sam's. "You got it," Sam said softly.

And from where he lay on the floor of the airboat, Jack said softly, "Dear God."

In the silence that followed his statement, they heard the whir of motors, saw approaching lights and heard the shouts of others.

More airboats and canoes arrived, and the area was suddenly aglow with floodlights.

"You got it?" Hugh called from another vessel.

Jesse realized that he was shaking. He nodded, turned, lowered his gun and found a seat.

The others began to haul the creature in.

"WELL, LORENA?" MICHAEL asked huskily.

Great, she thought.

She had a gun, and she was a crack shot. But she had let her eagerness to find the truth lead to stupidity, so here she was, boxed in by her main suspect, and he was challenging her....

She slid her hands backward on his desk. In all the old movies, there was a letter opener on a desk, ready to be used by a desperate victim as a weapon.

There was nothing on Michael Preston's desk but his computer and a few papers.

Not even a paperweight.

"Well..." she murmured, as he came closer. Closer.

There was nothing of use on the desk.

She told herself to scream!

It was all she had left.

"How could you?" Michael said suddenly, turning abruptly away from her.

She gulped down her scream.

"What?"

"How in the world could you suspect me of anything? Although what you think I've been doing, I still don't know. You've been on my computer. You've been searching this lab. What do you think that I've done? Or are *you* out to steal something from *me?*" he demanded.

She stared at him, a frown furrowing her brow. He seemed to be genuinely upset, and he also seemed to be as much at a loss as she was herself right now.

But if not Michael Preston…who? He was the scientist here.

The brains, not the brawn.

"What?" she repeated, stalling for time, rapidly trying to determine just what to say.

"Are you a thief?" he queried.

"Of course not!" she protested.

"Then what have you been doing?"

She sighed, looking downward. "Trying to understand," she murmured.

"Understand what?" he demanded.

"Well, you know, more of what's going on around here."

"Really. Didn't the concept of simply asking occur to you?"

Again she sighed. "Well…no. It's all so strange. This place, the people here."

"Except for Jesse Crane."

She stared at him, then shrugged. "He seems to be a decent guy. I like him," she murmured.

"In a way you don't like me?"

"Oh, Michael! You're great. You know that. Half the women you meet immediately start crushing on you," she told him.

He grinned ruefully, then shrugged. "The problem is," he said huskily, "it's the half of the female population I *want* that couldn't care less about me."

Lorena felt awkward then, not sure what to say. But feeling awkward was much better than feeling terrified.

"Michael…"

"Never mind. It's true. Women prefer brawn to brain."

She arched a brow. "Are you insinuating that men

with brawn can't have brains? I have the impression that you spend a fair amount of time in the gym."

He sat beside her on the desk, crossing his arms over his chest. He sounded amused as he admitted, "Yeah, I go to the gym. But do I want to be out looking for a giant gator? Not in this lifetime. I like hatchlings. They're little. They might bite fingers, but it's unlikely that I'll become dinner for them."

"Michael...have you ever altered a hatchling?"

"Altered?"

"When you crack the eggs. Have you ever experimented?"

"Yes," he said flatly. His eyes narrowed sharply as he stared at her. "Is that what you're after? Trying to steal my vitamin compounds?"

"Vitamins? No."

"Well, that's about all I've worked with. Vitamins in the egg. You want my password? You want to get into the files you haven't been able to crack?" he asked.

She was uneasy again, thinking that he might have refrained from harming her only because he hadn't decided what she was really doing, why she had come.

Was this a trap?

"Just what kind of work are you doing?" she inquired.

"What do you think?" he demanded. "The same kind of research as everyone else! Alligator meat is already lean and high in protein. I'm trying to make it even better, so someday it can feed the world."

He sounded like her father. But she wondered if he was driven by the same true passion to help, or if he was seeking renown—or just money.

He shook his head with disgust suddenly and walked

around to click on his computer. "What kind of work do I do? Research, and yes, experimentation. But you know what? Nothing I know about can create a giant killer gator. So you go ahead and take a look. I hope you're up on your enzymes, proteins, compounds, vitamins and minerals."

"Look, Michael," she began. "I—"

He was typing something when he suddenly looked up. "I just realized something. Why are you looking into *my* research? For a gator to have gotten as big as this one supposedly is, it would have to have been growing for years and years—while both of us were still kids, practically."

"Not that long," she murmured dryly.

He stared at her, then exhaled slowly. "Is there some kind of research out there that I don't know about? Some kind of discovery. That is…what you're saying is impossible."

"Hey," she murmured, keeping her eyes low. "I'm not a researcher. I'm not even an alligator expert."

"So what are you after?"

"I'm not sure. I'm just curious, I guess," she lied. She still wasn't certain she could trust Michael Preston.

He shook his head, studying the computer screen. "There have been big gators, but the biggest one on record wasn't even caught in this state. I suppose someone could have figured out a way to jump-start gator growth, or hybridize a gator with something else. I mean, we only have beefalo because of somebody's bright idea to breed a cow with a buffalo."

He seemed genuinely absorbed in seeking answers, but Lorena found that she was uncomfortable despite that fact.

"Come. Look," he demanded, staring at her belligerently.

She walked over to see the screen. He stood, urging her into the chair.

He had opened his research files. He had been telling her the truth—at least, as far as this proved. There were notes on the eggs with cracked shells. There was a study on albino alligators, with statistics regarding their life expectancy in the wild. There were side notes reminding him to speak to Harry about habitat changes, notations regarding the fact that he intended to set the temperature to create a male so they could eventually breed it with a number of females and track its genetic influence.

As she read his notes, she could feel him. He was standing directly behind her chair.

"Go on," he snapped, sounding angry again. "Keep reading."

Words began to swim before her eyes. She wondered how much time had passed.

It felt like forever.

She pushed the chair away from the desk, pushing him back, as well. "Michael, I told you, I'm not a researcher, so I don't even understand what I'm reading. I was just curious." She stood. "And I'm tired, really tired."

He shook his head. "You're not leaving here. Not until you tell me what you're up to."

"I'm not up to anything," she lied flatly.

"Then why break into my lab?"

She lowered her head, seeking a plausible explanation. She looked up at him again, knowing she had to be careful. "Michael…you're an attractive man."

"So?"

"I...well, frankly, I was interested in you. As a man. As a scientist. I was curious about you. I wanted to know what made you tick, why you're so fascinated with such strange creatures. But then..."

"Then you met Jesse."

She shrugged, not wanting to commit.

"You're sleeping with him," he accused her.

"Michael, that's really none of your business."

"Ah, I see. You break into my lab because of a crush on me—sorry, interest in my life, what makes me tick—but *your* life is none of my business."

She lifted her hands. "I'm sorry."

"I should report you to Harry."

"Do whatever you feel you have to," she murmured, looking down.

"You're making a mistake, you know."

He was close to her again. Just a foot away.

He reached out a hand. She nearly jumped.

He touched her face. "A big mistake," he told her.

"I'm afraid I've already made more than a few of those in my life," she murmured.

He tilted her chin upward, meeting her eyes earnestly. "No. You're making a big mistake with Jesse. You don't even know him."

"I know something about his past, if that's what you mean," she said.

"He's a loner, Lorena. Do you want to spend your entire life sitting on a mucky pile of saw grass? He belongs here. You don't. His passion is the land and the tribal council. He's decent enough as a human being. But he puts a wall up. He always will. Think about it."

She caught his hand and squeezed it. Like a friend.

She was more anxious than ever to get the hell out of his lab.

"Michael, we've got a bigger problem than my love life right now. There's a killer gator out there."

"People have been killed by alligators before," he said flatly.

"Yes, but this is different. And we breed gators here. People are liable to think we have something to do with it."

He laughed a little bitterly. "You think? Who cares? Maybe that gator will make things better here. Think about it. People love to stop and stare at accidents. They love horror movies. People don't mind watching terrible things happen to strangers. I think the fact that there's a man-eater out there will draw even bigger crowds."

"Michael, that's horrible!"

He shrugged. "A lot that's horrible is true."

She hesitated for a moment, feeling another tremendous surge of unease.

"They should be coming back soon," she murmured. "Very soon."

"Are you trying to get away from me?" he asked her.

She straightened determinedly. "I want to see if they're back yet, if they've caught that thing," she said.

She headed for the door.

She felt him following her.

For a minute she was terrified that she wouldn't be able to open the door easily, since it was locked.

She twisted the knob, feeling his heat as he moved up close behind her, almost touching her.

She was certain he was reaching out, about to grab her, but the door opened easily, and as she threw it open, Sally was coming down the hallway.

"Sally!" she exclaimed loudly.

If Michael had been about to touch her, his hand fell away. "Hey, Sally."

"I think they're coming back," Sally was saying excitedly. "Harry was just on the radio with someone. They've got something."

"They caught it?" Michael asked.

"Well, I don't know if they caught 'it,' but they caught something. Come on."

JESSE FELT DRAINED and uneasy when they arrived back at Harry's. Jack Pine had come too damn close to being that alligator's last meal.

But he was apparently the only one who felt uneasy. Everyone else, including the hunters who had come back empty-handed, seemed to be on some kind of a natural high—amazed and excited by the size of the creature.

"It's a record," Harry said as the men made their way to land, a number of them dragging the nearly headless carcass onto the hard ground.

Harry was barking out orders, getting people to take measurements. He, too, seemed pleased and excited.

Jack, who had been given the tape measure, cried out, "Son of a gun, we just beat Louisiana. Twenty-two feet, three inches!"

"I don't care what it costs, we need the best taxidermist in the country. What's left of this sucker is getting stuffed. Hell, who shot the thing so many times? Never mind, never mind, the bullet holes are good. They make him look tougher than a *Tyrannosaurus rex*," Harry said.

"Harry, it's going to a lab. There's going to be an

autopsy," Jesse said. He was drenched and covered in muck, and in no mood for the spirit of joviality going around. The thing had been a killer.

"An autopsy? On a gator?" Harry said.

Jesse felt his stomach turn. "We need to know for sure if this was the animal that took down Billy Ray."

Silence fell over the crowd at last as they all realized what Jesse was saying.

The gator would still have been digesting its last meal when it was killed.

"All right, Jesse. Have it taken to the lab." Harry sounded unhappy but resigned. "Do I get it when you're done?"

Jesse didn't answer, just turned away. Lorena was there, standing back in silence.

He felt a flip-flop of emotion.

In the heat of the hunt, he'd forgotten that he'd left her here. Alone.

But she appeared to be fine. More than fine. As ever, she was stunning. A rose in the midst of swamp grass.

"Are you taking the carcass to Doc Thiessen?" Harry asked.

Jesse kept staring at Lorena as he answered. "They'll have better facilities upstate, at the college," he said, turning away from Lorena at last.

Everyone had their cameras out now. They had hoisted the alligator up over one of the steel light poles. The thing was actually bending with the weight. Everyone had gone back to talking excitedly and having their pictures taken with the carcass.

The head...just the head...dear lord. The size of what was left was terrifying.

Lorena stayed apart from the crowd, but he saw that Michael and Sally were posing, Hugh snapping the picture.

"Harry, we'll see about getting the gator to you when we're done, okay?" he said congenially.

"Folks, we got the cafeteria open!" Harry called out, beaming at Jesse's words. "There's just coffee and sandwiches, but you're all welcome!"

Still grinning broadly at Jesse, Harry walked away.

Lorena was still a good twenty feet away, but her eyes were on him.

"Hey," he said softly.

"Hey." She smiled, apparently having forgiven him, and walked toward him slowly.

Damn, but he was in love with just the way she walked. The slow, easy sway of her hips. The slight look of something secretive, something shared, in the small curl of her lips. The way her hair picked up the lights, burning gold.

She reached him and touched his face, apparently heedless as to whether anyone noticed or not.

"You know, Officer Crane, you look good even in muck," she told him.

"I'd be happy to share my muck," he told her.

"Not here," she whispered. He thought she shivered slightly. "Not tonight."

"Are you coming home with me, then?"

Her head lowered; then she looked up, and her smile deepened. "Yeah, yeah, I guess I am."

The feeling of dread and weariness that had taken such a grip on him as they returned seemed to melt away. Strange, how life could be, how human emotions could be changed by something as simple as the sound of someone's voice.

The sway of someone's hips. Her smile.

Chemistry. She had been fascinating but unknown, and now she was known. Everything he knew now made her slightest movement all the more seductive. The thought of touching her again was deep, rich, combustible.

"Should we take my car?" she asked.

He arched a brow with a rueful smile, indicating the state he was in.

"I told you, I like you in muck."

"Down and dirty, eh?" he teased.

"I was thinking of a shower," she murmured.

"Jesse!" someone called excitedly.

He was startled from the absorption that had made him forget that dozens of people surrounded them.

"Jesse!" It was Sally. She came over and gave him a big hug. "Aren't you excited? That's the biggest gator on record, and you're the one who bagged it."

"It was a killer, Sally."

"That makes you one big, bad hunter, then, doesn't it?"

There was innuendo in her voice. Once it had amused him, but now it was an imposition.

She suddenly realized she had her back to Lorena and turned. "Oh, I'm sorry, Lorena. It's just so exciting."

Exciting? Yeah, Sally was excited, Jesse thought. Sally was the kind who found sensual stimulation in danger.

He looked at Lorena, and at that moment he realized that he was falling in love. She was clearly amused by the situation. Her eyes didn't fill with anger, fear or suspicion; there was even a slight smile on her face. She was willing to let him handle it. And she would wait.

"It was an alligator, Sally. Thousands of alligators

are killed on hunts. But I guess you're right. There are people who like the hunt. Frankly, I'm not a hunter."

"Jesse! Your people have lived off gators for over a century, hunting them, wrestling them."

For some reason, the way she said "your people" didn't sit right with him. He realized suddenly that Sally would always be fascinated with someone for what they did, not who they were. He hadn't really given it any thought before, but she'd never been more than someone with whom to enjoy a friendly flirtation. Tonight, he found that he was slightly repelled.

A wry smile came to his lips. That was, of course, because he'd never realized he could actually fall in love with anyone again.

"Isn't the casino the big moneymaker these days?" Lorena asked, her smile growing deeper as she and Jesse met each another's eyes.

"Oh, yeah. Bingo," Jesse agreed. "But we're all glad this guy's been caught. I think he's the one that got Billy Ray, and we'll know for certain soon enough. Good night, Sally."

He didn't actually step around her, just eased into a position that let him slip an arm around Lorena's shoulders.

"Good night, Sally," Lorena said.

The woman stared blankly at the two of them for a moment. Then she seemed to realize that they were leaving. Together.

"Oh! Uh, good night."

They avoided the cafeteria, where people had started massing. As they walked down the hallway, they could hear Jack talking. "I'm telling you, I thought I was a goner. If it hadn't been for Jesse, I'd have been chum."

Outside, Jesse protested again. "Lorena, this is swamp muck. Heavy, smelly dirt. The car—"

"There's a towel in back. You can throw it over the seat," she said. After rummaging for a moment, she found the towel and put it over the driver's seat.

"Hey, I'm the dirty one," he told her.

"And I don't know where I'm going. You need to drive."

She tossed him the keys. He shrugged. It was true. If you didn't know where to take an almost invisible road off the Trail, you were never going to find his house.

It was no more than a ten-minute drive, and both of them were too preoccupied to talk. And they were barely inside the door before she had slid into his arms, shivering slightly, clinging to him, her arms slipping around his neck, her body pressed to his, her lips seeking his mouth. It seemed an eon of ecstasy that they remained thus, and he felt a renewed sense not just of fervor and hunger, but of that deeper rise of emotion that came from the fact that they had made the subtle adjustment from wanting to needing, from carnal chemistry to a melding of body, heart and soul. She, too, was soon covered in swamp mud, and they made their way to the bathroom, where he managed to turn on the shower spray while disrobing himself and her, barely breaking contact the whole time.

Flesh, naked flesh, soap and suds, and hands. She touched him everywhere. He returned the favor. She had magic hands, taking a slow course of discovery. Light on his shoulders at first, and then with a pressure that both alleviated strain and created the sweetest strain of a very different kind.

Her fingers played down the length of his spine, over

his hips. He touched her in return. The darkness of his hands over the pale roundness of her breasts was arousing, his palms rubbing over her nipples before his head ducked and his mouth caressed them. The water sluiced through her hair. He caught it and cast it over her shoulder, turning her against him so that his lips could fall on her nape, below her ear, on her shoulders, her back. He turned her in his arms, continuing his erotic ministrations against her abdomen, her thighs, then between them. She gripped his shoulders, quivered at his touch, moaned slightly, then cried out, sliding down in sudsy sleekness to meet his mouth with the furious hunger of her own once again.

Her hands were delicate, then fierce, stroking against his chest. They knelt together in a steaming spray that seemed almost fantasy, something keener, sharper, than he'd ever known before. She stroked his sex with her hands and tongue, and he wound his arms around her, bringing them both to their feet, bracing her against the tile of the shower, lifting her until she came back down on him and the hard arousal of his sex slid easily into her. He nearly whispered the words to her then, that he was more than physically one with her, that he was falling in love. But he would never have her doubt such words, as she would if they were spoken in the urgent desperation of the desire that drummed through him like a storm tearing the Glades asunder, so he whispered instead that she was beautiful, and the words she returned were ever more arousing. He became aware of the ancient thunder throbbing through his body, his lungs and his heart, and in a matter of moments they climaxed together in the steamy spray. The winds began to ease while they remained entwined.

Later, when they had sudsed again, then slipped into each other's arms to sleep, but wound up making love again, he held her, spooned against him. He lay awake, stroking her hair, in wonder. He had thought he would never find a woman like his wife again, someone who had loved him fiercely, been brave and funny, sweet and strong, an equal, but able to make him feel his own strengths, that he was very much a man.

And, of course, he hadn't found his wife again. In a place in his heart, he would love and cherish her forever.

He had found someone unique, who was passionate and righteous, confident, her own self. Different, and yet with qualities that resonated in his heart and soul.

He adjusted his position slightly. Pressed his lips to the top of her head. "I think I'm falling in love," he whispered.

She gave no reply. He wondered if he had pushed her too fast, if his great epiphany was not exactly shared.

But neither did she move or deny him.

Then he realized that he had found the words to say what he was feeling too late, at least for that evening.

Her breathing was soft and even, her fingers curled around his.

And she was sound asleep.

He smiled to himself.

It changed what he was feeling, deepened it, to know that she would sleep beside him, that they would wake together in the morning.

That he wanted to sleep this way every night of his life, and wake beside her again and again.

Would she feel the same? he wondered. Enough to really love this place, where predators roamed, the mosquitoes seemed elephantine and bit like crazy...and the sunsets were the most glorious man would ever see, and the birds that flew overhead came in all the colors of a rainbow.

He rose in the night and padded naked to the back window, looking out on the eternal darkness.

He heard her, felt her, before she came behind him, arms winding around his back as she laid her cheek against him.

Words failed him again.

He simply turned and took her into his arms. Though tenderness reigned, he found himself afraid.

Afraid to break the moment…

Afraid she didn't feel the same.

And later, still awake, he wondered if there was even more that had stopped him.

Fear…?

They had almost certainly killed the man-eater that had gotten Billy Ray.

They had not, however, captured the man who had created it.

Chapter Eleven

The massive alligator was being taken upstate for examination, but that didn't stop Harry Rogers from trying to use it to improve his tourist trade.

When Lorena arrived bright and early for work, she discovered that Harry knew how to move quickly. Out front, next to the ticket stalls, he had a mounted enlarged photo of the giant crocodilian—his own arm around it.

Lorena hadn't seen what had gone on overnight, so she was amazed to see that a number of the television stations had arrived, along with radio and newspaper reporters.

The monster was, as Harry and Michael had known, good for business.

The day moved rapidly, in a whirl of tours. Lorena took only a few minutes for lunch. Besides helping with the tours, she had to pull out an ammonia capsule to revive an elderly lady who stood in the heat a bit too long, patch up two little boys who scraped their knees, and treat an allergic reaction to a mosquito bite.

Michael was either too harried to bother her about the previous night or he had just gotten bored with the subject and didn't care any longer.

Sam and Hugh were both still a bit on fire, talking about the hunt the night before. Jesse had turned off his phone during the night, so Jack and Hugh, with Harry's blessing, were delighted to keep busy providing the reporters with what they needed.

The place was jumping.

The police waited until closing to make their appearance.

Lorena had just been saying goodbye to a group of tourists near the main entrance when she heard Harry's booming voice, alive with protest.

"A search warrant—for *this* place? What do you guys think that I'm doing here, feeding drug runners to my critters? What the hell are you after at an alligator farm?"

She noted that although a number of cops had arrived in vans with all kinds of equipment, Lars Garcia and Abe were the ones talking to Harry.

Lars sighed. "Harry, look, I'm sorry—"

"This is Jesse's jurisdiction, or so I thought!"

"Tribal law stands, unless the county, state or federal authorities have to step in," Lars said unhappily. He saw Lorena and studied her absently as he spoke. "Look, Harry, Jesse knows that we're here, and he's not feeling that his toes are being stepped upon. Harry, that was a monster they brought down. We have to search all the farms."

"For what?" Harry demanded.

"Evidence that someone's genetically engineering monster gators," Lars explained.

"What?" Harry seemed incredulous. "Look here, that was no creature from a horror movie. It was big, but it was just a gator. Jesse shot it, and it died."

"There has never been an alligator that size in Florida before," Abe said.

"There hasn't been one on record. Doesn't mean there hasn't been one out there."

"It was way beyond the norm, Harry," Lars insisted.

"Harry," Abe interjected, "God knows, you're an opportunist. Let's just hope you're not a crook."

Harry looked at Abe, enraged.

"Harry, please," Lars said, glaring at his partner. "Let us just clear you and your group so we can move on."

"You idiot!" Harry said, still glaring at Abe. "Clear me of what? Hell, am I an idiot? If I could manufacture a creature like that, do you think I'd let it out in the Everglades? Hell, no! I'd be making money on it."

Lars tried once again to explain. "Harry, we all know that a hatchling could get out. Someone could get careless, or someone could steal one, then lose it."

Harry threw up his hands, really angry. "You know what you can do with your search warrant as far as I'm concerned. But you go right ahead. You look into anything that you want to look into. Search yourself silly. I'm calling my lawyer. You know, if you wanted to see something at my place, all you had to do was ask."

Harry walked away muttering. Lars gave a slight smile to Lorena, shrugged and turned away to talk to a distinguished-looking man in a special-unit suit.

She hadn't realized that Michael had come up behind her. "The suspicious cops are your fault, I imagine?" he asked softly.

A shiver shot down her spine as he spoke. She spun around quickly. She didn't have to answer. He shrugged.

"Not that I care. But if Harry finds out…mmm. You're in trouble. Big."

"Excuse me, Michael, I'm hungry," she said, and started for the cafeteria.

"I'm hungry, too," he said, trailing after her.

When they entered the cafeteria, Sally was rushing out. She didn't look at all amused. "Hey, sexy, what's up?" Michael demanded, stopping her.

She grated her teeth and cast Lorena what seemed like an evil stare, although she couldn't really be sure.

She might just be paranoid.

"They're inspecting everything, and Harry wants me there to explain the books. I don't get this—I don't get it at all! There was a giant alligator in the swamp—so we get *audited*? Not that there are any problems, I can assure you. My books are always perfect."

"I'm sure they are," Lorena murmured.

The woman might have been in a hurry, but she took time to glare at Lorena. "It's amazing, isn't it?" she murmured. "We were such a quiet place. Then you arrived and all hell broke loose. Did you have a nice time last night?"

"Yes, thank you," Lorena said evenly.

"What did you do last night?" Michael asked with a frown.

"Oh, come on, Dr. Preston! We have a budding romance in our midst, or didn't you know?" Sally asked.

Michael stared at Lorena. "You left with Jesse?"

"We're not required to stay on the premises," Lorena said.

"You're moving in with him?" Michael demanded. Lorena couldn't tell if he was angry or just surprised.

She looked at him incredulously, shaking her head.

"That's kind of a leap, isn't it?" she demanded. She kept smiling, but the curve of her lips was forced. "This is my business, okay?"

"We're just trying to watch out for you," Sally assured her, suddenly saccharine. "I mean, well, you work here, so you're one of us. Jesse is…well, Jesse keeps his distance."

"Doesn't seem that he's keeping much of a distance now," Michael murmured.

"Hey!" Lorena protested again.

"Think of us as one big family," Michael told her.

"Okay, *bro.* I'm not moving anywhere. If such a thing ever happens, I'll be sure to inform my *family,*" she said.

"How lovely," Sally murmured. "I'm off to see to my books. You children have a lovely dinner." She waved a hand in the air and left them.

"You know, you are going to have to tell us what's going on," Michael said, a hand at Lorena's back as he directed her toward a table.

She was saved from having to answer at that moment when Jack Pine joined them, sitting down with a weary grimace. "Busy day," he said.

"Oh? At your end, too?" Michael said.

"A bunch of scientist types, or so I'm told, will be in tomorrow. They want to investigate all our stock," Jack explained.

Michael stared at Lorena again. "How come I haven't heard anything about this?"

"Maybe they just haven't gotten to you yet," Jack suggested.

Hugh came over just then, settling down at the table across from Michael. "This is nuts."

"Are we closing tomorrow for all this?" Michael demanded.

"Oh, no. They can work around us. They're taking samples, bringing chemists and vets in, that kind of stuff," Hugh said cheerfully.

"It's absurd," Michael said indignantly. "I mean, my research is...well, it's *mine*. Where are my rights in all this?"

"I suppose the problem has something to do with giant alligators eating people," Jack said with a shrug.

"There are alligators everywhere," Michael protested. "Alligator farms abound in this state. Entrepreneurs run hunts on private property that aren't sanctioned or controlled by the state or federal government."

"Well, Michael, maybe they feel that your research will help them," Jack said. "Who the hell knows? Has anyone ordered dinner yet?"

Looking across the room, Lorena saw that Jesse had arrived. She was both startled and pleased, and jumped to her feet before she realized that despite the fact that their affair was growing obvious, she might have been a little more circumspect.

"Well, well," Hugh murmured.

Lorena ignored him.

Jesse was already walking over to them. He offered her a smile, held out her chair for her, then chose one for himself.

"So you reported Harry's as a hot bed of...what, exactly?" Michael asked.

Jesse frowned. "What?"

Michael leveled a finger at him. "Cops and the people from Fish and Wildlife are going to be crawling all over the place."

"I heard they're checking out a bunch of places," Jesse said with a shrug.

"Why assume that Harry's has anything to do with a giant alligator?" Michael demanded.

"Maybe because Harry sponsors a lot of research—*your* research—into improving gator meat and hides?" Jesse suggested.

"Can we order now?" Jack asked as one of the waiters arrived at the table.

"Sure. We're in the middle of a criminal investigation. Let's eat," Michael snorted.

"I'm hungry," Jack snapped back.

The tension was definitely growing, Lorena thought.

"Michael, they've got to find out what is going on," Jesse said. "There could be more of those creatures out there. And if they don't find the sustenance they need in the wild, that would put people in danger. Come on, Michael. How many attacks on humans do you want to see?"

"There's no reason to think there are more alligators that size out there," Michael insisted. "Maybe our gators are just getting bigger all around, catching up with some of their counterparts in other places. Maybe they should start investigating that before they come out here on Indian land and start poking their noses into things."

"Hey, this may be Indian land, but when it's a county-wide problem—"

"The alligator was caught on Indian land, too," Michael said testily, cutting Jesse off mid-sentence.

Lorena saw Jesse tense, but he wasn't the one who answered. "So what are you suggesting, Michael? That

it's all right because only Indians will be eaten?" Jack
Pine snapped.

"Don't be ridiculous!" Michael argued indignantly.
"I'm trying to be supportive of tribal law."

"Good of you to be concerned," Jesse replied.

"I think we should order dinner," Hugh murmured,
nodding to the waiter, who had continued hovering in
the background.

Fresh catfish was suggested and accepted all the way
around. Most of the tension around the table eased, but
a slight chill remained. Jesse seemed distracted, Jack
stiff, and Michael annoyed. Only Hugh seemed oblivious to the general air of discomfort.

"So, any clues as to how our gator got to be such a
monster?" Hugh asked Jesse.

"It's been sent off to Jacksonville. That's all I know
right now," Jesse said.

"Hey, there's Harry," Hugh said. "He looks happy."

Harry, smiling broadly, breezed by the table. "Looking good, looking good," he told them cheerfully.

"What looks good?" Michael asked skeptically.

"This place. The phones have been ringing off the
hook. People want to find out all about alligators. It's
kind of like Jurassic Park meets the Florida Everglades.
Hey, how's that catfish? Can't get any fresher."

"Harry, we don't know. We haven't got it yet," Hugh
said, amused.

"Well, it's going to be great. We're on a roll, all of
us. Keep up the good work."

Harry left just as their catfish arrived.

Lorena glanced at Jesse. Could Harry possibly be
guilty of anything if he was this happy while the authorities were crawling all over his holdings?

Just as Jack remarked that the catfish was indeed excellent, a slender, balding man in a typical tourist T-shirt and khakis walked up to the table. "Dr. Michael Preston?" he inquired.

Michael sat back tensely. "Yes."

The man offered a hand. "Jason Pratt, Wildlife Conservation. Can you give me a few minutes of your time? When you're done eating, of course."

"I guess I'm done," Michael said, throwing his napkin on the table.

"There's no reason for you to rush," Pratt protested. "I just wanted to catch you before you retired for the night."

Since it was still early, it was unlikely that Michael had been about to go to bed. Maybe Pratt was afraid Michael was about to flee?

Michael rose. "No. I'm done. How can I help you?"

He walked away with Pratt. Jesse rose, as well. "Want to take a ride with me?" he asked Lorena.

"Sure," she murmured, rising, too. Jack and Hugh were exchanging glances. She knew that along with the giant alligator, she was definitely a topic of conversation between them.

"See ya," Jesse said, nodding, taking Lorena's hand and heading out.

"Where are we going?" she asked as they got into his squad car.

"To see Theresa Manning."

"Theresa Manning?"

"The woman whose friend was…eaten," Jesse said.

"And what are we going to learn from her?"

"I'm not sure, but I called to see if we could speak with her, and she asked us over for tea and scones."

"Tea and scones?"

He shrugged. "Apparently she likes to bake."

"Jesse…do you think Michael is behind all this? I had the strangest conversation with him last night."

He scowled fiercely, looking at her in the rearview mirror. "You were alone with him?"

She ignored that. "He seriously believes that I'm here to cause him trouble."

"You need to stay away from him."

"But if he's doing anything illegal…he's about to face the music, right?"

Jesse shook his head. "Someone else has to be involved. Someone with money."

"Harry has money, but he seems as happy as a lark."

Jesse's cell phone started ringing. He answered it, then fell silent, frowning. Finally he said, "Call me as soon as you find out anything."

"What happened?" Lorena demanded.

He glanced quickly at her. "The alligator never made it to the university. Somewhere between here and Jacksonville, the truck it was on disappeared."

MICHAEL LEANED AGAINST his desk, scowling as Pratt and the other investigators—ridiculously casual in jeans and cotton island shirts or T's—went through his research records and his computer.

"What's this?" one of them asked.

Michael came around and looked over his shoulder.

"A record of the temperatures required to create the different sexes," he said patiently.

"And what's this?"

"Maturity level for the most tender meat," Michael said.

"And this…?"

"Breeding for the best skins," Michael said wearily.

The man rose suddenly. Others were still working in the filing cabinets, but most of his records were on the computer.

"I guess that's it for now," Pratt said, smiling cheerfully.

Michael realized that he had broken out in a cold sweat. Now he felt a debilitating rush of relief.

They hadn't found anything. Nothing. Nada. Zilch. Not a damned thing.

"You're done?"

"Yep. Thanks so much for your time and your patience," the man said.

"Hey, uh…sure," Michael said. "Anything to help. Not a problem. Anytime. Come back anytime you think I might be able to help." He couldn't seem to stop himself from babbling, he felt so relieved.

Pratt thanked him again as he and the others left the office. Michael sank into his chair with a sigh of relief.

"Yeah, any time," he muttered. Then he looked at his computer and quickly logged into his secret files.

"SUGAR? MILK? LEMON?" Theresa asked. "And…let me see. Those are blueberry in the middle, plain on the left side, and cinnamon on the right. I do so hope you enjoy them. I love to cook. My husband loved my cakes and pies."

Jesse had bitten into one of the blueberry scones. "It's wonderful," he told Theresa. "And it was so kind of you to make this offer. Delicious. Thank you. And for me, just tea is good."

"A touch of milk," Lorena murmured. "Thanks. And Jesse's right. These are just too good."

Theresa sat, beaming. "Well, I know you didn't come out for the scones. So how can I help you?"

"I know that this is painful for you, Theresa," Jesse said. "But you've heard all the ruckus about the alligator we caught last night."

Lips pursed, Theresa nodded grimly.

"Caught. It was caught," Lorena emphasized gently.

"That one was caught," Theresa said.

"So you think there are more?" Jesse asked.

"I think my friend was attacked by another one of your giant gators," Teresa said with assurance.

"Why?" Jesse asked her.

"They're territorial, aren't they? And yours was caught off the Trail. My friend was killed way out here."

Jesse cast a quick glance in Lorena's direction. "Was there anything strange going on at the time?" he asked Theresa.

"Strange?" Theresa repeated, then sat thinking for a while. "No. Nothing strange. Oh, now and then a few pets disappear, but…well, a small animal is natural prey, right?"

"I'm afraid so," Jesse said. "But you don't think there was anything else going on in the area?"

"Like what?" Theresa asked.

"Lights of any kind," Jesse said.

"Lights?" Theresa appeared confused. Then she gasped. "Why, yes, actually! There were lights in the sky several times right around the time when…" She paused, making a choking sound deep in her throat.

"Did they ever kill the alligator that took your friend?" Jesse asked. "Did animal control or the nuisance-animal division ever find the right gator?"

She shook her head, then returned to his previous

question. "We had been joking about aliens arriving," she murmured.

By the time they left, Jesse looked grim. He was silent when they got back in the car, and silent as they drove. At last Lorena asked him, "So...you believe that several of these creatures have grown up in the Everglades, and that big money is behind it. Enough big money so that someone is out in helicopters searching for their missing gators?"

"Yes," he said simply.

"But Harry is probably the one most involved with alligators who also has the most money," she said, lifting her hands in confusion. "And Harry is so happy he's practically singing!"

"We're moving forward," he said tensely. "The noose is tightening, and we will catch whoever we're looking for."

He didn't head back for the alligator farm but wound his way down the road that she would never have found herself, the road that led to his house.

As he parked, he looked at her, arching a brow. "Stay here tonight?"

"I should go back," she murmured.

"No, you shouldn't. Ever."

She sighed. "Jesse—"

"You want to catch a murderer. Well, you've done all the right things. The authorities are involved now. You don't need to go back."

She decided not to argue with him for the moment.

As they got out of the car, she glanced his way with a small smile. "You really are in the wilds out here."

"Pretty much," he agreed, watching her.

"It's been a long, hot day," she said.

"And…?"

"And the last one in is…a fried egg, I suppose!" she said, and dashed toward the door.

She began shedding her clothing once she had reached the patio. And she was definitely the first one in the pool.

The water hit her with a delicious sense of refreshing coolness. She swam from the deep end to the shallow, enjoying the cleansing of her flesh.

To her amazement, he was there, waiting for her, when she surfaced.

As she came up against the length of him, she was elated to feel the strength beneath the sleek flesh. His ink-dark hair was slicked back, and the green of his eyes seemed brilliant. His arms wrapped around her. "Skinny-dipping, Ms. Fortier? How undignified. Is this something you do frequently?"

She smiled and said softly, "Actually, no. This is the first time I've ever been skinny-dipping. In my whole life."

"I'm flattered. And honored."

He smoothed back a length of her hair, his lips brushing hers, hot and warm beneath the faint scent of chlorine. His arms tightened around her, bringing the full length of her body against his. Her breasts were crushed against the powerful muscles of his chest, her hips molded to his, and the perfectly placed thrust of his sex against hers was a titillation that thrilled and warmed her with a heady sense of anticipation.

"Does that mean," he asked huskily, "that the entire concept of sex in a pool is equally new?"

She started to answer, but his lips moved down the length of her neck and the words evaded her. He kicked away from the wall, the force slamming them more tightly together. She was scarcely aware of the slick feel of the tile steps when they landed there. For a breathless moment she met his eyes. Then she felt the full brunt of his body as he lifted her high against him, then thrust himself deeply inside her. She wrapped her limbs around him, and the fire that suddenly seemed to burn between them was an intoxicating contrast to the coolness of the water. She cast her head back, felt again the fury of his lips on her throat, breasts, the hollow of her collarbone.... Her lips met his again as they moved in the water, the night sky high above them, the whisper of the foliage around them, and the thunder of pulse and breath taking over. She buried her head against his shoulder as the power of need, and the agony-ecstasy of longing seemed to seep through her, spiral and grow, seize her and shut away the world. Her arms stroked his back; her fingers dug into his buttocks. She arched and writhed, and wondered that she didn't drown, but he kept them afloat, and in a cauldron of searing carnal mist until it seemed that the world exploded right along with the night stars, and she collapsed against him, still held tight and secure. Then she began to shiver, for the night, without the fire of him, was strangely cool.

"If I'd had any warning, we might have had towels," he said, amused, his lips handsomely curved as he pulled ever so slightly away.

"I was simply seized with overwhelming desire," she told him, and she smiled herself. "Quite frankly, I'm not sure I could have planned skinny-dipping."

"Stay, I'll get the towels," he said.

"But it's just as cold—"

She fell silent. He had already leapt out and, naked and dripping, headed for the house.

She realized that it was colder outside the water than in it, so she waited.

At first she eased her head back and simply smiled. She felt so wonderful that she refused to let herself wonder if she wasn't being a fool, falling in love with someone who made no promises, who was so distant.

But there wasn't a thing she would change, even if she could.

Her eyes opened suddenly, and she wondered why, aware that she was feeling the first twinge of unease.

She glanced around. Lights shone in and around the house, but beyond…

Beyond was the Everglades. Miles and miles of darkness and foliage and swamp, a land that was deep, dark and dangerous. A place where a million sins could be hidden.

She froze, aware then that she was in the light, that any eyes could be looking on from the darkness.

She was suddenly afraid, certain that the night could see.

"Here we are," Jesse murmured.

A towel was wrapped around his waist, and he had one for her in his hands. The sight of him seemed to turn back the darkness.

"Thanks," she murmured, rising, allowing him to wrap her in the soft fabric.

"Thank *you*," he murmured, and kissed her lightly on the lips.

The brilliance of his eyes touched hers, and he repeated the words very softly and tenderly. "Thank you."

He lifted her up, and they headed for the house.

In his arms, she forgot the darkness, and any thought that eyes might have gleamed at her from the black void of the night beyond.

Chapter Twelve

Jesse was gone in the morning. So was his car.

And she was furious. Despite the night they had spent together, she had no intention of listening to him about not going in to work. She was in no danger at the alligator farm. It was alive with officials—local, state and federal. Nothing was going to happen to her while she was working.

She walked around, fuming, for several long minutes while she brewed coffee.

Just how long would it take to get a taxi out to the middle of nowhere? In fact, was it even *possible* to get a taxi out to the middle of nowhere?

Come to think of it, she didn't know exactly where she was. What did one say? Come out and get me. There's a dirt road off Tamiami Trail, and it looks as if it leads into nothing but saw grass and a canal, but there's really a house out there. Quite a nice house, actually. Swimming pool, state-of-the-art kitchen...

She swore aloud and hesitated, wondering if she should call in to work or just pray that Jesse would show up and drive her to work.

She pulled out her cell phone and stared at it, ready to put through a call to his cell, tell him what she thought of his high-handed tactics and demand that he come back immediately so he could take her to work.

He might, of course, simply refuse. He might even be involved in a situation from which he couldn't extract himself. Too bad. There were others on his day crew. He could send someone for her, and damn it, he *would*.

Just as she was about to punch his number in, her cell rang. Caller ID said the number was the office at Harry's.

"Hello," she said quickly, expecting Harry, though a glance at her watch showed her that she wasn't late yet.

"Hey" came a soft voice. Male.

"Michael?"

"No, it's Jack. We didn't see you at breakfast. We were getting a bit worried."

"We?"

"Hugh, Sally and me."

"That was nice of you, but I'm fine."

"Glad to hear it. Not that you shouldn't be," he said hastily. "Things are just a bit strange around here right now, you know? I mean, who'd ever think *I* would be in any real danger from an alligator? So...we were worried."

"No, I'm fine, just..." She hesitated for only a second. "Jesse seems to have gotten caught up in something. He's not here, and I'm afraid I'm going to be late."

"We'll come get you."

"No, I'm sorry. You don't have to."

"No, no, it's fine. One of us will come. Fifteen minutes."

Jack hung up.

She clicked her phone shut. The hell with Jesse and his high-handedness. She was running her own life. No matter how much she cared for someone, she wasn't going to be ordered about or dissuaded from her course.

Her father had been murdered, and she had never felt so close to capturing the killer. No way was she going to back off now.

Inside, she poured a last cup and turned the coffee-pot off. And waited.

GEORGE OSCEOLA REPORTED on the missing van. It wasn't much of a report—the van was still missing. It had been on I-95. The driver had spoken to his wife at about ten-thirty in the morning, just after fueling up.

And then...

He and the van had just disappeared. County law enforcement throughout the state had been notified, along with the highway patrol, but so far, the van hadn't been spotted.

A call to Lars provided no further information.

Jesse looked at the phone and thought about calling Lorena. She was going to be really angry. But she hadn't called him to demand that he come back and take her in to work. Maybe she had fumed for a while, then decided on her own that the smart thing to do now would be to stay away from Harry's.

As he stared at his desk phone, it rang. A female voice greeted his ears, but not Lorena's. "Jesse, it's Julie. I was just calling in to see if...well, if anything else had happened."

"We're working on it, Julie, but I've got nothing to tell you."

He could sense her hesitation, then she said, "Jesse, I know it was probably foolish, but I went by the house last night. I mean, I have to go back inside eventually."

"I'd be happier if you'd stay away a little longer," he told her. "Just a few more days."

"A few more days," she echoed. "The police have asked me to wait a few more days, too. Before...before claiming the bodies. They're afraid the medical examiner might have missed something. But about the house... I'm going to need clothes."

"Julie, when you go, I'll go with you. And if you need my help at the funeral home or with the church..."

"It's all done, Jesse, thanks. I knew what they wanted," Julie said. "I didn't call you to cry."

"Sweetheart, you have the right to cry as much as you want," he assured her softly.

"Thanks, Jess, but what I need is to...to bug you and make sure no one stops until my parents' killer is caught. And also, I called because I keep thinking about the lights I saw out at the house."

"Plane lights? Helicopter lights? Men on the ground with flashlights?" Jesse asked. "What do you think?"

"I know they didn't come from anyone on the ground," Julie said. "To tell you the truth... I know why my mother thought aliens were landing. They hovered right above the trees. I didn't hear any noise. Of course, I was in the car, and they were at a distance."

"Thanks for calling, Julie. I'll look into it. Trust me. I want to help you. I loved your parents."

"I know you did, Jesse. And they thought the world of you. So do I. And I'll wait till we go inside together, okay?"

"Perfect."

He hung up after a minute, then called Lars back. "We need to start checking the airfields. More specifically, we need to find out who has been taking helicopters up."

Lars groaned. "Every television and radio station out there has a traffic and weather copter! And when we were out at Hector and Maria's, you said an airboat had been through."

"So?"

"So we've been talking to a lot of people with airboats, Jesse."

"Yes, and that was a move that needed to be made. Now we need to find out about helicopters."

He heard an even louder groan.

"Lars, I keep hearing stories about lights wherever there's been an event with an alligator. You have more resources at your disposal than I do. Can you get on it?"

He heard the deep sigh at the other end, but then Lars agreed. "All right. I'm on it."

Satisfied, Jesse hung up. He drummed his fingers on the desk. Something had been bothering him, and he wasn't quite sure why.

He looked at the phone and thought about calling his house, then decided not to.

He rose suddenly, since he wasn't getting anywhere sitting at his desk.

He grabbed his hat from the hook by the door. "Where are you going?" George asked him.

"To check with Doc Thiessen or Jim Hidalgo. See if anything else has happened over at the vet's. Call me if you hear anything," Jesse said.

LORENA EXPECTED EITHER Hugh or Jack to show up at the rear of the property with an airboat. Instead, it was

Sally who finally tooted her horn from the front. Lorena clicked the front lock and hurried out.

"Jesse's trying to keep you away from Harry's, huh?" Sally said.

"Why would he do that?" Lorena asked, hoping she wasn't giving anything away.

"Why? Killer gators, feds all over the place, something fishy in the air," Sally said with a laugh. "Actually, you should be happy. If he didn't care about you, he wouldn't be acting so much like an alpha dog. Well, maybe he's just the alpha-dog type. I don't know."

Lorena shrugged. "Thanks for getting me. I don't know what he got involved in, or when he might get back, but I don't like being late."

"Aren't you even a little bit worried about everything that's going on?" Sally asked her.

"Should I be?" Lorena asked.

Sally laughed. "Michael thinks you're a suspicious character."

"Michael is paranoid," Lorena murmured.

"Maybe. He's a scientist. Maybe all scientists get paranoid. They think their research is better than gold."

"Maybe it is. Sometimes."

Sally waved a hand in the air. "I don't think Michael has created a strain of giant killer alligators."

"Oh?"

Sally shook her head. "He always seems frustrated. He's a good-looking guy. I think he had the hots for you. Actually, until Jesse stepped into the picture, it kind of looked like you liked Michael."

"I like everyone at the farm," Lorena murmured.

"Just the slutty type, huh?" Sally queried.

"What?" Lorena snapped.

"Well, you *were* flirting pretty hard with everyone until you settled on Jesse."

Lorena stared out the front window. "Did you come to get me just so you could give me a hard time?" she asked.

Sally looked at her, eyes wide. "No! Of course not." A small smile curved her lips as she shook her head.

DR. THORNE THIESSEN wasn't in when Jesse arrived at the veterinary clinic.

Jim Hidalgo was there, though. "Hey, how are you feeling?" Jesse asked him.

"Fine. Just fine," Jim assured him.

"How come you're here? I thought you had the night shift? And where is the doc, anyway?" Jesse asked.

"This is the day he does calls. He covers a few of the alligator farms, you know. And he does cattle, as well. There are even a couple of folks with real exotics, snakes and things, and for them, he makes house calls. One day one week, two days the next. I guess it works for him."

Jesse chewed a blade of grass and nodded. "You still don't remember anything about what happened that night, huh?"

"Nothing. You still haven't caught the thief, huh?"

Jesse shook his head. "Tell me if I've got it right. You were in the back, then…wham! And then nothing, nothing at all, until Doc was standing over you?"

"Yeah, yeah, then lights, sirens, cops, med techs… You know the rest. You were here."

"Right."

Jesse shrugged. "So when will the doc be back?"

"Tomorrow morning," Jim told Jesse.

"Where is he?"

"Don't know. He works lots of places."

"And you're in charge until then? What about the day guy?"

"He works with Thiessen, travels with him. Weird goose, if you ask me."

"Because he's white?"

Jim laughed, shaking his head. "Because he never talks. Hey, lots of folks live and work out here who aren't part of the tribe. We all get along. His day guy, though. John Smith. Who ever heard such a name for real? He's a big goon. Never talks."

"To each his own," Jesse said. "Thiessen must trust him. Anyway, you feel safe enough out here alone now?"

"I'm not alone."

"Oh?"

Jim gave a whistle. A huge dog came crawling out from beneath the desk where Jim sat. He was quite a mix. Evidently a little bit shepherd, chow and pit bull. Whatever else, Jesse didn't know, but it made for one big beast of a canine.

"I just got him," Jim said happily. "I call him Bear."

Bear wagged his tail.

"He likes you," Jim continued.

"I'm glad," Jesse said.

"Anyway, he makes me feel safe. He was sniffing and woofing before you got out of your car. When I told him it was all right, he sat right back down. Got him from the animal shelter."

"Great."

"Doc isn't too fond of him," Jim admitted. "But he knows I'm not happy anymore about holding down the

fort by myself on the days he's gone and at night, so..."
He shrugged happily.

Jesse nodded. "See you. Don't forget—"

"Yeah, I know the drill. If I think of anything, I'll call you."

"Yep. Thanks."

When he reached his patrol car, Jesse put a call through to the office.

The van with the alligator carcass was still missing. And nothing had been found of the samples taken from the vet's office.

There were no known leads on the murders.

He clicked off, hesitated, and at last called his house.

She wasn't answering. He hung up, then called back, and spoke when he heard his own message. "Pick up, Lorena, please. It's Jesse."

But she didn't pick up. She might have been in the pool, in the shower or in another part of the house.

Or she might have called someone to take her in to work.

He tried her cell phone.

She wasn't picking up.

Okay, so she was angry.

He put a call through to the alligator farm. Harry answered. "Hey, Harry. I'm surprised to hear your voice."

"It's still my place, you know. Despite the goons crawling all over it," Harry said. But he sounded cheerful.

"You just don't usually answer the phone."

"This place is doing twice the business we used to. No one here but me to pick up. The feds said I didn't have to close, just as long as they could go through what they wanted. Hell, they can go through anything, as far as I'm concerned."

"I'm glad you're happy, Harry," Jesse said. "I guess it would be tough for you to find someone to search the throng of tourists and find Lorena for me, huh?"

"Yes, it would be. But I can put you through to the infirmary, in case she's there."

"So you've seen her?"

"Not this morning. But I'm sure she's working, no thanks to you."

"What do you mean?"

"You're trying to seduce my help away from here, aren't you, Jesse Crane?"

"Harry—"

"Hang on, I'll put you through. How do you work this ridiculous, pain-in-the-ass thing?" he muttered.

Harry didn't put him through. He hung up on him. Irritated, Jesse snapped his phone closed.

His house was between the vet's and the alligator farm, so he decided to make a quick stop, see if she was there fuming and swearing at his furniture, then head out to the farm.

A sense of genuine unease was beginning to fill him. It was as if puzzle pieces were beginning to fall together, yet they didn't quite seem to fit.

He closed his eyes for a moment. Someone from Harry's was definitely involved. There had to be a money connection. And someone who knew the Everglades well.

There was more than one person involved, for sure. A connection through Harry's, a money man, someone with a knowledge of genetic engineering, and someone else, a hired goon.

Thoughtful, he picked up the phone to make one last call, then hit the gas pedal.

THE PHONE RANG, and Sally answered it.

"Hey," she said cheerfully. Then she glanced sideways at Lorena. "Sure... No... Yes, of course."

She clicked off, then offered Lorena a rueful smile. "Jesse," she said.

"Jesse?"

"Yeah, he wants me to make a quick detour."

"Uh-uh. No way. Let's go in to work."

"I think he's found something."

"What?"

"I think he's made a discovery. Something to do with...if I heard him right, your father."

"My father!" Lorena said, startled.

"Yeah. I didn't know Jesse knew your family. Hey, it's your call. He wanted me to bring you out to what they call Little Rat hummock. It's barely a piece of land, but they have names for every little hellhole and cranny out here. From the days when they were running and hiding out here, I guess. Anyway, what should I do? Jesse sounded all excited."

Lorena's heart flipped; her pulse was racing. She was still furious with him. But if he had discovered something and needed her in any way, she had to be there.

"If Jesse were calling me," Sally said, sounding wistful, "I'd sure be going."

"I'm supposed to be working," Lorena murmured.

"Okay, we'll go to work."

Lorena lifted her hands. "No. Little Rat hummock it is."

"Good thing I brought the Jeep," Sally said. "There's no real road out there."

There wasn't. Lorena thought they were going to sink in mire once and, if not, be swallowed in the saw grass.

But Sally knew the terrain. Right when Lorena was gritting her teeth, certain they were about to perish in the swamp, the wheels hit solid ground. Ahead, she saw a cluster of pines.

"You're not scared out here, are you?" Sally asked her. "You don't need to be. Well, maybe you should have worn boots, but don't worry—the snakes won't get you, not if you leave them alone. Besides here, in the pines, all you really have to worry about are the Eastern diamondbacks and the pygmy rattlers. Well, and the coral snakes, but they don't have the jaws to bite you unless they get you just right." She glanced at Lorena, who could feel herself turning pale. "Sorry. I'm out in the Everglades all the time, and I've never been hit by anything more vicious than a mosquito."

Sally brought the Jeep to a halt.

Lorena looked around.

There was nothing. Nothing but a patch of high ground, a bunch of pines and the saw grass beyond.

"I don't see Jesse."

Sally was frowning, staring ahead.

Lorena heard the noise, too, then. A throb of engines.

"Airboat?" she murmured.

"Yeah. What the hell…?" Sally murmured.

"It's probably Jesse," Lorena said, getting out of the car.

Sally got out, as well. She walked around the car, staring ahead, still puzzled.

"It's not Jesse," she murmured after a minute.

The airboat came around the cluster of pines that lay ahead. "It's Jack. Jack Pine," Sally said.

"So it's Jack. Maybe Jesse asked him to come out here, too," Lorena said.

But Sally shook her head. "No...no...something's wrong here."

Jack brought his airboat to a halt and leapt out.

"Oh, man," Sally murmured. She turned again. Lorena realized that they had walked some distance from the Jeep.

"Hey!" Jack called. "Hey, Lorena! Stop!"

Sally shook her head wildly. "Run!" she advised, and immediately took her own advice.

Lorena stared from Jack to Sally, then back again.

There was a large machete hanging from Jack's belt.

"Run!" Sally called back to her.

"Run where?" Lorena cried, chasing after Sally.

"Follow me. I know where I'm going!"

THERE WERE TIRE tracks in front of his house. Jesse hunkered down and studied them.

A Jeep. Harry's had a number of Jeeps. Any of the senior staff had access to them.

He checked the house quickly, but he knew the minute he entered that she wasn't there. He paused in back, though.

There were tire tracks in the front, but the broken foliage in back indicated an airboat had been by, as well.

At that instant, his heart seemed to freeze in his chest. He headed back for the car, already flipping open his cell phone.

"George, I've got Lars checking on a few things, and I've asked him to get men out here. But we know the area better than they do. I want everyone available out here. Something is going down *now*. Cut a swath from the vet's to Harry's, pie-shaped, fanning south."

"Jess, what the hell...?"

"Do it. Just do it."

LORENA STOPPED BECAUSE she couldn't run anymore. Sally, ahead of her, had stopped, as well.

She looked back at Jack Pine, who'd been closing in on them.

Jack had stopped, too.

"What are you doing out here, Sally?" Jack demanded.

"Jesse called," Sally said.

Jack shook his head. "No."

"What the hell are you doing out here, Jack?" Sally demanded in return, sounding frightened.

"Following you. I saw the car from the airboat. I was on my way out to pick up Lorena, so I couldn't help but wonder why you were heading out there, too. What's going on, Sally?"

"Jack, you're a liar and a murderer!" Sally cried, her tone hysterical. "I couldn't let you get Lorena. I couldn't let it happen."

Jack shook his head, looking puzzled. "Lorena, get away from her. She must have been listening on the phone. She had to get to you before I did."

Lorena looked from one of them to the other.

Sally wasn't armed.

Jack was carrying one frighteningly big knife.

She had no idea where she was, only that she was far from the car.

"I have an idea," she said. "Let's all head back to the alligator farm and discuss this whole thing."

"Lorena, don't be ridiculous," Sally said.

Lorena realized that Jack was moving steadily closer to her.

"Get away, Jack," she said.

"Don't you get it yet?" Jack said.

"You're going to kill her—and me!" Sally cried. "Lorena, don't you see? He's going to chop us up and feed us to his alligators."

"No!" Jack cried. "You've got it all wrong. You have to listen."

"Come on," Sally cried. "Lorena, move! One swing of that machete…"

"Lorena," Jack pleaded as he took another step toward her.

"This way!" Sally cried to her.

Lorena tried to maneuver around the three pines that separated her from Sally.

"No!" Jack cried. "No!"

He was coming after her.

She turned to run more quickly.

But as she did, she was suddenly running on air. There was no earth.

No hummock, no ground.

She was falling through space.

Falling, falling, into the darkness of a pit.

She hit the ground with a thud, but after a moment of breathless shock, she realized that she hadn't broken any bones. The ground was not hard. It was muck and mire. Of course. They were below sea level. It would be impossible to dig a dry hole.

She let out a sigh of relief, then heard the thud next to her.

Someone else was in the hole.

And then...

She heard the noise. Loud. A grunting sound, like a pig. No, not a pig. A huge, furious boar. Or...

An alligator.

Chapter Thirteen

Jesse chose to take his own airboat, trying to follow the broken foliage across the Everglades, certain that time was of the essence. His heart felt heavy. There was so much ground to cover. The river of saw grass seemed endless. He'd already seen so much evil done out here. You could search forever to find a body.

No, he refused to think in that direction. She had to be alive. He was certain that Lorena had been lured somewhere, but where, he didn't know. Or even why. Except that she was a piece of the puzzle; she'd been the first to know that something very wrong was going on, and that they were talking technology.

Dangerous stolen technology.

They weren't going to find anything at Harry's Alligator Farm and Museum.

Because Harry wasn't guilty.

And if all went as the thieves had planned it, they wouldn't find the van or the alligator carcass, nor the specimens from Doc Thiessen's lab.

He still didn't have all the facts, but he was certain of one person who might be involved. And that person didn't intend for any of this to be discovered, and it wouldn't matter just how many people died. The frightening thing was that no matter how many people died, mysteriously or otherwise, the techno thief clearly believed he couldn't be caught.

Ahead, he saw one of the airboats from Harry's. And there was someone beside it, gesturing madly.

He cut his engine.

Sally.

"Jesse, Jesse! Help! Quickly. It's Lorena.... Help!"

His heart remained in his throat. "Lorena...?"

"Come with me. For the love of God, hurry. And be careful. It's Jack...he'll kill her!"

Jack? Jack Pine?

Sally was running. Jesse ran after her in a flash. She circled around the pines, then shouted to him.

"Hurry!"

He did. And then he plunged into the hole.

He should have seen it. Even concealed as it had been with bracken and brush, he should have seen it. Hell, this was his country. This god-forsaken swamp was his heritage. He knew it like the back of his hand. He should have seen the damned thing, and realized that it wasn't any natural gator hole.

No. This one had been dug intentionally. And it was deep. In the rain, it would flood. But in the dry season...

He landed hard. The hole was deep, and the thatch covering above kept out all but a hint of light.

"Oh, God, Jesse!" Lorena cried, recognizing him in the meager light. In a second she was next to him, warm and vital. He held her, damning himself a thousand times over. She'd come flying into his arms with such trust.

And he had no idea how to get them out of this mess. He pulled out his cell phone. No signal. Damn!

"Jesse?" Jack Pine moaned.

"What the hell?" Jesse said. He eased himself away from Lorena.

It was pitch black, and he wasn't a trigger-happy kid or a rookie, but Jesse pulled his gun, just in case.

"Stay where you are, Jack. I'm armed."

"I'm not your problem," Jack said.

Jesse blinked, trying to accustom his eyes to the eerie lack of light.

"Stay back," he said softly, his mind going a hundred miles an hour as he tried to figure out what the hell was going on.

Lorena backed up until she and Jack were both flat against the wall of earth and muck.

Above them, Jesse suddenly heard laughter.

Sally's laughter.

"What a pity I can't see you all down there. Sorry, Jack. You were really kind, likable. You shouldn't have been so determined to help Lorena. And Jesse...so gallant. See, Lorena? You were the problem. Everything was going just fine until you appeared. But it doesn't matter. They'll rip Harry's apart, but they won't find a thing. They'll just have to accept the fact that we've grown some big gators in the Everglades—and that they ate you all up."

She sounded as if she were happily reading a children's fairy tale.

"I have to go now. I have to get rid of both those airboats. Goodbye. Nice knowing you."

Jack exploded. "Dammit, Jesse. Do something. She's insane. I mean...she's not the brains behind things, I'd swear it, but when I realized she had Lorena, I knew something wasn't right."

It was then that Jesse heard it. The grunt…the grunt followed by the roar.

He'd been listening to alligators since he'd been a kid. He'd learned a lot about the sounds they made.

Those that had to do with mating.

And those that had to do with territoriality…and hunger. Or both.

"Hell," he muttered under his breath. He could barely see the other two. "Stay back," he warned them.

"Jesse," Lorena said softly. "What are you going to do?"

"I'm armed," he reminded her. But he was worried. Bullets at almost immediate range had barely pierced the tough hide of the alligator they had bagged two nights before.

He wanted to rush over to Lorena. He wanted to hold her, to place his body as a barrier between her and the creature in the darkness. He wanted to say a dozen things to her. He wanted to tell her that he loved her.

He stood dead still, listening, waiting.

The animal was moving. He heard it moving slowly at first, but he knew just how fast a gator could be.

Then there was the rush.

He spun, blinded, but going on instinct. He emptied the clip. The sound was deafening.

The animal bellowed and paused, then slammed into him.

In the dark, he heard the jaws slam shut.

Close. So close that he felt the wind the movement created….

He jumped back.

"Jesse!" It was Lorena, shouting his name.

"Jack, we've got to straddle it!" Jesse yelled.

"Are you insane?" Jack shouted back. "These are monsters. They can't be wrestled down like a five-or six-footer."

"Do you want to be eaten?" Jesse demanded.

The animal had apparently been wounded, because it continued bellowing. Its senses were far better than his own, Jesse knew, but it seemed to be disoriented. He tried desperately to get a sense of its whereabouts.

Then he threw himself on the animal.

He aimed accurately, hitting the back just behind the neck. But the creature was powerful and began thrashing. Right when Jesse thought that he was going to be tossed aside like a blown leaf, Jack landed behind him.

"What now?" Jack shouted.

"I've got to get on the jaws."

"I can't hold the weight!"

"You've got to."

"Wait! I'm here!" Lorena cried.

"Lorena, you don't—" Jesse began.

"We've done something sort of like this before," Jack panted. "Kind of."

There was a flurry of motion as the alligator gave a mighty bellow, tossing its head from side to side.

Lorena landed on the animal's back behind Jack.

"Now what?" Jack demanded.

"The jaw," Jesse said.

"You're mad," Jack responded.

"What? We can't ride this damned thing forever," Jesse said.

"But—"

"Big or little, if I can get the jaw clamped, we'll be safe."

"Yeah, yeah…if you don't get eaten first. Go for it."

He did. He had no choice. He tensed, feeling every inch of the creature beneath him, sensing with all his might, trying to ascertain what the creature's next twist would be.

And then he moved. He leapt forward, landing heavily on the open jaw, snapping it shut. The creature was mammoth; the jaws extended well beyond his perch.

He'd snapped the jaws shut, and still the animal was trying to fight him off. Its strength was incredible. It would shake them all off if they weren't careful.

Trying to maintain his seat, he reached into his pocket for a new clip. The animal bucked. He nearly fumbled the clip.

He tried again.

"Hurry," Jack breathed.

The alligator made a wild swing with its tail.

Lorena screamed. Jesse heard the whoosh as she flew through the air, the thud as she slammed against the mud wall of the pit.

The alligator bucked, fighting him wildly, beginning to get its jaws open, despite his weight.

"Jack, hold him!" he cried.

"Damn it, I can't. I can't!"

Then he heard Lorena, rising, breathless but as tenacious as the creature beneath him. "I'm coming."

"Watch it!"

The alligator swerved, knowing exactly where Lorena was, trying for her.

She moved like the wind, flying past him, landing behind Jack once again.

He could barely hold the gun, much less insert the clip. He had to. He had to, and he knew it.

He locked the clip into place.

He felt for the eyes, and he fired.

The ferocity of the bellow that erupted from the creature nearly threw him. The sound of the bullet exploding was terrible, almost deafening.

But he shot again.

And again.

At last the gator ceased to move.

For long, awful moments, none of them moved.

Jesse's ears were ringing when he finally said huskily, "Lorena, try getting up."

She did so, slowly, carefully.

The creature remained dead still.

"Jack."

Jack moved, but Jesse stayed. He groped around and found the base of the skull, then warned them, "I'm shooting again."

He delivered two more bullets into the creature.

Then, at last convinced that the creature had to be dead, he moved, too.

In the darkness, he felt her. But she didn't collapse against him the way a lesser woman might have. She strode over to him, and her arms wound around him as his wound around her.

Only then did she start to shake.

He heard Jack sink to the ground. "I think I'm moving north," Jack muttered. "Somewhere with ice and snow and no alligators."

Jesse allowed himself a moment to revel in simply holding Lorena, in feeling her, breathing her scent above the gunpowder and the muck.

"What the...?" Jack said suddenly. "Hell."

"What?" Jesse demanded sharply.

In the darkness, they could hear Jack swallow.

"What?" Jesse demanded again.

"There, uh, there was someone else down here," Jack said very softly. "There are...body parts."

"Oh, God!" Lorena breathed.

"Hey, we've got to keep it together," Jesse said sharply. "It's not over yet. We've got to get out of here. Quickly. They'll be back."

"They?" Jack said dully. Then he added, "Of course. They."

"Come on, Lorena," Jesse said. "I'll hike you up first."

He lifted her, and with Jack's help, he got her to his shoulders. From there, a shove sent her out of the pit.

"Hey! I found a big branch," Lorena called. "You guys can use it as a ladder."

She nearly hit Jesse in the head with it, but as soon as they got it in place, Jack reached upward, bracing against it. Jesse gave him a push.

They heard the tree limb cracking, but Jack was nimble for his size, and grasping for both the ground and Lorena's hand, he managed to throw himself to the edge of the pit. He turned then, ready to help Jesse. "Come on!"

Jesse eyed the height of the pit, the broken branch, and the length of Jack's arms. "Back off," he said.

"What?"

"Back off."

He gave himself a few feet, then ran at the tree limb, using it as a stepping-stone and no more.

He just made the rim of the pit, then hung there.

His grip slipped in the muck.

"Jack, where the hell are you?"

Jack didn't answer.

Jesse dangled. Then he got a grip, and at last, straining, he dragged himself over the rim of the pit. He rolled, then lay panting in the bright sunlight.

"Damn you, Jack," he said, turning.

And then he fell silent, knowing what had happened to Jack.

Both Jack and Lorena were still there. Completely covered in black muck and mire.

But the true killer, the thief, the one determined on getting rich at the expense of so many lives, had at last arrived himself.

Jesse made it to his feet, aware of the Smith & Wesson pointed at his face, and the grim features of the man he had once respected.

"Doc," he said. "Doc Thiessen. I've been expecting you."

"Damn, Jesse, why do you have to be so hard to kill?" Thorne Thiessen demanded.

"Hell, I don't know. I just like living, I suppose."

Sally was standing right behind Thiessen. Jesse noticed that she hadn't gotten rid of both airboats. There were two on the little hummock, his own and the one Doc had come in.

"So, Doc... I kind of figured you were involved in this," he said smoothly. He was playing for time now, but Doc didn't know that. Doc didn't know that the troops were already on the way.

"Oh, bull! You didn't have the least idea," Doc Thiessen said.

"Yeah, I did, Doc, but I was awful damn slow putting it all together. At first I thought it was Harry, because Harry has money. But so do you. I admit, I didn't figure out right away who you had working for you, and I

sure as hell didn't suspect Sally, but after I talked to Jim
Hidalgo a few times, I knew you had to be involved. He
gets whacked on the head, and the first one he sees is
you. And those samples... You should have had them
all prepared and studied and on their way somewhere
else. You had to steal your own samples. And I'm willing to bet that by now Lars Garcia has found out that
you own a helicopter, though I doubt you were the one
flying it around, looking for your gators. That was probably John Smith. I'm willing to bet that the altered gators are marked somehow. They would have found out
just exactly how if the one I shot had reached the veterinary school, as it was supposed to. I didn't suspect
Sally at first, but I should have. She was the one who
gave Roger a shove, wasn't she?

"So let me see if I've got it worked out. You were
the leader, and Sally and John were working for you.
Who did all the dirty work for you? The killing, Doc.
Who killed Maria and Hector—and Lorena's father?"

"I really don't have time for this," Thiessen said,
shaking his white head. The face that had always
seemed so kindly was now twisted in a mask of impa-
tience and cold cruelty.

"Come on. You beat me." Jesse tried to assess the
situation. Doc was the only one with a gun, and it was
now aimed at him. Jack and Lorena were standing to
one side, where they'd been forced in the last seconds
while he'd been getting himself out of the hole.

But neither Jack nor Lorena looked as if they were
about to collapse. As if they had been beaten. They
were survivors. Lorena had a steely strength to have
gotten this far.

In fact, she looked both defiant and angry. She wasn't going to go down easy.

And he couldn't count Jack out, either.

Thiessen smiled. "Actually, you'll find out who does my dirty work in just a minute or two. But first I've got to decide how to do this. You killed my gator, Jesse. In fact, damn it, you've killed two of them."

"C'mon, Doc, what else could I do?" Jesse said. "But listen, since I'm going to die anyway, do me a favor. Explain it all to me first, will you?"

Doc shrugged. "Easy enough. Sally heard about the research, made the contacts and came to me, since she didn't have the expertise to work with what she'd found. I've worked my fingers to the bone out here, and you can't imagine the millions to be made off a formula that can create an animal this size. The old man up in his research lab panicked. He didn't have to die. But he found out I'd gotten hold of a few of his specimens. Found out that they were growing, and he didn't keep his mouth shut, the old fool. He had to go and confront me about it. He hadn't figured out Sally's role yet, but I couldn't take the chance he would. She'd worked for him briefly, and if she'd been caught, that would have led back to me. So he had to die. Just the way things go," he said coldly. "Now, as to Lorena being the old man's daughter, well, it took me a while to make the connection, I'll admit."

"You bastard!" Lorena said softly.

For a moment Jesse thought she was going to fly at Doc, but she controlled herself, tense as a whip.

Her eyes touched Jesse's. He realized that she was trusting him to get them out of this.

He couldn't fail her.

Thiessen was on a roll. "You should have accepted that accident, Ms. Fortier. The cops would have gone on believing that Hector and Maria had been involved in drugs. As to old Billy Ray, well, I didn't kill him. The old drunk ran into one my gators, that's all."

"Just how many killer gators are there?" Lorena asked tightly.

Thiessen appeared amused. "There were four. One died on its own—near Hector and Maria's. You killed two, Jesse. There's still one of these beauties out there somewhere, and trust me, I'll find it. I've had Sally eavesdropping all along, and as soon as there's word, I'll know. None of this was as hard as you're trying to make it look, Jesse."

"And getting away with it won't be as easy as you think, Doc," Jesse said. All he needed was a distraction. He was certain that Doc knew how to shoot, but he was no ace, no trained officer. A distraction, and...

He swallowed hard. Did he dare? He'd be risking Lorena's life. And Jack's.

Lorena was staring at him, waiting. She still seemed to trust in the fact that he intended to do something.

And if he didn't?

Then they could all be dead anyway, unless the cavalry got here pronto.

"Lars Garcia will put all these pieces together, Doc."

"Don't be ridiculous. Other people out here have helicopters, and airboats? They must number in the thousands."

"People who know reptiles as well as you do are harder to find," Jesse commented. "And I've already mentioned your name to Lars. What was it, Thorne? Not enough money in what you were doing, or not enough glory?"

"The world is changing, Jesse. Genetic enhancement is being made on a daily basis. Clones are a dime a dozen now. You're got to be at the front of the flock."

"I'm telling you, Lars is on to you," Jesse said softly. "And you think that Metro-Dade Homicide will let go? You're out of your mind."

Thiessen looked troubled for an instant. "He has no proof."

"He will. I figure you marked those gators, tagged them in some way, and then let them loose on purpose, trying to see how they did in the wild. But you wanted to protect them from discovery at the same time, so you tracked them by helicopter, as well as by airboat. They're territorial creatures, so you probably shouldn't have let that one get so close to a populated area. That was a stupid-as-hell reason for Hector and Maria to die. Whoever killed Hector and Maria came on their property with an airboat. So tell me, Doc. Who did it?"

"I did," Sally offered, stepping around from behind Thiessen. "I did it, you fool. You thought I was nothing more than an attractive piece of ornamentation, a numbers cruncher. Background and nothing more. Well, get this. You underestimated me. You were friendly... you were even warm sometimes. But I could always see it in your eyes. I was nothing to you. But you were wrong. So wrong about me. I know how to be a mover and a shaker."

"And a killer," he said huskily.

She smiled. "And a killer."

She was slightly between him and Thiessen at that

point. Jesse cut a quick glance toward Lorena and realized that her eyes were on him.

She was afraid, but not panicking. She would fight until her last breath. He had never felt such a connection to another individual in his life.

A diversion. He needed a diversion.

She was staring at him so intently, he was certain she knew what he needed, how to help.

He prayed.

Then he gave a slight nod.

"Hey!" Lorena cried.

Startled, both Sally and Doc turned slightly.

And he made his move. He threw his body hard against Sally's, slamming her into Thiessen, bringing them all down to the ground.

The gun went off. A scream sounded sharply.

Still smoking, the gun lay on the ground in Thiessen's hand. Nearby was a pool of blood.

Jesse slammed his fist down on the man's wrist, and Thiessen released the gun. Jack Pine stepped forward, kicking it far from the man's grasp.

"Lorena!" Jesse cried, and leapt to his feet. She was standing. Unhurt.

Unbloodied.

She rushed into his arms.

He held her, shaking, feeling as if the world itself had begun to spin madly.

"Get up," Jack Pine was saying harshly to someone.

Jesse pulled away from Lorena long enough to turn and look.

Thiessen was getting up.

Sally lay on the ground, her eyes open but sightless.

A hole in her chest was surrounded by crimson.

"Is it over yet, Jesse?" Jack asked.

Jesse let out a sigh. "Not exactly. I imagine that, in a few minutes, John Smith will be arriving. He'll have been alerted by now to the fact that we're out here. If he does show, he'll be picked up. And I would also say that within minutes half the Miccosukee force will be out here. They'll be followed by the Metro-Dade cops. I can hear the airboats now."

Lorena looked up at him, then down at Sally. She shuddered, but only for a minute. Then she spun on Thiessen.

"Who killed my father?" she demanded.

"Ah, that," Thiessen murmured.

"Who actually killed my father!" Lorena repeated.

"Not me. I didn't kill anyone." He paused, and Jesse could see his mind working, trying to find a way out, to make himself look less guilty. "Sally...the whole thing was her idea. That woman was bloodthirsty. I was beside myself when I learned about the death of your poor father. And Hector and Maria. If she hadn't killed them... But she was certain they knew something and would get Fish and Wildlife in."

"Rather than Metro-Dade Homicide?" Jesse asked dryly.

"She was the one who forced me into everything," Thiessen said.

"Tell it to a jury," Jesse said.

"I intend to."

They heard the whir of an airboat motor coming closer. Jesse spun quickly, ready to dive for the gun if another of Thiessen's accomplices was arriving.

But it was George Osceola at the helm, and a number of tribal officers were with him. In seconds, they were rushing forward, shouting, going for Thiessen.

Seeing that the matter was in hand, George walked over to Jesse. "Everyone all right?"

"Except for Sally. She's dead," Jesse said.

"Sally!"

"Sally killed Hector and Maria," Jesse explained. "Were you able to pick up John Smith?"

"They're still looking for him. But, Jesse, you were right. Lars put out the APB, and Smith was spotted upstate. I'd bet money he abducted the van driver. We'll know more as soon as we get hold of him." George studied Jesse, then went silent. "Meanwhile, we need to get you all out of here."

"Hey!" Lorena cried suddenly. "Stop him! Doc's heading for the water!"

George Osceola swore; so did Jesse. They should have cuffed the man immediately.

Doc Thiessen was fast, and he knew the Everglades. He was tearing across the hummuck, heading for the water.

"Stop or I'll shoot!" George shouted.

Thiessen made a dive into the water. Jesse didn't think the man could make it—not with a trained force on his heels, several of them Miccosukees who had grown up in the area. It was a last desperate attempt at freedom by a desperate man.

They raced toward the canal. Thiessen had plunged deep, apparently hoping to surface at a distance, then disappear into the saw grass.

Jesse streaked toward the water himself, then stopped.

Everyone stopped behind him.

There was a thrashing in the water. Droplets splayed high and hard in every direction.

They were all dead still, watching the awful scene playing out before them.

Alligators were territorial.

And Thorne Thiessen had disturbed a large male in his territory. The dance of death was on.

There was no helping Thiessen.

He'd been caught in the middle of the abdomen, and now the mighty creature was thrashing insanely, trying to drown his prey.

Thiessen let out one agonized scream.

Then the alligator took him below the surface.

Gentle as dewdrops, the last glistening drops of water fell back on the surface of the canal.

And then all was still.

Jesse heard a soft gasp, but even without it, he had known she was there. He knew her scent. Felt the air tremble around her.

He turned, and her eyes were brilliant and beautiful and filled with tears. She had wanted justice, not vengeance, he realized.

It had been a fitting end to Thiessen, he thought himself. But maybe he needed to learn a bit more about mercy.

He took her into his arms. Felt the vibrance and life in her body.

He drew her tightly to him. And he didn't care about the tragedy they'd just witnessed, the mud that covered them both, or who heard his words.

"I love you," he said softly. "And it's going to be all right."

Epilogue

It was fall. The sun beat down on the water, but the air was gentle. Birds, in all their multihued plumage, flew above the glistening canal. Trees, hanging low, were a lush background for the chirps and cries that occasionally broke the silence.

There had been a picnic. A week had passed since the events at the hummock. They had all spent hours in questioning and doing paperwork for both the tribal police and Metro-Dade.

Michael Preston and Harry Rogers had both been horrified to discover that they had been under suspicion.

Hugh had merely been indignant that he hadn't been in on the finale.

They had all attended the funeral for Hector and Maria. Julie and Lorena were fast becoming friends, just as she was a friend of Jesse's.

Now, with the picnic cleaned up, with the others having talked over everything that had happened and finally gone home, Lorena stared out at the strange and savage beauty of the area and smiled.

Jesse, a cold beer in his hand, came up behind her, then took a seat at her side.

She leaned against him comfortably, taking his hand,

holding it to her cheek. "There's one more monster out there," she reminded him.

"Yeah.. We haven't heard any reports about it, but we'll arrange more hunts until we get it."

"And when you do...will you capture it or kill it?" she asked.

He smiled at her. "When an animal is altered, it's man's doing, not the creature's," he reminded her. "But these things could mate. Undo the balance in the Everglades. I don't like to make judgments, but if it's up to me... I think the creature is too much of a risk. Too many people have died already. Your father died to protect people from creatures like it, and so..."

"At least they didn't kill the van driver," Lorena said.

"They thought they did, though," Jesse said grimly. "John Smith thought the man was dead when he stole the carcass and drove the van into a canal. It's a miracle that he came to and escaped."

"Every once in a while, we get a miracle," Lorena said.

"So..." Jesse murmured.

"So...?"

"So somehow I doubt that you plan to keep your position at Harry's."

"I was thinking of doing something else."

"You want to leave," he said very softly.

"Actually, no."

"No?" His face seemed exceptionally strong then, handsome and compelling, his eyes that startling green against the bronze of his features.

She sighed. "I know it's soon, but I had been hoping you would ask me to stay here. My real love is the law. And causes. I'm great at causes, Jesse. It occurred to me that the tribal council could probably use a good lawyer now and then. And living here, with you…"

He laughed. "I love you. You know that. I have to admit, I've had my fears."

"You? Afraid?"

"This isn't just where I live. It's part of what I am. And you come from a world that's…glittering. Clean. Neat. Sophisticated. Not that we don't have our own 'Miami chic' down here, but… I'm not knocking anything, it's just that here…well, there are alligators in the canals. Water moccasins, and saw grass hardly stands in for a neatly manicured lawn. And my nearest neighbor is…well, not near."

She laughed softly. "Hmm. Water moccasins."

"I'm afraid so. Though they're not the vicious creatures they're made out to be. They're afraid of people."

"And alligators."

"Normally, they leave you alone if you leave them alone."

"Muck, mud, mosquitoes and saw grass."

"I'm afraid so."

She turned to him, touched his face. "But they all come with you," she said softly.

He caught her hand, eyes narrowing, a smile curving his lips. "Then you really would consider staying? I'd love a roommate, but I'd much rather have a wife."

Her heart seemed to stop. "Are you asking me?"

"I'm begging you."

She threw herself into his arms.

"Is that a yes?"

"A thousand times over."

He gently caught her chin in his hand, thumb sliding over the skin of her cheek. Then his lips touched hers.

The breeze was soft and easy. The birds went silent. The night was as breathtaking as his kiss.

THE WEDDING WAS a month later. They chose the Keys.

The bride wore white. The groom was dashing in his tux.

They were both barefoot, married in the sand at sunset.

They'd taken the whole of one of the mom-and-pop motels, as well as rooms in one of the nearby chains. The attendance was huge, with Seminoles, Miccosukees, whites, Hispanics and, as Hugh, the token Aussie, commented, a bit of everyone in between. Even Roger had made it out of the hospital in time to attend.

The sunset was glorious.

The reception was the South Florida party of the year.

And when the night wound down, they were alone in their room that looked onto the ocean, feeling the gentle breeze, aware of the salt scent on the air…

And then nothing else, nothing else at all…

Except for each other.

* * * * *

YOU HAVE
JUST READ A
HARLEQUIN®
INTRIGUE®
BOOK

If you were **captivated** by

the **gripping, page-turning**

romantic suspense, be sure

to look for all six Harlequin®

Intrigue® books every month.

The Stalking *by Heather Graham*

When a copycat killer stalks New Orleans,
FBI Special Agent Cheyenne Donegal teams up with
Special Agent Andre Rousseau from the elite
Krewe of Hunters unit to track them down in a race
against the clock to save the latest victim.

But the case is too close and too personal. It's tied to
Cheyenne's and Andre's pasts...

Cheyenne could have sworn that her cousin clutched her shoulder, that she felt her hand.

But of course, she did not. Her cousin was dead. Her earthly remains were being put into the family tomb, and there she would lie and decay, a year and a day in the blistering heat, down to bone and ash, scooped into the holding area, leaving room for the remains of family to come.

"That's him!" Janine cried. Her voice seemed to tremble. The hand that touched Cheyenne's shoulder was shaking. "That's him."

Him?

Cheyenne knew the police believed that Janine, her beautiful young cousin, had been killed by a man they called the Artiste.

His victims had been between the ages of sixteen and twenty-two, pretty, precocious and energetic. The first three had been working girls—vivacious, bright young women who had worked for an escort agency.

The fourth had gone missing after telling friends she was meeting with a drop-dead gorgeous man she had met through an online site.

The fifth had been a runaway, living in New Orleans.

And the sixth had been Janine.

Cheyenne looked at the man who was standing on the trail between the old plantation house and the tombs. She knew who he was. Ryan Lassiter, a substitute teacher, sometime guitar player with various bands in New Orleans and all the way out to Lafayette, New Iberia and beyond. He was young, cool and hot. The kids loved him.

"Mr. Lassiter?" she said aloud.

"Cheyenne, dammit, don't you think I know what happened to me?" Janine asked, a catch in her ghostly voice. "I was so stupid! I thought I was so cool. Yes, I flirted with him. I had a ridiculous crush on him, and I thought he was… I thought I was so hot, and I was flattered, since for sure I had to be something…something for him to want to be with me. You have to stop him, Cheyenne," Janine pleaded. "Tell them, tell them that he did it, that he killed me, that he stole my life, that he left me…there!"

Janine pointed to her casket.

The priest was still speaking. The members of the funerary jazz band were preparing to start another song. The cemetery workers were waiting for them all to leave so that Janine, in her coffin, might be sealed into the family tomb.

Cheyenne was looking at her cousin's killer.

Don't miss the latest thrilling case in the
Krewe of Hunters series!
The Stalking by Heather Graham.
Available September 24, 2019 from
MIRA® Books, wherever books are sold.

MIRABooks.com

MHGEXP0919

INTRIGUE

EDGE-OF-YOUR-SEAT INTRIGUE, FEARLESS ROMANCE.

Save $1.00

on the purchase of ANY

Harlequin Intrigue® book.

Available wherever books are sold, including most bookstores, supermarkets, drugstores and discount stores.

Save $1.00

on the purchase of any Harlequin Intrigue book.

Coupon valid until November 30, 2019.
Redeemable at participating outlets in the U.S. and Canada only.
Not redeemable at Barnes & Noble stores. Limit one coupon per customer.

52616453

5 65373 00076 2   (8100)0 12428

Get 4 FREE REWARDS!

We'll send you 2 FREE Books plus 2 FREE Mystery Gifts.

Harlequin Intrigue® books feature heroes and heroines that confront and survive danger while finding themselves irresistibly drawn to one another.

FREE
Value Over
$20

Get 4 FREE REWARDS!

We'll send you 2 FREE Books <u>plus</u> 2 FREE Mystery Gifts.

FREE
Value Over
$20

Both the **Romance** and **Suspense** collections feature compelling novels written by many of today's best-selling authors.

YES! Please send me 2 FREE novels from the Essential Romance or Essential Suspense Collection and my 2 FREE gifts (gifts are worth about $10 retail). After receiving them, if I don't wish to receive any more books, I can return the shipping statement marked "cancel." If I don't cancel, I will receive 4 brand-new novels every month and be billed just $6.99 each in the U.S. or $7.24 each in Canada. That's a savings of at least 13% off the cover price. It's quite a bargain! Shipping and handling is just 50¢ per book in the U.S. and $1.25 per book in Canada.* I understand that accepting the 2 free books and gifts places me under no obligation to buy anything. I can always return a shipment and cancel at any time. The free books and gifts are mine to keep no matter what I decide.

Choose one: ☐ **Essential Romance**
(194/394 MDN GNNP)
☐ **Essential Suspense**
(191/391 MDN GNNP)

Name (please print)

Address   Apt. #

City   State/Province   Zip/Postal Code

Mail to the Reader Service:
IN U.S.A.: P.O. Box 1341, Buffalo, NY 14240-8531
IN CANADA: P.O. Box 603, Fort Erie, Ontario L2A 5X3

Want to try 2 free books from another series! Call 1-800-873-8635 or visit www.ReaderService.com.

*Terms and prices subject to change without notice. Prices do not include sales taxes, which will be charged (if applicable) based on your state or country of residence. Canadian residents will be charged applicable taxes. Offer not valid in Quebec. This offer is limited to one order per household. Books received may not be as shown. Not valid for current subscribers to the Essential Romance or Essential Suspense Collection. All orders subject to approval. Credit or debit balances in a customer's account(s) may be offset by any other outstanding balance owed by or to the customer. Please allow 4 to 6 weeks for delivery. Offer available while quantities last.

Your Privacy—The Reader Service is committed to protecting your privacy. Our Privacy Policy is available online at www.ReaderService.com or upon request from the Reader Service. We make a portion of our mailing list available to reputable third parties that offer products we believe may interest you. If you prefer that we not exchange your name with third parties, or if you wish to clarify or modify your communication preferences, please visit us at www.ReaderService.com/consumerschoice or write to us at Reader Service Preference Service, P.O. Box 9062, Buffalo, NY 14240-9062. Include your complete name and address.

STRS19R3